To Dona

Who constantly teaches me how precious an old friendship can be —

With love

Jean Dell

THE TOSCA TAUNT

This is a work of fiction. Characters, names, incidents and places are products of the author's imagination, or are used fictitiously, and are not to be construed as real. Any resemblances to actual persons, living or dead, events, locales, or organizations, is entirely coincidental.

© Copyright 2005 Jean Dell

All rights reserved. No part of this publication may be reproduced, stored in a retrieval system, or transmitted, in any form or by any means, electronic, mechanical, photocopying, recording, or otherwise, without the written prior permission of the author.

Note for Librarians: A cataloguing record for this book is available from Library and Archives Canada at www.collectionscanada.ca/amicus/index-e.html
ISBN 1-4120-6793-6

Printed in Victoria, BC, Canada. Printed on paper with minimum 30% recycled fibre. Trafford's print shop runs on "green energy" from solar, wind and other environmentally-friendly power sources.

TRAFFORD
PUBLISHING

Offices in Canada, USA, Ireland and UK

This book was published *on-demand* in cooperation with Trafford Publishing. On-demand publishing is a unique process and service of making a book available for retail sale to the public taking advantage of on-demand manufacturing and Internet marketing. On-demand publishing includes promotions, retail sales, manufacturing, order fulfilment, accounting and collecting royalties on behalf of the author.

Book sales for North America and international:
Trafford Publishing, 6E–2333 Government St.,
Victoria, BC v8t 4p4 CANADA
phone 250 383 6864 (toll-free 1 888 232 4444)
fax 250 383 6804; email to orders@trafford.com

Book sales in Europe:
Trafford Publishing (UK) Limited, 9 Park End Street, 2nd Floor
Oxford, UK ox1 1hh UNITED KINGDOM
phone 44 (0)1865 722 113 (local rate 0845 230 9601)
facsimile 44 (0)1865 722 868; info.uk@trafford.com

Order online at:
trafford.com/05-1704

10 9 8 7 6 5 4 3

For E.W.S.

ALSO BY JEAN DELL

The Otello Omen

The Fanciulla Fate

THE TOSCA TAUNT

Jean Dell

One

The screams woke Jenetta Maclean Amato. Her head shot up from the pillow as she peered around the room, lit now by an eerie red glow. Reaching quickly towards the lamp she could see on the bedside table, she flicked the switch. Nothing happened. The luminous dial on the clock beside the lamp no longer shed its bilious green light. Now, as she remembered that she was in a hotel, she recognised the acrid smell; it was smoke. She grabbed the tiny flashlight she carried when she travelled, which last night she had put beside her bed. Switching it on, she swung its beam towards the door. To her horror she saw smoke slowly snaking its way into her room through the crack under the door.

For one moment Jen succumbed to a comforting thought.

The Tosca Taunt

This is a dream, every hotel guest's dark fantasy. I'll force myself to wake up, I'm being ridiculous ... But as she willed herself awake, she heard again the screams and crashing sounds, and she realized that this nightmare was real.

Her stomach contracted. *Tony!* No, she realised she was confused; her husband was not here—but her children—where were her children? Could she reach them in time, could she guide them to safety? Then she remembered she was travelling alone. But there was somebody in the other bed. Oh yes, of course, that was her unexpected roommate, Bridget Jennifer Noonan. Jen's eyes burned as the smoke in the room grew more dense. Could she safely reach the emergency exit she had taken note of, four doors down the hall? She always forced herself to notice the whereabouts of exits, just in case.

Hurrying to the door, she put her palms against it. It felt hot. Did she dare open it? Now the fear roaring in her head was reinforced by another roar, and she realized that the fire already blazed in the corridor just outside her door. The smoke seared her lungs each time she breathed. Running back to her roommate she shook her roughly by the shoulder. But Bridget Jennifer slept a deep, drugged sleep.

"Bridget, wake up, wake up, there's a fire, we've got to get out of here, we can climb out the window ..." Jen shook Bridget hard by both her shoulders. But Bridget slumbered on.

What can I do, how can I save her? Clutching Bridget's arms, Jen tried to drag her from the bed, just as the door slammed open and fire blasted into the room. Jen held Bridget's arms tightly and gave a mighty pull just as a fierce pain stabbed into her back. A small explosion hurled her away from Bridget

Jean Dell

towards the window. Jen had a nanosecond's glance at the narrow path one storey below, and at the sloping cliff below that.

Exactly at ten p.m an enormous explosion blew the blazing hotel apart, and Bridget's heavy suitcase hit against Jen's head as she, the case, a mattress and part of the room went tumbling to the path and down the cliff. Jen was briefly unconscious as she and the suitcase, flukily shielded from harm by the mattress and bed covers, slipped and slid down through the forest below. She came to a stop finally in a sitting position, her hand resting on the suitcase. And to her amazement, she was sure she saw her personal trainer, Harrison, coming towards her through the bright moonlit woods, lit as though with a spotlight. Only why were there bright flowers floating all around him? She could make no sense of it.

"Come on, Mrs A, no pain no gain, weight training today, I want you to pick up the suitcase and walk down this slope."

A deeply confused Jen, hurting all over, did his bidding. She walked, and walked, and walked, exhorted by Harrison's "no pain, no gain", until, fit though she was, she could walk no longer. The forest spun wildly around her, and then all was dark.

Mercifully, miles above, Jen's room-mate Bridget Jennifer Noonan remained drugged and unconscious as she and the rest of the blazing, exploding hotel tumbled into an inferno that would burn her beyond any kind of recognition.

....

Jen finally awoke, shivering violently. *This is the most uncomfortable bed I've ever been in. Am I ill? I hurt all over and I'm*

The Tosca Taunt

cold and why do my eyelids feel so heavy?
Her eyes seemed glued shut. Finally she pried the lids open with her curiously stiff fingers. She looked up, blinked hard, shook her head and looked again. Above her, two tall fir trees swayed, their long branches rising and dipping in the breeze. A slight drizzle seeped from the overcast sky. Jen put her hand down to feel her bed; she discovered she was lying on a damp pile of leaves.

She struggled to push herself into a sitting position. *My head hurts, my back hurts, what am I doing sleeping here? What are these filthy torn pyjama tops I'm wearing? Where are the bottoms? No wonder I'm so cold—I'm half naked. This doesn't make any sense. I must be ill and I'm having chills and one of those dreams in which I've gone out and forgotten to put my pants on ...*

A raccoon emerged catlike from the brush and peered curiously at Jen. A second raccoon followed the first, repeating his actions. Jen realized it was just possible she was not dreaming. She struggled to get up out of the moist leaves, but a sharp pain in her head sent her crashing dizzily to her knees.

What's happening to me? I feel so sick. I must find some clothes, I'll freeze, wherever am I? She looked wildly around her.

She saw the blue suitcase nearby, battered and streaked with smoky dirt. *Oh, thank goodness, I hope that's mine, I hope there are some clothes in it, this is so strange. What am I doing in this place? Was I camping?*

She tried to stand; pain and dizziness defeated her. Finally she crawled over the uneven, scratchy forest floor to the suitcase. She could scarcely focus her eyes because of the pain in her head, but she finally deciphered the printing on the luggage's name tag, which said "Bridget Jennifer Noonan".

"Bridget Jennifer Noonan," said Jenetta Maclean Amato aloud. "This must be my suitcase."

Jen opened the luggage, which she found jammed with a pile of what looked like very expensive clothes, shoes and handbags. She quickly donned underwear in pale blue silk and lace, a pair of grey cashmere wool slacks and a matching sweater; grey socks, grey loafers which seemed too loose, and a soft beige leather aviator type jacket.

Jen explored the handbag. She found a comb, lipstick, mascara and a powder compact with a tiny mirror. Opening the compact she peered at herself; her face was streaked with dirt, she had bruised eyes, one considerably worse than the other, and a lacerated cheek. Her fair hair was matted and snarled with bits of leaves and twigs. Gently she untangled her curls with the small comb, and winced as it hit what she discovered was an egg-sized bump on the back of her head.

Maybe that's why my head aches so. Is the sticky stuff I'm feeling, blood? She looked at her fingers; they were dark with almost congealed blood.

Who am I camping with? I wonder where they've gone? I must try to remember. Let's see, yesterday I was—I was doing—what? I'm not sure I know who—who am I? I must be this—this—Bridget Jennifer Noonan—but who is Bridget Jennifer Noonan?

Jen rummaged in the handbag. And there she found a hand printed letter without an envelope which read,

"*Dearest Mama;*

I'm so sorry Mama, you must be crazy with worry. I'm okay, I really am. I would have contacted you sooner, but I've been so upset

and scared. He'll kill me, he will, I didn't want you to know but I was in hospital for three weeks the last time. He found me even though I was supposed to be safe in that shelter for battered women. Maybe it's because he's a respected professional man that he can find out where those sanctuaries are, even though their addresses are secret. While I was in the hospital I finally realised that what I must do is disappear, escape somewhere where he'll never find me. But he's so clever. Oh Mama why did I ever marry him? Maybe for just that reason—that he is clever, and he wanted me, God, how he wanted me. I'm glad we never had children. I thought when he kicked me and I miscarried that it was a tragedy but it wasn't really. How could I have protected my baby from him?

I don't dare tell you too much. He'll come to you for information and I'm scared he'll hurt you to try to make you talk. Oh, I wish Papa were still alive; at least you had some protection then.

The postmark on this letter has nothing to do with where I am— I'm going to ask a woman who's on the bus with me to mail it when she goes home. I have to trust her—I don't see what choice I have. I've even changed my name. Oh, how can I tell you without telling you? The one I nicknamed Briggie.

I'll phone you when I get up the courage, but it will have to be from a pay phone. I'm so scared he might trace the call back to me. Maybe if I call collect, or should it be the other way around—oh, I just don't know, I can't think straight tonight.

I've dyed my hair—bleached it, actually. Can you imagine me blonde? Believe it or not, it doesn't look too bad.

Read this and burn it. Oh I'm so sorry, Mama. Who will look after you when you get older if not me? Maybe he'll die soon. I hope he does—is that wicked? Please, please know I love you; know that I'm

doing this to stay alive, so that one day I can see you again, hug you again, oh Mama!
                    I love you,
                            ME"

P.S. You always told me to write my letters in longhand, but I had to print this; my hands are shaking so much tonight I can't write legibly—no, not alcohol, not any more, just nerves."

....

Jen thought, *but I don't remember any of this. I'm escaping from a brutal husband? My Dad is dead, and my Mama—I can't remember anything about my Mama. Was I camping with friends of mine—of Bridget Jennifer's? Where are they? Maybe if I call?* But calling loudly and repeatedly had only one result; it made Jen's throat hurt.

Frantically now Jen rummaged in the suitcase, and again she found something enlightening. It was another letter, from which the recipient's address had been carefully cut out. The letter, from a catering company in Timmins, Ontario, confirmed that Bridget Jennifer Noonan had been hired for the position of *sous-chef*, and was to appear at the Delson Mine, reachable by helicopter from Timmins, on October 14, to start her new job.

Jen felt faintly hopeful. *Surely I'll remember some of this soon. But at least I know where I'm supposed to be going. I wonder what date today is.* She looked down at her watch and saw it was a Cartier, an expensive brand. The watch told her the date was October 11. *Obviously I've got some money to be able to afford these luxurious clothes and this brand of watch ... money! I need money to go where I ...* She looked in the wallet. No identification there. But to her utter amazement there were five thousand dollars in it, in fifty and

The Tosca Taunt

hundred dollar bills.

Whatever am I to do? I guess I've no choice but to go on up to this Delson Mine place. Maybe on the way I'll remember something, but if I don't, surely they'll be able to help me ... only, do I admit to them I don't know who I am? If I'm escaping from something—someone—terrible, would they try to find out who I was and would that tip off this man as to my whereabouts? This brute—my—my husband?

I'd better try to find a road. I'll climb down this hill—I'm too tired to try climbing up—oh my head hurts—I have to drag this luggage—I surely don't pack light! I wonder if there's any painkiller in the handbag?

Jen dug into the bag and, not finding anything, tried the suitcase. She came up with a bottle of prescription painkillers on which all traces that might identify the patient had been torn off. Only the name of the drug, Demerol, remained.

I wonder if this is really Demerol? I guess I'll have to gamble; I can't stay here, I'll freeze. And I can't I walk with this pain.

Jen had no water, so with difficulty she swallowed one pill, gagging unpleasantly before she got it down. And presently, buoyed by the effects of the drug, she was able to start dragging Bridget Jennifer Noonan's heavy suitcase down the rocky, treed slope.

From time to time she stopped, breathing painfully hard from her exertions, wondering how she could have managed to get herself into this unnerving predicament.

Two

Doctor Victor Macready Kilbride twisted the steering wheel of his Lexus hard and the car skidded, tires squealing, into his semi-circular driveway, a type of driveway *de rigueur* on this New Orleans street.

Damn aeroplanes, never on time, thank God I parked my car in the airport parking lot, cost a bloody fortune but convenient, convenient.

Because Bryony would be waiting. She'd better be waiting this time; he had brought her a beautiful present from his dental convention in Chicago. A Rolex diamond studded watch.

That was one of the good things about being a dentist; it was marvellously lucrative. Even so, the watch was expensive, but he needed Bryony to know that he was sorry, really sorry this time; he had hit her too hard; he hadn't meant to give her a concussion and broken ribs that would keep her in the hospital so long.

But damn! She did provoke it; it was her fault, after all. Couldn't she just do what he asked? Was it really so much to expect, that your wife would stop fooling around with your

The Tosca Taunt

colleagues? Well, maybe not fooling around exactly, but all that flirting at parties, that laughing, that acting up, couldn't she just be quiet and modest like his mother had been? His mother would never have joined in the men's conversations at parties; she would have stayed with the women like she was supposed to do.

Victor needed Bryony trained, so that when he became the "grey eminence" for his pal Leonard LeComte, once Leonard succeeded in getting elected as Governor of Louisiana, then Bryony would be his perfect helpmeet.

Dignified, supportive, not a flirty, flighty, goddam stupid woman.

Maybe he should never have married. Or maybe he should have chosen a wife nearer his own age, after his mother's death. Bryony was after all fifteen years younger than he. Only thirty-six, even now. Was that at the root of her problem? But she couldn't be looking for more sex, surely, from the men she flirted with; she even flirted with Len LeComte and she knew perfectly well Leonard could hardly keep up with the woman he already had, that gorgeous new wife Delphine. God knew Bryony was so damn sexy Victor himself wanted it every night, but he was lucky if she gave it to him once a week. Gave it to him, what a laugh. What he got he had to force out of her. Lately she had accused him of rape. Damn fool thing to say. You can't rape your own wife. Well, you could under the law—his own lawyer had successfully defended one client against such a charge—but in that situation, the law was definitely an ass.

Victor was surprised to see only one light burning in the two storey Georgian facade of his house, the light in the study. Bryony must be reading again. Lately she had been taking a course in African-American Literature from the television; he didn't like her to go out alone at night to the school. Fat lot of good that course was going to do her, he told her she'd be far better off to take a cooking class. Not to mention how much better off he'd be.

He unlocked the front door and called out, "Bryony! I'm home!"

Silence.

Oh for God's sake don't tell me she forgot I was coming home tonight. Bloody damn woman. She should have known I'd have a special present for her this time, given recent events.

"Bryony, God damn it, where are you?"

Silence.

Victor strode through the house, flicking lights on in each room as he sought his wife.

"Bryony! Bryony! Bryony! I know you're here somewhere, where are you?"

But in each room silence greeted him. Until the last room, the bedroom Bryony had shared with him for seven years. On a small cushion covered with lace and eyelet embroidery there was a letter to him, to his astonishment impaled with their small meat cleaver in the now shredded cloth.

"What the ... ?" Victor thrust away the cleaver and picked up the letter. Typed on their computer, it said;

I've gone, Victor. This time you will never find me. Don't even bother to try, you'll just be throwing your money away. This time, I tell nobody where I'm going, not even dear Mama. Because I would be afraid for her if you thought she knew.

Can you even begin to imagine how much I hate you? You have taken

The Tosca Taunt

from me everything I wanted—all my dreams of a loving husband and a baby, and now you have even separated me, maybe forever, from Mama and the rest of my family that I care so much about.

I thought there was protection for someone like me, from someone like you. I was wrong. You came so close to killing me, Victor. Next time I figure you will—that's why I'm making sure there will NEVER be a next time.

Goodbye.

Bryony

Victor stared at the letter in disbelief. Then, with a fury even he could not measure, he grabbed the diamond Rolex from its case and threw it on the bedside table. He stooped to pick up the meat cleaver, and swung the blade at the watch with all the strength in his compact, muscular body. The watch made a curious crunching sound, as Victor hit it again and again. Diamonds and gold spewed over the white wool broadloom, and the small antique table, rent beyond enduring, suddenly groaned and collapsed in a heap of splinters. Spent now, breathing hard, Victor stopped. He stared in the Venetian mirror above Bryony's dressing table at the handsome, flushed face under the grey curly hair.

No next time? Oh Bryony, you're wrong. There'll be a next time, never fear, unless you stop this nonsense. And you're right. Next time, you may not get out alive. But don't ever think I'll pay for it. Not Victor Macready Kilbride. Not with my connections in this state. Never. Never. Never.

Victor ran downstairs, hitting the balustrade once with the cleaver as he went. In the study, he flipped through the Yellow

Pages to remind himself of the name of the private investigator Leonard LeComte had mentioned recently; just for the moment, the name had slipped his mind. Oh yes, there it was, the PI Leonard had said was the cleverest and most reliably secretive in the whole state. Gerald Geraint, PI.

Quickly, Victor dialled the number and left a brief message on Gerald Geraint's voice mail.

Three

Jenetta Maclean Amato would never remember how she came to be with Bridget Jennifer Noonan the day before the fire. During that afternoon the two women were seat mates on a crowded bus going from Toronto to Sudbury, Ontario, but they had talked little. Engine problems forced them to stop for the night in the picturesque town of Hadley's Ridge; the sputtering bus deposited its passengers at a historical site, a splendid wooden Victorian-style hotel, situated on the edge of a cliff. It reminded Jen of the beautiful wooden lodge at Waterton Lakes, in the Canadian Rockies. The already frustrated travellers were dismayed to learn that a gas leak, now fixed at least temporarily, but compounded by a plumbing problem, had forced the hotel manager to close half the hotel.

In desperation, desk clerks were asking this unexpected busload of patrons to double up, if necessary with strangers. The choice they were offered was either to share a room, or to sleep in one of several hastily recruited private homes, for the town of

Hadley's Ridge was not overrun with tourist accommodation. Nobody had ever been able to compete successfully with what the townspeople called the "big" hotel. Bridget Jennifer and her seat-mate had agreed to share a room.

Ravenous after their trip, they devoured a cold supper, the kitchen stoves being still out of commission because of the earlier gas leak. Afterwards, satiated and sleepy, the two women climbed the curving wooden staircase to their second floor room.

Bridget Jennifer settled at the small pseudo-Victorian desk and, with shaking hands, printed her letter to Mama. That done, she stuffed the page into her blue Louis Vuitton handbag and threw the bag into her matching large leather suitcase. Drawing out a bright blue cashmere dressing gown, she draped it across a wing chair; when she emerged from the bathroom a while later, her roommate, wearing the gown, sat in the chair staring out of the window and sketching the rapidly darkening view on a small pad. Incensed, Bridget Jennifer snapped, "Why are you wearing my dressing gown?"

Her roommate looked down, astonished. "Am I? I thought it was mine. I ..." She rose quickly to look into her own luggage where, to her embarrassment, she found her own identical robe.

"I'm sorry! I don't know what I was thinking. When I'm sketching I'm hopeless! We do seem to be the same size." She smiled. "We're even both blonde. Practically twins." She thought, *I'm so embarrassed I'm babbling*. Hastily she removed the offending garment and put on her own.

Bridget appraised her room-mate. " We must be about the same height."

"I'm five foot six, size ten, size seven shoes."

The Tosca Taunt

"I'm the same, but my feet are size eight." They grinned at one another, their similarities creating a tentative bond.

A distant, sharp noise, like the pop of a huge champagne cork, startled them. They stopped talking to listen, but no sound followed.

"What was that?"

"I don't know," answered Bridget Jennifer. She sat down on the edge of her bed. "I've got to get into bed, I've taken a sleeping pill and I'll fall over if I don't lie down." The drug emphasized Bridget Jennifer's Southern United States accent; all the words were drawled now.

Each woman climbed into her narrow bed. Jen was the last to flick off the light on her bedside table. She shifted position several times, trying to get comfortable, and repeatedly snagged the soft, fuzzy synthetic blanket with her rings. Realizing if that continued she would keep waking herself up, she debated removing the blanket, but it was a cool night and the heating system had produced no heat so far. So she reluctantly did what she had vowed never to do; she removed her two diamond rings and placed them on the bedside table. One was her engagement ring, the other had, many moons past, belonged to the renowned early twentieth century watercolourist, John Marin. Jen's husband, an avid collector of antiques, had given it to her for their tenth wedding anniversary.

She felt for the comforting presence of her broad wedding band, which she had never removed since the wedding ceremony, when her husband had lifted her hand to his lips to kiss the finger on which he had just slipped the ring.

In the pseudo-intimacy created by the dark, Bridget Jennifer sleepily asked her room-mate, "I'm sorry, but what's your name again?"

" Jenetta Amato. Everyone calls me Jen."

"Amato? The only other person I've heard of with your name is that Italian tenor, Antonio Amato. I think he's gorgeous."

Jen Amato smiled into the darkness. "Join the club."

"You sound like a fan too," Bridget Jennifer said. "Did you ever see him in person?"

"Oh yes."

"Is he as attractive in real life as he is photogenic? Did you get an autograph?"

"Yes, he's as attractive—actually, Antonio Amato is my husband."

"Oh my goodness!" Bridget's drawl became almost a caricature. "Lucky you! If he's as nice as he is gorgeous; you-all must have a great marriage—if there is such a thing ... "

"We have a fantastic marriage."

"Good for you," Bridget Jennifer said. "Don't ever let it go."

"Don't worry, I won't."

Bridget Jennifer was silent a while. Then she said, "I hope I'm not being rude, but I see pictures of your husband with a lot of women, sometimes one particular woman, that opera singer with the Greek name, is it Mia Mitsouros? What's it like, being married to a man so many women are crazy about?"

"Scary. You wonder how a man can resist all that adoration. But Tony and I have been married thirteen years, and so far so good."

In the dark, the superstitious Jen crossed her fingers and

The Tosca Taunt

touched the wood of her headboard.

Bridget Jennifer asked, "You've got kids?"

"Two. One of each. How about you?"

"No, I—once I had a miscarriage. I was heartbroken."

"That's sad. We had a premature baby, Gianni, who lived just three weeks. Tony and I grieved so for him. I imagine a miscarriage feels a bit like that."

Another muffled explosive sound interrupted their conversation.

"That's got to be the repair men trying to get this place fixed up." said Bridget Jennifer. "Where did you say *you* were going? I'm on my way to work for a gold mining company."

"I'm the official opener of an arts college in Sudbury. I'll give seminars in art there for two weeks."

"And where's your divine husband?"

"Right this second my divine husband should be singing in *Tosca* at the Metropolitan Opera."

"New York's home?"

"Yes. And you?"

"New—I mean, Savannah, in Georgia..."

"This is embarrassing, but what did you say *your* name was?" Jen asked.

"Bryony—I mean Bridget, it's Bridget, I can't imagine why I said Bryony,—these sleeping pills make me so—m-m-m-m-m-m." Bridget Jennifer was asleep.

Jen smiled indulgently into the darkness. Then, to help put herself to sleep, she began drowsily to go over yesterday's phone conversation with Tony, after he had finished singing a *Tosca* in Berlin. She had reached him in his hotel room at dawn, just as he was getting up to catch his flight back to New York.

"Tony love! Don't tell me; let me tell *you* how your *Tosca* went. It was a triumph—I've been feeling it for hours."

Tony laughed, and superstitiously clutched the Saint Cecilia medallion on the gold chain around his neck before answering her, his Italian accent still thick with sleep.

"*Amore*, if we told to other people that we can communicate without words and not even being on the same continent, they would say, the Amatos, they have finally gone crazy. But you are right, it was *molto* excellent as usual, my *Tosca*."

"Well, now we've accounted for the amazing health of your ego, love," Jen said, "how are *you*? Your trip had such a fiendishly tight schedule."

There was a pause, which surprised Jen. Her question had been rhetorical, for Tony was so ebulliently healthy she could not imagine him saying anything except that he felt fine.

"I am okay, Jen," he said, his voice flat. "You know if I could not do it I would not let them schedule me so tight. But I am better always if you are with me."

"Tony, please, don't make me feel guilty."

"Don't be *assurdito*—absurd; I don't expect you should give up your life to come every time with me, any more than I can give up mine to come with you. I am a reasonable man. Only when I don't have my Jen fix—"

"Flatterer!" Her body ached to be close to him, to give him the tenderness on which he thrived. "I miss you, Tony. You're so far away."

"It's hard, Jen, because I'm so addicted to you," he said, only half in jest. "Do you remember the night I learned I was addicted

The Tosca Taunt

to you, *cara mia?*"

"Yes. Oh Tony. I wish I'd refused this invitation, even though it *is* an honour. I'd much rather be with you. I'll talk to you tomorrow night, my darling. I do love you."

"Goodnight, my Jen. Soon, soon."

Now in the narrow hotel bed Jen turned onto her left side and, wistfully imagining that she was tucked into what she called the envelope of Tony, with his strong hard body folded against her back and his hand holding her breast, she fell asleep.

Downstairs there was another explosion as the flames which had been contained in a little used basement store-room broke out and licked their way quickly down a corridor. And not long after, there came the massive explosions, those that changed Jen's and Bridget Jennifer's lives forever.

Four

Antonio Amato stared out of his bedroom window at the hazy skyline of Manhattan. He had planned a day of vocal silence before he sang *Tosca* tonight at the Metropolitan Opera. He had sung in this production before; he knew what would be required of him. But he was uncomfortable with what his tight schedule too often imposed on him, this parachuting into operas without adequate rehearsal with a particular cast. Often cast members resented being unable to practice properly with him, even though he would (he hoped) duplicate the moves of the rehearsal tenor.

So the least a jet-lagged Tony—who had flown to New York from Berlin yesterday—could do for his fellow performers, would be to sing well. Hence the planned day of silence to rest his musical instrument, his vocal cords.

Nevertheless, the same afternoon that Jen and Bridget Jennifer were agreeing to share a hotel room, Antonio Amato let himself be summoned by the telephone ringing in his untidy,

The Tosca Taunt

book-and-toy strewn library. He picked up the receiver just as he remembered vocal silence. But since he had the phone in his hand, he might as well speak briefly with whoever it was. It could be Jen. But the voice that greeted him was deep and male.

"Tony! How's my favourite tenor? How was Europe?"

"Hello Gareth," Tony said morosely to his manager. "You forget already my day of silence? You sound too cheerful; what are you going to say that I don't want to hear? Don't tell me you have another booking. Is enough already."

"You have such a suspicious mind. Actually I..."

"I knew it! Your timing is terrible. Ask me tomorrow."

"If it wasn't urgent, I would. But hear me out, Tony; this is a benefit for handicapped children in the third world. You've already dealt with this organization; you sang for them last June."

"*Grazie a Dio,* Gareth, at least that was in New York, you say it is urgent but if I can sing here, as long as it does not conflict."

There was a silence. Gareth, as usual thinking first with his wallet, reflected on how best to break the news of the venue to an overworked Tony. An oblique appeal to his sympathies might be best.

"Did you hear that Carlo Paoli decided to learn to ski and broke his leg first time out? A bad break—he's in traction and will be for some days."

"No I did not hear, poor Carlo, what does he think of, trying to learn such a sport at his age? He must be fifty-five."

"That's hardly senility, Tony, I'm fifty-three myself. Just because you're a young fellow of forty—"

"You are maybe avoiding the subject? First we talk benefit,

then suddenly we are talking Carlo's leg and my age, what is it you are not telling me, Gareth?"

"I'm telling you that Carlo can't sing and the organizers need you to replace him."

"I just finish telling you I will; so what is the problem?"

"The problem is that the concert is in Buenos Aires, on Sunday."

"*Cielo!* Are you crazy? I cannot do that; I am singing a run of *Tosca*, you know already this. Why are you even asking me?"

"Well, for openers, it will make marvellous publicity. Amato the indefatigable tenor, over-booked though he is, steps in at the last minute to replace his good friend Carlo Paoli, because Amato is so moved by the plight of the children—it's irresistible, Tony."

"Maybe to you," Tony replied glumly.

"They're willing to triple your usual fee."

"Which triples your usual fee, right, Gareth? But you know I always—"

"I know, I know. You sing for free so the charity gets more funds, and you won't even let us use that as publicity. You're impossible."

"Thank you very much."

"So will you do this benefit? You can fly down Saturday, sing Sunday night, fly back Monday, and you'll have a whole day before you do *Tosca* on Tuesday. You won't even have jet lag; Buenos Aires is only two hours ahead of New York."

"You think I don't know this already? All right, all right, make the arrangements, I wish I could go Friday night, who can sleep right after they sing? But I am recording a CD that night

The Tosca Taunt

after *Tosca*, remember? That was the only time we could all get together."

Tony now thought about the best way to organise this trip to spare himself exhaustion.

"So book me two first class seats Saturday, so I can sleep, Gareth, *cielo!* And get me a suite in a quieter hotel this time. Tell the organisers I will waive my fee; just they pay me my expenses. What am I to sing?"

"Carlo was doing two arias and six light songs. But under the circumstances the organisers will take anything not too grim. I mean, don't trot out *Otello.*"

"Okay okay. I have to stop using the voice right now, Gareth, unless you want to see tomorrow a review of how rusty Amato sounded tonight."

"Okay, Tony. And thanks. You're one hell of a nice guy, you know." Gareth chuckled. "Good thing you have a hard-headed manager like me or you'd go broke giving away your hard earned money. 'Break a Leg' tonight. We'll talk."

Tony hung up the phone. *Madre mia,* he thought, *they will kill me. What I would not give for two weeks off. I wish Jen were here. She always makes me feel better.* He smiled to himself. *I am truly addicted to my wife.*

He went into the kitchen and made himself a cup of strong espresso. He was hungry, but knowing he, like most opera singers, sang better on an empty stomach, he decided the large lunch he had eaten three hours ago—steak, salad, pasta, and ice cream, would have to do. An empty stomach gives singers more control over their diaphragms, as well as reducing the risk of having to sing with indigestion. But after the performance tonight, full of adrenalin and ravenous as usual, he would eat an enormous Italian supper across the street from Lincoln Centre at Fiorello's, and afterwards, sleepy at last, go home to bed. *A lonely bed for me*, thought Tony.

Time for his pre-performance walk, he decided, putting on a coat, winding a scarf around his throat and heading for the door.

....

That evening Tony arrived early at the Metropolitan Opera. His chauffeur-driven car deposited him at the stage door, under Lincoln Centre in the brightly lit parking area. After signing autographs for five thrilled die-hard fans who had been waiting an hour to see him arrive, he hurried through the outside corridor to the stage door. The two guards acknowledged his greeting with big, welcoming grins.

He strode down the long yellow locker-lined passage and, before entering his dressing room, he knocked at the door marked Valentina Welles. The young black American soprano was making her Metropolitan Opera debut with this run of *Tosca*. Her career had risen rapidly in the past three years, the leavening having been her triumphantly replacing Tony's friend, the great diva Mia Mitsouros, twice, at short notice, in highly publicized situations.

Valentina herself opened the door, and Tony was surprised to see her already in costume, since her entrance on stage in *Tosca* did not come until the middle of the first act. She was visibly shaking. If Tony had not sung with her before, he would have been unnerved by this display of stage panic; but he had learned that her fear gave a special, exciting edge to her performances.

The Tosca Taunt

He hugged her tightly, saying, "You don't be afraid, you will be wonderful; when have you not sung well?"

"Tony darling. You always say the right thing. You will— you will—" Her eloquent eyes beseeched, saying what she was too proud to utter.

"Will I help you? There will not be any need, but of course I will ... we will help each other."

She laughed. "Me? Help the unshakeable Antonio Amato? Don't be ridiculous. Have you ever needed help on stage?"

Tony made as if to think hard. He said, "Maybe once when I was seventeen. He hugged her again. "*In bocca al lupo*, Valentina. I'll see you on stage."

He continued on to his small, brightly lit dressing room. He hoped, after he was costumed and made up, to have his cherished half hour of mental preparation and vocal warmup just before the performance. He always wished for Jen close beside him then, while he thought his way into the character he was about to portray. He felt a mysterious flow of support from her that he could find nowhere else.

As curtain time approached, Tony, concerned that he had not yet heard from Jen, consulted his notebook and dialled the number of her hotel. Jen had phoned that afternoon when Tony was out walking in Central park. She had told their children's nanny of the unscheduled stop at Hadley's Ridge, and that the hotel phones were to be disconnected for a short while but that she would call Tony before his performance as usual.

There was no answer to Tony's call. Tony tried the number through the operator, but she could get no reply either. She made an enquiry, to learn that the hotel lines were still down due, it was theorised, to continuing electrical and other problems. Dismayed, for the superstitious Tony never wanted to sing without hearing "Break a Leg" or "*In bocca al lupo*" from his wife, he said two prayers instead of his usual one, as he clutched his medallion of Saint Cecilia, the patron saint of musicians. Only then did he feel ready to perform.

"Beginners on stage please," boomed the loudspeaker.

Tony started out the door to stand in the wings, waiting for his entrance which came partway through the first act, when the phone rang. His crew-cut blonde assistant Eric, who had just returned to the dressing room, said, "I'll get it, Tony."

"No, I don't go on right away, I am sure it is Jen; listen for my cue if I am talking to her," Tony said, as he dashed back across the small room and picked up the phone.

"*In bocca al lupo,* Tony darling!"

"Mia! You call me all the way from England just to say this; is very nice."

"I had to wish you good fortune," said Mia in her lilting voice. "How will you ever get through a *Tosca* without me? How many *Toscas* in a row have we sung together before Valentina Welles usurped me in your affections?"

Tony laughed. His close friend, the American singer Mia Mitsouros was by far his favourite soprano. He felt he sang better with her than with any other soprano. He knew how good they looked together on stage, he tall and dark, she small, with bright brown hair, round turquoise eyes and an unusual, off-beat beauty. But it was not only the way they looked together that had casting directors eager to pair them on stage, for the chemistry between them was electrifying.

The Tosca Taunt

"Mia, I have to make this short, they have started the overture."

"Actually, I'm calling Jen—is she there? What a silly question, where else would she be but with you just before you sing? I need to consult with my matron of honour about the wedding."

Tony's assistant was beckoning him; it was nearing time for his entrance on stage.

"I have to go, Mia. Jen is not here; she is opening an art college in Canada. Quickly, tell me what do you want?"

"I need to know what shade of rose is her dress for the wedding."

"*Cielo,* I am a singer, not a fashion designer. Let me see. It exactly matches the silk on our bedroom walls. Okay?"

"Perfect, Tony darling. So we'll see you and Jen in London in three weeks. I can hardly believe Cedric and I are finally getting married after all our troubles."

"You are happy, Mia? Is okay?"

There was a short silence. Then Mia replied, her voice soft, "Of course I'm happy, Tony darling. Since I can't marry you—or—or Placido or Luciano or Roberto, you know how I love tenors but you lot are all spoken for, I'll settle for Cedric. He is so good to me and to my children—but I hardly need to tell *you* that."

"I know. But he better be good *for* you too."

"Mr Amato on stage, Mr Amato," said the loudspeaker.

"Well of course, Tony darling. That goes without saying."

"I have to run away, Mia, they call me now on stage. We will talk soon, and we will see you at the wedding."

Jean Dell

Mia Mitsouros distractedly put down the phone in her suite at Ridlough Hall, the ancestral chateau in Hertfordshire belonging to her fiance Cedric Tyhurst, Viscount Ridlough. Absent-mindedly she sat down in a yellow armchair and chewed at her thumbnail. There was a peremptory knock at the door.

"Come," called Mia, and Cedric, too well mannered to barge in, even on his fiancé, without signalling first, strode into the room. Mia was constantly bemused that a man of such power and wealth—he was the owner and chairman of Ridlo Consolidated—could appear so ordinary, so bland and blonde. He was far from unattractive, but his physical appeal was understated, not at all like Tony and other flamboyant, vivid singers in the operatic world, with whom Mia often worked.

Cedric seized her outstretched hands, pulled her from the chair and kissed her with a passion belied by his composed appearance. He had waited a long time to possess Mia. He had forced himself through a divorce so painful to Alexandra, the wife who had been his childhood sweetheart, that he thought she would kill him, kill herself, or die of grief. But that was finished; Alexandra had finally survived her sadness, and in three weeks Mia would be his wife. He still could scarcely believe his good fortune. The great American soprano Mia Mitsouros, at last his.

"Time for today's mystery gift."

"Darling Cedric, you must stop giving me presents every day, you'll bankrupt yourself."

"Don't fret over that, darling. You fret over singing, I'll fret

The Tosca Taunt

over money."

He took from his pocket a small jewel case. "This time you'll be surprised."

Mia opened the case. Lying on the dark green velvet inside was an enamel miniature of a bewigged youth in a rose coloured coat and ivory weskit. She peered more closely. It was obviously antique, and the miniature was of—why, it was of Mozart. Cedric gave such appropriate gifts. She hugged him tightly and drew back, smiling and shaking her head, wordless with pleasure.

Suddenly his expression changed; he looked like a child expecting a lollipop. He took her hands in his. "I must tell you. I did hope I could wait for our wedding day to announce it. But I've just this morning managed to get a commitment, if he can begin straight away, from the architect I must have. Actually he's engaged, for years. So I'll tell you what my wedding gift to you is, since you must be in on the designing from the beginning."

He paused, and she wondered why he was out of breath. She bit her bottom lip, both excited and uncertain.

"My wedding gift to you is the Mia Mitsouros Opera Theatre, which I will build on our estate, and which we will use for operatic festivals like Glyndebourne, but focussed around your talents, your tastes, your ideas."

Mia was deeply moved. Years before, in the heat of a terrible quarrel, he had tried to coerce her into marrying him with the promise of her own opera house, but she had been far too angry to even consider accepting. Now, she hugged him painfully hard, overwhelmed by the generosity of his gift. But in her secret self there was dismay as well as joy. She wished—oh how she wished! that her love and need for him, real though they were, came somewhere near to equalling his. But her good friend Tony Amato cast a long shadow over her emotions.

"Darling Cedric," she said, "I don't deserve such generosity—I hope I never let you down, I hope you are never disappointed in me—"

"Disappointed? In you? I can only conceive of one thing you could do now that would disappoint me."

Mia did not want to pursue that. She held his hand, tracing his fingers one by one with hers. "You really don't care that I've been married twice before, do you, Cedric."

"But I've been married too. We are both the sum of our pasts. How could I resent what created you?"

And although he should have been leaving for an important meeting in London, he pulled her purposefully into her bedroom, as she resolutely put aside her disquieting, unwelcome thoughts.

....

The fire in the Hadley's Ridge Hotel was exploding out of control, while in New York Tony's *Tosca* was progressing well despite a delayed beginning. Tonight, to his relief, Tony detected little animosity from the cast members who might have liked at least one rehearsal with him. And Valentina Welles was, as usual, a small miracle.

The second act was now splendidly under way. Tony, as *Cavaradossi*, was standing in the wings supposedly being tortured, and was singing loud moans somewhat too melodic to be convincing. *Scarpia*, onstage, sang to *Tosca* that a band of sharply spiked steel around *Cavaradossi's* head was slowly being

The Tosca Taunt

tightened.

At exactly ten p.m, Tony was astonished by a fleeting vision of Jen's face contorted in fear, and by a pain in his head so sharp that the cry he was singing became absolutely convincing. He lost his breath for a moment, dreading the performing opera singer's nightmare, a headache, which causes the resonation in a singer's head to become agonizing.

Tony took several deep breaths before, in his character as *Cavaradossi*, being dragged onstage in a faint from having been tortured. To his relief the violent pain in his head subsided as quickly as it had come, leaving him feeling strangely detached. He floated through the rest of the opera, singing only adequately, and puzzled as to why he was suddenly unable to connect either to the music or the drama. His performance had become just form with no substance. He hoped fervently that nobody else would notice.

After the final applause had died down, he and Valentina Welles descended the short corridor to their dressing rooms where baritone Bruce Grey, already in his street clothes since his character *Scarpia* died at the end of the second act, waited to go to supper. Tony, ravenous earlier, now went to Fiorello's with several of his fellow singers only because he had promised. Valentina's relief and excitement were in proportion to her previous terror, and would have enlivened any party, let alone one of opera singers feeling triumphant. But Tony was inexplicably despondent. Still, he was a convincing actor, so his dinner companions had no reason to suspect that Tony felt restless, unhappy, almost afraid.

He worried as he struggled to do justice to a large plateful of pasta with marinara sauce. *I have read about these—what do they call them—panic attacks; don't tell me I am starting that. For there is absolutely no reason why I should feel like this; of what should I be afraid? My life goes so well these days ...*

Finally at three a.m. Tony climbed into the antique four poster bed in the bedroom that was his favourite place in the world, when Jen was there. He reached over to turn off the light, extinguishing the glow cast by the rosy brocaded silk on the walls. He lay on his back, disagreeably wide-awake. Imagining Jen beside him did no good; it only made him long for her always passionate response to him. He was oddly cold, although the duvet was thick and the bedroom warm despite the window open to the cool October evening.

It is because my body is still on Berlin time. Almost lunch time, not bedtime. I will just lie here anyway; I am bound to sleep sooner or later. I will not think about how big this bed is for one person. It is strange I have not been able to contact Jen at that hotel. We have never gone a whole day without phoning when we were apart. We did not speak now for—let me see—forty-six hours. Feels like forty-six days.

What are you doing now, my Jen?

Five

Stumbling, panting, Jen dragged the heavy suitcase down a steep and seemingly endless incline. She could find no path, and she struggled through damp leaves, underbrush, tangled weeds and half concealed roots that tripped her. Her uncomfortably loose shoes kept slipping off her heels. Above her the pines whispered to the misty rain. At least the sharp pain in her head had lessened, so she concluded that the pill she had ingested might well be what it was labelled, Demerol. She certainly had a good supply. For what severe pain it had been first prescribed? No recollection came to her.

Does this hill ever end? I'm so tired ... what if there is no road at the bottom? I'll never make it with this suitcase if I have to go back. I'd better not trouble trouble until trouble troubles me—good grief, am I the sort of person given to hearty slogans like that? What sort of person am I? I can't waste my energy worrying about that. I won't even think about it until I get to the bottom of this hill.

A faint noise gradually grew louder—the sound of a

powerful engine straining hard. Somewhere near, there must be a road, because that was a truck hauling a heavy load up an incline, she was sure of it.

Hurrying, she lost her footing and began to slide down the slippery fallen leaves as bushes tore at her face. She knew she was being scratched but felt little, and wondered uneasily how high the dosage of that Demerol was. She hung on to the suitcase handle, barely managing to keep her footing as she emerged from the bushes and saw a most welcome sight, a well-kept gravel road. To her left the road descended sharply into a deep forested valley, and she saw what was making the roaring noise—a large tan-coloured truck pulling a double load of logs up the steep incline towards her.

She let go of the handle of her suitcase and, as the truck approached her, stuck out her thumb in the universally recognised hitchhiker's gesture.

The trucker, Charlie Demchuk, glanced, then frankly stared at the woman beside the road just ahead, who apparently wanted a ride. What was a woman doing hitching on this road? Charlie had just come from the sawmill, and there was nothing between the sawmill and the main highway several miles to the north of here except this gravel road. How did that woman get here? She looked young, pretty, well dressed.

I'd better pick her up, he thought. *Likely nobody will come along this road again for several hours, and it's wet and cold.* He slowed his rig to a grinding, shrieking halt—he'd better get those brakes seen to again, damn noisy things—and leaned over to open the door on the opposite side from him.

"Come on, lady, you better get in, it's cold out there. Put

The Tosca Taunt

your suitcase in the back, no, no, this door, there where my bunk is, yeah, you've got it." He laughed at her attempts to get into the high truck. "Too short at one end, eh, lady? Here, grab my hand."

The hand she put into his was soft and small. He pulled, getting a good look at her as she got into the cab. Blonde, two good shiners, a couple of long scratches on her face, but the face itself now, she looked a bit like that French actress who used to do ads for that expensive perfume he bought every Christmas for his wife Barb, *Chanel Number Five*. This woman looked like whatsername, DeNiro, no, Deneuve, something like that, Cathleen or maybe Catherine.

"Wherya going?"

Jen thought hard. Where was that mine?

"I'm going up north to work in the Delson mine, you go in to it from Timmins."

He took his eyes off the road to look at her again. She must be a mining engineer or geologist, something professional, judging from the way she was dressed, expensive stuff. But if she was a mining engineer, she could certainly afford the train or bus fare; what was she doing hitching?

"Whatcha going to do there?"

"Kitchen work. I'm a—" Jen remembered the phrase from the letter she had found. "—I'm a *sous-chef*."

"A cook? You don't look like a cook."

"I didn't know there was a mold for cooks."

Charlie laughed. "I guess there isn't. But what I mean is, you don't look like a cook in a mine."

This worried Jen a bit. She said, "Why? I didn't know there

was a mold for them either."

"Well, I dunno, maybe I'm not being fair, but the camp cooks I've known, not that I've know very many, have been, well, either guys, or women who were, um, kinda husky, know what I mean?"

"Sort of a Marjorie Main type?"

"Who's Marjorie Main?"

"A movie actress who was popular in the 1940s."

He stared at her again. "You like old movies? For sure you're not old enough to remember that. You weren't born then, me either, fifty-six I was born."

"Oh no, of course I wasn't born then, I just ...it seems to me we like old movies..."

Jen struggled with a memory that would not come. Who was the person making up the "we" with whom she had watched old films? She hoped she sounded more normal than she felt. Tentatively she smiled at Charlie, who had turned again to look at her curiously.

"What were you doing where I picked you up? Nobody goes on this road except to go back and forth to the sawmill." He looked again at her battered face. "You maybe have some trouble with your last ride? He turned off the highway to get you on a quieter road?"

"I'm not sure what you mean—"

"Well, a pretty woman like you, hitching all by herself, some guys might try to take advantage of the situation, know what I mean? Is that what happened? You've got two real good black eyes and you're kinda scratched up."

Jen, her stomach knotting suddenly, thought maybe that was

The Tosca Taunt

what had happened, maybe that's what she was doing there, but—but she had been in pyjamas. With no bottoms. And way up on the hill.

Have I been—could I possibly have been raped? Is that why I feel so sick and achy all over? I'm getting really scared.

"Yes, yes." Jen rubbed her forehead uncertainly. "That must be what happened."

"Must be? Dontcha know?"

"Actually, I can't seem to—" but some instinct warned Jen not to reveal that she could remember nothing. Somehow she would feel even more alone and vulnerable if she had to admit that at the moment she could not remember who she was. Even though she knew she was Bridget Jennifer Noonan. Had to be Bridget Jennifer Noonan.

So she extemporized. "I'm sorry to be so vague. I hit my head on something ... maybe fighting with the ... see this lump?" She showed him the back of her head, not realising how swollen and blood encrusted it looked. He whistled.

She continued, "I—I've got such a headache."

"Geezus lady I'm not surprised. You sure you don't have a concussion? You don't feel dizzy or sick to your stomach or anything? Maybe we should go to the hospital up in—"

"No, I don't think so, I don't feel particularly sick or even dizzy any more. Just, my head hurts, you know?"

"I've got aspirin, you want some? There's a thermos with coffee too if you're thirsty. Just over there. The aspirin's in the glove compartment. You could even lie down in the back if you want."

Jen reached over, took out three aspirins, and, pouring

herself a mug of coffee, swallowed them, choking a bit on the last one. Only then did she remember that she had taken Demerol a while before. She had a moment's panic, wondering how the two drugs mixed.

"You're very kind," she said finally.

"Hey lady, why would I be mean to you? We're not supposed to pick hitchers up, company policy you know, I could get fired for this, but every once in a while it gets damn lonely and it's nice to have someone to talk to. You want to listen to music? What kind do you like—I've got everything."

"Opera. I like—" Jen was astonished. Where had *that* come from? "I like opera."

"I guess I *haven't* got everything. No opera here. Country, Broadway musicals, soft rock, oh yeah, I have got one CD of some opera singer singing with John Denver, it's not bad, you want that? Domingo, the other guy's name is."

"That would be nice."

Charlie asked her to flip through his CDs to find the right one, and he put it on.

"I saw a program says there's big time competition between this guy Domingo and that other one, you know, the big one, Pavrot, some such name. You know about that?" Charlie asked.

"Um, yes. I think I like Domingo better."

"How can you tell the difference between those two guys? Their singing I mean. They all sound the same to me."

Jen thought, *Isn't this peculiar, I can remember about that but I can't remember about me.*

She explained, "Domingo is a great singing actor and Pavarotti is a singer with a gorgeous voice, but I think he doesn't

The Tosca Taunt

aspire to be a great actor. I like singing actors best. But lots of people think Pavarotti is the best tenor alive."

They drove along in companionable silence for some miles, listening to the CD. After a while Charlie said, "I'm Charlie. What's your name?"

Before she could think, Jen said, "I'm Jen." Why Jen, she wondered? Surely I'm Bridget, aren't I? But somehow the name Bridget doesn't feel right. Surely it will come back to me, surely, as soon as this awful lump goes down and my head stops hurting ...

She could not stop the tears. She surreptitiously wiped them away, sure that she had hidden her emotion, when Charlie said to her, "There's Kleenex in the glove compartment."

"Thanks," Jen said. Then, "I'm sorry. I don't know what's the matter with me."

He looked at her kindly. "You been knocked around, that's what's the matter with you. Don't worry, lady, I mean Jen, I've got three sisters, I been married eighteen years and I got four daughters, two sons, I understand all about women. Sometimes I think I should write a book how to understand women. Anyway, you cry some if you want. I don't mind."

Jen blew her noise quietly, and, for reasons she wished she could understand, now began to cry in earnest. Charlie said, "That's okay, I won't watch you, you'll feel better in a while," and, turning up his Domingo-Denver CD, he kept his eyes steadfastly on the road.

Six

Slowly the adrenalin from performing his Metropolitan Opera *Tosca* dissipated, and Tony drifted into restless sleep. But he kept waking; he missed Jen. Thinking of his last conversation with her, he tried repeatedly to put himself back to sleep by recollecting the night of which he had reminded her, the night when he realised that to his surprise he was already addicted to her.

....

Thirteen years before, just after Tony and Jen's wedding, they had planned to embark on his latest European singing tour together, going directly from their honeymoon in Barbados. But those well-laid plans were abruptly changed.

Late on a steamy Caribbean morning Tony and Jen were debating whether they should get up, when the phone rang. Jen reached lazily for the receiver across a supine Tony, whose immediate reaction had been to ignore the telephone. Then she sat bolt upright in the bed, shocked at the shaking voice of her

The Tosca Taunt

usually phlegmatic British brother-in-law.

"Gordon, dear Gordon, slow down, catch your breath, you sound terrible—" for Gordon had stopped speaking and sounded to Jen as though he were choking.

"What is it, " she continued gently, for she was very fond of her sister's husband, "are you ill?"

"Oh God Jen, no, it's not me, it's—it's Allison, she's—" and he broke down again. Jen's insides knotted. Allison, her fraternal twin sister, her alter ego, her best friend ... She grabbed Tony's hand, holding it so tightly it hurt, as she listened.

"For goodness' sake, Gordon, what? You're scaring me—"

"Alli's gone into labour and—"

"Already? But Gordon, it's too early—"

"I know, Jen, please come, she's asking for you—"

"What do you mean, she's asking for me, you sound as though you think she's—"

Gordon was for a moment completely incoherent. Then he continued, "The doctors think there's an outside chance they may be able to save the baby but Allison is—" He could not go on.

"She's what? What are you saying? Are you telling me she's dying?"

Silence. Then, "Yes. For the love of God come, Jen. But hurry, or you may not get here in time ... "

Jen started to respond, then realised she was speaking to the dial tone. She turned to Tony, still tightly holding her hand, and, her voice a hoarse whisper, told him that they were about to be plunged into tragedy.

A pain stabbed into Tony's head as he realized he was

forced to inflict even more misery on her. He had hoped she would not have to come to terms with the sweet tyranny of his career until later, when their marriage was better established, more secure and solid. Her next words added to his apprehension.

"Darling, we must hurry, you call the airline and make reservations, I'll pack, I've just realised I've never even asked you what happens in a case like this, I mean, you're going to miss rehearsal time, do you cancel the performance or what?"

She started out of bed; he pulled her back, and, holding her tightly against him, caressed her hair, as he said, "No, I don't cancel. I can likely come with you for two days and —"

She pulled sharply away from him. "*Two days*? What do you mean, *two days*? Tony, I *need* you, the only close blood relative I have left is dying! Oh God, I can't take it in—" and Jen slumped against him, weeping.

He stroked her back, the pain in his head stabbing like an ice pick. After he had calmed her a little he said, "Let me call Vienna and see what can be done. This is a difficult situation, you have to understand—"

Disbelieving, Jen cried, "There's nothing to understand. Surely my needs come before some little opera—"

"It's not just *some little* opera, Jen, it's my life, it's our lives, our future."

"You mean you're actually considering *not* staying with me until Allie's situation is resolved? Tony, please, I thought you were—you've always been so kind—I can't believe these are your priorities. We won't *have* a future if you can't put your family first even in a frightening situation like this."

The Tosca Taunt

"Jen, try to understand. There are a lot of people involved who are counting on me. This is only my second time at the Staatsoper, this *Faust* is a new production they have created especially for me and that soprano Mia Mitsouros, the first time we sing together. Naturally I don't know yet the blocking or stage directions, and besides I have never worked with the conductor, Sheldon Wasserman, before. *Cielo,* Jen, don't you understand how hard this is for me?" Grimacing, he clutched his forehead with his hand.

"Hard for *you*? Just a bit self-centred, aren't you?"

Tony almost responded in kind, but realised that would only make this quarrel worse. "*Per favore,* Jen, it is crucial for me to sing this *Faust.* I don't have a choice."

Jen's anger was compounded by her fear. She was out of control now. "Oh—yes—you— do. You have a choice, and you can make it right now. You can choose your career or me."

"Don't do this to me. Let me call Vienna."

She put her face in her hands and whispered, her voice muffled. "I knew there had to be an argument—I'm told there always is one on a honeymoon, but I never dreamed our first quarrel could destroy us. Any more than I dreamed you could be so disloyal to me. I can't believe this is happening."

Tony was crumbling inside. He had put his singing before everything else in his life, because he believed his voice was a sacred trust that he was obligated to share. Up to now this decision had inconvenienced nobody but him. But now the foundation on which his life was built was shaking in an emotional earthquake, and Tony knew his career decisions would never be simple again.

Jean Dell

Jen leapt out of bed and, pulling her luggage from the bottom of the closet, began to pack, hurling aside any of Tony's clothes that were intertwined with hers.

Tony quickly reached over to pick up the phone. After repeated tries, he got through to Vienna. With difficulty he convinced an irate director, who had reluctantly agreed to Tony's previous request to arrive late for rehearsal because of his honeymoon, to give him three extra days. Tony could feel the animosity behind this concession. He was perturbed; these were early days in a promising career, and he needed to maintain his growing reputation for reliability.

"I can come with you for three days," he told Jen miserably. "You think I like this? You think I would not rather stay with you? This is the price I pay for the gift of the voice. Often I want to be in one place, but the voice has to be in another."

"And if Allison dies?" Jen's voice was bitter. "Will you be able to get an hour or two off for the funeral or will your *Faust* take precedence? Have *you* sold your soul too?"

The superstitious Tony was horrified. He grabbed at the medallion of Saint Cecilia that he always wore, and held it tightly as his words tumbled over one another. "How can you even think of planning for if Allison dies? How can you even say the words? You're inviting disaster—take back the words, Jen, here, take them back and touch my medallion, my Santa Cecilia, we must pray they both live!"

Jen stared at him, her face contorted with her pain. "Of course, of course you're right—how could I be making a plan for if she dies?" She reached out and clutched the medallion that he held out to her. "I take it back I take it back oh God oh God let

The Tosca Taunt

her live, oh Tony I can't bear it—"

He was not sure she wanted his arms around her but he thought he would risk it. She did not resist; she leaned against him unhappily.

"I don't understand why you have to do what you're doing, Tony, but I—I apologise for asking you to choose between me and your career. I promised myself I'd never ask that, and here we are, married only a few days—"

This was by far the most difficult choice Tony and his voice had yet had to make. There were worse to come, of course, but fortunately he did not know that. He did not know what he knew now as he recollected all this, that for example years later, because he had to finish singing the last act of *Boheme* in San Francisco, he would not be able to reach Jen, in hospital in New York, in time to support her when she nearly died from premature labour with their doomed son Gianni.

But now his mouth was against Jen's hair as he said, "I told you life with a singer would sometimes be hard, Jen, you cannot say I did not warn you, but, oh *cara mia*, you must understand, I do love you."

....

The doctors in Oxford announced after three anxious days, that Allison and her tiny son, though still both weak, would live. So the newlyweds, still reeling from their quarrel, said a tense goodbye in London Airport, from where Tony would fly to Vienna and a satisfyingly successful *Faust*. Critics were almost unanimously ecstatic over the new pairing of Amato and Mitsouros, of the mellifluous blend of their voices, of their attractive appearance together, and of their electrifying stage presences.

Six weeks later, an uneasy Tony stood in the middle of the Charles de Gaulle airport concourse on the outskirts of Paris, waiting for Jen to come through Customs. When he caught sight of her, pulling her suitcase and looking all around for him, he broke into a run. Throwing his arms around her he kissed her as though they had been apart for years. Finally he drew back, slightly breathless.

"Does this by any chance indicate you're glad to see me?" Tony was moved to hear Jen's voice trembling.

"It indicates," he said, and kissed her again. "I missed you. You feel like a part of my life I don't want to do without."

"More than your vocal cords?" she whispered, her mouth still against his cheek.

He drew back, looking at her reproachfully. "Low blow, Jen, let us start with a truce ... "

They climbed into the back seat of a taxi, and clutched each other's hands fearfully. Each wondered if their beautiful closeness would return, or whether they had maimed it beyond repair.

"Is for sure all okay now with your family?"

"I think so, Tony. It was good to be with them; I felt so needed. Of course if Mom and Dad were still alive Alli would have their support too; we are so alone, Alli and I."

"Except for Gordon and me, we count for something, surely?"

She turned tentatively to him and they embraced again. Then, with one thing and another, they were surprised to find themselves already at their hotel. Firmly, so as to shut out the world, they closed the door of their Grand Hotel suite. They did not even glance from the windows that gave a splendid view of the old Paris Opera House, the Palais Garnier. But views of anything except one another seemed at least temporarily unimportant.

Both now feeling a little more confident, they caressed one another, shedding clothes on the way to the bedroom. Tenderly, hungrily, Tony kissed the rosy aureole of Jen's breasts. Knowing he risked her rejection, still he whispered, "It will be wonderful to have you always with me. Sometimes I have been so lonely ... but now, I will never be lonely again."

Jen had the fleeting thought that his sentiment was operatic, dramatic, possibly self-deceiving. But, at last no longer angry, who was she to disabuse him if he believed it? And soon she became utterly engrossed with other things.

After a long while, they lay still, her naked body tightly against his. Then she propped herself up on her elbow and looked down at him teasingly. "You're in pretty good shape for a man who's been on such a busy tour ..."

"Why would I not be? I am strong, you know. I truly never feel tired except maybe one or two times a year, and then I am black depressed until I get a couple of good nights' sleep, you will laugh at me, Jen."

"I doubt it. I'll sympathise and look after you. Tony, don't laugh at me, but I—I really need to believe your life will be better because you married me."

Jen's words were what Tony had hoped to hear. They revealed to him a welcome depth, a desire to devote herself to his career (he hoped) as well as to him. His spirits soared. He jumped from the bed and pulled his bride up into a joyous impromptu dance. Then he tumbled her back on the bed. They tried to count ecstasies. Losing count, they finally fell quiet together, entwined on the rumpled sheets. He began to hum.

"What are you humming, Tony?"

"You don't recognise? I must be losing my touch. Listen. "There's a somebody I'm so glad to see, I know that she's turned out to be someone who'll watch over me—".

"You're playing fast and loose with the words."

"And with you. I think already I am addicted to you, *cara mia*."

Now, thirteen years later, Tony thought how welcome these memories were. He turned over on to his stomach and dozed, dreaming that Jen was asleep beside him, one arm across his back.

Seven

The air conditioning had finally been fixed in Doctor Victor Macready Kilbride's dental office, situated in a dignified old house in a suburb of New Orleans. In one of his cubicles, Doctor Kilbride peered enthusiastically at Shelley Smith's molars. Pretty little thing she was, this Shelley, although her dignified mother, also his patient, must have been dismayed when she saw the green spiked hair. Shelley had another cavity; if she insisted on ignoring milk for soft drinks, forgetting meals, and smoking marijuana, well, it probably all added to the cavities and helped increase Doctor Kilbride's large bank balance.

He'd better freeze her up a little, to convince her she would not feel the drill. He had no intention of freezing her enough, but she wouldn't know it until the drill hit the nerve. Doctor Kilbride poked the needle into the soft shiny pink gum and twisted it a bit as Shelley squirmed, said, "Ow!" and glowered at him. He said soothingly, "There now, just a little more and you won't feel anything." He pulled out the needle and massaged her cheek hard.

"This better not hurt, or I won't come back," said Shelley almost intelligibly, the implicit threat lost on Doctor Kilbride. She was there now, nubile lissome creature, what did he give a damn whether she came back or not? He caressed her hand and said, "Don't worry, you shouldn't feel a thing."

Down came the drill. Doctor Kilbride knew he had better get started before the freezing took hold altogether, just in case he had accidentally given her enough. Gently he passed the drill over the edges of the cavity, and without warning plunged its vibrator into the tender exposed nerve. Shelley jumped, shouted "Ah-h-h-h," and pushed his hand away just after he hit the nerve a second time with the drill.

He had a most pleasurable sensation. This was remarkably bracing. He said to her, "I'm sorry, Shelley, I can't understand how that happened, I'll put in some more freezing." Again he thrust the syringe in, this time not depressing the plunger at all, just moving the needle so it would feel to Shelley like freezing filling her gum. Her dark eyes filled with tears, though from the expression on her face he could tell she was furious with herself for showing him that she was not brave. The tear-shiny eyes looking helplessly at him augmented his enjoyment.

Again he plunged in the drill. She leapt, shrieked, and began to weep in earnest. He had better really freeze the gum this time, and leave her for a minute for the anaesthetic to take effect. Gently he inserted the needle one more time and filled her gum so full of anaesthetic she would be unable to smile symmetrically for hours. He said, "I'll leave that for a minute, Shelley, and we'll test when I come back to make sure it's really frozen. I'm sorry we're having such a problem this morning."

Scarcely able to contain himself, he went into the bathroom. There he scarcely had time to touch himself before he shuddered with pleasure as he came. Shelley would complain to her mother; all his teenage girl patients did, but he treated their mothers with such care they never felt a moment's pain under his treatment. And they could not understand why their daughters complained so bitterly about such a kind, gentle dentist. Best one the mothers had ever had.

His private phone rang insistently. He decided to answer it before he finished with Shelley. He was glad he had, because it was his great good buddy, Leonard LeComte.

"So! Len! What's up?"

"What's up is a meeting tomorrow, Vic; I've finally decided it's now or never, for me to run. About time, I hear you thinking. Anyway, dinner at our place tomorrow night, seven o'clock. Wives included: Delphine's rented a movie for them after dinner while we have our meeting—I've got to show off our new entertainment room."

"Uh ... Bryony's ... uh, Bryony's away," Victor said. "Visiting her mother. She'll be sorry she missed the party."

"Yeah. Well. See you Thursday. I'll let you go. You're probably filling the cavities of some gorgeous creature, as usual, eh Vic?"

"You've got it, Len. This one's a smasher. See you tomorrow night"

Smasher is right, thought Victor as he strolled back into the room where the lovely Shelley waited nervously for his next ministrations. *And wouldn't that old bigot Len have a fit if he knew I could be so turned on by a smasher who is black.*

Eight

Tony Amato lay in his four poster bed, planning his day. Surely this morning he would at last be able to contact Jen. Other than doing that, his day consisted of approving the choice of songs for his CD recording session, and giving an interview to a magazine journalist from California. Otherwise, today was pleasantly free. He reached across to the bedside table and pulled the phone towards him.

But when he dialled Jen's hotel, the phone did not ring at all. His next attempt was through the operator who told him there was trouble on that line; she admitted she was puzzled about it. Tony hung up the phone, feeling unaccountably uneasy.

I am doing what Jen always says; I am making an opera out of my problems. Except I think this time I am inventing a problem to make an opera out of. It must be that I need a break. Is there enough time for Jen and me to get away? Maybe we could go back to the Canary Islands after Mia and Cedric's wedding? He reached for his maroon silk dressing gown, his last birthday gift from his children Anton

Jean Dell

and Janina.

In his always untidy library he took the book that held his schedule for the next two years, from a drawer of the massive, cluttered mahogany desk. Brushing aside his daughter's doll and the doll's wardrobe to make room, he laid the schedule on the desktop. While he was scanning what he had on for the next month, the phone on the desk rang; he pushed books, toys and papers aside and eagerly reached for the receiver.

"Jen? Is about time!"

He was greeted first by a moment's silence and then by his manager's voice. "Sorry to disappoint you, Tony, but it's me, to tell you we're all set for Buenos Aires, you leave Saturday morning at nine. Have you lost Jen?"

What an ugly phrase, Tony thought. "Of course not, I mean, only temporarily. But while you're on the line, Gareth, I'm thinking Jen and I can spend a week in the Canary Islands after Mia's wedding. Can you look into arrangements?"

"You can't, Tony, you've got the concert in Madrid."

"I can just fly out for the concert and come right back to the Canaries. I need a holiday, Gareth. You don't want I should get sick or lose the voice, do you?"

"Always very persuasive, that argument, Tony. I'll get back to you about arrangements. Now, go find Jen. You two really are extraordinary. After—how many years have you been married?—you still act like newlyweds."

"Thirteen years, but we figure with all my travelling we've only been together about five. And jealousy will get you nowhere, Gareth."

"I know. Pity!"

The Tosca Taunt

Later Tony, not yet having found Jen, and still sitting in the big leather easy chair in his library, stopped studying a *Romeo et Juliet* score, rubbed his eyes, and idly switched on the radio to a newscast.

" ... investigators have arrived on the scene to search the still smouldering ruins for four people who are missing and presumed dead. Their names as well as the sixteen known dead are being withheld pending notification of next of kin."

Tony switched off the radio. *Poor people*, he thought. *There will be families crying today when they learn who they have lost.*

He changed from his dressing gown to what Jen called his great-Italian-tenor-going-to-a-meeting look, black turtleneck and slacks and expensive light grey wool Italian blazer. Then he phoned the limousine company and ordered a car.

As Tony was driven along the Manhattan streets, he stared out the smoked window, idly admiring the ornate buildings that appealed to his sense of decoration and symmetry, and reminded him of Italy. But the architectural gems of his native Italy held for him a warmth, a special flair that he found in no other country, however beautiful.

At his meeting with the record producer, in Gareth's office Tony found himself dissatisfied when presented with the list of songs to be recorded. "Who chose these? The name of the album is sad; these songs are not all sad."

"What did you expect? The CD is called, *To Have, to Hold, Perhaps to Lose.* You were maybe expecting *Otello?*" asked Tony's frequently exasperated producer. "There's a couple sad songs—*We'll Meet Again*, for instance."

"Okay okay, I don't have time to argue, but next one we

name it better to fit the songs."

"Whatever, Tony. You liked the name last month, and you approved most of these songs then, don't you remember? This name should attract buyers. If you know anyone who hasn't loved and lost, tell me about it."

"Well, me, for instance."

The producer shook his head and winked knowingly at Tony. "Sure, sure, you don't have to put on that act for me. I mean, I know that's what your publicity says, except of course for the tabloids that talk about Tony Amato's roving eye. But you're not going to tell *me* all your public lovey dovey stuff is for real."

"I *am* going to tell you."

The producer glanced at Gareth, raised one eyebrow and grinned at Tony. "Yeah, right." And then, seeing Tony's expression, said quickly, "Okay, okay, some guys have all the luck!"

"*Grazie a Dio,*" Tony muttered, rubbing his hand against his medallion of Saint Cecilia. Sometimes he felt almost too lucky; should he be looking over his shoulder, just in case?

On Tony's drive home he impulsively had the car stop at a florist's shop. There he ordered two dozen red roses to be waiting for Jen on her arrival at the Sudbury art college.

He dismissed the car at the Plaza Hotel, and, savouring sudden sunlight after rain, he strolled up Fifth Avenue towards the Metropolitan Museum and home. This great avenue, flanked by Central Park on one side and some of Manhattan's handsomest apartment buildings on the other, was on Tony's list of favourite streets down which to stroll. When he entered his

The Tosca Taunt

own elegant apartment, expecting to see the interviewer, Mrs Burns, his children's nanny, met him in the front hall. He was surprised to see her pale, trembling.

"Mrs Burns? Is something wrong? You look not so good — are you all right?"

Mrs Burns nervously caught her lower lip with her teeth.

Tony panicked. "The children? Are the children —?"

"The children are fine, Mr Amato. But — but I am anxious, there are two policemen here in the living room, they want to speak to you."

Policemen? Why would policemen come to his apartment? His only contact with the police was over occasional speeding tickets. But they never came to his home about those. Especially not in twos. *Policemen in twos in his home could only mean bad news*, thought a perturbed Tony as he unwillingly entered his living room.

He was met there by two tall New York police constables, one young and black, the other older, pale and grizzled. The older one cleared his throat and said quietly, "Antonio Amato?"

"Yes," said Tony. His heart suddenly began to thump disagreeably hard.

"You'd better sit down, sir."

Tony sank slowly into the soft-cushioned rose chesterfield, his eyes never leaving the constable's face. It seemed to him that everything had gone into slow motion — Mrs Burns standing in the doorway clasping her hands tightly in front of her; the two policemen with not a shadow of a smile on their faces; and he, wondering whose name from among those he loved would emerge from a constable's lips.

"There has been an accident, sir, in Ontario. The Hadley's Ridge Hotel has burned to the ground; sixteen people have been killed and four are missing. I'm sorry to have to tell you that your wife Jenetta Amato is among the missing. The fire was very intense, sir; the missing people are presumed dead. There is almost no chance they could have survived."

Constable Murphy hated this aspect of his job. He watched the great Italian tenor's dark eyes open into an unblinking stare, like the stare of the dead. Then came what the constable expected.

"No! No! This cannot be; she—she was not at that hotel last night, I am sure she cannot have been there, how can you know she is one of the missing? This is a mistake, it has to be!"

"Mr Amato, the clerk at the desk of Hadley's Ridge Hotel had the presence of mind to grab the hotel register as he escaped from the building. Your wife had signed the register. Everyone else is accounted for; everyone is identified, except the four missing people. Your wife is one of them. I'm really sorry."

"No! I am sure it is a misunderstanding, you will see, when they find the missing people they will learn—"

"Apparently the centre of the fire was very fierce, sir. It's doubtful the few remains they have found so far can ever be identified. Please, Mr Amato, don't get your hopes up. I'm sorry, but your wife is almost certainly dead."

It hit home. Tony slumped as though he had been struck in the stomach. And though the policemen would not have been surprised at tears, Tony, that consummate actor who had no trouble crying tears of real grief when they were required on stage, was dry-eyed, stunned, disbelieving.

The Tosca Taunt

Tony thought, *Jen. I need you, Jen. Come to me—I am so afraid. Per favore. Comfort me, oh my Jen.*

Come to me.

Nine

Charlie Demchuk brought his rig to its usual squealing stop in a small village, but the exhausted, battered Jen, fast asleep beside him with her head fallen against his shoulder, did not waken.

Whatever was he going to do with her, he asked himself worriedly? A looker like her shouldn't be hitching, no way. He guessed he'd have to help her, to trust her. He drew from his breast pocket a small notepad and a pencil, and wrote out his name and address. Then he fished around in his back pocket for his wallet and took out three one hundred dollar bills. He had a number of mouths to feed, but his company paid their drivers generously. Jen's head fell further against him, her pale hair brushing his cheek. *Geezus,* he thought, *if I were a different kinda guy* ... He gently pushed her upright, and said quietly, "Jen, wake up, this is as far as I go in your direction."

She opened her eyes and looked around her, puzzled. Charlie grinned broadly. "Forgot for a minute where you were?

The Tosca Taunt

You're with me, Charlie Demchuk, in my rig, remember?"

Jen frowned. "Y-yes, I remember, but what am I doing with you? Where—where am I going?"

"You said you were going up to the Delson gold mine."

Slowly Jen's mind focussed. Of course. She was Bridget Jennifer Noonan and she was going to work in that mine as a *sous-chef*. But who was Bridget Jennifer Noonan? She felt slightly sick.

Charlie stuck out his hand suddenly; she thought he wanted to shake hers until she saw something in his. She looked at him, questioning.

"Look, Jen, I think you're in some kinda trouble you don't wanna tell me about. That's okay, I don't expect confidences, but the way you're dressed and all, you've had some money somewhere along the way, and now you're so down on your luck you have to hitch. But a looker like you—well, hitching's dangerous. So I can spare a coupla hundred, I'd feel better if you take the bus up to where you're going, here's my address, pay me back when you can. I trust you."

Jen again tried to hold back tears and could not. What on earth was the matter with her? She was so deeply touched by this gesture.

"Oh Charlie, that's—you're so kind. I can hardly believe you'd do something like this for a total stranger."

But I seem to remember that someone else in my life does kind things like this; why can't I remember who?

She continued, "I'm not broke, really, I don't know why I was hitch-hiking, well, except there was no other way to get off that logging road, I realise that now, but why I was hitching before—I just don't remember. I'll catch the bus from here, I promise. I won't take your money, but I'll take your name and address; I'll send you a card when I get where I'm going. I'm so glad it was you who picked me up. Thank you, Charlie."

Jen climbed down from the cab and Charlie got out to hand her down the suitcase. He pointed towards a clearing beside the road, in front of a one-pump gas station.

"The bus stops over there, one should come along in about half an hour, you just flag them down out here and buy your ticket when you get on if you haven't already got one. I've got to get going. Just in case you need it, behind the gas station around that corner there's a sort of bed and breakfast, there's good people there, the Adamsons, if you have to go there tell them Charlie Demchuk sent you."

Jen held out her hand. "Thank you, Charlie. You've been wonderful." Impulsively she leaned forward and kissed her saviour on the cheek. Charlie reddened, and quickly climbed back into his truck.

The last Jen saw of him was one arm waving out the driver's window as he turned down the road with his cumbersome load. She looked around at the forest through which the road made so small an impact. She felt small, threatened by an unknown menace. She forced herself to walk purposefully over to the bus stop and to sit by the roadside on her battered luggage, waiting for the bus to appear so she could flag it down.

....

"Sixteen people have died and four are missing and presumed dead in a hotel fire in Hadley's Ridge, in Ontario, Canada. Among the missing are Jenetta Maclean Amato, the

The Tosca Taunt

well-known watercolour artist and wife of Italian tenor Antonio Amato. According to investigators there is virtually no chance that any of the missing have survived the fierce blaze."

That story was blaring out on radio and television newscasts all over North America. Tony knew he must confront his children with this devastating news before they heard it elsewhere. He could hear them playing in the library, alternately laughing and arguing over a board game he had bought for them in London. For one hideous hour he had procrastinated, sitting in the living room numbly sipping the whiskey-laden tea that Mrs Burns kept bringing him after the police left. Now with reluctant steps he walked down the hall to the library. Tony reached the door and stood, hesitant, watching. Ten-year-old Anton, a dark, intense miniature of his father, did not look up from his game. Janina, four years younger, had Tony's dark colouring but her delicate features echoed Jen's. She glanced at him, said "Hi Daddy," without interest, and shook the dice for her turn at the game.

Tony took a deep breath. He tried to speak but nothing emerged. He tried again. "Anton ... Janina, I want you to be brave because I have to tell you something frightening ... "

Tony ran his hand distractedly over his dark hair and sat down on the brown leather sofa. He told his children to sit beside him, one on each side. Reluctantly they complied; all they really wanted to do was finish their game.

He put his arms around their shoulders and clutched them against him, so they could not see his face when he told them. The highly disciplined Tony knew that in this situation he was nearly out of control.

Jean Dell

He cleared his throat roughly; he had to find a voice. "There has been a hotel fire and your Mama—she was—there are four people missing in the fire and the police—" Tony swallowed hard. "The police say the missing people are likely—" His voice disappeared.

Anton drew back, stared at his father and was horrified by the expression on Tony's face. Rather than confront that, Anton turned his face away and drew again into the tight, protecting circle of Tony's arm.

Tony tried to continue. "The missing people may be—may be dead, the police say, but—"

Now it was Janina's turn to stare at her father, fear replacing puzzlement on her face. "Dead? What do you mean, Daddy? Who's dead? You said something about Mommy," Janina said, her vulnerability piercing Tony. "But—but when Sandidog died, she never came back, she went away and she never—oh, Daddy!"

Tony drew his children even closer and hugged them tightly, these children who were the tangible witness of his love for Jen. Urgently he sought strength. He summoned what remained of his failing resources.

"No, no, you don't understand," he said. "The police say these missing four *may* be dead, but I am certain they are wrong about Mama. There is just a—a confusion, there is always a confusion around such a disaster, but Mama is all right, I am sure of it, I believe this with all of myself."

Tony saw the doubt, the fear on the faces of his children. He mustered the last argument he possessed. "Anton, Janina, have you ever known me to tell you a lie?"

The Tosca Taunt

Anton knew he had not. Even at the age of ten, with some knowledge of the outside world, Anton still considered his parents to be the rocks on which his world was built. So if Daddy said Mama was alive, then Mama was alive.

But Janina began to sob. All she knew was that the words "Mama" and "dead" had been spoken in context with one another, and that nothing had brought back their dear dead Sandidog. Tears beget tears, and Tony hid his by burying his face in her dark curls.

"Nina, Nina, don't, I am telling you, Mama is all right. It will be hard for a while because the papers and the news broadcasts are all going to say Mama is dead, and likely at school they will also, but we must go on as though she is just away for a while, because she is, soon we will hear that all is okay—"

Tony caught back a sob. He believed. He did believe. He must believe.

Anton wiped away tears, and Janina's sobs slowly subsided. They heard Mrs Burns' heels clattering on the marble floor as she went to answer the telephone. It was the doorman in the lobby announcing a visitor. The first caller arrived, presaging a flood of distressed relatives, friends and colleagues who would soon be on the phone, at the door, sending flowers, notes, cards, and generally making sure there was no way the Amatos could forget for a moment what they refused adamantly to believe.

This first caller was Tony's manager Gareth Ryan. Gareth had heard the news when, in his usual evening state of martini-induced good cheer, he had arrived home after work and had turned on the TV news. Dismayed, he said to his wife, "Oh hell, Naomi, Jen's death is the one thing I've always said would cost me Tony Amato. You remember when Jen nearly died in that awful childbirth, and Tony was so upset we thought we'd lose him too? They are symbiotic, those two. What can I do? Tony's not our bread and butter; he's our caviar; I'm not prepared to do without him."

"You'd better get over there, Gar," his wife said. "I sympathize with you. If we lose Tony for a client ... Here, supper's ready, have a quick bite while I run out and pick up flowers for you to take. Should I come to Tony's too? No, you go first, you know him so well, he'll be comfortable with you. I'll come over afterwards if you think it would be politic, once you feel out the situation."

Now, in Tony's apartment, the three Amatos, who had gone into the living room to receive the caller, heard whispers between Gareth and Nanny Burns, and then Gareth came slowly into the living room carrying a huge bouquet of white lilies. He looked at Tony and the children for a long moment, and finally said, "Tony, Anton, Nina, what can I say? I'm so sorry ... "

Tony stood up and moved forward so the children could not see his face. Staring at Gareth, he put one finger to his lips, and said, "Is all right, Gareth, you don't understand. The children and I—we are absolutely certain Jen is all right. Missing and presumed dead does not mean dead, and in the case of Jen, it is all a mistake, you will see."

Gareth frowned. He knew denial was one of the stages of grief, but this seemed somewhat exaggerated. Still, he supposed there was always a chance Jen could be alive, although, having heard the news reports, Gareth thought that chance was slim to non-existent. But since his carefully rehearsed speech of

The Tosca Taunt

condolence was obviously the last thing that was wanted, Gareth decided to get on with necessary business.

"Tony, the Met has just been in touch with me, they're getting Raffaele Ricordi to sing your *Tosca* for the rest of the run."

"*What?*" Tony's face contorted with anger. "But they haven't even spoken to me about this, how can they? This is breach of contract!"

"Tony, Tony, calm down, it's only natural, of course they realise you can't sing under the circumstances and they're speaking to you through me, how else should they do it? They're just covering their—" Gareth stopped. The children were sitting wide-eyed on the chesterfield, staring at him.

"What do you mean, I can't sing under the circumstances? What circumstances? Of course I sing! There is nothing wrong, don't you understand? Jen, she is fine, she is just—somewhere—where she cannot get in touch with me yet, don't you see?"

Gareth glanced anxiously at Nanny Burns, who had come to the doorway of the living room. She shook her head slightly and gave an almost imperceptible shrug.

"You phone back the Met *right now,* Gareth," Tony shouted. "You tell them I sing, you understand? Right now or I fire you!"

Gareth thought Tony was in worse shape than he could have imagined. Placatingly he said, "Of course, Tony, I should have—er—have realised that Jen was likely—was likely okay—just—er—do I use this phone or the one in the library?"

"Use the one in the library, Mr Ryan," Nanny Burns said. "I'll show you."

"I know where—" Gareth stopped. He had just realised

Nanny Burns needed to talk privately to him. They left the living room together and had a worried whispered conversation. The Scottish Mrs Burns, unusually agitated for someone so calm-natured, asked Gareth's advice on what to do in this most bewildering situation. But neither of them was able to come up with a helpful plan to deal with this tragedy or with Tony's denial.

Soon Gareth was on the phone to the conductor of *Tosca*, Sir Sheldon Wasserman. Sir Sheldon had worked with Tony many times and knew his nature and his voice well.

"But I cannot let Amato do this, Mr Ryan," Sir Sheldon responded in measured British tones. "I know he likes to challenge himself; I have known him to sing in stressful situations that would have daunted many singers, and he has come through successfully. But I have always credited Mrs Amato for a lot of Amato's *sang-froid* when performing. She has been such a supportive, steadying influence on him; they seem to have—have had—something rich and rare together. How sad this is. But what happens now, if in the middle of a performance of *Tosca*, Amato finally comes to the realisation that Mrs Amato is dead?"

Gareth made decisions based first on his wallet. "I know, Sir Sheldon. But what can we do? He absolutely insists that she's alive. I think we've got no choice but to pretend we believe she's alive too; otherwise we risk damaging him even more. There are so few great tenors—they're an endangered species—let's try to keep this one going if we can."

Sir Sheldon took his time replying. Finally he said, "We are certainly taking a risk, Mr Ryan, both with Amato and with the

The Tosca Taunt

performance. I'll do it, but I will see to it that Raffaele Ricordi is in costume and ready to go on at any moment throughout the evening. I'm sure the Met will not balk at the expense, given the circumstances. The only person who may not like it much is Ricordi, though he'll get excellent wages whether he does anything or not. Let me see what I can arrange. I would like to speak to Amato if you think I should."

"I don't know what the 'shoulds' are in these circumstances, I don't have much experience. Sure, talk to him. It can't do any harm."

Gareth called a reluctant Tony from the living room.

"Tony, I am so dreadfully sorry about—" Sir Sheldon began.

"No, Sir Sheldon, don't say it. Is just a mistake, you will see, Jen she is all right, my children and I are sure of it ... "

Sir Sheldon's voice sounded grating to Tony. "Er—what I was going to say, Tony, was—er—that I am so sorry you have to go through this period of anxiety. We will all be glad when it is resolved. Now, Tony, I understand you propose to sing *Tosca* tomorrow night."

"Of course, why would I not? Everything is going to be okay, the voice is fine, I am not sick, why should I not sing?"

"Because you are under considerable stress. But I want you to know I'll support your decision to sing and we'll all do everything we can to help you through."

"Is no need," Tony replied stiffly. "I have never needed help to get through an opera, you know this."

"Of course not, I worded it badly. Forgive me. Er—you take care of yourself between now and tomorrow night, Tony, and if there is anything I can do, please don't hesitate to call me."

Jean Dell

Sir Sheldon debated telling Tony that Raffaele Ricordi would be ready to go on throughout the performance, and thought better of it. It might be politic to keep that from Tony entirely, even during the opera if possible. No use letting an emotionally fragile Tony know how little Sir Sheldon believed in his ability to sing the opera tomorrow night.

....

Though it was still the middle of the night in New York, it was morning in Europe. Mia and Cedric had ordered breakfast served in her suite and were watching the television news as they poured maple syrup lavishly on their fat free oat bran waffles, somewhat defeating the purpose. One for waist, one for taste, Mia said of that particular breakfast.

Cedric reached abruptly across the yellow tablecloth and stroked Mia's hand, putting at risk the delicate white china and crystal. He was stopped in mid-caress by the bombshell television news of Jen Amato's disappearance and virtually certain death.

Cedric's chest tightened. He suddenly remembered how he and Mia had quarrelled three years before, a bitter disagreement that had precipitated a year's separation from her.

At that time he had exploded at her, "Has it ever occurred to you that you are more than a little in love with Tony Amato? I knew you hadn't learned to love me enough, but I was certain that would come when we were married. Now I think it may never happen, because between you and me stands Amato. You have to know how I feel, because between you and Amato stands Jen."

And now? Now if Jen Amato were dead? What had Mia

replied during that terrible scene?

"Oh my dear," she had said, "oh please, try to understand. You may think I am a bit in love with Tony ... and maybe I am; it's all so complicated! But part of me loves you, Cedric, much more than you seem to understand ... "

Ultimately Cedric had rested his destiny on the knowledge that in her own fragmented way Mia did love him, and that Tony and Jen Amato were a happy and united pair.

But if all obstacles were removed between Mia and Tony?

Cedric made it his life's work never to lose out on anything he wanted. But he was not prepared to wager that he could win a battle against Tony Amato for Mia, on a newly levelled playing field. The timing could not be worse. For if this had happened only three weeks later, Cedric would have his sanctified marriage to Mia as a formidable weapon with which to fight to keep her.

Cedric watched the colour drain from Mia's face as she said, "Cedric, how horrible! Burned to death? I can't take it in—We must go to Tony, we're the best friends he has, oh darling, he'll die of grief, he'll do something terrible like commit suicide."

"Darling, you're being operatic. Tony has more guts than that."

But tears filled her eyes and spilled over. "You don't understand. I'll phone Tony as soon as it's morning for him and I'll tell him we're on our way. Is the plane available or should we make arrangements for the Concorde?"

"Mia, my love," Cedric began, feeling overcome, but not only with grief for the Amatos. Like many people who knew her he liked and admired Jen Amato—and what a hideous way for anyone to die. "Surely first you should talk to Tony, to see what we can do that would help him the most."

It transpired that Cedric's jet was out of England being used by Alexandra his ex-wife, a small item Cedric had not previously bothered to mention to Mia. Faintly annoyed, Mia phoned to her assistant to book tickets on the Concorde from London to New York for later that day, so they could be by Tony's side as soon as possible.

The newscasts about the hotel fire grew increasingly horrific. Cedric watched for inauspicious signs as Mia waited for time to pass, waited for it to be late enough in New York that Tony would be awake. He watched her pace the floor, pick at a sandwich lunch, wring her hands, and make herself three very dry vodka martinis.

Finally she dialled Tony. He came on the line, his voice hoarse.

"Darling, we've just heard," said Mia. "I'm so, so sorry. I know nothing worse could have happened to you. Cedric and I will be in New York with you tonight, I just wanted you to know we're on our way."

There was a long silence. Mia said, "Tony, are you there? Are you all right?"

"I am fine. I am touched you should phone, and even more that you and Cedric should want to come, but there is no need."

Mia was taken aback by the calm finality of his tone. She said, "What do you mean? What kind of friends would we be if we left you to face this alone? Don't say another word, darling. We'll be there soon."

"No. *Per favore.* I don't want you to come. I appreciate, you must believe, but—"

"But what? What is it, Tony darling? Why don't you want us?"

"No, Mia, you don't understand. Is not that I don't want you, is that there is no reason for you to come, because Jen is all right."

Mia was shocked into momentary silence. What was this? "You mean they've found her? She's safe? Oh Tony, that's the most wonderful thing you could have told me—"

"No. No. It is not like that. It is that the children and I are sure this is all a mistake. Jen is only missing, this is temporary, she is not dead, Mia, she cannot be dead, *Madre de Dio*, she cannot ... "

Suddenly Mia understood that Tony could not yet face losing Jen. However was she going to help him out of this? She could think of only one way.

"Tony darling, whatever, we're coming."

"No!" The word exploded over the telephone. "Don't you understand? If you come, if everyone acts as though Jen is—as though Jen is dead, then that means we have given up the faith, that means maybe she *will* be dead, no, no, *per favore,* don't come—"

Mia felt a sudden fear for him.

"All right, Tony darling, if you believe, then we will believe with you. Of course there is always a chance, since they haven't found the—I mean—oh Tony, are you sure we can't help if we come?"

"I am sure," said Tony. "I am even so okay I will sing tomorrow *Cavaradossi* as scheduled."

Mia could scarcely believe this. She had performed with Tony when he was singing under difficult circumstances and he had always managed to pull off a creditable performance. But this time? How could he even imagine he could perform? Unless his self-delusion about Jen's fate was total... Mia gradually surmised that all she and Cedric could do was to give him long distance support. She hoped she was wording it right.

"Tony darling, I think that is very courageous, very admirable. Cedric and I will be pulling for you, we'll be with you in our thoughts every moment, and if you change your mind and want us, we'll be there right away. I'll call you every day. *In bocca al lupo*, darling."

Before Mia could say goodbye Tony had hung up the phone. Shaking her head, she looked apprehensively at Cedric and told him what Tony had said. Then she threw her arms around his neck, and wept.

....

Before Tony was able to contact them, Tony's parents and his two brothers in Italy all heard newscasts announcing the death of their beloved in-law Jen. But when they phoned Tony to say they were on their way to him, they received the same message; don't come, because that will mean that Jen is really dead. Frightened at what this meant about Tony's mental state, they nevertheless felt they had no choice but to do what he asked. To violate his request would seem to show such a lack of respect for his confused grief.

Ten

In Manhattan the day had dawned grey, drizzly, sad, unredeemable. With only a few hours to go before he performed in *Tosca*, Tony re-routed all calls to his assistant. He asked Eric to put nobody through to him except Jen. Eric was to explain to other callers that Jen was safe, and that rumours to the contrary were caused by a misunderstanding arising from the confusion surrounding the fire. Tony also told Eric to say that he would be singing that evening, and, as he usually did before performing, that he was spending the day resting his voice, taking solitary walks, and having a late afternoon nap.

But all that was easier said than done. When the worried, well-meaning Mrs Burns prepared Tony's favourite brunch— eggs Benedict with smoked salmon, a rich creamy Hollandaise sauce, and a plate of pasta with tomato sauce, he feigned enthusiasm and sat down at his glass-topped dining room table to eat the large meal. But his throat closed at the first mouthful; he had to make a superhuman effort to swallow it. The second mouthful was not much more successful. He sipped a bit of orange juice, a bit of coffee, all the while admonishing himself.

If Jen is all right—and I truly believe she is, I do, I do—then why am I like this? Since she is okay then she is thinking about me; she is supporting me as she always does if I perform when we are apart, she is saying "In bocca al lupo" as usual. I must not lose faith. I must act normally. For if I once act as though I believe she is ... as though she ... then that will mean she really is ... dead ...

He forced his rising gorge to accept the rich filling brunch, and came very close to losing the meal immediately after. But that he could not allow. Nothing must indicate to the watching fates that Tony believed anything was amiss.

....

Jen sat on the northbound bus, apprehensively wishing its arrival in Timmins could be indefinitely postponed. From Timmins she would, according to the instructions she had found in the luggage, travel on a helicopter belonging to the mine company, to the mine where the job was waiting for her.

Beside Jen sat a teenage girl with fuschia hair, who, although every once in a while she smiled at Jen, was immersed in the music emanating from the earphones of her Walkman. The girl had the volume up so high that Jen could hear the sound. Presently the teenager tired of her program and fiddled with the dial on the tiny radio, assailing Jen's ears with various sounds from rap to news to, at one point, a long high C from a distinctive voice Jen recognised as belonging to the tenor Luciano Pavarotti.

Jen frowned. She had the unexpected notion that there was something she should be remembering, something she should be

The Tosca Taunt

doing that had to do with—with Luciano Pavarotti? What on earth could she have to do with him? But tantalisingly at the edge of her memory was whatever she should be doing at this moment.

An Italian phrase came into her mind, *"In bocca al lupo"*. She realized she knew what it meant—"in the mouth of the wolf"—but why did she know it, and what did it have to do with anything, least of all with Luciano Pavarotti? Was she, like Pavarotti, of Italian extraction? The mystery of her identity seemed only to deepen with these odd bits of revelation. Once again she fought back tears. She stared resolutely out the window so nobody would notice her emotion.

She became aware of the teenager staring at her, and she realised Pavarotti was still blaring forth from the headphones.

"Can you hear my music?" the girl asked.

"I can, actually," Jen smiled, pretending to brush away a strand of her hair as she quickly wiped away a stray tear. "Why?"

"Because when this guy sang whatever he's singing, I was looking at you and you started to—like—cry, you know? So I figured you must like this stuff."

Feeling faintly ridiculous, Jen took a Kleenex from her handbag and blew her nose. "I do, actually. I'm surprised that you do; you were listening to rock for a long while before."

"I hope it didn't drive you crazy. I keep forgetting how loud I like my music. But yeah, I like this Pavarotti guy. Although my fave is that good-looking one, you know, Antonio Amato. Who's your fave?"

Jen couldn't conjure up a picture of Antonio Amato,

whoever he was. So she replied, "I'm a Placido Domingo fan myself."

The girl grinned. "Well, yeah, him too, he's okay. You go to operas?"

Seems to me I do, Jen thought. *I can remember seeing some, was it on TV or for real?*

"Not much, but I watch a lot on TV." *But what is it I should be doing today, and why does Luciano Pavarotti remind me of whatever it is? Why isn't my memory coming back at all? What if I never remember? ...*

The Tosca Taunt

Eleven

As soon as she heard the terrible news about Jen Amato, Valentina Welles phoned the Metropolitan Opera to find out who would be singing *Cavaradossi* to her *Floria Tosca* tomorrow night. She was dumbfounded to hear that Tony Amato himself would still be singing. And even more astonished when she heard the reason Tony was performing.

This new situation exacerbated her chronic stage fright until she was nearly catatonic. She had absolutely counted on the unflappable Tony to help her in this debut run of Met performances. But what now? She, the tense debutante, might even be called on to help Tony, on the stage of the Metropolitan Opera.

She tried to phone Tony but was stonewalled by his assistant. Then, desperately needing reassurance, she called Sir Sheldon Wasserman. He sounded uncharacteristically apprehensive as he told her of the arrangements that had been made—that Raffaele Ricordi would be costumed and ready to go on stage at any time should Tony be unable to continue. Wasserman told her they would all have to make extra efforts tonight to help Tony—but, he said, he was sure she realized that.

Valentina sat rigidly in her easy chair and hugged the knees she had drawn up. She would phone her dear friend, the author Julian LeComte. His common sense would help her. She once had believed fiction writers lived in a never-never land of dreams, so Julian's practicality had surprised her. He remained a mainstay for her in times of stress, even though they had not seen each other for more than two years. Not since that last surreptitious weekend they had arranged to spend together, when they were so certain they were safe, so certain they had set it up to circumvent any surveillance.

The peace and solitude of Julian LeComte's townhouse in New Orleans cushioned and stimulated his Muse. He thought he had turned off the bell on his phone, so when it rang in the midst of the scene he was painstakingly creating, he debated whether to interrupt himself in full flight. Reluctantly he picked up the receiver.

"Julian, can we talk?"

All thoughts of writing fled and were replaced by a vision of Valentina. He swung his chair around to look at the small framed picture she had just sent him, placed carefully on the shelf behind him so as not to be a distraction except when he wanted it to be. It showed her in a red bejewelled evening gown for the second act of this *Tosca* at the Met. She looked to Julian like an exotic blossom.

"We can talk, dear Val. How are you? Is everything going well? Are you all set for the second performance?"

The Tosca Taunt

He sounded so cheerful.

"Julian, have you been writing non-stop since day before yesterday? You haven't heard the news, have you."

"Uh, well, no, I haven't been away from my computer for two days, except to sleep for a few hours. The Muse feeds and I have to devour. Why? What's going on?"

"Oh, Julian ... " Valentina's voice was shaking.

Julian knew how uncontrollably she trembled before each opera and it amazed him that the shaking did not affect her performances; indeed, to his surprise, her nervousness gave her an extra edge of emotion that seemed to move audiences deeply.

"Julian, darling, there's been a terrible hotel fire in Canada and Jenetta Amato is dead—"

"What? Good God! I can't believe it! However will Tony survive that? They had such a good marriage—and what happens now, I mean tonight, with your *Tosca*? Who sings *Cavaradossi*?"

"This will sound unbelievable, but Tony says he's singing."

"*What?*"

"I know. I can't get any of it through my head." Valentina told Julian everything she had heard about the fire, including Tony's illusory belief that Jen was still alive.

"But I've absolutely counted on Tony to help me, he's so unflappable on stage, and now I'm going to have to pull myself out of any problems, and maybe help pull Tony out too. There's no way he can really be in any condition to sing. I'm so scared. That's why I phoned. I thought you might—I mean, you always seem to be able to—"

"Make some sense for you? Actually I think you're

underestimating yourself. Remember the emergency replacements you've done, and how capably—no, more than capably—how splendidly you did them."

"Yes, darling, I know, but then everybody knew *I* needed help and they gave their all for me, and to me. This time—"

"This time it's your turn to put a little back into the general 'help pot'. Surely that's one of the things being a great performer is all about. Look at Tony; he's at the top of the heap, and yet he has a reputation for kindness and generosity on, and, come to think of it, off stage."

"Of course you're right, you have so much common sense, this is why I needed to call you."

"Darling Val, don't be afraid tonight, there's no need. I'll be there with you on stage, remember that; I'll play my CDs with you singing *Tosca* and I'll think about you non-stop from eight to midnight, I promise."

He laughed. "I don't know why I imagine I'll stop thinking about you at midnight. That's usually the time when I think about you the most, actually."

Valentina hugged herself tightly with her free arm. "Oh Julian I do miss you. You always make me feel so much better. Now I guess I have to go. Always, Julian."

"I know. Break a leg, my sweet Val."

Abruptly, he was gone. She sat holding the receiver until a recorded message interrupted her reverie. At least her conversation had given her something besides her terror to reflect on. Slowly she rose and, her feet bare on the thick carpet of her hotel room, she walked into the large bathroom. She filled the bathtub, poured in a generous amount of musky smelling oil,

The Tosca Taunt

climbed in, and tried to relax by savouring a tender memory.

Three years before, when Julian LeComte's father Leonard had realised his only son was actually in love and not just infatuated with a black woman, he tried various schemes to separate them. He talked "sense" to Julian, but the "sense" of the Ku Klux Klan only infuriated Leonard's young and idealistic son. And Valentina proved to be equally intractable.

Finally, in desperation, the determined Leonard had ordered his bodyguard to disguise himself and to beat Valentina, threatening her with worse if she continued to see Julian. At that point the unhappy lovers realised they could not win any contest with the wealthy and powerful Leonard.

But Julian and Valentina had been unable to break contact completely. So they kept in touch by telephone. And as the weeks turned into months and Leonard did not even mention Valentina, let alone remonstrate with his son, Julian grew confident enough to try to arrange a tryst with her.

The most auspicious time for it seemed to be when Valentina was in Geneva singing *Minnie* in *Fanciulla del West*. During a period when Leonard planned to be away on a cruise of the Pacific Rim, Julian had arranged a book promotion trip to London and Paris. And in addition to booking hotels in those two cities, he arranged for a suite in a charming hotel in the out of the way, fortified mountaintop village of Conques, in southern France. Julian, who had toured this area as a teenager with a group from his high school, had pleasing memories of this site whose impressive gold stone cathedral had been one of the way stations for the Crusaders centuries ago. Julian surmised this old town knew how to keep its secrets.

Jean Dell

So Julian and Valentina had arranged to meet in the town of Rodez, thirty-seven kilometres from Conques. Air Inter flew out of Paris into the small airport there; Julian would arrive first, rent a car, and be waiting when Valentina took her two days off between performances. Their ruse would entail her missing a rehearsal for the second opera she was scheduled to sing in Geneva. For the first time in her career the ambitious Valentina would put her private life before her singing, and would feign exhaustion, in order to get these two unexpected, precious days.

Her director in both operas needed her in peak condition to continue singing her difficult role in *Fanciulla*, so he excused her from rehearsals for the next opera when she told him that she was tired and needed to rest. She said she needed to get away completely, and would go to a quiet village in France for a brief change of scene. Hardly a naive man, the director had for some time been curious as to why anyone as exquisite as Valentina Welles not only seemed to have no close relationship with a man, but did not even encourage any of the men who flocked hopefully around her. Even the married director himself had made a tentative, unsuccessful advance towards the exotic singer.

But since Valentina's reputation for reliability was impeccable, her director eventually castigated himself for a suspicious wretch when she complained of fatigue, and made penance to himself by driving her to the airport. He gave her a warm kiss on the cheek and almost tripped himself up by saying, "Have a wonderful time—I mean rest, rest is what I meant to say—"

Of course Valentina realized he suspected something, and

she was assailed by guilt for deserting her career for what she hoped would be pleasure. Once seated in the small plane she began to tremble. *I don't believe this,* she thought. *I only shake when I'm about to go on stage. Have I actually got stage fright about seeing Julian again?* Her palms were wet, and as the plane began its steep descent she felt light-headed. She had fainted only once in her life, after Leonard's minion Hugo Violle had so viciously beaten her. Ruefully she asked herself whether everything to do with Julian was going to make her dizzy.

The plane touched down. She pulled her flight bag from under the seat ahead of her and, first in line, dashed out the door and down the steps of the plane. And there was Julian, standing at the gate in the small airport, a dozen red roses in his arms, and a smile on his face so wide Valentina wondered whether he would ever be able to wipe it off. He did, of course, when he seized her and kissed her, heedlessly crushing roses as he did so.

Eventually, Julian led her through the airport and across the parking lot to their rented car. Arriving at the intersection to the highway, he said doubtfully, "Do you want to see the Rodez cathedral? It's very old, very large, you can see a bit of it over there." She looked through the shimmer of heat at the soaring pink edifice. "Julian, no. I want to see you. Cathedrals I can see any time."

So they made their way along the winding roads that led upwards to Conques. Small high clouds danced across the sky; The closer hills glowed green against the dark dappled blue of those farther away on the horizon. Valentina caressed the back of Julian's head, then put her arm around him and gently stroked his throat, which made him swerve dangerously into the path of an oncoming truck. The driver mouthed imprecations and made a universal gesture of disgust with his middle finger.

"Quit, Val, please!"

"If you order me not to, my lord and master ... "

They exchanged a quick glance as Valentina withdrew her arm, and Julian stepped harder on the gas. Short, bushy trees framed the road that was becoming winding, perilous. The medieval village of Conques waited patiently at the summit, to the lovers only a setting, a backdrop for their play, as it had for centuries been the backdrop for divers other dramas. Their hotel, in a narrow street seemingly unscathed by time, maintained the medieval atmosphere of the village, except in its surprisingly modern comforts.

"Do you want lunch?" Julian asked rather breathlessly as they parked their car.

"Do you?"

"Not necessarily ... "

So they registered, and were taken up to their suite. It overwhelmed them with flowers, from the matching wallpaper and draperies patterned with spring blossoms in yellows, blues, and pinks, to the huge multicoloured bouquet of real flowers on the antique fruitwood desk. From the dormer window they could reach out and almost touch the tower of the Romanesque pilgrimage church of Ste Foy, across the narrow street.

"Oh Julian, it's perfect—" began Valentina, but he stopped her words with a kiss. Now with a hunger intensified by their enforced separation, they slowly undressed one another, and fell onto the bed in an ecstasy of longing.

By dinnertime they had only begun to be satiated, and a

The Tosca Taunt

little hungry. Julian phoned down for room service, and they ate a leisurely French meal, made even more leisurely by the necessary interruptions of lovemaking.

At noon the next day they pulled themselves together enough to dress and to wander through the out-of-time village. They wondered at the ancient houses and shops; they were suitably awe-stricken by the eleventh-century ochre stone church with its vigorous representation of the Last Judgement in the tympan over the main doorway. Julian showed Valentina a devil pointing to an inscription accusing a man and woman underneath of fornication.

"That's us, love. We're doomed forever in Hell."

"I don't care, Julian, as long as we're doomed together. Do you?"

He took her in his arms and kissed her yet again, kissed her in full view of the stone devils, the stone God.

"Will that do as an answer?"

They went into the church, their eyes repeatedly drawn upwards to the arches, to the lofty ceiling. Valentina, used to the symbolism of stage settings, began to feel the weight of centuries of rigorous judgement. A dark thought assailed her.

"Julian, can you really believe that anything as lovely as we have, could doom us forever in Hell?"

Julian was moved by the tremor in her voice. Could she actually be afraid of such a thing, in this the late twentieth century?

"No, of course not." He tightened his arm around her shoulders. "I believe love is the best part of humanity; surely it's because we are still capable of love that the Deity hasn't lost all patience with us as a species. And sex? Isn't it the best, the holiest expression of love between lovers? How can it possibly be wrong?"

She leaned her head against his shoulder, comforted. He could not really know the answer to the riddle of the universe, and yet, and yet!

"You talk like you write," she said. "It's beautiful."

They walked out from the church, under the tympan, turning left into the quiet cloister from where they entered the museum to see the famous treasury. Why, Valentina wondered, did these lovely medieval and Renaissance treasures move her so? She and Julian admired in silence the Reliquary of Ste Foy, spotlighted in a niche at the end of the room. The saint was portrayed enthroned, covered in gold and silver and precious stones, some faceted and some not, depending in what century they were added to the hollow statue.

When Julian and Valentina reluctantly left what seemed a holy splendour, they turned automatically back towards the hotel, realising they had but one more night together, and then — what? They passed a tiny jewellery shop, and he impulsively pulled her inside.

"I want you to have something to remember these days by," he said, his voice tight, husky.

"Julian, do you really think I would forget? This loveliness will nourish me — will *have* to nourish me — for how long?"

"Nevertheless, Val."

He quickly sought the small showcase which housed medallions. Already Valentina had around her neck an intricate gold chain, and, like Antonio Amato, she wore a Saint Cecilia

The Tosca Taunt

pendant. Julian was looking now at the famous circular medallion of love. It had a plus sign, set with diamonds, and a minus sign, set with rubies, signifying the quotation, "I love you more (+) than yesterday and less (-) than tomorrow." The medallion Julian chose was encircled with diamonds.

Julian paid for the pendant, waved away the box the shopkeeper offered him, and unclasped the chain from Valentina's throat. He added the sparkling medallion of love as a companion to the image of the more sober Saint.

"Wear it always, dear Val, and know that whatever happens I can't forget you."

Leaving the shop, they hurried, arms about one another, back to the hotel where they spent a joyful, wakeful night. The next morning they unwillingly arose, both happy and sad, and took their luggage down to the rented car in the parking lot. They were about to climb in when they heard footsteps in the gravel behind them, and, both turning, were dumbfounded to see Leonard's burly bodyguard Hugo Violle and another equally husky man walking towards them.

"Christ, Hugo," Julian exploded. "What the hell!"

"Look, Mr J, we're supposed to beat the shit out of her. Just to let you guys know you can't hide anything from Mr LeComte. But I'm not gonna do it. I think you get the message."

Julian nodded, speechless. Valentina, frightened, remembered the power of Hugo's fists. She let Julian move protectively in front of her. He said, "Get in the car, Val."

"No, Mr J." Hugo growled. "You say goodbye right now. For good, you understand? Mr LeComte says you guys are never gonna see each other again, or one of you's gonna get hurt bad, and it's not likely to be you, Mr J. I could hit her in the throat and stop her career real fast. I could hit her different in the throat and stop everything. You get it?"

Trembling uncontrollably, Valentina hung on to Julian's shoulders from behind him.

"Hugo, for God's sake. I get the message. You'll have to disable me before you can get to her here though, do *you* get *that* message? Dad doesn't want me hurt and you know it. Now you let her get in the car with me. I'm taking her to Rodez airport, she's on her way back to Geneva, she sings an opera tonight. I'll drive so you can follow me, but just let me take her—"

"Can I trust you, Mr J?"

"Under the circumstances, Hugo, what choices do I have?"

"You could get away from us in the car."

"Yeah, right, on these narrow roads? And down below they're virtually traffic jams—"

"Okay. I'll be in the car right behind you. Don't try anything."

Julian put his arm around Valentina and ushered her into the car. Slowly, so that Hugo and his sidekick could pull in behind them and stay there, he drove out of Conques and down, down the perilous road towards Rodez.

Valentina fought waves of nausea. "We're really beaten this time, Julian. We can never meet again, otherwise your father will do something terrible to—oh Julian, he's won."

Julian took her hand. "It looks like it, doesn't it, my sweet Val, oh God I love you so much. What are we going to do?"

Valentina's voice was little more than a whisper. "We're going to s-say goodbye."

The Tosca Taunt

"Say goodbye and be sad and lonely for the rest of our lives?"

"What else can we do? Maybe *not* say a real goodbye — maybe just set each other free, but keep in touch any way we can —"

"Nothing can set me free from you." He sounded definite, sure, defeated.

"Oh Julian, I feel that way too, this is so *Romeo and Juliet*. Must we each die a slow death because we have to stay apart?"

They arrived at the airport at Rodez and they parked the car in the rental car lot. Very slowly they got out of the car and moved towards each other, but Hugo stepped between them, forcing them apart.

"No way you're gonna make a run for it and get on a plane to god-knows-where with her, Mr J. Just say your sweet goodbyes and I'll take her to her plane."

Hugo stepped aside, staying very close. He was not a monster; he simply knew on which side his bread was buttered. More to the point, he knew what Leonard LeComte held over him and what Leonard was willing to do with that bit of evidence if Hugo got out of line. Still, he would not now stop these lovers from embracing one last time.

Julian and Valentina stared at one another. They did not dare a final kiss; they were too close to the edge of madness. Their hands clutched, then only their fingers touched, then each held only a handful of air.

....

This afternoon Valentina, oddly comforted by her long reverie, climbed from the bath, towelled herself dry with a soft white towel, and realized she must hurry if she wanted her usual two hours at the theatre before the *Tosca* performance.

She pulled into herself all the strength that her love for Julian continued to bring her. Tonight she would need it, for herself and for Tony Amato.

....

Backstage at the Metropolitan Opera, Valentina, dressed for the first scene of *Tosca*, emerged from her dressing room to see Tony and his assistant hurrying down the yellow corridor towards the dressing rooms. Her heart sank. Tony's dark eyes blazed in his pale face, and the lines beside his mouth were set deep. He looked ten years older than he had three days ago. He came abreast of where she stood.

What should I say, she wondered? *I can't say I'm sorry, because he professes to believe Jen is still alive so what would I be sorry for?* Valentina's instincts took over. She stepped in front of him and, stopping his rapid progress down the hall, put her arms around him and hugged him hard, kissing him on the cheek. As she drew back, still holding him, she saw him catch his bottom lip fiercely with his teeth. His eyes filled with tears.

"Tony. I'm so—I—you've been such a help to me every time we've sung together. It's time I reciprocated."

"There is no need, Val, but I appreciate." He swallowed hard. "I am just fine. I am fine because you see, Jen is fine too, this is all just a—" He could not go on. He pulled away from her and walked into his dressing room.

And Valentina continued her trembling, which tonight slowly became uncontrollable.

....

The Tosca Taunt

Raffaele Ricordi had been instructed to be in costume but if possible to stay out of Tony Amato's sight for the duration of the opera. So he paced the floor in the dressing room allotted to the male singers performing secondary roles, until he was sure Tony was in the wings ready to go on stage to sing his first aria, *Recondite Armonia*.

Only then did Ricordi creep out, anxious to see what state Tony was in, and to assess his own chances of having to replace his unfortunate colleague tonight. But he miscalculated, because Tony, trying to hide from himself how shaky he felt, had delayed leaving his dressing room to go into the wings until the last minute. He came face to face with a dismayed Ricordi. At first Tony smiled a greeting, puzzled but pleased to see his colleague there, until he realized that Ricordi was in a costume identical to his.

"*Cielo!* Have they so little faith in me? This is intolerable, Raffaele. Why did you not tell me?"

"Tony, that's your cue, you'd better get on stage, I'll explain later, but—"

"I know, is not you, is that Wasserman, why does he not trust me? I have put his iron from the fire often enough. What is the matter with everybody? I am fine!"

And he ran onto the stage, much to the relief of the perspiring conductor, for the orchestra was already three bars beyond the cue for Tony's entrance.

Tony, as always taking the emotional temperature of the audience, imagined he could feel their morbid anticipation. *Madre de Dio!* He felt like a human sacrifice; was *everybody* expecting him to fall apart on stage tonight? Why should he?

Everything was fine. Jen was safe. He would sing splendidly; he would show them—and the watching fates—that he too was fine.

Carefully, carefully he sang his first big aria, reminding himself of his singing techniques as though he were a novice. The high notes were a little tight, but clarion enough, he hoped, to thrill an audience which felt to him as though they wanted to see him shatter. He had never felt this way about his public before. In a pause before Valentina came on stage he asked himself whether he was imagining it; surely all those fans who professed to adore him should be sympathetic, supportive, tonight of all nights?

Tony's first act love duet with *Floria Tosca* went well until he had to sing the line "My whole life is bound up in those eyes of yours". He looked into Valentina Welles' brown eyes but saw only the deep blue eyes of his Jen. Carefully he paused, breathed, and pushed his diaphragm against his lungs, to make his usual honeyed gold sound. He began "My whole life is bound up in—" and ran out of air. He pulled in a ragged breath as Valentina did exactly what he needed her to do; she held his face for a moment in her two hands and then hugged him, not in just a stage embrace, but in a genuine one. He could feel real warmth, real support, just as he could feel her pounding heart against his chest. He drew back, ruefully nodded his gratitude, and found his voice.

As soon as the curtain descended for the first intermission Sir Sheldon Wasserman rushed to Tony's dressing room. The last thing Sir Sheldon wanted to do was to disturb Tony further, but he needed to know whether he should try to stop Tony singing now and let Ricordi finish the opera. Wasserman knocked on Tony's door and was greeted by Eric. The pale Tony, sitting at his makeup mirror, saw the reflection of the conductor and turned to snarl, "How could you have in me so little faith that you have Ricordi ready any minute to step on stage? Have I let you down so often?"

Damnation, Sir Sheldon thought. *I hoped Ricordi would have had the sense to stay out of the way. Now what do I say?*

"Of course not." He came over to Tony and put his long thin hand on Tony's shoulder. "You know perfectly well you've never let me down. You've even rescued situations for me several times. I was just trying to do the same for you. If you become unable to sing tonight, don't you feel better knowing Ricordi is ready to go on immediately for you?"

"But you should have told me. Anyway, why should I not be able to sing? I am not sick, and the voice is fine, except you paced the orchestra too quick and I did not have the time to breathe, you be more careful in this next act."

Sir Sheldon was unused to being told how to conduct. He was about to make a sharp retort when he realised Tony was trying to save face. In order to keep his star tenor calm, Sir Sheldon called on his own minuscule acting talent and made himself apologise.

"Is there anything else I can do to help you, Tony?"

"What you mean, help? Who needs help? Now I need to concentrate for five minutes alone, you leave me *per favore.*"

Act two went well, partly because Tony's role in it was small, and required much more in the way of acting distraught, than of singing. Sir Sheldon knew it was easy for Tony to act distraught tonight.

Act Three began with Tony in his character as *Cavaradossi* bribing the jailer, holding out a ring and singing "This ring is the only possession I have left."

....

Sitting on the darkened bus, Jen fiddled absently with the wide gold wedding band on the third finger of her left hand. She pushed and pulled at it until inadvertently she slipped it off. This caused her an inexplicable pang. She was about to put the thick ring back on when marks inside it caught her eye. Holding it up to the dim light on the panel between the windows, she strained her eyes to make out what the inscription said. Finally she made it out; it said "J, *sempre*, T." What was it? "J" for Jen; "*sempre*" which means "always" in Italian—she seemed to know a lot of Italian; was she of Italian descent, she wondered again? —and "T", which must be the initial of the name of her husband. The husband who according to the unmailed letter to Mama, beat her so badly she feared for her life. "T"—the reason she was making her final escape. If "T" was such a horror, then Jen should take the ring off, shouldn't she? She should just take it off and throw it away.

Slowly she opened the unused ashtray in the armrest, planning to put the ring in and leave it there. It had obviously done her no good, but a finder might get some pleasure and some money from it, since it was eighteen karat gold. Deliberately not watching what she did, because somehow she couldn't bear to see herself doing it, she dropped the ring into the small container and the ashtray lid fell shut by itself. She was surprised by an anguish so devastating that she had to put her head in her hands.

Her young seat mate now spoke to her again. "I bet you don't know what you just lost."

Jen took her head from her hands and looked at the girl. "I don't," she said, the words ringing in her head with double meaning.

"You—like—dropped this ring into the ashtray, I don't know what you were thinking about, but anyway here it is, I think it's your wedding ring, you wouldn't want to lose it, you know?"

She handed Jen the ring, and under her curious gaze Jen thanked her. As soon as the ring was back on Jen's finger her strange anguish subsided.

What is this? If "T" is such a monster, why can't I leave his ring behind? Did I once really love him? Why won't any memory of this come back to me?

....

Two investigators, one a police officer and the other from the fire department, were working overtime at the now brilliantly floodlit site of the hotel fire. The officer bent down and picked up two blackened rings near where they had found remains so burned they were hard to recognise as human. He wiped the rings carefully and peered closely at them. One was a diamond solitaire, the other an oddly shaped band of diamonds.

He held them out to his colleague. "Bill, have a look at these. I'm surprised they didn't melt. There's something engraved inside, can you make it out without the magnifying glass?"

Bill stepped over and took the rings. He held them up so they would be well lit by the spotlights illuminating their work, and said, "Well, yeah, this is clear enough, you must need new glasses."

"So what do they say?"

"This one," Bill held up the solitaire, "says, 'Cara mia; Antonio'. This queer shaped one says 'Mia amore, Tony'. So whose, do you think?"

"Somebody with money, judging from the size of these stones. Maybe belonged to her—or him, if that's human." The officer nodded in the direction of the charred remains.

"Maybe these belong to Jenetta Amato, the artist, the wife of the tenor? There's got to be money in that family, and the names on the rings work; his name is Antonio, and he's known as Tony."

"He can likely identify them then. We'll have to phone him, and he can come to the site if he thinks they're his wife's. God I hate this part of the business. The detecting part is great; the people part is lousy."

....

At the Metropolitan Opera Tony was beginning the aria from *Tosca* that the audience was waiting to hear, *E lucevan le stelle*. This time he would give them an aria they would never forget; he was so sure they were just waiting for him to fall apart.

His voice soared thrillingly over the orchestra and into the vast auditorium where the audience, far from waiting for this well-loved tenor to fail, was mentally trying to support the stricken singer through this most emotional of scenes.

The voice rolled out, all molten gold, until Tony came to the last lines. He had to get through them somehow ... *Saint Cecilia,*

The Tosca Taunt

patron saint of musicians, help me, help me!

"Now my dream of love has vanished forever," said Tony's aria, "and I die—" The rest of the line should have emerged "in despair." But Saint Cecilia's blessing and Tony's voice disappeared at the same time. His dream of love, said the libretto, his dream of love vanished forever vanished forever vanished forever ...

As his stage directions required, Tony put his head into his hands and simulated weeping. Even now the tears were not real. The audience applauded, and Tony felt the wave of emotion roll from them to him. It was adulation, support, concern—but all he read in it was malevolent pleasure in the fact that for the second time tonight he had been unable to finish an aria. *Maledetto!* He would finish this opera and miss no more notes; he would show them.

Valentina-*Tosca* rushed on stage as the action required. Again she hugged Tony in a true, supportive embrace, and this time she whispered, "Hang on, Tony, we'll make it."

His head felt heavy as he nodded almost imperceptibly; he sang "You gave my life all its splendour, all its joy and desire, they radiate from you like heat, you alone give beauty a voice and colour." His voice cracked on the final note. Valentina, in Tony's arms, now had a long aria about their love; maybe, just maybe he could find his voice during this respite and could make it through the opera. He had very little left to sing. But when he opened his mouth for his next line nothing emerged. Holding Valentina close, he whispered, "I am finished."

A sudden strength, the strength of the great artist who comes through under stress, took hold of Valentina. Whispering to Tony, "Stay in character; I can carry us both," she altered the Italian libretto slightly as she sang, the new words making it seem as though his silence was what the role actually called for.

Sir Sheldon, who a moment ago had wondered whether to stop the production and have Ricordi take over, was now filled with admiration. He decided to go with Valentina's improvisations and Amato's considerable acting talent. Now Valentina bent over Tony's "dead" body, crying out "How could it end like this?"

At this Tony almost lost his control. *No, no, I cannot*, he thought; *if I cry, then I am admitting that Jen could be ... no! Jen is fine, I know she is, maybe tonight finally she will be able to get in touch with me ...*

The audience applauded, not really knowing how to cheer for a bravura performance they had not understood. Those who believed Jenetta Maclean Amato was dead could not comprehend how or why the grieving Antonio Amato sang tonight. Some, particularly the elderly among them, thought Tony was noble, rather like Sir Harry Lauder, the British vaudevillian who went on stage to give a performance to soldiers during the First World War, the same night he learned his own son had been killed in the trenches. Others thought Tony was heartless, or maybe slightly mad, to insist on singing regardless. But only a few of Tony's close associates knew he professed to believe Jen was still alive.

The singers took their last curtain call. Backstage Tony took Valentina's hands in his, and said, "How do I thank you for rescuing me?"

"Tony, there's no need. Remember how we met, remember

when I replaced Mia at the very last minute in *Fanciulla?* Tell me you didn't save me a hundred times during that terrifying filming! I owe you a forever debt."

She looked closely at him, her admiration and affection for him palpable. No longer was she awed as she had been when she first met this superstar. "Now, are you going to be okay? I hope you are coming with us to supper; you look like you need care and feeding."

But Tony declined all invitations to dine with the cast, as well as invitations from worried friends and colleagues to accompany him home. He suddenly found being sociable and polite difficult. He left with his assistant, but waved goodbye to Eric at the stage door and stepped alone into the car he had ordered. It felt huge, empty. Jen was so often there with him after a performance. He asked the chauffeur to take him home.

An anxious Mrs Burns was still awake and waiting for him in the apartment. Just for a moment Tony hoped that—but her first words quelled his hopes.

"How did it go, Mr Amato?"

"I have sung better, I even ran out of breath, Wasserman conducted so fast tonight. I don't know what was the rush. But I made it, with a big help from Valentina Welles. I thought maybe there would be—is there—there is—no news?"

"No news, Mr Amato. I'm so sorry."

"The children?"

"The children are still doing quite well, all things considered. They are trying to believe as you do, that their mother is all right."

Tony examined Mrs Burns pale face. Something was wrong

here.

"But—but you believe too, do you not? Of course you do!"

Mrs Burns averted her gaze. "Oh ... I ... well, of course, Mr Amato, of course I do."

Tony needed to have faith in her. But he was not willing to push the conversation further. "I go to bed now. Thank you for ...for ... *Buona notte.*"

He walked heavily down the hallway to the bedroom. Wearily he shed his clothes onto a chair and climbed into bed. He forced himself not to think of Jen. Tomorrow, surely by tomorrow there would be news. He tried to put himself to sleep by making himself think about nothing else except his upcoming CD recording.

But sleep was a long time coming. And when it did, he had the oddest dream; he was descending the escalator at the Charles DeGaulle airport in Paris, moving through a large transparent plastic tube. He looked across at the tube that held the up escalator, and saw Jen ascending. He called out to her, shouted her name, and finally, crying her name over and over, he beat on the side of his tube in a frenzied attempt to get her attention. But she did not look at him. She just kept going up, up, up, into the place you could not get to from where he was. Never. Not ever.

....

Jen dozed on the bus, and dreamed a strange dream. She was ascending an escalator which was in a transparent tube. Across from her she saw a similar tube that held a descending escalator. She was perfectly happy going up, until she looked more carefully at the down escalator. On it, his back turned to her, stood a tall man with curly dark hair. "Turn around, turn

The Tosca Taunt

around," she called frantically to him, "let me see your face. I must see who you are." But he did not turn; he continued descending down and down into the place you could not get to from where she was. Never. Not ever. And in her dream Jen felt such a sorrow, such a yearning, such a need for the unknown, unknowable dark man ...

Twelve

The manager of the Delson gold mines in Northern Ontario, Mark Reinhard, looked up from his desk, and, clasping his hands behind his head, stared out the window at the mine buildings, silhouetted against the pines in the opalescent light of the full moon. It occurred to him that it was two years ago this month that he had given up smoking, and that, like now, he still fought cravings. Hearing someone climbing the stairs to the second storey administrative offices where he and his accountant were working overtime, he stared through the glass tops of the partitions. A pretty woman with bruised eyes came around the corner and spoke to the accountant in the first office. Mark saw the accountant waving her towards Mark's cluttered office.

The well-dressed woman who walked through the door towards Mark looked more like a sophisticated big city woman than a potential cook in a mine kitchen, but he reminded himself of his father's frequently uttered saying, that you could never tell

The Tosca Taunt

how far a frog could jump from looking at it. He grinned at her and held out his hand. The hand she put into his was small and cold, but the handshake was firm. Her look was direct and unwavering. *Impressive*, he thought.

"Sit down, sit down, Mrs—er," he glanced down at his notepad. "—Noonan. I've been appointed the welcoming committee. You'll have been expecting the cook but he's off sick tonight and asked me to do the honours. I'm glad to see you; we're short two assistant cooks, and the quality of meals has gone way downhill. Now the cook wants you to fill in this short form, although we should have some of this information on file—the caterer's staff files are on the computer system—just let me bring them up."

But try as he might, Mark Reinhard could not access Bridget Jennifer Noonan's file. No matter what he did, the message he got was invariably "Bad file name".

"Apparently you don't exist, Mrs Noonan. But the cook gave me a file on you, let's see ..." He shuffled papers on his cluttered desk and finally turned up a flat grey file folder. It contained nothing except a sheet of blank paper to which was stapled a photograph with a name underneath, but something dense and brown had been spilled over the picture so that little was identifiable.

"They obviously filed this in the coffee urn" said Mark in disgust, holding up the picture of her and looking at it closely. "All I can tell from this is that the woman in the picture has red hair; otherwise it could be anybody." He looked at her appraisingly. "You don't have red hair any more." He wanted to say he liked her blonde, but mindful that almost anything could be construed as sexual harassment these days, he kept quiet.

"Would you mind filling in another form so the catering company can have the information? I'm sorry we've—they've—lost all your previous material—things usually run better than that around here."

Jen thought, *How can I fill in a form? What do I know about Bridget Jennifer Noonan? How do I get around this? I can fake it and fill something in, but what if they eventually turn up my file in the computer and see that the two don't match?*

Summoning a skill at lying that she hadn't known she had, a new fact about herself that made her wince inwardly, she said in her most charming voice, "Seems a waste of time filling in forms I've already done, but if you need them, of course I will."

She waited. He handed them to her, saying, "Why don't you take them to your quarters and fill them in once you're settled? I'm sure the company's in no rush."

Jen felt relieved. After a moment she asked, "When do you want me to start work?"

"Is tomorrow too soon? The cook says he needs you on the day shift. They have two twelve-hour shifts here. Still, you must be tired from your trip, so if you'd just as soon have tomorrow off ... "

"No, of course not, I'd like to get started. I'll settle in and have an early night and appear in the kitchen—what time?"

"The cook said not to come for the first breakfast. He's willing to wait for you until lunch preparations, being as it's your first day. He said to come to the kitchen at ten."

"Thank you. Now," Jen wanted suddenly to be alone, "could I be shown to my room, please? I'd like to get my things

The Tosca Taunt

organised."

Mark picked up his phone and called someone to his office.

"I think you'll like your accommodations," he said with some pride. "They're surprisingly big for mine rooms, and most of them have private bathrooms. You'll have one of those. We're so isolated up here, I guess the planners figured we needed to be adequately housed or we'd go stir crazy. We have good recreation facilities too—a hobby room, a card room, a common room for watching TV, a video machine, a CD player... I hope someone let you know that if you want a TV or a radio in your room, you have to bring your own."

"They didn't, actually."

"There was an extra radio-CD player someone left behind, I think it's still sitting in the hobby room. Would you like to use it until you can arrange to get your own sent up here?"

"That would be great."

"You can take CDs from the common room but please don't keep them in your room too long." He looked at her curiously. "What kind of music do you like?"

Again it came out of nowhere; "Opera, actually."

He grinned, an attractive grin in a craggy, weatherbeaten face. *A Clint Eastwood sort of look,* thought Jen. *How can I remember a film star's look and not faces from my own life?*

"I'm afraid you won't find opera CDs up here, Mrs Noonan, or many opera fans either. Sorry about that. You'll have to get your opera on the Saturday afternoon broadcasts."

"You like opera too? Since you know when the broadcasts are ..."

"Neither like nor dislike. But my wife used to listen to it."

"Doesn't she listen any more?"

"I don't know. I haven't seen her for—she's my ex-wife, actually."

A short square man in a lumberjack shirt appeared in the open doorway. He ushered Jen back down the stairs to the luggage she had left beside the open door to the first aid room. Short-and-square picked up the suitcase and held a door for her. It opened on the path to the dormitory, a building which she saw also contained the kitchen facilities and recreation areas.

The room assigned to Jen was in the centre of the hall on the second storey. She found herself delighted with it, her happiness quite out of proportion to its relatively modest attributes. But it seemed a safe refuge, from which she might venture out in search of herself, and come back to, if doubt overwhelmed her. It was perhaps fourteen feet by ten, and contained a comfortable looking bed tucked under the window, an upholstered side chair, and a plain light oak chair and desk with an ivory coloured phone on it. A door on the right opened to a generous closet, another door on the left led to a tiny bathroom complete with shower. A fanciful previous occupant had painted the walls bright peach, which cast an almost gaudy glow. A rosy glow—something in Jen's maimed memory stirred—she reached eagerly for the thought, but before she could seize it, it slipped away.

Short-and-square fetched the borrowed radio and put it on the bedside table where it took up most of the space. He then left her alone and almost contented. Now she was going to be able to settle somewhere, and to get into some sort of routine. She looked down at the form in her hand, which asked for such

The Tosca Taunt

details as her home address. She put it carefully down on the small desk.

For the first time since she had come down the mountainside, she completely unpacked the battered, expensive suitcase with "Bridget Jennifer Noonan" in gilt on the name tag. She found layers of luxurious designer labelled casual clothes, good casual shoes which seemed big on her feet, exquisite lacy lingerie, and two handbags, one of which, a Louis Vuitton royal blue, matched the suitcase. Surprisingly, at the very bottom, scrunched up behind a fold in the suitcase's lining, she found a paper with a name and a telephone number typed on it--"Mama, new, (912) 786-0389".

Jen's heart lurched. Her mother's phone number? But did she dare try to phone that number? The letter to "Mama" that she had found in the handbag had said Bridget would phone whenever the call couldn't be traced, would call from a pay phone.

But how can I wait, she asked herself urgently. *I can't stand this, not knowing anything about myself. Surely there's not that much risk, surely my husband—"T" or whatever his name is, surely he wouldn't have put a trace on my mother's phone line. Surely you have to be the police or the FBI to do something like that.*

I've got to gamble. Because soon they're going to ask me for this form, and I don't know the answer to any of these questions except for my name. I'm glad they didn't ask me in the office how old I am, I don't even know that. Oh dear God! Let this be my Mama's phone number, she'll be upset when she hears I can't remember anything, but she'll help me, my Mama will help me.

If I'm scared my call is going to be traced, like I say in my letter to

Jean Dell

Mama, maybe I shouldn't call from this phone. But anyone here would wonder why I was asking to use their phone, since they would know I have one of my own. I guess I have no choice. I can't remember; if I call collect does that make the call untraceable back to me? I think so, I think collect calls show up on my bill, not on hers. I'm almost sure it's not the other way around. Why can't I remember about collect phone calls, why can't I reason out even the simplest things?

Before she dialled the number she had found, she phoned the long distance operator to inquire where it was located. She was told it was a Savannah, Georgia number. In her confusion and excitement she forgot that she could have asked the operator about collect calls too. With trepidation she began to dial. But before she came to the last digit she slammed down the receiver, suddenly unable to face what she might learn. Twice she dialled before she found the courage to let the phone ring its summons to the operator to put through the collect call. And afterwards there were seven rings before the call was picked up, by a woman who sounded vague, as though she had just been awakened.

"Hello, Amanda Rees here," she said with a heavy southern drawl.

"I have a collect call for anyone from Bridget Jennifer Noonan," the operator said. There was a silence. "Ma'am, hello? Will you take this call?"

The woman answered finally, her drawl less pronounced. "Who did you say?"

The operator repeated the name. Amanda Rees said hesitantly, "Yes, ah'll accept the call."

"Go ahead, ma'am," said the operator.

The Tosca Taunt

"Mama?" said Jen tentatively.

There was no reply. Then, "Bryony? Bryony darling ah've been worried out of mah mind, where are you? What's happening, darling?"

"Oh, Mama, you really are my ... I'm in such trouble, I need your help, oh please..."

There was another pause, longer than the last. Then, "Well now just one minute, you don't sound one bit like—you're not Bryony, don't be playing silly games with me, nobody who sounds like you has a right to call me Mama."

"But ... but I don't understand, why do you keep calling me Bryony, I'm Bridget Jennifer Noonan."

Jen heard a sharp intake of breath. Then the woman Jen was calling Mama said, "Ah don't know who you are, but ah know perfectly well you're not mah daughter; mah daughter doesn't sound a bit like you, her voice is higher and she doesn't have your accent. But the name you just said, it's mah grandmama's name. Only grandmama's been dead for years."

Jen thought, *what is this?* She replied, "That's very strange. I—I'm sorry—I seem to have made a mistake; I was sure I had my Mama's number. I must have—" (must have what, Jen?) "—written it down wrong. Do you—where is your daughter?"

Mama's voice suddenly became hard. "Oh, ah see. You're trying to find Bryony. Did Victor put you up to this? Ah have no idea where Bryony is."

The receiver was slammed down so hard it hurt Jen's ear.

Good grief, I'm glad I'm not her daughter because I don't want any part of whatever that's about. I wonder who Victor is? Obviously not the man I'm married to—his name has to start with a "T", doesn't it?

Thirteen

The voice over the phone was deep and, if the words it had uttered had been different, would have been soothing. But to Tony who listened, heart pounding faster and faster, the message was what he had hoped never to hear.

"Mr Amato, we have found some objects we believe may have belonged to Mrs Amato. I'll describe them to you, and if you think they might be hers, we will arrange for you to identify them." Moses O'Brien, the police constable at Cedar Grove, which housed the police station closest to Hadley's Ridge, paused.

"Go on, I am listening, but I am sure what you have found will not be Jen's. What is it?"

"We've found two rings." The constable described them and read the messages inside.

Slowly Tony sat down on the chair at his desk. He whispered, *"Madre de Dio,* it is not true, it cannot be!"

Jean Dell

What am I going to do next, how can I help myself remember? I had such hopes for a moment ...

Shivering though the room was warm, Jen showered and put on a pale yellow nightgown and a white cashmere sweater. She thought she would have trouble getting to sleep; for the first part of the night she was wrong. The bed was soft and surprisingly comfortable.

Meanwhile, Mark Reinhard finished working overtime and, winning his debate with himself against tidying his desk tonight, locked his office. He left the administration building and made his way along the path to his room, which was at the other end of the hall from Jen's, and only slightly larger. He closed the door behind him, reflected a moment, then emerged again and ambled down the hall to the bar where he drank a convivial mug of beer with a geologist who was reading in the common room. That night it took Mark a while to get to sleep; he kept seeing the remarkably pretty face, despite the bruised eyes, of their new cook's helper.

Jean Dell

The constable said, "What did you say, Mr Amato? We seem to have a bad connection."

"The connection is fine, it is just that ... " Again Tony's voice faded to a whisper.

"Do you think these might have belonged to Mrs Amato?"

"I know they—they did—they do. But Jen never would take off her rings, I used always to tease her about this, why would she take them off this time?"

The constable thought some things did not bear saying but must be said all the same.

"She didn't necessarily take them off, Mr Amato. These rings were found near what may be human remains, but so badly burned they are probably unidentifiable."

Tony shut his eyes tightly. He could barely hold on to the receiver, let alone to his emotions. Somewhere behind his eyes he could see the flames creeping, licking, snaking upwards ... The horror, the pain of being burned alive—his Jen, her cool pale skin, her ardent lips and soft pale hair—aflame, a screaming pillar of fire—Jen, like Joan of Arc, sacrificed—but to what? He covered his eyes with his free hand.

"Do you mean—" He cleared his throat in order to find his voice again. "—do you mean the fire was so fierce that you cannot do tests?"

There was a short silence. Some questions were better left hanging.

"Mr Amato, I know how terrible this must be for you," the constable finally said. "Please know you have my sympathy."

"How can you know how terrible it is for me?" Tony cried. "Have *you* lost the best part of yourself in a stupid fire? I *need*

The Tosca Taunt

her, don't you understand? She—she cannot be dead!"

The constable ran his finger around inside his collar. He hated this part of this work. "I'm really sorry, Mr Amato. Uh, we would like you to identify these as soon as possible—"

But Tony had abruptly made up his mind. This was not happening. This was an unfortunate coincidence, but that was all it was, he was sure of it—he had to be sure of it. He would go and see for himself, he would prove to himself that this was a mistake.

"*Per favore,* I apologize for the shouting, is not your fault. You are just doing your job. I will come as soon as I can get there. But you will see—I will find Jen. She is not dead. You will see."

The receiver fell from his hand as the constable was saying uncomfortably, "We'll see you soon then, Mr Amato."

Tony sat staring at nothing as the receiver spluttered, "Please hang up now. If you need assistance, please dial your operator," and then began the double squawks that prompted anyone who could hear them to hang it up. Anton heard, and raced into the living room in the red jogging suit-style pyjamas Jen had bought for him before she left on her trip. He stopped abruptly at the sight of his father. Perceptive like his mother, he had no trouble discerning the distress Tony tried to hide.

"Daddy? What is it? Why are you looking so—Daddy, have they—have we found—is there news of Mom?"

Tony stared at his son, through his son. "No," he said, but the voice came out a whisper. "No, but they have found her rings," and then realised what he had said. Because Anton had been in on some of the teasing when Jen would not remove her precious rings for any reason.

"Mom's *rings?* But Daddy, she never took them off. What—what does that mean?"

Tony, his courage failing, tried to save the situation for himself with a quick, "Maybe it means something good, Anton, I am sure—"

But Anton was clever, knowledgeable, imaginative. "You *can't* be sure of anything, Daddy, not if they've found Mom's rings and not—and not Mom. That means—that could mean—oh, Daddy!" Anton drew on knowledge gleaned in television programs he was not supposed to have watched. After a moment of reflection that caused him more pain than anything had yet in his young life, he cried, "That could mean that Mom is b-burned up and all that's l-left are her rings!" Anton's lips trembled; that was the end of his sophistication. Now he was a frightened boy, needing his father to come up with a convincing reason why the hideous evocation could not be true. Tony knew it, and from his own pain he drew inspiration.

"Anton, Anton, don't, *per favore,* don't cry, because they—they have not found Jen's wedding ring, and the reason they have not found her wedding ring is that she is wearing it, wherever she is, I am sure of it. If she had been—if the rings had fallen off her—*o Madre de Dio!* Surely all three rings would have come off... "

But Anton was too frightened by his own imagination to be convinced. He crumpled on the chesterfield into Tony's encircling arm, sobbing with terror and grief. Tony held him, trying to control himself for the sake of his son. *Grazie a Dio* that Janina was asleep. Tony could not have dealt right now with

The Tosca Taunt

both his children's fear.

He kissed the top of his son's head, the curly dark hair so much like his own. But Anton drew back suddenly and, pulling away from his father, said brokenly between hiccuping sobs, "You lied to me, Daddy. You promised you would never lie, but you did. You told us Mommy was alive. And now you're lying again." The young voice rose, pitched at the edge of hysteria. "She isn't alive, she's dead, she's burned, Daddy I need Mom, it must have hurt her when the fire was burning her, oh Daddy oh Daddy!" The last words were a scream of pain.

Mrs Burns came rushing from her bed-sitting room, her dressing gown awry. When she saw the two stricken faces, so alike, the father and the son, she knew that reality had struck at last. She had no idea how she would begin to help with this raw and tangible grief. Before she had a chance to collect her thoughts, Janina, tugging at her flowered nightgown, came sleepily around the corner, awakened by her brother's scream. She looked at him doubtfully.

'Whatsamatter, Anton? You got a tummy ache?'

But Anton was beyond caring how he told his small sister that their world had crumbled. "Mom's dead, Nina!" he shouted.

For a moment she was uncomprehending, and then she said quietly, "That's wrong, Daddy says she's okay. Stop yelling, Daddy says everything's fine."

"Daddy's lying! Daddy lies and Mom's dead, she's all burned up!"

Now Tony pulled himself from this nightmare enough to do something constructive. He put his hand gently over his son's

Jean Dell

mouth, just long enough to stop the shouting. He said as calmly as he could "Stop it, Anton. Nina darling, come here, sit with Anton and me, sit down, Mrs Burns. I'll tell you what has happened, and what I must do."

So Tony told an edited version of the finding of the rings, and how he must now go up to the site of the fire. He paused, unsure of how to proceed. He said, "I am not a liar, Anton, Nina; I want never that you should say such a thing to me or even believe secretly in your hearts. I believe Mommy is alive; I cannot explain why, the evidence is not so good, but I just do. Don't lose your hopes yet, *per favore*, believe with me, just a little longer, let me try to—to find Jen—"

Anton was weeping quietly now, held tightly in the circle of Tony's right arm. Janina sat on Tony's knee, bewildered but prepared to believe a father who had not let her down yet.

Mrs Burns dabbed at her eyes with a lace handkerchief, willing her reserved Scots blood to help her control her emotions in front of the stricken Amatos. She had cared deeply for Jen Amato, and was devastated that the two children would now grow up without the love and influence of their kind, gentle, talented mother. As she watched Tony controlling his grief in order not to further upset his children, she was filled with admiration.

Finally she and Tony got the children to sleep. Tony told Mrs Burns that he would leave for the site of the fire the next day, and that he would probably have to cancel both his Friday *Tosca* and his part in the charity concert he was to give in Buenos Aires on Sunday. His Friday night CD recording session could be postponed; that at least would not be lost.

The Tosca Taunt

He said goodnight to Mrs Burns and went to bed. To bed but not to sleep. Everything hurt; his head felt like it was being repeatedly bludgeoned. He found himself going over and over the night he first met Jen, fourteen years ago at a dinner, after his debut at Glyndebourne in England. He had been singing *Tosca* then too. *Madre de Dio,* was that an omen? That their love should begin during a *Tosca* run and end during a *Tosca* run? Why did he let himself think like this? It was surely, surely! only a coincidence.

Again he forced himself to think only about the night of their meeting. Jen, repeatedly insulted by the very drunk man to whom she was engaged, had run from the chateau into a maze on the grounds, in order to regain her poise so she could return to the party. But the floodlights illuminating the maze were on a timer which shut them down. Tony, who had just been introduced to Jen an hour before, inexplicably knew she was lost and afraid in the darkened maze; to his bewilderment he seemed able to feel her thoughts. Following instincts he did not then understand but had since come to marvel at and accept, he sought and found her there, claustrophobic and hysterical. He, who until then had scarcely spoken to her, had held her, comforted her, kissed her—and their destiny together was sealed.

Tonight the clock ticked the hours away. Finally Tony fell asleep. And dreamed that he was looking for Jen in the maze, but that he could not find her, and, searching ever more feverishly, finally became hopelessly lost himself.

....

Jen, restless because tomorrow she had to start work and

pretend to know something about a profession for which she had never trained, tossed and turned and had nightmares. One in particular disturbed her, although she did not remember in her new incarnation that she had been claustrophobic in the old. She was walking in a beautiful sunlit forest. Gradually the light faded, and the trees closed malevolently around her, making a series of narrow pathways. What she could still see of the sky was darkening quickly, as she walked faster and faster through the channels, desperately seeking a way out.

In her dream she sobbed and cried out. A man called back to her, the voice gentle, calming. It said, "I will sing; follow the sound, *cara mia,* you will find me." Then the most glorious song filled her dream. She knew it to be an aria, but she could not identify it. She sought frantically to locate the singer. She made a final turn and there he was, a dark haired man with his back to her, dressed in a white shirt with flowing sleeves, dark trouser tucked into tight, high boots. She wanted to call his name but could not think what it was. Just as she came up to him, hoping he would turn so she could see his face, there was the sound of bullets, and he crumpled face down at her feet. Even the back of his shirt was covered in blood.

Jen started awake, her heart pounding. What a ghastly dream. It seemed to her that the dark man in this dream was the same as in the other dream, the one on the down escalator in the plastic tube, although she had not seen his face either time. Then she had a most unwelcome thought. There had been bullets in her dream, and the dark man appeared to be dead. A man, shot and killed. Was she by any chance running away from more than a violent husband? Was her husband dead? Had she

The Tosca Taunt

witnessed a killing? Had she had anything to do with it? Was she—was Bridget Jennifer Noonan possibly a murderess?

Fourteen

It was the dinner hour in England, but noon for Tony in New York—time for Mia and Cedric's now daily call to him. In the great dining room at Ridlough Hall, Cedric sat at the head of his long table but Mia, who according to the etiquette bred in Cedric's bones should have been at its foot, sat at his right, where he could touch her when he needed to. He put his hand over hers now.

"Eat your soup before it gets cold, Mia darling, Tony can wait five minutes. You won't be any use to him if you become ill because you're not eating properly."

Cedric searched Mia's face, needing to penetrate the wall set up by her acting talent so he could discern what she really felt. He could see immeasurable sympathy for Tony, but in her glittering turquoise eyes was there anything beyond that? Was he wrong to suspect that she felt anything more for Tony than a close, profound friendship? An almost inevitable friendship, given their community of shared interests and how often they had sung together over the years. But now the tabloids were having a field day rehashing the years of rumours about Tony and Mia, and writing up the death of Jen, which removed the barrier to the alleged romance. And though Cedric knew all about those papers, knew how they dealt in lies and innuendo, he knew that sometimes they also dealt in truth.

But it hadn't only been the tabloids in the past that had conspired to arouse Cedric's jealousy. Those who cast operas, and who were mesmerised by the look of the attractive pair on stage, and by the electricity between them, had never been averse to publicity about a possible covert romance between Mia and the married Tony.

Mia cast her eyes down at the cream of watercress and mushroom soup, usually one of her favourites. She had better eat it; she knew Cedric was uneasy about her feelings for her colleague, and it was pointless to exacerbate his discomfort by showing him how little appetite her worries had left her. So she smiled her prettiest stage smile at him and forced down her soup.

Then she rang for Thomson the butler and asked him to bring her cellphone. She dialled Tony, and, waiting for someone to answer, reached across and reassuringly caressed Cedric's cheek.

Soon the Scottish voice of Mrs Burns traversed the Atlantic, saying, "Mr Amato has just gone down to the lobby to speak to the doormen about his trip—"

"Trip? What trip?"

"I'm afraid I'm the bearer of bad news. The fire investigators have found Mrs Amato's rings."

"Jen's *rings?* How on earth is Tony taking that news?"

"It's difficult to judge. You see, Mrs Amato's wedding ring has not been found, and Mr Amato says Mrs Amato is alive somewhere and is wearing it. But the authorities in Ontario want Mr Amato to try to identify the rings, so he's going to the site of the fire. He's convinced he's going to find Mrs Amato alive somewhere there. Oh, here he is."

Tony greeted Mia in a voice so husky it was almost unrecognisable.

"Tony my dear, Mrs Burns just told us about your trip; I'm so sorry! Who's going with you?"

Tony's voice was flat, uninflected. "You don't understand, Mia. I have to go alone. This is only between Jen and me. She is not—she cannot be dead. How can she be dead when I can still feel her thoughts like I always do?"

Cedric could hear none of this, and so did not fully understand the look of panic on Mia's face as she said, "Please, Tony, postpone going until Cedric and I can get to you. Of course we'll let you go wherever you need, to be alone, but at least let us make the trip to the fire site, we can just be there for you."

"Mia, I appreciate, you cannot imagine how much such a friendship means to me now, but I will not wait for you. I might phone you tonight or tomorrow night, maybe I will need. Goodbye, Mia."

Tony abruptly hung up the phone, and Mia, closing her eyes for a moment against the pain of her sympathy, gave Cedric an emotional account of what was happening.

"We've got to go to him today, Cedric; I'm afraid he might

be suicidal and that's why he insists on travelling alone."

Cedric listened carefully to her voice; he discerned no secret passion in it for Tony, just the concern of a frantic friend. *So far so good*, he thought. But he had a major problem.

"I can't go straight away, have you forgotten?"

"Yes, I guess I have, what is it?"

"I must chair that conference in Brussels; I must be there tomorrow night and for the four following days, remember?"

"Oh Cedric, how could it possibly have slipped my mind? It's such an important conference, you've slaved to put it together—and what about the dinner we were to host together for the conferees?"

She took his hand and held it against her cheek; then she kissed his palm. "Cedric, I—I *love* you; but—but I'm terrified Tony might do something crazy—where on earth should my priorities be?"

Cedric figured that since she was about to become his wife, there should be no question in her mind about her priorities. For him the duel had at last really begun; he was oddly, surprisingly invigorated. He was gambling for high stakes, and he immediately decided his trump card in this situation would be altruism.

Staring at her pale face he said, "Your priority must be to save Tony. Go to him, Mia. He's in such desperate trouble, and he still has much to do, starting with raising his unfortunate children. We mustn't let him go down. After Jen, you're surely his best friend. Go. I'll come as soon as possible."

Mia lost control of her fragile composure and burst into tears of relief. Cedric felt a sudden fear. Was he playing the wrong card? Should he have asked her to wait until he could come to New York with her?

....

Jen's restless first night at the mine ended and she looked through her handsome wardrobe and put on suitable—she hoped—clothes for professional kitchen work—a pair of designer jeans and a bright blue blouse which matched her eyes. Apprehensively she made her way down the corridor and the stairs to the kitchen, guided unerringly by the clatter of dishes.

A man stood with his back to her, dressed in a yellow golf shirt and jeans, with a chef's hat at a precarious angle. He wore an apron tied around his back.

At her "Hello, I'm Jen Noonan, your new *sous-chef*," he turned and they mutually appraised one another. She saw a man of medium height, wiry and muscular, with a thin face, soft brown hair and eyes.

"Pleased to meet you. I'm Steve Macdonald. I'm going to be glad of the help, I'm telling you. We can get to know each other after lunch; for now, there're the aprons. You can chop up those vegetables and then make a *roux* to serve fifty guys. I was just starting, there's the ingredients."

Jen donned an apron and began labouriously to chop up a large pile of vegetables. Never particularly well co-ordinated, she took a long time over her task, and she noticed Steve covertly watching her.

I'm not going to get away with this, she thought. *It seems to me I know how to cook, but just knowing that isn't going to be good enough; I'm likely going to have to tell him I don't know how to be a sous-chef.*

Finally she finished chopping the vegetables, and she was

faced with making a *roux*. Only she couldn't remember what a *roux* was, if ever she had known. She didn't seem to know much. She did not know who Bridget Jennifer Noonan was; she did not know whether the cause of her bruises and lacerations was rape; she did not know if she was implicated in a violent death; she did not know if she herself was a murderess; and now she did not know something that doubtless was basic to any chef's training, how to make a *roux*. No, she was not going to cry, she was absolutely not going to.

"Hey, hey," Steve said softly, coming up beside her. "What's the matter? First day nerves? Come on, you're doing fine, just make me a nice big *roux*, you'll be okay."

She said miserably, "I don't know *how* to make a *roux*."

"Yeah," he said, looking at her with resignation. "It figures. You've got no training, have you. Nobody with training chops vegetables like that. So why'd you apply for this job? Running away from something? Like from whoever gave you the shiners?"

What could she say? Could she make enough of a convincing story from the little bit she knew about Bridget Jennifer Noonan? She decided to try an oblique approach.

"Yes, that's why I came, I'm running away from—" she put her hand up to her bruised face. "Are you going to fire me?"

"You got any place to go?"

"No, not really. Please, I'm sure I'm a good worker; will you give me a chance? Let me stay for a week, let me learn from you, you must have books I could study that would help me—"

The harassed, overworked Steve was in the mood to give her just enough time for him to replace her with a trained *sous-chef*.

There was no lack of people looking for work, even to come up here—maybe especially to come up here where the pay was so good. But she looked so damn vulnerable. What was a guy to do?

"Okay, okay, I'll give you the fastest training a *sous-chef* ever had, and I'll lend you the books I've got here, but you better be a quick learner because there's no time to fool around. If you're any good after one week you can stay."

She held her hand tightly across her mouth. Then she said simply, "Thank you, Steve. You've no idea how badly I need the help ..."

....

Cedric had played one of his trumps, but it had not taken the trick. All it had done was make Mia reveal—or so Cedric believed—one of her most important cards. She had shown Cedric how much it meant to her to go to the stricken Tony Amato. And how much would it mean to her to stay with Cedric if he asked her to? If he told her how much he needed her support and help at this crucial Brussels conference?

But did he? Was he actually just replacing one supportive woman, his ex-wife Alexandra, with another, his Mia? Cedric Tyhurst, Viscount Ridlough thought of himself as tough, self-reliant. Could he conceivably be this dependent on the support and love of his latest woman, indeed, of *any* woman? He did not like the picture. But he was forced to face it all the same, and admit that possibly its colours were true.

....

Mia had made a reservation on the Concorde to New York for later that day; the car was ordered to take her to the airport,

The Tosca Taunt

and she and her personal maid had decided quickly which clothes the maid must pack. Mia had half an hour before it would be time to leave. She ran down the wide staircase looking for Cedric, but he was nowhere to be seen.

"Thomson, where is he?" Mia asked Cedric's longtime butler.

"I'm not sure, madame. But he asked me to give you this."

He handed her a note. Hastily she tore at the envelope. She read;

Mia my darling;
Odd, I cannot say goodbye. I will miss you too much as it is; if I have to go through a goodbye it will seem longer before you return. This way I won't be absolutely certain you've gone—
Two weeks to the wedding, my love. After the conference, after you—we—have supported Tony, then—us.
Always,
Cedric

Thomson was still in the room with Mia, although he had, like the good butler that he was, averted his gaze from her as she read. Of course he had seen everything—had seen her expression change dramatically.

"Thomson, I know where your loyalties are, where they must be, but please, I must see him before I go ... "

Thomson hesitated. He had been Cedric's faithful butler since before Cedric's marriage to Alexandra. Now he sensed his employer's need. There was a way to tell without betrayal.

"Perhaps, madame, you would like to take a bit of fresh air

before your long journey? The winter pansies over near the potting shed are blooming particularly well at the moment."

"Oh Thomson thank you. I won't tell him you—but of course you didn't, did you?" She smiled. "You *are* clever."

From the large back scullery closet she snatched up the first wrap that came to hand, an Aran sweater, and she stepped out into the garden. In case Cedric were watching, she ambled casually through the well-kept autumnal gardens behind the chateau in what would appear to be an aimless walk, but coming always closer to the potting shed. Finally she reached it and leaned against its wall, ostensibly looking at the winter pansies smiling and nodding mauvely around her feet. Then she opened the door and saw Cedric leaning against a table, his back to her.

"Cedric, whatever are you—"

"Go away, my love. Did Thomson give you my note?"

"Yes, but darling, I don't understand, what is it?"

He turned to her, and the look of sorrow and longing on his pale face shocked her.

She hesitated only a second, then went quickly to him and put her arms around him. "Darling whatever is wrong? Are you—you're not ill and hiding something from me, are you?"

"No, no, I'm not ill, although—"

"What? Although what?"

"I don't want to tell you, Mia. It's too bloody selfish."

"For heaven's sake, my dear, in two weeks I'll be your wife, I want to know *everything* about you, please don't start keeping things from me now!"

She put up her hands and caressed his face, touched his soft hair, then kissed him gently and held her cheek against his. And

The Tosca Taunt

he made his decision; he would play a risky card this time. But he had to know.

"Tony needs you, Mia. But I—I have this crucial conference going on—I counted on you to help me—I need you too. Not like Tony needs a good friend just now, but in a different way my need is as great as his."

"Are you asking me not to go? To stay with you?"

"Yes."

"But Cedric," asked Mia, bewildered, "whatever am I to do?"

Cedric could not realise that what was about to happen to him, something entirely out of his control, would turn out to be the highest trump card he could have played in his high stakes game. He was assailed by a sudden, agonizing pain. He put his hand on his chest, grimaced, drew in his breath sharply and said, "I've got a terrible pain—I can't breathe—Mia—help me—"

The perspiration began to roll down his face as Mia panicked. She put her arms around him and helped him down onto the old wooden chair beside the potting table.

"Darling, of course I'll stay, you're not well, oh Cedric, why didn't you tell me? I'll run and get Thomson, oh darling, you're scaring me—"

She let go of him and ran for the door.

"Stay with me, my love. Please."

He's dying, she thought, so used to singing in operas where tragic love and death took precedence over all other plots. She could not think in terms of muscle spasms, of severe heartburn; all was immediately catastrophic.

Cedric's pain, whatever it had been, was passing. But he

looked alarmingly grey and drawn to Mia as he said, "I feel better, I'm all right, God knows what that was about. I—I had no right to ask you to stay. What Tony must be going through is unimaginable. Go, go to him. He needs you."

But Mia looked at Cedric, haggard and perspiring, and knew her duty as his soon-to-be-wife was to stay with him. She felt rent in two.

"No, Cedric darling, of course I'll stay with you. We'll go to the conference together. You—you frightened me so badly just now. After the conference is over, then we can go together to Tony."

Fifteen

Despite his best efforts, Tony was prevented from going alone to the actual site of the fire, even though, having successfully fended off his assistant and his anxious friends, he travelled by himself to the town nearest the fire. Once Tony had checked into the Biltmore Hotel and Motel he asked the desk clerk where the police station was. The desk clerk hated operatic music with a passion, his thing being good jazz. But hey, this was a famous guy asking him for directions. He stared at the tall singer as he said that yes, you could certainly walk to the station from here, it was only two blocks, but they did have a taxi service in town, did Mr Amato –

Mr Amato said he would walk.

Now Tony found himself in driving autumn rain, forcing himself down a street that looked to him like a setting for a film. On the main street of this small city, time had stopped. Tony walked more and more slowly; he wanted time to stop for him as well, to stop before he had to see those rings, those rings that could not, could not! be Jen's ...

Not even raincoats as expensive as Tony's are impervious to the driving rain of November in northern Ontario. He was damp and uncomfortable as he walked through the door of the small old-fashioned police station and stood before a high counter. The same young policeman who had phoned Tony with the news about the rings, Moses O'Brien, his chair swivelled around so he had his back to the public, was saying into the phone, "Listen, Sharry, you think I got nothing better to do than talk to you all day? You saw *who* in town? Oh yeah, that opera singer. So he's good looking, so what? I suppose you're gonna decide you like opera now you caught a glimpse of him. You think I'm jealous of some *opera* singer?"

Tony cleared his throat noisily. Moses said "I gotta go," and hung up the phone before he swivelled in his chair and looked carefully at whoever this member of the complaining general public might be. Then, remembering what he had just been saying on the phone, he muttered "Ojeeze" as Tony, grinning now at the policeman's obvious discomfiture, said, "I am the good looking opera singer."

"Um—yeah, I guess you are." Moses shook Tony's outstretched hand. "I'm Moses O'Brien—Mr Amato, I presume."

"Well, I am not Mr Livingstone."

Moses forgot his embarrassment with the recollection of why Tony Amato was here. He said, "You'll be wanting to—"

"No. It is the last thing I am wanting to do. But let us get on with it."

"They're here, in this locker, my superior wants to be here when you identify the rings—"

The Tosca Taunt

"Or if I am truly lucky, when I don't."

Moses' superior was a woman. She said it was an honour to meet Tony, and guided him to the lockers in the back room of the station. Unlocking one, she removed two sealed plastic bags, tagged, accompanied by photos which looked to Tony to show where the rings had been found. The woman gave Tony the plastic bags. He took them into his hands reverentially, as though they were sacred; two vessels holding the bread and the wine of communion. But the communion was only with Jen, for there winking in the light were her rings. Jen's rings ...

He took out the solitaire and remembered, remembered giving it to Jen over dinner in the Dorchester Hotel in London, on that luminous evening when they had become formally engaged.

He put the solitaire back in its bag and took the "eternity" ring from the other. This jewel he had sought for a long time; it had belonged to the noted painter and watercolourist John Marin, and Tony had wanted an antique ring with a special provenance to give to his artist wife. He had put it on Jen's finger on their tenth wedding anniversary, when he had dashed back from London to New York on the Concorde, to be with her. She had been prevented from coming to England to celebrate their anniversary because one of their children was ill. So, as she had dined that evening in the Rainbow Room with a friend, he had made a surprise appearance on the stage singing a love song.

She had been so happy then. He had said, "Never take the ring off, Jen," and she had promised she would not. Now, he held these rings again in his hands. He closed his eyes, trying to

Jean Dell

recapture some of the joy these rings had symbolised. But he could not. There was nothing but this darkness, this appalling, unimaginable pain.

"Yes," he said to the woman who stood before him, "yes, these belong to my Jen. I have given them to her."

"I'm so sorry, Mr Amato. Now that you have identified these, you may take them with you."

"*Grazie.*" Tony slipped the little bags into his pocket.

The juxtaposition of the rings with the doubtful bones was explained to Tony. Finally he said, "But you have not found her wedding ring. Maybe there is still a hope?"

The policewoman said, "Mr Amato, a fire like this is an odd business. The wedding ring may have melted. I don't know why it would melt and these not, but with fires—"

Tony threw his head back and stared at the ceiling. He was afraid he was going to be sick. He took a deep breath, held it and closed his eyes, and for a moment closed his mind, against what he was hearing. And, exhaling, finally knew he must accept this. *Jen was dead. Jen was dead was dead was dead* ... Only he imagined he could feel her thoughts still, as he could when she was alive. He thought he felt her being afraid. But how could he feel her thoughts if she were dead?

"I believe you, and at the same time I do not believe you." Tony stared at the policewoman, unseeing. "I seem to be quoting *Otello*—only you are not *Iago*."

"Mr Amato, I realise how hard this must be for you. It is even hard for me to have to tell you these things; I cannot imagine how you must be feeling. All I can say is that I hope in time your grief will—er—"

The Tosca Taunt

"*Time!*" Tony exploded. "You think *time* is going to help me? Nothing will help me, can you not understand? Jen and I, we are—*Dio*, we are like two halves of one person. And now I go on for the rest of my life being only half a person? Tell me how to do that, tell me, oh, *Madre de Dio*—" Tony turned away, breathing hard.

The people in the police station with Tony thought miserably, *this is sometimes a lousy profession.*

Finally Tony said, "I would like to see the site of the fire. How do I do this? Can I hire a car or—"

The policewoman said, "You can, but if you like, I can spare Moses for the afternoon. His job for the rest of the day is to drive you to Hadley's Ridge and back."

So Tony and Moses set out in an unmarked police car for Hadley's Ridge. But the easy conviviality of Tony's first words with Moses had disappeared. Usually Tony was sympathetic with people's nervousness in the presence of a celebrity, and he was at pains to make them realise that he was, in his own view, an ordinary man with an extraordinary gift, just working hard doing his job. But today was different.

While Moses drove, racking his brains for conversation that would not be inappropriate in the circumstances, Tony sat beside him, white-faced and silent, staring out at the pelting autumn rain. Any attempts Moses made to comment on the passing scenery, an endless panorama of dripping trees and pines, were met with monosyllables. Finally he gave it up. He had seen pictures of Jenetta Amato. He figured if he had just been given proof that he had lost such a woman, burned beyond knowing in a savage fire, he might be monosyllabic too.

Finally he had to say, "We're here, Mr Amato, the hotel is—was—just around this bend."

Tony had not known what to expect, but he was not prepared for what he saw. Because the hotel had been made of wood and the fire so ferocious, there was nothing left of the building itself except a great pile of ashes with the odd charred beam and pieces of pipe and plumbing protruding. Tony clapped a hand to his mouth and stared at Moses in helpless shock.

"I know. I'm sorry, Mr Amato."

Tony responded after a long moment of gazing at the ruin. "I would like—if I could just—could I be alone a little bit, *per favore*."

"Of course. I just have to speak to my colleague."

Once Tony and Moses had emerged from the car they could smell the smoke still hovering like a pale, rank ghost, despite the rain. A fire truck was parked at the side of the road in front of them.

The ruins were surrounded by a barrier of wide yellow arson investigator tape, with Do Not Cross printed repeatedly on it. A policeman stood impassively guarding access. He gave a stolid sign of greeting to Moses as they approached

"This is Joe MacMahon, this here's Mr Amato, you know, the singer, the husband of the missing artist," said Moses, gesturing awkwardly. "He'd like to walk around the site a bit."

"I would like to go inside the tapes, is possible?"

Joe said, "I'm sorry, Mr Amato, I can't, not even for you. But you're welcome to walk around the outside all you want."

Tony slowly approached the pile of ashes where a small,

scattered group of people worked. One by one they looked up, did the double take Tony was so used to seeing when he appeared somewhere unexpectedly, and then for once in his life they, without exception, lowered their heads to their work and did not stare. Did not stare at the pain that was so private, so destructive that he would conceal it from them if he could. This was only between him and Jen.

Very slowly he walked around what had been a beautiful Victorian building, the terrible sickness in him growing, growing. This was the funeral pyre of his Jen. She had perished here in an awesome inferno, alone, terrified, in inconceivable agony. And he had not been here, had not been able to share, had not been able to help, had not been able to die with her. Would it have been too much to ask, that they might have been allowed to die together? Was there any other destiny that was fitting for the end of his life?

O Madre de Dio, pray for us now and in the hour of our death, pray for us pray for us now now now and in the hour of our death of our death of our ...

It was not only the relentless rain that wet his cheeks. His pain, the pain that was for him and Jen alone to share, would have to be shared with others whether he wanted or no. With great care he made his way around the pile of ashes, staring only at it. Then he went to the waiting Moses and, shakily poised, said, "I like to walk around again one time, *per favore*, before I go."

"Of course, Mr Amato. I didn't think at the station, but do you want pictures—we take photos of course, we could let you have copies."

Jean Dell

"I have pictures in my head now I will never forget. Thank you but no, the photographs, I don't want them."

He walked away from Moses, and, forlorn, soaked with rain, went once more slowly around the site, head down. On the cliff side of the hotel a small patch of cloth, caught on a partly concealed twig, caught Tony's eye. He bent to pick it up. It was a rain-sodden, filthy scrap of fine pale green silk, rather like the travelling pyjamas Jen had bought for that trip. He held it tightly to him; should he show it to one of the investigators? What good would that do? It was just one more proof of Jen's death. This he would keep, this would be between him and Jen alone. He pressed it to his lips, but unlike the clothes still in her closet in New York, it had lost her scent. He could not even have that consolation.

Now night was falling. Moses drove Tony silently back to his hotel. He said, as he dropped Tony off, "You're not here alone, are you?"

"Actually, I am. I cannot explain why; many people said they would come with me, I am lucky in my friends. But some things nobody can help you with."

"I think I understand. When do you go back? Are you okay tonight alone?"

"I go back tomorrow. I have to be okay tonight alone. I have to be okay for the rest of my life alone ... " Tony's voice faltered. Finally he was able to continue. "You see, is wonderful to have been given the voice, but is such a big responsibility, and I have counted very much on my wife to share what I have to do."

Tony paused, wondering why he could not stop blurting all this out. "She always brings me the luck, she chases away the

The Tosca Taunt

sadness ... *Dio,* how do I live without my Jen?"

Moses said hesitantly, "Would you like to have supper with me and my girlfriend? There's a nice quiet restaurant over on—"

"I thank you, I truly appreciate that you invite me, but no. I am not hungry—and I would not be good company tonight." Tony smiled wanly. He held out his hand and shook that of the young policeman. "*Grazie* for your kindness. Goodbye."

When had gone from the car, even though Moses was disappointed that he would not be able to produce Antonio Amato to impress Sharry with, he still felt lighter, as though a great sadness had been lifted off his shoulders.

"Who'd want my job?" he asked himself mournfully as he drove off.

....

Tony let himself into his hotel room. It was one of those generic hotel rooms in generic northern Canadian towns—scrupulously clean, with a comfortable bed, the not quite adequate lighting making the beige and brown decor seem like a perpetual twilight. A deeply depressing room, thought Tony, wondering whether he should rent a car and leave tonight. But knowing how badly he drove when stressed—he had long since given up driving on days when he performed, because the first time he tried he had driven into a parked car—he decided to stay. However much he might long tonight for abiding peace, he knew he had responsibilities that were bigger than his grief: he had two children to nurture, and a voice which belonged not to him but to the world.

"*Maledetto,* Jen! How could you do this to me?" he cried. "How could you leave me to do all this alone?"

In a sudden rage he tore the bedclothes from the bed and threw them on the floor; he swept the bedside lamp off the table, breaking its bulb; he hurled the Gideon Bible across the room where it hit the door with a crash; then he sank down on the bare mattress, stunned by his outburst.

There was a book of matches in an ashtray on the chest of drawers that held the television set. Tony sat staring at them, wondering what they were doing in his "No Smoking" room. His mind segued to the fire, to Jen, burning alive, screaming for him, needing him in her agony; maybe if he had been there he could have found a way out for them both. *Why had she gone on that trip, curse her, curse her!* How could she have left him alone? How soon did you lose consciousness when you were being burned alive, how much had she suffered before the mercy of unconsciousness, of oblivion and death came to her, *o Dio o Madre de Dio ...*

He walked like an automaton to the small book of matches and lit one. He held the flame to his palm until the pain became unbearable. He lit a second match, a third, a fourth, and held them one by one in the same place until he too was in agony. He had to know; he had to share Jen's pain. He lit a fifth match. *Burn burn burn Jen oh my Jen oh my Jen ...*

He fell to his knees finally, and sank sobbing to the rug where, overtaken by pain and a vast sickness, he fell into an exhausted sleep.

Sixteen

Victor Macready Kilbride's morning at the office, during which he treated a nervous middle-aged man and several attractive young women, was over. After his receptionist went off to lunch, he sat down at her desk and pulled the telephone towards him. He jumped as it rang under his hand, but the caller was welcome; it was Gerald Geraint, P.I.

"Doctor Kilbride, I've given your case some thought and in my opinion the best and fastest way to go is through your mother-in-law. What say I go to Savannah next week and sniff around? I'm hoping by now Bryony will have phoned her mother; you say Mrs Rees is an incurable pack rat, keeps everything; anyway she's bound to keep some records for Income Tax purposes. So, I figure she's likely to have her telephone bills around. I'll do a little break and enter if I have to, whatever is necessary for me to find if there have been calls—if we're real lucky, your wife will have called collect—and I can find out from where."

Victor demurred; the last thing he wanted was to be connected with an illegal break and enter. Geraint continued, "Don't worry, my talents are impeccable. Surely Len LeComte told you that. Anyway, if Bryony hasn't made any collect calls, well, I can always do an illegal tap with a little help from my Savannah connections. I'll check all possible numbers on the bills first, and we'll see what we come up with, what say?"

"Okay fine, as long as *I'm* not implicated in anything illegal, you do whatever it takes, and whatever it costs, you find her. Effing bitch, nobody leaves me like that, nobody humiliates me like that! Don't even *think* of telling Len LeComte about this, y'hear? You just find that bitch."

"Okay, okay, Doctor Kilbride, keep your shirt on, I've never failed to find a missing person yet. I'll be in touch with you real soon. You all take care now."

Victor slowly replaced the receiver. His throat felt tight. He was going to teach that Bryony never ever to leave him again — she would never leave after he got through with her this time. Why did she want to provoke him so? What alternatives had he ever had, from the beginning, except to discipline her in order to teach her to behave like a wife in his social circle should behave? For example, like his dear mother had behaved, throughout her marriage to Papa.

....

There were traces of snow staying on the ground at the Delson Mine site. Although the heating system was working in the building where Jen cooked, she felt chilly and out of sorts as the day progressed. When she finally got to her room that evening she undressed with relief; the waist of her jeans had

The Tosca Taunt

seemed to tighten hourly. She examined her naked self in the full length mirror, tracing the slightly raised scar on her abdomen with her finger, wondering what it had been for. Hysterectomy? Fibroid tumours? Intestinal disease? Caesarean section? Cancer? She wondered why she had been prescribed painkillers as strong as Demerol. Was she by any unfortunate chance chronically ill? There was an echo of memory about the scar, but try as she might she could summon only half-remembered grief for unremembered loss.

During the night some of her questions were answered by the onset of menstruation. She wondered whether such heavy bleeding was normal for her, and again asked herself how old she was. Then she realised she had something to be thankful for. If her fading bruises had been due to rape, at least she was not pregnant from it.

But a new fear assailed her; AIDS. A rapist would not likely take precautions. She lay in her narrow bed, her cramps worsening, as she wondered about AIDS, about herself, about whether she would ever remember who she was, about whether, in the light of the dream she had dreamt about the dark man falling dead at her feet, she wanted to remember. She began to think up ways she might look for her identity. What were distinctive things about her that might make her traceable?

As far as she could tell, she spoke with a generic North American accent. She knew it was not French-Canadian English, nor was it Boston, or New York or New Jersey or the Southern States. That left her most of North America to begin searching in. Was there an atlas in the library here? If she checked a list of cities and towns in North America, maybe one would ring a bell.

And then she might call the police station there and ask about missing persons. It was worth a try, surely. She turned over on to her stomach to try to ease her discomfort.

These cramps are terrible, she thought; *I can't stand them. I'm going to have to take some Demerol; maybe this is why I have the prescription.* She got up and swallowed a pill, then paced around the room, fists clenched against the pain, until the Demerol took hold. *This is not normal*, she thought; *this pain is as severe as childbirth. But how do I know that? Do I have children?* She lay down again, pushing her vacuum of memory to evoke children, any children, her children? But there was only the semi-anaesthetized remnant of an arresting pain.

Maybe if I go to sleep now the Demerol will give me different dreams, she thought, feeling inexplicably bereft; *maybe I will dream of my children, if I have children, oh dear God*!

She drifted into sleep. But the only child who invaded her dreams was a pitiful dead baby, tiny and obviously premature, which she held in her arms while other arms held her tightly around the shoulders. When she looked to see whose arms they were, the dark curly head was turned away. And then the dream shifted; she was walking, this time on the large flat roof of a building, and the view was Rome—she could make out Saint Peter's Basilica in the distance. Just as she was feeling thrilled to be in Rome again, she turned to see, at some distance from her and with his back to her, the dark man, again dressed in the white shirt and high boots. She ran towards him, hoping at last to see his face, but just as she reached him gunshots rang out and he fell forward, blood soaking through the back of his shirt.

Jen awakened with a start. What *was* this horrible repeating

The Tosca Taunt

dream? This one had been different, she remembered. This one had begun with a baby. A dead baby—her baby? The name Gianni suddenly entered her mind. *Gianni—my son; Gianni?* It seemed right, and yet ... As she was trying to pull herself from the black mood created by these dreams, her alarm clock sounded and she slowly got out of bed, showered and dressed for work.

Her cramps started again. She thought, *if I take a whole Demerol I won't be able to work, they make me so drunk. I'll try half.*

Finally she appeared at the door of the kitchen. Steve, already sweating from the heat in the room and the work he had to do, turned to her and said, "Hey, you look awful."

"Thanks a lot, Steve, I've always thought I was semi-attractive."

He grinned. "Semi-attractive, yeah, right, you know damn well on a scale of one to ten you're an eleven, that's not what I mean. You look kind of green, you know? You sick?"

"A bit. But I've taken a pill and I should be okay."

"I had a night's stomach flu earlier this week, is that what you've got?"

"No."

"Well, here, sit on the stool and stir this, see how you feel. You look terrible."

In a short while Steve put a plate in front of her, with two poached eggs on toast, prettily garnished with watercress and twists of lemon peel.

"Breakfast for invalids, enjoy."

Jen looked at this and swallowed hard. "You're too nice to me, Steve, but I'm not hungry. Thanks anyway."

Jean Dell

After the breakfast and lunch flurries were over, Steve said suddenly, "Okay okay you're fired."

"What?" Jen turned towards him, shocked.

"Hey, hey, I don't mean for good, I just mean for this afternoon. Take the rest of the day off, I can't stand watching you trying not to throw up."

She laughed. "But I can't take time off. You've given me a week to learn my job, I can't afford not to take advantage of all the teaching time you can give me."

"You know damn well I'm not going to let you go. You're doing fine, just go away before *I* throw up watching you. If you feel better, come back and help me with dinner; if you don't, I'll see you in the morning, okay?"

"You're a nice guy, Steve."

"Yeah, yeah, so my girlfriend tells me."

....

Before Jen went back to her bedroom, she made a detour past the library where she found a comprehensive and modern world atlas. Pleased, she took it to her room where she removed her tight clothes and put on a loose peacock blue dressing gown. She needed more Demerol; then she lay down on the bed and began painstakingly to study the list of North American cities and towns. When she reached the last listing, Zwolle, Louisiana, she reluctantly admitted that no memory had been stimulated. But she would try again; she would try every week until something clicked. Something had to, one day. Still, she was disappointed, and consoled herself with a *Time Magazine* she had brought from the library along with the atlas.

She was looking over the Milestones column, to see what

The Tosca Taunt

had happened to whom and if the "whoms" triggered any memories, when she came across "Missing, Presumed Dead: Jenetta Maclean Amato, well-known watercolour artist; wife of superstar tenor Antonio Amato. Mrs Amato was listed as one of four people missing in a hotel fire in northern Ontario, Canada."

Jen looked at the top of the column to see if there was a picture of this woman, but the three photos were of other people in the news. Something about the phrase, "well-known watercolour artist", stirred her. Was she—was Bridget Jennifer Noonan—an art connoisseur, maybe a collector, and might she own a picture painted by this now dead Jenetta Amato? Certainly judging by the expensive clothes in her suitcase, she had previously had the kind of money that would allow her to own original works of art. Or maybe she herself was a teacher, an art teacher?

Surely the puzzle of her identity would soon be solved. But Jen remembered again the dark man in her dreams, shot, bleeding; and her ambivalence grew. She had to learn who she was; or did she have to forget who she was? She dozed, and, waking to severe cramps again, did not go to help Steve for dinner

Half an hour later Jen's phone rang. It was Mark Reinhard.

"Jen, I was just talking to Steve; he said you weren't feeling well. Would you like a visitor for a few minutes?"

"You? I'd like that. I'm not so sick that I wouldn't enjoy company."

That was what he had hoped she would say. He would be lying to himself if he said he did not find her interesting. Very attractive, faintly mysterious, and definitely, definitely intriguing. So he hurried to her room, and when she had let him in, he sat down, judiciously leaving the door open. Jen was giggly and amusing under the influence of the Demerol, but he realised after he left her that he had learned nothing at all about her, and that she had learned a great deal about him. He would have to remedy that in the future.

But he had better go carefully; there were secrets here. This was a woman who had a story, almost certainly a sad one, and he did not want to upset her before ... before ... he could not finish that idea. He was not falling in love. He absolutely, definitely, was not falling in love. Would not, could not, should not—would, could, should—he grinned to himself.

Now he was stuck with taking the month's leave of absence he had been given, to teach a course in Toronto. Damnation! Would she still be here when he came back?

He had rarely been with a woman who charmed him more.

Seventeen

Tony arrived in New York from Cedar Grove to a profusion of phone calls, telegrams, faxes, and E-mails telling him about the coming invasion of loving relatives and friends. Before the first arrivals, and the first lamentations, he knew he must tell his children that their mother was dead.

"Do you want me there, Mr Amato?" asked a nervous Mrs Burns.

"No, not when I tell. But if you hear things are getting bad, you come, *per favore,* I may need your help then. The children should be any minute home from school, when the chauffeur brings them up you send them to the library; tell them I need to talk to them."

Anton and Janina soon came into the library where Tony sat, fidgeting with a magnet he kept on his desk. Janina hurled herself at Tony and cried happily "Daddy, Daddy, you're home!" She gave him a huge hug before sitting herself on his knee. Anton came in slowly, vigilant and apprehensive. His father's grey, drawn face frightened him.

"Sit with me, my darlings, we have to talk—" Tony put his arm around his son, and continued cradling Nina on his knee.

"I have to tell you—I was wrong." Tony paused. "I did not lie to you, *sinceramente* I did not, and I would not ever. I told you what I believed myself, I believed that Jen—that Mama was alive."

He stopped and shook his head, wondering in pained bewilderment how she could be dead when he kept feeling her thoughts just as he had since the day they met.

His children watched him, their dark eyes, so much like his own, mirroring the uncertainty and fear he felt himself. He forced himself to continue.

"But I have been to the fire site now, I have seen the—I have Mama's rings, I have to—I *have to* believe, *o mi bambini*, Mama is dead, I am so sorry, she is gone, we will not see her, ever again."

Nina looked up at her father, dry-eyed. "Not see Mama? But—but I want her, Daddy, I want her, make her come, won't she come, Daddy? Is this *really* like Sandidog?"

"This is really like Sandidog, Nina," said Anton, his young face grim, his voice without expression.

The children sat as still as sculptures. What was happening? Tony had expected tears, lamentations, hysteria. Now he wondered whether Anton had accepted Jen's death before Tony had gone to Hadley's Ridge. And was Nina simply too young to take this in? Tony hoped desperately that he would be up to the task of helping his children cope with grief, so they would not be maimed forever ... as he knew he was ... *is ... and ever shall be, world without end, grief without end, amen ...*

The Tosca Taunt

What was Nina saying? She had drawn away and was staring at Tony, her eyes wide, serious.

"Daddy, you're wrong. Mama isn't dead. I know if I'm a really really good girl Mama will come back. She's just gone away because I was bad and she's mad at me."

Tony pulled her tightly to him. "No, Nina darling, no, I am so sorry—"

"I don't believe you, Daddy. It's because I was scratching pictures on the side of her dresser with a pin and she got real mad at me. That's why she went away. If I promise not to do that any more she'll come back, I know she will."

Anton withdrew from Tony's hug and stood up. He couldn't bear this. He knew this wasn't Mama punishing Nina. It was God punishing him, that was what it was. Because Anton had done a terrible thing.

He and two schoolmates had been caught smoking a joint of marijuana brought to the school by one of the senior boys. Naturally the headmaster had informed the boys' parents, in Anton's case only Jen, because as so often happened Tony was singing in another part of the world and would not be able to participate in the immediate disciplining of his son.

Jen had come down heavily on Anton, with a severe lecture and with punishments, deprivations of Anton's pleasures. In truth this smoking episode had unnerved Jen badly, for she had close friends who just the month before had lost a teenaged daughter to a drug overdose. And since Jen often had to deal by herself with problems involving the children, she had of necessity evolved her own system of discipline whereby she saved strict punishments only for very heavy transgressions.

She and Anton had a stormy scene when Jen imposed the punishments on Anton. He had tried everything to stop her, finally breaking into hysterical fury. And then he had said the terrible thing.

How would he forget, let alone forgive himself for his unforgivable act? Anton put his hand on Nina's shoulder and said, "It's not your fault, Nina, it's mine."

"What are you talking about, Anton?" asked Tony, bewildered by the turn this was taking.

"Send her away, Daddy."

Tony looked at his young son, blenched and obviously afraid, and at his daughter, confused but not yet accepting the inevitable. He saw the greater need.

"Nina, *cara mia*, you go get your chocolate milk from Nanny Burns, we'll talk later, is that okay?"

Nina was now so puzzled she could not put any of this together. She might as well go and have her chocolate milk. Maybe Nanny Burns would give her cookies too. She gave her father another huge hug, frowned, stared at him, and went into the kitchen where Nanny Burns waited apprehensively.

"If I'm a really really good girl, Nanny," Nina said, "Mama will come back. Can I have my chocolate milk now?"

In the library, Anton stood before his father and said, "I did this, Daddy. Did Mama tell you about the pot?"

"What are you talking about, Anton? What pot?"

Anton saw that his father did not comprehend the word. "Carl and Rob and I smoked marijuana and Mr Cairnwell told Mom. Oh Daddy she was so mad, you wouldn't believe how mad she can get, I'm sure you've never seen her like that."

The Tosca Taunt

Tony surprised himself by bursting into half-hysterical laughter. Jen was one of those glacial looking women whose appearance conceals white heat. Nobody looking at her expected her to have much passion. *Wrong,* thought Tony, *totally wrong, my Jen is so– my Jen is—she is dead—even now I have not accepted it. How can I expect acceptance of my son?*

Anton, momentarily nonplussed by his father's laughter, continued.

"She—Mama—she said I couldn't watch television for a week, she said I couldn't play that game you brought me back from London, Daddy, she made me so mad, and I– I—" he looked at his father, his face naked, stripped of all defences. "I said I wished she was dead."

The superstitious Tony grabbed at his medallion of Saint Cecilia and stared at his white-faced son, standing before him so bent on confession, on doing the honourable thing in this most terrible of situations.

With difficulty Anton continued. "And now God is punishing me. It's my fault, Daddy, it's all my fault."

Abruptly Anton covered his face with his hands and sank down beside his father, leaning against Tony's arm. His hot tears scalded what was left of Tony's *sang-froid*. What could Tony say? He had to convince his distraught child that he was not to blame for any of this tragedy.

"But, Anton, Anton, no! Of course God is not punishing you by making Mama die. Because that would mean we are all being punished for what *you* said, and does that make any sense? Why would God give me such pain for something you said? Cry for her, *o mio Dio* yes, cry for her, but not like this, not blaming yourself, oh Anton!"

And Jen's husband held Jen's son as they wept tears of utter desolation.

....

As soon as they heard the confirmation of Jen's death, Tony's parents and his brothers flew to Manhattan from their Italian homes. Immediately on their arrival, Tony's mother Isabella had sent the rest of her family away for an hour; she needed to be alone with her distraught Tony. She made *cafe latte*, and sat drinking it with him in his library. What could she do to help him, this son she knew both so well and so little? She had always been able tap into some of his emotions; he was very much like her. But his need, once he had realised the implications of possessing a superb voice, to give himself regardless of the cost to a public that devoured him, she admired but could not completely comprehend. Yet she had given herself utterly to her family. But she was unable to shift her understanding to Tony's compulsion to give. She could only regard him with awe and respect.

But love, now, love real and lasting, that was in her ken. She had grown up in a caring family, and, knowing how that worked, had created a caring family of her own, with her husband, a cellist who had spent his life as a professor at the Guiseppe Verdi Conservatory of Music in Milan. He could have been a world-famous soloist, busy on the exhilarating, exhausting international circuit, had his health not been permanently compromised by war wounds.

Isabella had borne Alessandro three sons. One was a violinist, a professor of music like his father and at the same

The Tosca Taunt

conservatory; one was a lawyer in Rome.

And then there was Tony. He had been different from the start. The family love of music was there, but until he discovered his voice, he had quite seriously intended to be a professional soccer player. He had been a skilled amateur, but possibly not skilled enough. In the event he never had to find out. For once the family realised that Tony had an extraordinarily beautiful tenor voice, his future was sealed. He who had been lackadaisical in his studies, enthusiastic only about sports, was willing now to work himself tirelessly turning himself into a professional singer. Isabella and Alessandro had rejoiced in his triumphs, but had never dreamed he would reach this superstardom, this bittersweet slavery to his voice.

Now Isabella took Tony's hand into hers and held it. She searched his face; he looked much older than in summer when she last had seen him. She was afraid for him. He was the most emotional of her intense, volatile children, and he was by far the most tightly self-controlled. He had needed to learn that, of course, to be a successful singer, but Isabella knew there was a cost to hiding emotions. She knew, for Jen had told her, how Tony was prey to deep depression at those rare times when his great stamina was spent. And in the slump of his shoulders, the relaxing of the corners of his mouth almost to slackness, she saw emotional and physical exhaustion.

What could she do, how could she help her son over this most difficult hurdle and back into the career and the parenting that would now need to be his life's blood? She repeated what she had been rehearsing to say to him, that he must have a farewell ceremony for Jen, a memorial service of some kind.

Speaking Italian, for that language came more easily just now to her weary son, she said, "The children need it, Tonio, and so do you; you need some kind of closure, an end point, a starting point if you will for the rest of your lives without our dear Jen."

"Yes, Mama, I have been thinking, and you are right. You will help me organise this?"

"Of course; we must find the perfect place to say goodbye to our Jen," and Isabella realised how desperately he needed her now as he rubbed a hand tiredly over his face and momentarily covered his eyes.

He finally looked at her. "Jen loved The Cloisters so much, Mama. I know it is a public museum, but do you think they might let us have a service there? In the Fuentiduena chapel maybe, and we could use the cloister alongside, you know, the Saint-Guilhem. Jen used to stand with me under the arches for so long a time, and look at the fresco of the Virgin and Child, and say to me, 'Oh Tony, oh Tony!' Even once she did two paintings of the chapel. I think my Jen wants us to say *addio* to her there."

So, between them, they arranged for Jen's memorial service at The Cloisters, to be held in five days. In return for a generous donation, the Museum authorities agreed to let Tony use Jen's favourite space, when the building opened at 9:30 a.m. They would close the upper floor to visitors for the first hour, letting them wait among the exhibits on the lower floor for that time.

Tony found an Episcopalian minister who knew Jen, mostly as an artist, having met her when he had wandered in to the gallery where Jen regularly exhibited, and had bought one of her Fuentiduena chapel paintings. The minister interviewed Tony, his family, Jen's stricken twin Allison, Allison's husband, and Jen's friends, for details about her life and personality. This Tony found difficult, although the minister assured him at the beginning of their chat that most people are comforted when they talk of their dead loved ones; that at least while they are speaking, the deceased come alive again. But not for Tony. For him, eulogising Jen only emphasized that for the first time in thirteen years she did not stand beside him, ready to shoulder half his burdens and, by sharing his joys, double them.

At last the dreaded morning of the service came. The family breakfasted early, each pushing food around his plate in an attempt to appear to eat. After breakfast, Tony went into his bedroom to dress. Opening the door of the clothes closet he shared—*had* shared—with Jen, he was assailed by her scent, not only by her perfume but by the lingering, sweet smell of her skin. He had to walk past her clothes to get to his. It was the shoes, the shoes that had taken on the shape of her feet, which touched him most. There was something so vulnerable about her shoes. He bent slowly and picked one up, a slender navy pump, the leather soft as butter. He stared at it. *The clothes could belong to anyone, but only Jen's feet could have shaped her shoes like that. Stop it, stop it,* he admonished himself, carefully putting the shoe beside its mate. *At least,* he thought, *at least it has a mate.*

He walked past her clothes to his side of the closet. There he stood looking at his suits. Jen used to say to him, wear this one or wear that one, I like it on you ... he shook his head slowly.

Wear this suit, Tony, I like it so much, he heard her say, so close to him that he was sure if he turned around she would be there ... He was not about to turn around and test the thesis. He pulled out the new navy pin striped suit she had chosen with him just before he went to Germany. Why had he accepted that Berlin engagement? At the beginning of their marriage they had travelled joyfully together as he sang all over the world, but so often lately the needs of their children, and her own career, prevented that.

Why had he taken on so many engagements that took him away from her? He could have refused; he did not need to sing so often. He had sung as though his voice would only last a short time and he had to use it while he had it. She always said to him, there's lots of voice there, Tony love, don't worry so much about it. But he never dreamed his relationship with Jen would end before his voice had given out.

He shook his head to clear it, to try to remember why he stood there staring at his clothes. He opened a drawer and took out the cream double cuffed silk shirt she had insisted on him buying to go with the suit, and he found at the back of his closet a black silk tie, his usual funeral tie. *Black for mourning, for mourning this morning. Black. "Black is the Colour of my True Love's Hair," when I was learning to sing I remember singing this song, it was hard to learn the "h" in the right places, "Black His the Colour of my True Love's Air," I would sing, and Professor Sandani would be angry, what a temper he had but such a good teacher, he helped me a lot. But gold, gold is the colour of my true love's hair; no, my true love's hair is black, burnt black, mio Dio, what am I doing, why am I standing in this closet?*

"Tonio," his mother knocked on his door and called out from the hall. "Tonio, it is almost time, we are ready."

Oh yes, I am here to dress for Jen's service. Her memorial service.

The Tosca Taunt

Yes, of course.

He put on the clothes he had chosen. *He* had chosen? But surely Jen had just finished telling him to wear these today? He searched in his full, untidy cufflink case for one particular pair, by no means his most dressy. They were simple squares of hand-beaten gold, nothing more, but they were Jen's first gift to him, she had fashioned them herself and inside she had inscribed in minuscule letters, "All my life, Jen." All her life. Tony sat down heavily on edge of the bed. He had thought that meant all his life too, that she would be with him all his life.

But it can mean that if I want it to ... I can go to the service and then I can find a way to end this ...

"Daddy, daddy, are you ready? We're waiting for you," called Janina from the hall.

That. That is what stops me. That and the singing, this terrible gift of a voice that was never mine to keep. Tony took a deep breath and summoned his composure. He had never needed it more nor felt less sure of it. Suddenly he hit the wall hard with his fist, and Jen's impressionistic Arabian Nights painting, the one he liked so, came tumbling down to the soft dark rose carpet.

He went down on his knees to make sure it was not damaged. He cried, "*Maledetto,* Jen! How could you leave me? You promised you would always be with me, I need you, don't you understand? How could you do so cruel a thing to me?"

Another knock on the door. His father's voice, concerned. "Tonio? Come, son, we must go."

Tony swallowed hard. "I come, Papa. *Momento.*"

Now he clutched at his medallion of Saint Cecilia, desperately summoning, if not his self-control, at least his acting talent.

He opened the bedroom door to see his family costumed in funereal colours; his parents and Mrs Burns in black, his children in navy and grey. Silently they left the apartment and descended to the waiting limousine. Photographers at the door snapped pictures, their flashes momentarily brightening a dull autumn morning. Tony, usually amiable with the press, looked through them; today they did not exist.

But then today nothing exists. This is not reality. This is a piece of theatre, a new and tragic opera I have to get through somehow, is it not? Is it not? Jen always teased him about making an opera out of his problems. Maybe she was right. And maybe for once this tendency would help him.

The ubiquitous press was again waiting outside the Cloisters Museum. Tony clenched his teeth hard, fighting for composure, and was grateful that it did not fail him as he and his family entered the building. They climbed the stairs of this medieval appearing stone edifice, and made their way into the Romanesque Hall and through the massive, iron adorned wooden doors into the Fuentiduena Chapel. Tony looked up at the fresco of the Virgin and Child that Jen so loved, and at the ancient cross with its burden, the suffering Christ. *O Madre de Dio, pray for me, see me through this, hold me, hold me ...*

The long chapel was crowded with friends, relatives, colleagues. As Tony walked to the front down a centre aisle created by stacking chairs set in rows, he noticed the designer-director Alain Bonenfant sitting at the back. Long ago, Jen had abruptly broken her engagement to Bonenfant, in order to marry Tony, and Tony had long suspected Bonenfant was still in love

The Tosca Taunt

with her. He thought, in an unusual burst of sympathy for Bonenfant whom he disliked, *I keep forgetting that other people maybe have the broken heart over my Jen, not only me and my family ...*

Tony, Anton and Janina took their places in the front row. Tony would get through this harrowing service somehow, for his children; for them he wanted to demonstrate fortitude in the face of tribulation. But somewhere along the way, in the ministerial phrases that should have comforted him, he almost lost himself. He heard, "The Lord gave, and the Lord hath taken away ... in the midst of life we are in death ... the Lord thy God is a just God ..." *A just God?*

Anton, holding Tony's right hand, began to weep, big silent tears coursing down his cheeks. Janina squeezed Tony's left hand hard, then turned to look at her brother; soon she had joined him, weeping soft hiccuping sobs. Tony began to shake. He felt as though he had a severe case of stage fright.

" ... ashes to ashes, dust to dust ... " *How could the minister include this,* thought Mia miserably, holding tightly to Cedric's hand for comfort. She glanced at her fiance; he looked pale, grave. He shook his head slowly at her, as they shared a thought—*it must be disturbing enough for Tony to know how Jen died, without this unbearable Biblical reminder.*

Finally the minister finished. He had evoked God; he had evoked Jen, her spirit, her life, the tragedy of such a death for one so young, so talented, with so much to live for. Nothing that might give Tony pain had been spared.

Tony had chosen Jen's favourite hymn to finish the service. Now he would sing it for her, would sing it as a love song.

The congregation stood; the string ensemble played one

verse, and the mourners joined in to sing the words "O love that will not let me go." *No,* thought Tony, *do not let me go, love, never let me go, stay with me, stay with me ...*

The opera singers in the congregation, used to projecting their voices, in this circumstance produced exquisite *pianissimi.*

"I rest my weary soul in thee;
I give thee back the life I owe,
That in thine ocean depths its flow
May richer, fuller be."

Tony did not realise, so intent was he on singing every syllable, every note of this hymn for his Jen, that he was unleashing the full power of his voice.

"O Light that followest all my way,
I yield my flickering torch to thee,
My heart restores its borrowed ray
That in thy sunshine blaze, its day
May brighter, fairer be."

Gradually the congregation stopped singing to listen, until only Mia Mitsouros and Tony sang:

"O Joy that seekest me through pain,
I cannot close my heart to thee;
I trace the rainbow through the rain,
And feel the promise is not vain,
That morn shall tearless be."

Now Mia's throat closed with emotion. She stopped singing, and Tony, all unaware, sang alone. The congregation and a few people on the lower floor who were waiting for access to the rest of the museum, listened in awe as one of the world's most beautiful voices, perhaps more beautiful at this moment than it

The Tosca Taunt

would ever be again, soared, mysterious, holy:

"O Cross that liftest up my head,
I dare not ask to fly from thee;
I lay in dust life's glory dead,
And from the ground there blossoms red
Life that shall endless be."

Tony stopped, looked around him, bewildered. How could he feel Jen in his thoughts so clearly when he knew she was dead? The congregation slowly sat down, then rose once more as the minister uttered the benediction.

The service was over.

Jen's sun had set.

Tomorrow held a new and darker dawn.

....

That morning in the mine kitchen Steve Macdonald looked across at Jen, chopping vegetables and humming. He laughed.

"What's with you? You coming over all religious?"

Jen looked at him, surprised. "Why? What was I doing?"

"Don't you know what you were humming?"

She thought a minute. "Yes, I guess so, that was my favourite hymn—" She stopped. How did she know that was her favourite hymn?

"I know that one," Steve said, "my parents were big on sending their kids to church, but I've forgotten the words."

Jen said, "I only remember the first line—'Oh love that will not let me go'." She smiled. "That sounds more like a love song than a hymn. I can't get it out of my mind."

And now for no discernible reason her morning, which had begun happily enough, became indescribably sad.

Eighteen

"No, Mama, *per favore*," Tony said, "you must not stay here with me, you know you must return with Papa; he needs you with him always. One day Jen and I will be just like you ... " He faltered. For one sublime moment he had forgotten. Then, "I will be okay, I promise you."

Isabella reluctantly acceded to his firmly expressed wishes. Never separated from her husband for the forty-four years of their marriage except in the direst of circumstances, she was deeply torn. This was certainly a dire circumstance, this loss of their cherished Jenetta, but three weeks had passed since the terrible fire; the memorial service had closed the sad doors and, Isabella hoped, opened up the future for her son and his children.

She was comforted knowing that Tony was surrounded by attentive friends and supportive colleagues. His close friends Cedric and Mia had even postponed their wedding in order to

The Tosca Taunt

fly repeatedly back and forth across the Atlantic to support Tony. Her son was blessed in his friendships. Though deeply unhappy about him, for she realised that he was hiding his grief behind his extraordinary self-control, she decided that since he was able to control himself he must be dealing at least adequately with his loss.

So Tony's parents returned to Italy, his children returned to school, and Nanny Burns hired a new housekeeper-cook for Tony, to come in every other day and work under her tutelage. Tony's home resumed a semblance of order.

....

"*Six months?* Have you lost your mind?" shouted Gareth, Tony's manager, although Tony was only two feet away from him as they strode down Madison Avenue. Heads turned around them to see who was doing the yelling.

"Probably," answered Tony.

"What the hell does that mean?" asked Gareth, realising he had better try to seem calm even though he could see six months of his fees going down the drain.

"It means I don't want to sing for six months. You know how the operas are, all love and death, you cannot expect I should be able to deal with that right now."

"But—but your public will forget you exist if you go into seclusion for six months!"

"Don't be crazy, Gareth. Placido—you know—Domingo, he has taken a leave from opera for six months when his aunt and cousins were killed in that earthquake in Mexico City; his public did not forget about him that I can see."

"You're not Placido Domingo."

Tony glowered at Gareth.

Gareth said uncomfortably, "Okay, okay, I admit you're included among the star tenors but still—"

"Is no 'but still'. You want to ruin my career, just try to force me to sing now. Even if I only *think* of some of those libretti— *Otello*, for instance—my throat goes tight. I have to be about this realistic, Gareth."

His manager could tell from the deterioration in Tony's English that he was becoming upset. Gareth would simply have to go along with this, postpone the caviar now for longtime caviar later. And then he had an inspiration, just possibly a glimmer of hope. He proceeded with caution.

"Okay, Tony. I'll start cancelling everything for you in a week, if you still feel the same way by then."

"Tomorrow! You start tomorrow to cancel everything for six months, you hear me, Gareth? We have to be considerate, is not easy to replace someone like me on short notice, you know that."

"Sure, Tony, sure," agreed Gareth, mentally crossing his fingers. He knew his volatile client well. He would cancel only one or two weeks at a time if he could. And he would wait and see.

Tony had decided how he would occupy his six months. He would spend time with friends; with his children; walking in Central Park; exercising at his club; perhaps studying operatic scores; reading; contemplating; gradually coming to terms with his desolation ...

Only, reality came like a splash of ice water in his face. His friends were working or singing in far places; his children, who seemed lately to have forgotten how to play, were at school and busy after school with organised activities; Central Park was cold and grey at this time of year and, during the walks he did take, he was chilled to the bone and could not warm up afterwards; his nearby sports club was temporarily closed for renovations; he was singing nothing six months from now which he didn't already know and which might have required study; and the only books that appealed to him at the moment were all disagreeably sad.

So as empty day followed empty day he thought endlessly of Jen, and his mood spiralled downwards. Finally he phoned Gareth.

"Tell me Gareth, did you cancel everything for six months already?"

Gareth's spirits rose slightly. "Why, Tony?"

"First, you tell me."

"No, not yet."

"Good. Because six months are too long. I want you to cancel only three."

Privately Gareth thought he would continue cancelling week by week, until the next phone call. But he said to Tony, "Fine, fine, I'll attend to that, you keep in touch."

Ten lonely days later, Tony made another call to Gareth.

"Okay, okay, I know you, you haven't cancelled one thing beyond next week, is just as well. You phone the Met, you tell them I will be back there next week."

"Right. I do know you, Tony. Give me some credit."

"I do. Only you have never known me in this situation before."

"I'll phone the Met as soon as I hang up. There will be a collective sigh of relief when you are back singing, I can tell you. I've had calls from Covent Garden and La Scala that would set your teeth on edge."

"Tell them to keep on the shirt. Amato will be singing again right away."

....

Tony's first singing commitment was to begin rehearsals for a new production of Gounod's *Romeo et Juliette*, the Met's first production of this opera in some years. This had been designed and would be directed by Alain Bonenfant, Jen's ex-fiance. Tony was relieved that Juliette was to be the lustrous-voiced Mia. She understood him well—at times disconcertingly so. And her affection for him would make her indulgent of his possible problems, vocal and otherwise. *Dear Mia*, he thought. *If only*...

Mia, still in England, was now trying to re-schedule her postponed wedding to Cedric, to take place sometime in between various important singing commitments. Tony wondered how much the bridegroom minded being shunted aside for operas. The British Cedric seemed always unnaturally calm to Tony.

This was the first time in three years that Tony had worked with Alain Bonenfant, and he did not look forward to it. Their relationship had been prickly from its beginning. Bonenfant, blaming Tony for the breakup of his engagement to Jen, had hoped and even plotted for the failure of Jen and Tony's marriage so that he might have another a chance with her. But now of course it was too late for anything but bitterness and regret.

The Tosca Taunt

Still grieving though he was, Tony had little choice but to work with Bonenfant if he wanted to work right now. Either he fulfilled this commitment or he cancelled singing in the Met opera and went on to his next scheduled performances, weeks away. They were of *Les Contes d'Hoffmann* in London, again with Mia who would be replaced after three performances by Valentina Welles. Welles was at the moment singing *Madama Butterfly* in her home town of San Francisco, and Tony was gratified to see that the American critics and media were outdoing one another in fulsome praise of her work.

Nineteen

Evangelina Welles, cousin to soprano Valentina Welles, had suffered from mental illness for almost half her life. She looked so much like her famous singing cousin that opera fans stopped Evangelina on the streets of San Francisco where she lived and, though puzzled by her sixties hippie type of clothing, nevertheless asked for autographs. All the Welles family, from Evangelina's parents to her extended family including her cousin Valentina, had agonized over Evangelina for years. They had sought repeatedly to help her, until finally they realised that she meant it when she said she wanted to live on the streets, wanted to sleep out of doors despite the dangers, wanted, as she said, to be free.

Occasionally she would show up on the doorstep of one of her relatives, where she would ask, plaintively, if she could take a shower and launder her clothes. It did not seem to bother her that she went for long periods without properly washing herself or her garments; these desires for cleanliness were sporadic. The members of her family were invariably relieved to see her. They let her do as she asked, tried yet once more to prevail upon her to allow herself to be helped, pressed money on her, and resignedly let her wander off once more into the streets of the city. She was, after all, an adult, and not yet certifiable.

Valentina was flamboyantly in San Francisco singing a run of *Madama Butterfly*. Opening night was a tremendous success, but no sooner had the American press decided to make a vast fuss over their increasingly successful prima donna than she began to have singing problems. She was having trouble relaxing her throat; she was uncertain as to why, although it might be because she was going through an unusual time when she could not discipline her thoughts about Julian LeComte. She supposed it was a side effect of having seen Tony Amato so distraught at *his* loss. But her singing was definitely suffering. In particular her usual soaring high notes were tight and shrill, as a result of which she was starting to panic. Tonight after the performance she had dined with her leading man and his wife, and they had commiserated with her well-warranted concern by plying her with that excellent tranquilliser, champagne.

So, returning home, Valentina was not sober as she descended from the taxi outside her building. She was not reeling of course, for she would not abuse her singer's body like that, but she was at the point of being unsure whether she would go off into unmanageable giggles or equally uncontrollable tears.

After paying her regular taxi driver and asking him not to drive away until he had seen her into her apartment, she shut his car door and made her slightly unsteady way up the walk. She inserted her key into the lock of the outer door, when from the large clump of evergreen bushes beside her there emerged a tall figure. Valentina jumped back, frightened, as her driver leapt from his taxi. The figure spoke, the voice flat, without expression.

"Geez, Valley, don't be scared, it's only me. I wondered if I could—"

The taxi driver grabbed the figure from the back just as Valentina said, "Gerry, thanks so much, but it's okay, this is Evangelina Welles, my cousin, she did scare me. Lina, this is Gerry Jonas."

Evangelina looked at Gerry reproachfully. "You don't think I'd hurt her, do you? She's my famous cousin Valley. Did you know that?"

Gerry was unnerved. "Yeah, yeah, I did know that. Uh, pleased to meet you. You'll be okay?" This last was addressed to Valentina.

"We'll be fine."

Soon Evangelina and her cousin were in Valentina's kitchen, drinking instant coffee while Evangelina, always slow to come to the point, finally said, "Can I sleep on the rug? Can I have a shower? Can I wash my clothes, just what I've got on? You still got that fuzzy pink kimono, the one I wore last time? Can I wear it, can I, can I?"

"Of course, Lina, only you can't sleep on the rug, don't be silly, remember, last time you came and you took a shower and washed your hair and we made up the hide-a-bed and you slept there, you stayed two nights."

"You still got the fuzzy pink kimono and the fuzzy pink sheets?"

The Tosca Taunt

"Kimono, yes. I don't remember the fuzzy pink sheets."

"Maybe it's auntie-your-mom who has the fuzzy pink sheets. I dunno. You got any pink sheets?"

"Yes, and you shall have them tonight. Go shower, dear, I'll wait up for you, I'm not a bit sleepy. I'll hang the kimono inside the door while you're showering. Come out when you're done. You'll find shampoo on the shelf in the shower."

Evangelina shuffled into the bathroom, shedding clothes as she went so that before she reached the bathroom door she was naked. There were odd marks on her poor arms, Valentina saw, and though her body was still beautiful, it looked thinner, more emaciated than Valentina remembered from the last time she had seen her cousin about seven months ago. Valentina hoped urgently that this time, this time at last she might persuade Evangelina to accept help. For Valentina cared about her cousin, and feared for her. But she would wait until morning to speak to Evangelina, until both their minds were cleared by a night's sleep.

Valentina picked up the dropped pieces of clothing and threw them into her washing machine. She started the machine, pouring in a little strong disinfectant along with the laundry soap. Then she fetched from her store of multi-vitamin and mineral preparations a large, full bottle. She could at least do this for Evangelina. And once the clothes were out of the dryer she would stuff money into a pocket of one of the three blouses Evangelina had removed.

Valentina searched her linen closet for her prettiest and most pink sheets. She pulled open the sofa bed and made it up, with the sheets and a feminine, floral patterned comforter in shades of pink and mauve. She hoped these would make Evangelina happy. Having organised herself to this point, Valentina sat sipping coffee and waiting for Evangelina to come from the shower. And though she tried hard to keep her thoughts from him, Julian crept into her consciousness just as surely as if he had tiptoed into the room.

She went across the room to her CD holder and pulled out an Antonio Amato CD, called, *"Remembering"*. She had bought it two days ago, but had not yet had the courage to play it for herself. She knew well how powerful was the emotional impact Tony had when he sang. But in this crepuscular light, with the sound of traffic silenced and the only sound the swish of water in the shower, Valentina decided to listen. To listen, and soon to regret. As *"Give Me Something to Remember You By"* was followed by *"Autumn Leaves,"* Valentina could not stop the alcohol-induced tears. Then Tony launched into *"There's a Place for Us, Somewhere a Place for Us,"* and Valentina sank sobbing to her knees, all that champagne and Tony's voice ripping apart her composure, just as Evangelina, wrapped in the fuzzy kimono, came smiling out of the shower.

She stood above Valentina, puzzled. Then she too knelt on the rug and put her arms around Valentina. She swayed gently back and forth, saying, "Don't cry, baby, my baby, don't cry, Valley, Valley, please, you're making me sad, baby, please—"

But Valentina could not stop. Hysterically she clung to Evangelina, saying, "Oh Lina, help me!"

Nobody had asked Evangelina for help, for years. She frowned, aware that she had just been given an awesome responsibility.

The Tosca Taunt

"How, help you, how? Tell Lina."

As Tony's voice soared with its evocative, passionate beauty, Valentina blurted out her Romeo and Juliet story, with names, with places. She finished with a rather drunken statement, "'—so you see, Lina, there's no hope. Leonard stands forever in our way. Oh God!"

Evangelina held her cousin, rocked her, crooned a tuneless but to Valentina curiously comforting lullaby. Finally the two women rose from the rug. Evangelina tucked Valentina in bed, where she would toss restlessly for yet another night. Evangelina slept for a short while on the sofa bed.

Very early she arose, and, remembering Valentina's often repeated injunction to take whatever clothes she wanted any time, she tiptoed into Valentina's bedroom, and took from the closet a three piece outfit of black silk pants and jacket and patterned blouse. She bent to get a pair of shoes, reached up for a black handbag, and went back into the living room where she folded these clothes into two large Safeway shopping bags. She returned to the bedroom and looked into what Valentina called her money pot. Evangelina knew Valentina kept a large amount of cash there; indeed Valentina had told her cousin that she could take whatever money she found there, any time, that she did not even need to ask. Otherwise Evangelina would not have touched any of these things; she was not a thief. She grabbed five hundred dollars and stuffed them into her bra.

Then she sought a piece of paper.

Valley;

Thanks again. Iv taken the money like you always said I can, seems an awful lot this time but youl see, you wont be sorry. And I took that black suit and blouse, very nice, and the shoes and the purse says Gucci on it. Honest Valley dear youl see, youl be glad. Im so sorry about your troubles. Theyl get better, youl see. Please dont cry without me. Il comfort you. Life is awful. Some times Id be happy to die. Id die for you, dear Valley. But dont you die. I think part of me is in you. Do you unerstand? As long as your alive and famous Im not dead even if Im dead. Dont cry for me. I love you. Thank you dear Valley.

    Love,

    Your Lina

Then Evangelina took her clothes from the dryer, dressed herself, shook her head at the bottle of vitamins on the table, for Valentina was always trying to give her those, and sneaked quietly from Valentina's apartment. Her first call that morning was at a shop which displayed a variety of objects, including revolvers, in its shop window.

Twenty

The day before Mia was to arrive in New York from England, for rehearsals of *Romeo et Juliette*, Mia's two young children left Cedric's chateau in the Rolls Royce. The chauffeur was to drive Simon and Gilda to their boarding schools, after an especially happy weekend with their mother. The demands of Mia's career had parted her too often from her children, she felt, for she was a deeply maternal woman. Reluctantly she accepted the pain of separation as part of the price she paid for having the voice, but she had never been able to rid herself of dejection after she said goodbye to her children, even for a brief period. As the Rolls disappeared around a bend in the driveway, Cedric suggested a ride on horseback to cheer her.

Soon Cedric and Mia were reining in their horses to a walk and riding contentedly beside one another down a wide path through pines and leafless woods on his estate. Misty late afternoon sunlight filtered through the bare branches. The scenery was gentle, mild, melancholy. Mia found she was always glad to arrive at Cedric's home, because of its beauty and its peace, and always glad to leave for the unpredictable excitement of her career. She felt faintly disloyal about this. But she was definitely looking forward to her rehearsals for *Romeo et Juliette*, looking forward to seeing Tony after three weeks away from him, hoping she would find him a shade—just a shade was all she dared hope for—more reconciled to the loss of Jen.

She reached across and clasped the hand Cedric stretched out to her. They rode along in companionable silence. How grateful she was to him; she had not known he cared so much about Tony, had not known he would be willing to spend so much time criss-crossing the Atlantic in order to help not only Tony but her as well. She reluctantly admitted to herself that, even after years of knowing him, a lot of Cedric's character still remained an enigma to her.

She would have been dismayed had she known one of the reasons Cedric had stayed so close to her on their mission to console Tony. He was about to surprise her with his next announcement, because he was not going to let his Mia and the still-stricken Tony Amato have any time alone together. He knew his passionate, maternal Mia too well. If the tightly controlled Tony finally broke in front of her, and if they were alone—what then? No, before he risked that, Mia would have to become Cedric's wife. Only then would he trust her a little. A very little.

"I've got good news for you, Mia darling."

"Wonderful! We could use a bit of good news; it's been in scarce supply since the fire. So, tell, tell!"

"I've cleared my business slate here; I can work out of the New York office, so I'm coming with you now for your rehearsals instead of just for the performances." He watched her carefully as he announced this.

For a millisecond her hand in his went slack, then she squeezed his hand hard and said happily, "That's great news. Tony will be so pleased."

"I was hoping Mia would be pleased too."

"Oh, Cedric, don't be silly, darling, that goes without saying."

"No, it doesn't. Not for me. I want to hear it."

Mia was faintly exasperated. "Of course I'm happy you're coming. How could I be anything but pleased about that? You're so foolish sometimes, my darling."

He pulled her hand to his mouth, and kissed its palm. "Am I? Am I really so foolish?" He dropped her hand, jerked the reins to turn his horse around and galloped away from the path and into the trees.

Mia, surprised, turned her mount and followed, but Cedric's was the faster, wilder horse and he disappeared quickly into the dusky woods. She caught up with his riderless horse after several minutes of hard riding. Dismounting and leaving her gelding beside Cedric's stallion, she called out to her fiance. Nothing answered her but the soft rustle of the bare branches, moving in a gentle wind. Did he want her to look for him, or did he want solitude? Had she really sounded unenthused over the prospect of him coming to New York? She weighed her emotions carefully. Actually she was much more pleased than not, and did not know how he could have construed her response as anything but pleasure. She decided she had better look for him.

Her boots made little soft swishing sounds as she strode through soggy leaves. The woods smelled faintly smoky. She was probably going in the wrong direction anyway; she would likely get lost and he would have to send out a search party for her. It would serve him right. Fortunately she could not get too lost; Cedric's huge property was fenced, so she could only be on his land. She called his name but there was no answer. Then, quite suddenly before she could cry out, someone put a hand across her mouth from behind and pulled her roughly down onto the leaves.

It all happened so fast. Her first instinct was to try to turn, to knee him and scratch at his eyes, but when she did turn, it was Cedric's face she saw. She was angry.

"Cedric, what are you doing? You could have given me a heart attack; I thought I was about to be raped!"

His voice sounded choked. "You are."

She laughed. She trusted him; he would never do such a thing to her; after all, why would he need to? They had been lovers for years. *But—but what was he doing?* He was on top of her now, and the buttons flew from her riding jacket as he tried to rip it off her.

"Cedric, stop it. This isn't amusing any more. Just—oh! You're hurting me!"

He stopped, as abruptly as he had begun. "Am I? Does it matter? It didn't matter to you that you hurt me when I told you I was coming to New York with you. Why don't I have the right to hurt you back?"

The Tosca Taunt

Mia, dishevelled now, pushed him hard and sat up. "Well, this *is* a new school of courtship. I'm not sure I like it much. This is a side of you I don't know, Cedric."

He was breathing hard. "Yes, I suppose it is. It's a side of me you'd be better not knowing, Mia my darling." The appellation was uttered with deep sarcasm. She looked at him in the failing light, and saw he was as pale as when he had so frightened her with the pain in his chest. Tenderness welled up in her. She did love this man after her fashion, and she did not want to hurt him. She put her arms around him and, lying back, pulled him down to her. And soon to the susurring of the branches were added other sounds, words of love and little moans of pleasure.

Twenty-One

In New York, Tony, Alain Bonenfant and Sir Sheldon Wasserman, who was to be the conductor of *Romeo et Juliette*, were having a pre-rehearsal meeting, requested by Tony, in a small brightly lit rehearsal room on the lower level of the Metropolitan Opera building.

"I have one condition, Sir Sheldon—Bonenfant—and if you want me to do your *Romeo* you will say yes. If you say no, I do not sing, I take right away another leave of absence. Who will not understand if I do?"

"Tony, you know I give no quarter for any reason, I've never been able to work that way," Bonenfant said edgily.

Sir Sheldon, less volatile, soothed. "Wait, Bonenfant, let's hear him out first before we decide..."

Tony did not wait for Bonenfant to reply. "Here it is, my condition. I will not rehearse—and I will not watch—the second scene of the last act. I will go through the motions of that scene for the dress rehearsal; but until opening night I will not sing the

The Tosca Taunt

words."

"*Sacre nom de Dieu,* how do you think we can work around that?" Bonenfant exploded.

"It does not matter to me how you can work around it. Do whatever you have to do. Else I do not sing for you."

"But why? This is blackmail!" shouted an imperceptive Bonenfant.

But Sir Sheldon, reserved British knight though he was, understood. "Think a moment, Bonenfant. Do you recollect the words of that last scene?"

"Well of course I remember the words, how do you suppose I designed the opera, how do you imagine I can direct it if I don't rememb—oh. I see what you mean."

"Is about time," said Tony. "The less I should be exposed to such words right now, the better."

Sir Sheldon nodded reflectively. He addressed the director as though Tony were not there.

"Bonenfant, since we want Amato, we have to agree. Tony knows the role, he has sung it before, the last time with me and Mia at La Scala. I say we go along with this; what choice do we have?"

"I *never* make exceptions for this kind of thing," Bonenfant said, looking at Tony with distaste. He was ill disposed to make concessions, especially to Tony Amato, but he did not want to hurt his own carefully thought out production. Could Tony really get away with doing the last scene of a new production without one rehearsal? He was a quick study, but still...

Insultingly, calculatingly, Bonenfant asked Sir Sheldon, "Who else could we get to sing this *Romeo*?" He knew it was a rhetorical question; Sir Sheldon would have no answers to it. But the insult was hardly lost on Tony. He took a deep breath and held it, waiting for Sir Sheldon's response.

Sir Sheldon was nobody's fool. He wanted Tony and Mia together for this opera, and he would have them, regardless. He smiled at Tony, and calmly answered Bonenfant with, "Nobody of Tony's stature at this late date, they're all booked. We could get an adequate but less experienced tenor, someone on his way up. Or Raffaele Ricordi might be available. But we'll not get anyone else with Tony's drawing power—nor for that matter anyone who looks as good on stage with Mia."

"*Bon, bon,* if you put it that way, what choice do I have? But I want it recorded, Amato, that I object vigorously to this concession. There's no way you'd get it under any other circumstance. Jen's death, of course, is a blow," Bonenfant's voice lost its hard edge, "to us all."

....

Rehearsals for *Romeo et Juliette* proceeded at a bumpy pace. *Thank God for the magical Mia Mitsouros,* thought Bonenfant over and over, as she consistently gave to her interpretation of *Juliette* an incandescent charm that amazed him. How was she able to glow with that aura of virginity—she, who had had two husbands with children by each, several lovers, and who was now about to marry her tycoon Viscount Ridlough? Yet she radiated naive, obsessive, girlish love all over Tony's *Romeo.*

Bonenfant had wondered for a long time whether there was more between Tony and Mia than musical collaboration and an obviously warm friendship. The tabloids had been creating rumours about each of them for years, together or with other

The Tosca Taunt

putative (or possibly real) lovers. These two photogenic singers were unwilling fodder for the general tabloid feeding frenzy.

Today's rehearsals were just ending. Bonenfant noted with wry amusement that Mia's fiance Cedric was still in attendance. He had been highly visible at the edge of the stage for every rehearsal of *Romeo et Juliette*, at Mia's request. She insisted it would help not only her but Tony if her supportive fiance were around. Sir Sheldon and Bonenfant were only too happy to do whatever was necessary to keep their valuable tenor afloat. Now Cedric rose from a folding director's chair and ambled towards Bonenfant, while at the far end of the stage Mia and Tony conferred over a point of interpretation.

"Still here I see," said Bonenfant to Cedric. "Are you enjoying the rehearsals?"

Cedric smiled with his lips; his eyes did not follow. "Not particularly. I'm not enough of a musician to be interested in how an opera is put together. It rather spoils the effect of the final version for me. And I do enjoy the polished performance."

"Why come then?" Bonenfant asked. "Life's a bit short for spending this much time doing something you don't like."

"I have my reasons."

Bonenfant looked across at Mia and Tony, heads close together, Tony's eloquent hands waving as he emphasized the point he was making.

"I'll bet you do."

Cedric's mental antennae shot up. This was an implication that Cedric did not want to hear. He needed to believe his apprehensions were baseless. He asked curtly, "What are you insinuating?"

Bonenfant smiled, his expression ingratiating. "Not much. But if you really want to take a day off from these sessions, I'll chaperone your Mia for you. She'll get away with none of her usual tricks while I'm around."

The inoffensive, bland looking Cedric drew himself up. "I will not forgive you for saying that, Bonenfant." Cedric was angry. "What usual tricks? I dislike you speaking of my fiance as though she were some sort of trained seal."

"Sorry." Bonenfant was positively gloating.

What, Cedric wondered, did Bonenfant know that Cedric did not? He realised that just after a difficult rehearsal was not the most opportune time for such a discussion, but at dinner he would tell Mia he was growing impatient now, and that she must make time available soon, so their wedding and honeymoon could finally take place. Only then, if she were married to him, could Cedric be sure that when Tony finally came to terms with his loss, he would not pursue Mia. Cedric was certain Tony Amato would not deliberately break up someone else's marriage. Tony had appeared to hold marriage sacred even before Jen was killed; how much stronger his feelings must be now.

But when Cedric introduced the subject of their wedding date, over dinner that evening in Cedric's Manhattan apartment, Mia said to him, "Darling, do I have to look at my schedule right now? These rehearsals are so difficult. Let's wait until the performances are under way before we start looking for a break in my timetable."

"Is it that complicated?"

"No; it's just me, darling. I'm nervous about this *Juliette*.

The Tosca Taunt

You're being so helpful to me and Tony; please, don't put pressure on me right now."

She looked down at her plate of *pasta marinara*, her appetite gone. Because she knew she had a window of time in her schedule. If she cancelled her small part in a concert in Hamburg—and she was only one of eleven soloists—she had three weeks free after her *Carmen* engagement in Paris. She did not want to explore her reasons for hiding this knowledge from Cedric. Before Jen died, she had been so eager to marry him.

But explore those reasons she must. Was she grieving too much for Jen? Certainly she continued to feel sad, to feel as though a hole had been punched in the fabric of her friendships and that the fabric would never be properly mended. But to grieve so much that she would deliberately not give the man she believed she loved what he wanted so? *No, it was not grief. It was something much more complex.*

Cedric had told her long ago that before he would marry her she had to resolve her love for Tony Amato. He had surprised her, for before that she had never given a label to her complicated feelings for Tony. *Flirty friendship? Platonic love? Unrequited love? Requited but unadmitted love? None of the above?* Even when Cedric had named it, she was not certain he was right.

But now Jen was dead.

Mia twisted her engagement ring around and around, dismayed by the surge of emotion that filled her. *For Jen was dead, and Tony was free.*

....

Mia's notion that Cedric was supporting and helping Tony

by conscientiously attending their rehearsals, was to say the least fanciful, in Bonenfant's opinion. Nobody could help Tony. All through these days of preparation the usually reliable tenor stumbled over his blocking, forgot his lyrics, lost his famous equanimity, and was forced to miss three rehearsals because of hoarseness.

"We should never have gambled on him, Sir Sheldon," the worried Bonenfant said, two days before the final dress rehearsal. "He's trying to do the impossible. What singer in history has succeeded in singing well immediately after a loss like his?"

"Damned if I know, maybe Harry Lauder," Sir Sheldon answered. Somewhat less than sanguine himself, he called on his memories of performing with Amato, and tried to comfort Bonenfant and himself. "I know Amato, he'll pull it off, I'm certain of it. I've conducted him under appalling circumstances, even once when he had a concussion, and he performed more than adequately. He'll surprise us both, you'll see." *And I am whistling in the dark,* thought Sir Sheldon fearfully.

Now at last it was time for the dress rehearsal, when Tony would do a walk-through of the final scene with Mia. For the sake of the orchestra and Mia, Sir Sheldon had wanted a rehearsal tenor to sing the words while Tony went through the actions.

"If you force those words on me before I am ready, I will quit right now!" a costumed Tony had stormed, when this was suggested to him just before the rehearsal began. "You will have to find yourself another star. Where do you find one now? You think maybe Pavarotti or Domingo are free on such short

The Tosca Taunt

notice?"

Several times during that dress rehearsal Tony lost his temper and stopped the performance, mostly over minuscule problems. Even Mia rolled her eyes heavenwards as Tony stopped singing yet again and walked to the front of the stage to confer with Sir Sheldon.

Sir Sheldon said to Bonenfant afterwards, "I've never seen Amato this difficult. I hope it does not bode badly for opening night when he actually has to sing that last scene. Maybe you are right, maybe we should have stopped him from performing so soon after—"

"*Dieu*, don't even think it now," said Bonenfant. "I won't say I told you so, but –"

On opening night Tony and his assistant waited for his call to go onstage. To his consternation, everywhere Tony looked tonight he saw Jen, Jen who had so often been with him in this bright little dressing room giving him the support he needed. She knew exactly what to do for him; she knew him so well. Correction; she *had* known him so well.

Mia knocked on his door, and he summoned a smile of encouragement for her and the faithful Cedric, standing just behind her. Tony knew how many people involved in this production were concerned about whether he would get through it, especially through that last act. He embraced Mia, and they said to each other in unison, "*In bocca al lupo.*"

"Are you going to be okay, Tony?" Mia asked, drawing back from him and looking anxiously at his set face.

"Yes. For Jen. She would expect that of me." He bit his bottom lip hard.

"Here we go, darling," Mia smiled at him as the call came over the loudspeakers, "Beginners on stage please."

Before the famous gold curtain went up the audience was surprised to see, not the House Manager, but Sir Sheldon Wasserman coming on stage to make an announcement.

"Ladies and gentlemen, Antonio Amato—" The audience groaned; this often meant the named singer would not sing tonight. Sir Sheldon smiled and held up his hands. "Antonio Amato *will* sing tonight; he has asked me to tell you that he dedicates his performance tonight to the memory of his wife, Jenetta Maclean Amato, who was tragically killed in a fire two months ago. The Amato family has set up the Jenetta Maclean Amato Scholarship Fund, which will be given to singers and painters of unusual promise, alternating between each discipline from year to year. You will find an insert about the scholarship in your program. All the singers performing tonight, including the chorus, have volunteered part of their salaries for this evening to the fund; Mr Amato will learn about this gift for the first time as I speak. Thank you, ladies and gentlemen."

Tony, standing in the wings to hear the announcement, was stunned by this generosity to his Jen. He knew she had been well loved by the employees at the Met who knew her, but this was a tribute beyond anything he expected. He felt almost overcome. His throat tightened with emotion. But with a strength buoyed by the resolve that he sang tonight for Jen, Tony forced his throat to relax, so he would be able to sing.

Throughout the evening Tony concentrated fiercely on his singing technique. Under the circumstances the acting out of a tragic love story came easily to him. But he was also determined

The Tosca Taunt

to sing well. He would tolerate no mistakes from himself tonight. To everyone's secret surprise except Tony's, all went smoothly as a dream until the last scene. Only Tony could know how much that might cost him.

On stage, Tony-*Romeo* opened the door to the tomb where lay his *Juliette*. He walked towards the slab of marble on which she had been placed, and he began the loveliest of laments. Soon he sang, "Oh my wife, my well-beloved, death has not altered thy beauty," and was transported in memory to the mound of ashes that was Jen's funeral pyre. Her beauty– her beauty– altered—to that—to that gritty, grisly blackness...

"Death, this is the only joy my heart longs for," Tony sang, as his audience, hearing emotion almost out of control, wondered uneasily how much of this could be true.

"Come, let us flee to the ends of the earth, to a profound peace, oh pure joy ... be consoled, poor soul, the dream was too beautiful ... "

As the action required, the revived Mia-*Juliette* held Tony tightly. She felt him begin to shake. She knew she had to help him sing to the end, and she whispered the one thing she knew would work; "For our Jen." It was enough. Tony-*Romeo* was dying now, singing softly, his part in the opera almost over. He would make it through.

Tony was grateful to Gounod's librettists that they had given the line, "O infinite, supreme joy, to die with you," to *Juliette*. Tony could not have sung it now. It was too perilously apt...

The two voices soared in a final, "Lord, Lord, forgive us," as the lovers expired together.

The gold curtains lowered to clamorous applause. Mia

disentangled herself and stood up, but Tony lay unmoving, his eyes closed, holding back sobs that he dared not let go, for if he began he knew he would not be able to stop. The first curtain calls were being organised, as Tony continued to lie there. Mia went quickly back to him.

"Come on, Tony darling, we must take our call."

"Just leave me, *momento*—I cannot—"

"Yes you can."

"Yes. I can. Yes." He rose slowly and walked with Mia through the opening in the gold curtains to receive the thunderous roar of the audience. He could not smile his famous little-boy smile for them, but he knew they would understand, for he had never been able to muster a smile immediately after performing a tragic opera; he was too caught up in his often real emotions. But tonight he could have mustered nothing but tears—tears that fortunately he was able hold back, for his own pride, and for his Jen.

When he took his curtain call alone, flowers rained down upon him, and an audience who had loved him for years stood and cried out their admiration for his singing, for his dignity, for his courage.

This is the hardest part, let me get through this, Santa Cecilia, don't let me break now, this is for you, my Jen.

The curtain calls at last over, a joyful, relieved group milled around backstage, pleased with the opera's premiere, pleased with themselves, pleased with life generally. But Tony shut himself in his dressing room and would let nobody in but his assistant. Very quickly he showered and changed. Mia came to his door finally to say, "What are you going to do, Tony darling?

The Tosca Taunt

Are you coming to supper with us all, or would you prefer if just Cedric and I—?"

"No. I go right away home," he said, and when he opened the door he looked, to her, utterly forlorn. "Forgive me, *per favore*, but I must go."

"Do you want—do you need me—I mean us, darling? What would help?"

"You know what would help. What I can never have again. I thank you, Mia, you and Cedric are to me such good friends, but please, understand that now I must be alone ... *Buona notte*."

He and Eric slipped out quickly, before the long line formed for autographs and congratulations. There was a small group of ardent fans already at the stage door, but not even they got a smile from the usually friendly Antonio Amato. The most he could do was nod at them courteously, wave his assistant goodbye, climb into his limousine and say, "Take me home, *per favore*."

But as the limousine was entering Central Park, Tony said to his driver, "Stop now, I will walk from here."

The driver was doubtful. "It's late, Mr Amato, you're not thinking of walking in the park, are you?"

This annoyed Tony. "I don't know. Just stop the car, I am not a small fellow, I am strong, I will be fine wherever I walk."

The driver reluctantly braked, and the big dark limousine glided to a stop. Tony climbed out. He stood for a long moment, and then slowly, aimlessly began to wander along the lower edge of the park, watching and being watched by the sad, often homeless people of the night. He was tired, but the last thing he wanted was to take his weary heart home to his empty bed.

Jean Dell

O my Jen. Were you too good for this world? I was a fortunate man—I had you for a little while, and now it is finished. Was I trying to say goodbye to you tonight? Am I really ready to go on without you? Dio. This is impossible.

"Death; this is the only joy my heart longs for," said tonight's libretto.

The pain in his soul transmuted itself into physical pain; his very bones hurt him. He walked on, crossing a street, turning unheeding down Fifth Avenue.

Is there no peace for me? I am in such chaos. Never before have I felt like this. Yes, I have our children; yes, I have the singing; yes, I have a long way to go—how does that poem go that Jen loved so? "Miles to go before I sleep..." Jen, my Jen, you always knew how to help me. But I am so tired ...

"I salute you, silent dark tomb," said tonight's libretto.

Silence.

Darkness.

"The peace of God which passeth all understanding," said the minister at Jen's memorial.

Is death the peace of God, Tony wondered uneasily? *Is it peace at all?*

"I look without fear at the tomb where I will rest beside her at last," said tonight's libretto.

Rest, to rest, beside Jen, but how could he rest beside Jen? Where was Jen? Ashes in the wind ... if he died, he would ask to be cremated and his ashes scattered over the hotel site, maybe his ashes would somehow mingle with hers, was it possible? If he died. *When* he died. For life is a terminal illness. How soon could he hope for the peace of death?

The Tosca Taunt

"I thought you were dead, and I drank this poison; the dream was too beautiful—but love, that celestial flame, will survive death," said tonight's libretto.

High balconies, tall bridges, sleeping pills, sharp razors, electrified subway tracks, let me count the ways ...

"Lord, Lord forgive us," said tonight's libretto.

Dazed, Tony looked up and saw that he had arrived at St. Thomas' Church, a church which remained open at night to give refuge to the homeless.

I am homeless; home was Jen and Jen is not.

He lurched like a drunken man up the stairs and into the dim reaches of the church. It was the style of building Jen loved, French-Gothic; he had shared its beauty with her and now he was for a moment comforted as he stared down the main aisle at the Great Reredos, remembering when he had first seen it with Jen. She had such a capacity for awe, and she had caught her breath at her first sight of the white waterfall-like wall, rich with carved figures of saints and three tall blue windows that drew the eye up and up.

But the comforting memory passed like mist in the breeze.

Lord forgive me my thoughts, Lord forgive me my weakness, Jen forgive me ... I cannot go on like this.

Tony stumbled unsteadily to his left and found himself before the bronze statue of Our Lady of Fifth Avenue. He knelt suddenly as his knees gave way, and read with tear-blurred eyes the prayer inscribed there to Our Lady. "I come to you, Holy Mother, to ask your prayers for ..." *Oh Madre Mia, pray for me, for your son Antonio, per favore, help me, are you really there, Holy Mother? Were you ever there, or are you a myth created to give our absurd lives meaning?"* The inscription continued, "You give us all encouragement to approach you as your children, whose brother your son Jesus Christ we claim as our blessed Saviour and yours. Help me now I ask you with a prayer to him on my behalf, and for his sake, Amen."

Words. Nothing but words, invented by the trivial speck that is man, to console man. Out of emptiness. Bitter gall and wormwood.

Nothing.

Nulla.

Tony felt sick. He stood up, but again his legs faltered and he edged into the first pew, sinking down on the red velour cushion.

He closed his eyes and lowered his forehead to the back of the pew in front of him. He felt Jen's arms around him, holding him tightly, and knew they were not. He saw her face before his, all her love for him in her eyes, and knew she was not.

The peace of God ... death, where is thy sting ... Tony had read somewhere that if you could just hang on for twenty minutes, only twenty, without giving in to the impulse, you would not commit the deed, at least for that one time.

....

Maria McGinn plied her trade along Fifth Avenue. But this night she was tired, and she came into the church, as she often did, to escape her pimp for a little while. Now she sat slumped on the comfortable church bench, eyes closed, knowing she would soon need another fix. She heard someone sit heavily down on the seat behind her. Whoever it was groaned quietly.

Somebody's hurting, she thought, opening her eyes and slowly turning to her left. Just beside her shoulder she saw a head of dark curly hair, the forehead resting on the back of her pew. Then hands gripped the pew on each side of the head, and again the man groaned softly.

Maria put her right hand over his. "You sick, honey?" she whispered. "You need help?"

The man lifted his head. Maria's first impression was of unspeakable despair; then she thought the face was familiar; then with a shock she recognised who he was.

"But you're—aren't you—you're Antonio Amato!" She gave a little laugh, embarrassed, almost girlish. "What are *you* doing here?"

She had the impression that Tony looked at her but did not see. Then he seemed to bring her into focus. He shook his head and whispered, "Is a good question," and grimaced as though in pain.

Maria's awe dissolved quickly into sympathy. "What's the matter? You want me to fetch one of the volunteers?"

Now Tony smiled, the famous little-boy grin whose power he knew very well. He did not want to be fussed over by well-meaning volunteers, especially as the church was sheltering people he believed to be infinitely needier than he, at least in the material sense.

Infinitely needier than he. Yes. Perhaps like this woman, whoever she was. Tony felt a sudden affinity with this stranger who was offering him warmth and kindness.

"No, *grazie*, I am okay." He rubbed his hand wearily over his face, and peered at her. From out of his pain came an unconditional compassion for all living creatures; he asked her, "Is this where you sleep? Do you have a place to go besides here?"

"Well sure, honey, course I do, but if you must know I came in here for a little peace. It's just the usual working girl's life." Her hand was still on his, moving slightly, caressing him, gentle, maternal.

Now Tony looked at her more carefully. A wide mass of curly red hair (not, he could see from the shadow of dark roots, its original colour), a short black leather skirt, black stockings over superb legs, black shoes with exceptionally high heels, an elegant black suede jacket over a low-necked red top. A lot of makeup, well applied. *Of course, poor woman, she is not as young as she pretends; we have to play the cards we are dealt but she likely got not very many trumps.*

For a long time I had all the trumps, he thought. *And now they are all played, except ... I have the voice and ... and what? ...*

Maria kept staring at him. "It's funny, me meeting you like this," she said finally. "I never thought I'd ever get to talk to someone like *you*, though—don't laugh—I've rehearsed what I'd say if I ever did. I was to the Met—once in my life would you believe I got taken to the Met, and it was you singing, I can't remember the name of the opera but you were playing a poor Parisian poet and—"

"*La Boheme*," he said. "I haven't sung that at the Met since four years ago."

"That would be about right. I loved it. It was so sad when your girlfriend died, you didn't know she was dead and then when you realised, you called out to her and you sobbed, it broke my heart it was so real; I cried and cried, even afterwards I couldn't stop crying. Hey, what did I—did I say something

The Tosca Taunt

wrong?"

For Tony had shut his eyes tightly and had made a gesture as if to push away the words. He shook his head and looked away. He had called out to her, called to his dead beloved, *Jen oh my Jen oh my Jen* ...

"*Scusi,*" he said. "It's just something ... personal."

"Oh geez, I'm sorry; I put my foot in my mouth, didn't I. I've just remembered. Your wife was killed in a fire a couple months ago, right? *Entertainment Tonight* said you guys had a great marriage." Her hand squeezed his. "God but that's tough. I know, believe me. I was married once. He was real good to me. He died too. Well, he didn't just die, he was killed in a car accident. The driver of the other car was blind drunk. Why am I telling you this?"

"I don't know," said Tony.

"Do you mind?"

"No. I never thought I was the only person in the world that got hurt. Only—" he looked at her hard but pretty face, kind, full of concern. He felt frighteningly vulnerable to this unexpected kindness. "Only, how do you survive losing someone you love so much? I feel like half a person. I don't know what to do."

They were silent for a moment. Then she spoke.

"I've been trying to figure out what someone like you was doing here alone this time of night, and I think I've got it." Maria looked at him almost tenderly. "You want to die too, don't you, honey. You're walking the damn streets looking for a reason— *any* reason—not to throw yourself under a bus."

Tony looked at her in awe. "How do you know this?"

"You think I haven't been there?"

Tony again rubbed his hand tiredly over his face. "Is strange I should meet you tonight."

She smiled. After a moment of reflection she said, almost shyly, "I don't know how much weight it will carry with you, but I can give you one reason not to throw yourself under that bus. It's your music—you must know how much you give people with your music. I listen to you singing and sometimes it keeps me going. I've got a kid, you see. He's beautiful. My mom has him, upstate. I send money for him ... I don't want him ever to know what I am ... but the more I can send, the better his future will be."

Tony said, "But I don't have an Antonio Amato whose music can keep me going."

"No, but you have all the people like me who listen to your voice and are braver and happier because of it."

He swallowed hard. After a long while he said, "My music is both a—a Cross and a joy for me. But tonight I am grateful to you for reminding me of the part that is joy." He put his other hand over hers. "I feel better for talking to you."

But Maria had begun to shake. She needed a fix now. Reluctantly she would have to leave this church, leave Antonio Amato to his sad, unique destiny. She took her hand from his and started to rise, but he clutched her arm and pulled her back. He needed to let this woman know, without actually saying the words, that she had stopped him, at least for now, from committing an irrevocable act. But how to do this?

"Before you go, *per favore* do not be offended," he said. "You have given me something ... *molto* ... valuable, and I would like to give you something in return."

The Tosca Taunt

"I told you, you already have. So, no, honey, I won't take anything from you, unless you happen to be buying what I'm selling, and I don't think you are."

Tony did not know what to do. He had an inexplicable sense of urgency, a deep need to return the favour to this unknown woman. Finally he said, "Will you at least accept a memento of me, something to remember this meeting? I would like to think there had been something for you too in our coming together."

"Do you really think I'm going to forget meeting you?"

He frowned at her. But then he had an inspiration. He had a splendid watch, given to him by the company for which he had done a commercial endorsement. The watch had no sentimental attachment for him; indeed, it was so new even Jen had never seen it.

"I have no jewelry on me that doesn't come from my Jen, except this watch. It is a good watch the company gives me for saying I like this brand. *Per favore,* I will be very happy if you will take it. If not for yourself, for your child one day." Tony fished around in his pocket until he found a narrow gold card case. He pulled out a card which said merely "Antonio Amato". No address, no profession. The card of a supremely confident man. He wrote his private phone number on the back.

"Maybe someday I could do for you what you did for me. You have given me back ... " He could not finish. He stretched out his hand to her, holding the watch and the card.

True to Maria's profession, she could read people, and she saw that the power of whatever she had done would be diminished for him, if she did not accept his memento. Slowly she took the proffered gift.

"I won't forget this, Mr Amato, not ever. And I'll be listening to your songs all the rest of my life. Don't give up. There's a whole lot of us that need you. Thank you—good luck—goodbye." She rose, fuelled by her sudden emotion and by her increasing need for a fix, and quickly left the church before Tony could say more.

Slowly Tony got up from the pew. He felt odd, still sick at heart yet lighter somehow. Quietly he passed the pews where people were stretched out for a few hours of tranquillity. At the door he took out his wallet and stuffed almost all the cash he carried, three hundred dollars, into the container for donations. Then he stepped outside and hailed a passing cab.

Tony let himself into his apartment and walked quietly through the entry hall when he heard, "Tony! Thank God! We were about to call the police!"

He rounded the corner. All the lights were on in his living room. Mia rushed towards him, while Cedric sat unsmiling and a pale perspiring Gareth was getting out of his chair.

"What are you doing here so late?" Tony asked, astonished.

"You can't be serious!" Mia looked to Tony to be on the verge of tears. "We've been panic stricken; don't ever do that again!"

Tony knew they were justified; the knowledge made him angry. "Do what? I can't take an evening walk now without asking your permission?"

"Good God, Tony," exclaimed Gareth. "What did you expect? Your driver got the wind up after you left him at Central Park. He didn't know what to do so he came back to the Met, found Mia and Cedric and told them. She immediately phoned me; we called Mrs Burns but you weren't here so we drove around looking for you until we realised that was futile. Then we came back here and tried to decide what to do."

"You are all crazy. I am not free to do what I want now? I am not a child."

But now Mia was angry too. "Tony, you weren't in a good frame of mind when you left the Met tonight; you refused my company for the first time since we've known each other, and frankly I was—" She glanced at Cedric. "Cedric and I were very concerned about you. And when the driver came back—"

"Okay, okay, I appreciate you are worried, but as you can see I am okay. Except I am tired, I go now to bed, *scusi, per favore.*" He strode down the hall to his bedroom and shut the door with a resounding crash.

Twenty-Two

Relaxed and unambitious though she was, Victor Macready Kilbride's mother-in-law Amanda Rees still did not have enough to do. Being a widow was bad enough; being a widow with few interests and enough money that she did not have to worry about her future was in her dour view a kind of disaster. She lived alone in her big brick house in Savannah, Georgia, with nothing on her hands but time. Not many friends left—they had dropped her because she was an attractive, unattached woman, who either made an odd number at dinner or might be a threat, or, they had moved away, or died. So she had too much time to ponder, to fret, even to panic.

To panic, these days, about her daughter Bryony. Wherever was she? Of Amanda's two children Bryony was the only one who kept in touch regularly. When Bryony's sister Leah was very young she had married a diplomat, and except for letting her mother know which country she was in and what her telephone number was in case of emergency, and sending a

The Tosca Taunt

letter and an expensive gift for Christmas and birthdays, she rarely communicated with her family. Only dear Bryony cared.

During Bryony's last phone calls to her mother, she had indicated that she had finally decided to leave Victor. Amanda suspected that once Bryony actually left him, she would be so emotionally bruised she would hide for a while without getting in touch with anyone, including her mother. However this did not help Amanda deal with the lengthening, frightening silence. After all these years she still thought of Bryony as a beautiful, pampered child, in many ways unable to take care of herself, yet so appealing to men she would always find someone to care for her. How could Victor have treated a lovely child-woman like Bryony so badly?

So it was worrying enough that Bryony had disappeared, without Amanda's detested son-in-law trying to locate his wife in that underhanded way, having some woman phone and call her Mama. And then having the woman use Amanda's grandmother's name, Bridget Jennifer Noonan—to what purpose? Amanda pondered this, growing increasingly puzzled, but for some time her distaste for Victor kept her from contacting him.

This night she sat in a soft easy chair in the parlour of the big house, sipping her nightcap, which had long since changed from one cup of Ovaltine to three or four gins and tonic, or, truth to tell, three or four drinks of whatever alcohol came to hand. Slowly she sipped the last long drink of the evening, building up her courage. She would phone that dreadful Victor and stop him from putting his accomplice up to such stupid calls. Using the Noonan name too! Outrageous behaviour, but then in her view

Victor had always been showy, vulgar, somewhat beyond the pale despite his wealth and impressive earning ability.

She dialled his number. At the other end the phone rang several times, and the answering machine had just begun its spiel when Victor picked up the receiver and shouted, "Don't hang up, whoever you are, I'm here, the machine will shut itself off—hello, hello?"

"Victor. Amanda Rees here."

Victor disliked his mother-in-law almost as much as she despised him. No "Mother Rees" for him.

"Yes Mrs Rees. I was half expecting you to call, but I'm sorry you did."

"Why?"

"Because it probably means you're looking for Bryony too—unless you know where she is and you're calling to say you don't, to put me off the track. Which is it?"

"You must know perfectly well I don't know where she is. And now I know you don't either."

"Enigmatic as ever, my dear Mrs Rees. So, if you haven't phoned to tell me where Bryony is, to what do I owe this—"

"This pleasure?"

"Your word. If you insist. That's not quite the word I had in mind."

"I've called to tell you to quit this telephone nonsense."

Amanda waited; Victor must be contemplating this. Then he said, sounding surprisingly genuine, "What telephone nonsense? What are you talking about? I haven't phoned you for at least two years."

"I know *you* haven't. You leave that to your henchpersons,

don't you. And how dare you use my grandmother's name!"

"I haven't any idea to what you're alluding, Mrs Rees."

"I'm alluding to the woman with the sexy voice who calls herself by Grandmama's name and who is trying to find out where Bryony is."

Again Amanda had to wait for a response.

"I really don't understand what you're telling me," Victor said, puzzled now. "You say a woman called you and wanted to know about Bryony? But this has nothing to do with me."

Victor again paused to think. Bryony was hellish devious. Could she have put someone up to doing that for reasons of her own? Who else would know the name of Bryony's great-grandmother? But what could be the purpose of using it to phone his mother-in-law? Better gentle down and see what he could find out from her.

"What name did this woman use?"

Amanda Rees finished her drink at a gulp. "You know perfectly well what name; you have that painting of Grandmama in your dining room and the name's on the back. Victor, I want you to quit this stupidity right—" Amanda found she was speaking to the dial tone.

For Victor had a sudden inspiration and hung up. He rushed into his dining room and took down the oil painting of Bryony's ancestor. On the back, sure enough, was the name of the model; Bridget Jennifer Noonan.

Quickly he hung the painting back on its hook and dialled Gerald Geraint.

"Good to hear your voice, Geraint; you obviously haven't left yet for Savannah. I've got some information and some instructions for you. If and when you get into my mother-in-law's house, and for God's sake be careful, after you check her phone records, of course you'll be phoning any numbers that look promising. Try asking to speak to Bridget Jennifer Noonan and see what you get." Victor explained what had just happened.

"Hey doc," Geraint growled, "If you happen to get unfrocked or extracted or whatever they do to dentists, you can have my job."

Victor was not amused. "Never mind that, just get on with it."

"Right, doc."

....

The day after Tony's *Romeo et Juliette*, he took a long walk alone against a cutting wind in Central Park, head down so he would not be recognised.

This cowardly behaviour is not what Jen would expect from me — nor is it what I expect from myself. All those years of sacrifice, all the times we could have been — should have been together and were not, because my voice had to be somewhere where Jen could not be. Were the sacrifices ultimately for nothing? All the people who want to hear my singing, those people to whom I have given a loyalty greater even than I gave to Jen, because they were so many and she was only one, will I be able to sing reliably for them, ever again? Dio! Jen and I have lived by the credo of the greatest good for the greatest number. We have given ourselves to the people who demanded the voice.

If I had only known. Oh my Jen. What can give me back the time I could have spent with you?

He stopped walking and stood, staring at what only he

could see.

Jen, per favore, show me the way. I am lost. Nothing will make me really happy, not ever again, I am sure of it. But—if that is so—what reason is left for me to live, except to make other people happy? At least I still have this one glorious thing, the power to alleviate suffering, to bring joy with my voice.

Passers-by jostled him as he stood, a tall sturdy man in the middle of the path, blocking the easy flow of pedestrians. It didn't matter. He was going to pull himself out of this free fall. He had to. For the sake of his Jen.

The determined Tony was able to sing the broadcast on Saturday afternoon, but not without some difficulty during the scene he dreaded. He did not of course fully realise how moving his private grief made his public performance.

....

Jen paced around in her room, her radio tuned to the Canadian Broadcasting Corporation station, listening to the Saturday afternoon broadcast of *Romeo et Juliette*. She became increasingly involved and moved by this music as the afternoon wore on. During an intermission Mark Reinhard appeared, framed in her open doorway.

"You're finally back from Toronto!" she said with pleasure. "I *am* glad to see you."

"That's promising," he said, and grinned what she thought of as his Clint Eastwood grin.

"I don't know *what* it's promising," she said. "Come in. I've just fetched a pot of coffee from the kitchen; let's share it and the end of this glorious opera."

He stepped inside, leaving the door wide open. "You look a

lot better than the last time I saw you," he said. "You've been okay?"

"I've been fine." The Metropolitan Opera announcer Peter Allen said Sir Sheldon Wasserman had just stepped up to the podium. Jen said with a smile, "Please, sit down. You get to keep quiet now until this last act is over."

"What opera is it?"

"*Romeo et Juliette*, with Mia Mitsouros and Antonio Amato. It's so lovely."

He sat opposite her. She poured their coffee, and then sat down, her head against the high back of her easy chair. As the words and music grew increasingly more emotional, she felt mysteriously disturbed. What was it about Antonio Amato's voice that so moved her? She was puzzled by the intensity of her reaction. She had been listening earlier to a Jussi Bjoerling CD she had unearthed in the common room, and though the voice was exquisite, almost perfect in its interpretation, she found that music enjoyable but nothing more. Yet now, as Amato's sob-edged tenor soared in the sad phrases of the last scene, Jen's feelings were physical, orgasmic. Nearly out of control, she rose from her chair and stood looking from the window, her back to Mark.

During a brief quiet interlude in the music she turned and said to him, "Do you have the feeling Antonio Amato is singing inside your bones?"

"No, can't say I do. I'm enjoying it though."

She turned back to the window. The libretto said, "Oh infinite, supreme joy to die with you, come! One kiss! Lord, Lord, forgive us..." Jen was embarrassed that she seemed unable

The Tosca Taunt

to control her body, her deeply orgasmic reaction to this music. She began to tremble.

Mark had scarcely taken his eyes off her since he had entered the room. Now he stood up, hesitated a moment, then walked over to her and put his hands on her shoulders from behind, saying, "Hey, hey, don't be upset, it's only a story."

"I'm not upset, it's just that beauty does this to me—there's something about his voice ... "

She turned to face him, trembling still, her dark blue eyes shining. And, without giving himself time to think, Mark bent and kissed her. In a moment she responded to his kiss. He could feel her quivering with passion and somehow trying to hold it back; he wondered why—unless her passion were not for him? But it surely couldn't be only for the music, could it?

They drew apart, and she closed her eyes for a moment as though reflecting on what had just happened. Then she disentangled herself completely from his embrace. They stood awkwardly, like youngsters after a first kiss. Finally he said, "Do you realise how little I know about you, and how much I want to know?"

Her response was quick. "Do you realise how little I know about myself?"

"Oh, you want to play games, do you?" He smiled at her.

"No."

"Then I'll sit down, and you'll tell me all about you."

"You first, Mark."

"I told you all about me the day you were sick."

This gave Jen her out. She said, "But I was so drugged on Demerol I've forgotten, and I really would like to know, for example, what brings someone like you to a place like this?"

She watched him anxiously. Would he, like most men, respond enthusiastically to earnest questions about himself? And, she wondered, how did she know this about most men? What had her husband really been like, this "T"? And what other men had she known? Was she a sexually liberated woman, was she perhaps even promiscuous, or had she been a faithful wife to "T"?

She was relieved when Mark immediately launched on a long story about the reasons for his choice of profession.

"I became an engineer because I couldn't get into law school the year I tried for it. My dad is a lawyer, head of a big firm in Toronto; he wanted his only son to join him. It was the best thing that ever happened to me, not getting into law school; I didn't want it, and I would have been an ineffectual, unhappy lawyer. No, I'm a born engineer. Talk about getting lucky! And the family wasn't a total washout as far as Dad was concerned; my two sisters joined him in the firm, and one of them will succeed him eventually as head of it. So there you are; it's an ill wind that doesn't blow somebody good!"

It was easy for Jen to draw him into other stories about himself, his five almost grown children, and his marriage—at least the happy parts of the marriage. Jen was impressed with the way he spoke of his ex-wife; he seemed to have a friendship with her, and had nothing critical to say about her. He merely said he and she had chosen badly, had married too young and for all the wrong reasons.

His stories relieved Jen, at least for today, of having to talk, of perhaps having to tell him the truth about herself—which was that she didn't *know* the truth about herself. After a long while he stood up and said, "I'll see you at dinner then, thanks for the coffee. Are you coming to the common room later? I hope so." He left her standing by the open door.

Watching him retreat down the hall, she wondered uneasily what she should do. As day had followed blank day during his absence, she had felt increasingly frustrated about recovering her past. While exploring ways to stimulate her memory and to find out who she was, she realized it would be possible to contact the police in Timmins and tell them she had amnesia. They would then publicise her situation, and try to find her identity. But almost every night now she dreamed of the dark man who collapsed face down, bleeding and dying in front of her, and an instinct for self-preservation kept her from rushing headlong into advertising her amnesiac plight. Because a medical book in the library had told her that amnesia was sometimes self-inflicted, that the amnesiac was avoiding memories too painful to face. She reflected miserably that if she had fled both physically and emotionally from murdering someone, then perhaps she would rather not know.

But now there was Mark's kiss, which had been anything but perfunctory. She could see a disconcerting new problem brewing. She liked Mark a lot, but was she free to pursue any kind of relationship with a man?

Should she tell him she didn't know who she was? Would he immediately instigate a search for her identity? Would she then find out not only her identity but that of the dark dead man of her nightmares? Was he "T"? Could any of this possibly be fair to Mark, who was obviously becoming interested in her?

Jean Dell

In the television room that evening several of the mine employees watched a video of a Goldie Hahn film in which the actress had amnesia. In the end, after numerous comic adventures, Hahn left her real husband and stayed with the man she had met after her memory loss.

Mark walked Jen upstairs to the door of her room, and kissed her goodnight with a passion that disturbed her dreams.

Twenty-Three

In the hobby room at the mine Jen found some rather good watercolours, some indifferently cared for brushes and some excellent paper. She picked up one of the brushes and ran her fingers over its hairs, feeling a sudden powerful urge to try her hand at this medium.

"Do these belong to someone, or may I help myself?" she called out to Mark who was in the next room.

"Go ahead," he said. "The cook before Steve fancied himself an artist and brought more equipment in though we already had some, but he didn't bother taking any of his stuff when he left. You sure can't paint any worse than he did."

Jen grinned. "Thanks a lot. Just for that I'll do a portrait of you."

"Good God. Do I have to sit for it? Are you any good?"

"You'll just have to wait and see. No, I don't want you to sit for it, just give me a photo of yourself and I'll work from it and from my knowledge of you."

"You talk like a pro."

"Have you known many professional artists?"

"Now that you ask, no."

Mark searched in his wallet and produced a picture of himself with one of his teen-aged sons, fishing. In the photograph they stood on a riverbank with low bushes in the background, arms around each other's shoulders, hair blowing in the wind, contentment and affection on their faces.

"See what you can make of this," he said. "You may surprise me."

"I may surprise myself," said Jen.

"Speaking of surprises, will you please fill in that form? The catering company sent me a memo; they are updating records and they need the data about you now."

Jen felt her stomach tighten. How to postpone this? "Yes, of course. It keeps slipping my mind."

She would put Mark off once again, this time with a handsome painting of him and his son. Only why did she think she was capable of producing anything in the way of good portraiture?

....

She was alone as she set herself up in a corner of the hobby room near the north window which would give the light she needed, and began to conceive the portrait. Slowly, very slowly she realised that she had considerable knowledge of this craft, and presently she could see she had a formidable talent.

Abruptly, eerily, the certitude came to her that she was an artist. She was a professional artist, and she had a vivid flash of memory of some pictures she had painted. And of the room in which she had painted them, a high-ceilinged loft with skylights and a view of tall buildings.

Biting her lip hard, she wiped a paint-stained hand across her face, turning one cheek lavender. Not trusting her suddenly shaky legs, she backed against the built-in storage bench and sat down. Dread mingled with relief. This was the first real indication that significant portions of her memory might come back. She found herself hoping desperately that it would be better to remember than not to remember, particularly since she was unable to stop herself. And if recollection brought misery in its wake, perhaps that would be no worse than her frequent moments of amnesiac terror.

....

Jen wanted Mark to be so dazzled by her painting that he would temporarily forget about her filling in the form. For she believed that now she had begun to remember, complete memory would rush back any time. And then she could fill in that form with, she hoped, no qualms.

She held the portrait in her two hands and went out into the cold afternoon, down the path to the building that housed the administration. She was surprised to find Mark's office door closed today. It was usually open, Mark being a friendly, involved manager. She knocked.

"Come in," he called, his voice abrupt.

She opened his door to see him sitting at his desk, looking grim.

"What's the matter?"

"Nothing you need worry about, Jen; just a bit of trouble with the assay lab."

"I've got something that will cheer you up." She turned the portrait towards him. He frowned, and then his eyes opened in astonishment. He stood up, took it carefully from her, and examined it closely. Then he looked accusingly at her.

"I don't know one damn thing about you, except that you are obviously a professional artist, and a gifted one at that. Why on earth didn't you tell me?"

She looked away and was silent. The dreaded cross-examination could not be long coming.

"Jen, what is it you're hiding? Have you run away from something that embarrasses you? Whatever it is, I'm not your judge."

He stared again at the portrait. "This is excellent. Of course I'll buy it from you."

"Buy it? It's a gift, Mark."

"I can't accept a gift of this calibre from an obvious professional. That's not how my world works." He grinned, not knowing how close to the truth he was. "And, for the record, this doesn't stop me insisting about the form. Whatever you don't want us to know, it won't lose you your job here, unless of course you're hiding from the law. But of course that can't be..." He was stopped by the expression on her face. "Hey, hey, don't be upset, Jen, what the hell is going on here?"

He put the portrait carefully down on his desk, and moved quickly to put his arms around her. But she brushed him away.

"No. You sit on your side of the desk and I'll sit here. I can't put off telling you any longer. But will you promise me something? Will you promise not to do anything for a couple of weeks, about what I'm going to tell you?"

The Tosca Taunt

"I can't promise that. If you're escaping the law—"

"Oh, Mark," Jen cried desolately, "I—I don't know!"

"What do you mean, you don't know?"

"I can't remember!"

"Can't remember what? What are you talking about?"

"I can't remember who—" Her voice disappeared. She whispered, "—who I am." At his incredulous look, she added, "I mean, I seem to have lost my—I seem to have amnesia."

"Are you putting me on?"

"I wish."

"You're not saying this because there's something you want to hide—" But she was looking at him with such confused honesty in her dark blue eyes, that he, who prided himself on being a good judge of people, felt she had to be telling him the truth.

Now it came out in a tumble of words; the forest, the bruises, the logging road, the truck driver, the letter to Mama, the phone number in the luggage that had given her a moment of hope soon dashed, her constantly recurring dream about the dark man shot and dropping dead at her feet, and now the first glimmer that her memory might be returning, this certitude about her profession. And her hope that since her memory had begun to return it might come back completely in a few days or weeks.

"Will you help me, Mark? Will you give me my window of time to try to—and if I don't, will you let me run away someplace else? I'm afraid to know, and I'm afraid not to know."

"Let you run away? No, I won't let you do that. I'll give you time, of course. But I—we're not prepared to lose you—from the kitchens, I mean—" But he got up then, and, pulling her gently up from her chair, he kissed her, and she knew at least one thing for certain.

....

Gerald Geraint P.I. sat in a car across the street from Amanda Rees' home, hoping for her to go out on this moonless dark night and give him his chance to reconnoitre. He had sized up the big red brick house last night. No burglar alarm, just a notice on the front and back doors saying there was one. A low window leading into a small library had a feeble looking closure, and once he was sure Amanda Rees was out of the house he would gain access that way and do his research rapidly and in peace.

Was he about to be in luck? Her inside porch light and her verandah light had just been turned on. Yes, there she was, a slender smartly dressed woman, locking her front door and stepping quickly down the street to a similar house three doors down. Victor Macready Kilbride had mentioned Amanda's neighbourhood bridge group. Gerald hoped that was where she was going; bridge evenings took a while.

Donning surgical gloves, Gerald quickly opened the feeble lock and let himself into the library where he began to look methodically through the tidy drawers of the desk. Nothing interesting. Then he turned to the matching oak filing cabinet. Meticulous, Mrs Rees. Everything filed under easily deciphered headings. In the file called Bryony, souvenirs of a childhood; letters to her mother, school art, but nothing recent enough to be of any use. Gerald rifled through other semi-promising files. Finally he came to the file for phone bills, and there he struck, if

The Tosca Taunt

not gold, at least fool's gold. He copied down collect calls, and any other numbers that might be of interest; one bill had so many of them he simply stuffed it into his pocket. Mrs Rees would think she had misplaced it if she looked for it at all. Gerald would not have taken two bills; their absence might arouse suspicion if she happened to look through her phone file. One bill could be misplaced; the disappearance of more could seem odd.

Now Gerald looked through the rest of the house. Beside Mrs Rees' bed, on her table, he found a journal, not a diary so much as a record of daily thoughts. He looked over the pages he arbitrarily assumed to be for the past two months since the disappearance of Bryony—unfortunately Amanda Rees did not date her journal. But he found there one thing of interest—a reference to the call from Bridget Jennifer Noonan, with descriptions of the woman's voice, and an account of Mrs Rees' puzzlement and unhappiness about this call. This seemed to confirm to Gerald Victor's suspicion that Bryony was using that name. Gerald decided he would ask for this Bridget Jennifer person at these phone numbers.

The next day from his hotel room he made call after call in an attempt to find a lead to Bryony. It was beginning to seem like a fruitless morning until he called a Canadian number, billed to Amanda Rees as a collect call, and was answered at the other end with, "Delson Mines, Horvath speaking."

Gerald used his most convincing old southern accent. "Mr Horvath, this is Norman Wilson of Wilson, Ketchum and Schaft, attorneys, in Savannah, Georgia. We are trying to locate two people who have just come into a considerable sum of money through an estate. We have a lead that one or both of them could be working for your company. One is a woman named Bryony Kilbride, do you have an employee there by that name?"

"No, we don't."

"The other one is, just a moment, I have it right here, seems to me the name was — er—Noonan, it's on my desk somewhere here—"

He got the response he was fishing for. "You mean Bridget Jennifer Noonan? Goes by Jen?"

"Yes, here it is, that's right. Now, we found another woman of the same name but the description was entirely wrong, turned out to be no relation whatsoever, odd about names isn't it. What—er—what does your—"

"What does she look like? Well, I'll tell you," volunteered Bill Horvath, a member of the cleaning staff who had just absent mindedly answered the phone in Jen's room when it rang while he was mopping the floor.

As he pumped this willing fellow, Gerald Geraint held his breath, as well as a picture and a paper of the vital statistics of Bryony Kilbride. Gerald had a hunch that Bryony and Bridget were one and the same, despite Amanda's doubts and Victor's puzzlement. The voice came over the line.

"She's a real looker, great legs, good figure," volunteered Mr Horvath. He was two weeks overdue for a leave home to visit his new wife.

"That's very descriptive, but hardly helpful in identifying whether she is the woman we are looking for. Could you elaborate?"

"Sure. Um—she's got short blonde hair, dark blue eyes and

The Tosca Taunt

she looks a bit like that French actress, um, what's her name again, she sold that perfume, oh yeah, Cathleen de Niro, or some name like that. I'd say she's about, um, five foot six, same height as my wife, and weighs maybe a hundred and thirty? Nice dresser." He paused. "Well, good for her, if she's inherited some money. So? Is it her?"

Gerald thought, *Damn right it's her. Bridget Jennifer is Bryony. I knew it! Damned if I understand what game she's playing though.*

He told Mr Horvath that he couldn't be certain, and that possibly he would be sending someone up to find out.

"Should I tell her?" asked the young man with enthusiasm.

"No, she might get her hopes up and be disappointed. We wouldn't want to disappoint such a nice person, would we? Thank you for your help, you have been extremely co-operative."

Gerald Geraint hung up the phone and shouted "Yahoo!" He dialled Victor Macready Kilbride's number. When Doctor Kilbride answered he heard, "If I haven't found your wife, you don't need to pay me one more cent, I'm that sure of it!" And he explained what he had done, and why he was so sure.

"Now of course we have to figure out a way to smoke her out," Gerald said.

"Smoke her out, hell! Give me her number, I'll phone her anonymously and I'll know by her voice—"

"I wouldn't, if I were you. She may have call tracing and she could trace the call

"From a payphone?"

"The area is traceable, Dr Kilbride. I really wouldn't if I were you. She'll run away again if she thinks you're on to her. I'll go up and reconnoitre—"

"The hell you will. I can take a couple days off. I'll go and see for myself. Bryony is damn well coming home now. Enough of this fucking embarrassing little caprice of hers. Just give me the details of where to find her and I'll be gone. And since you say you don't want any more money from me until I verify that she's Bryony, well, you'll hear from me after I get back."

"You can't just go up there like that, the mine is hard to get to, you go in by the mining company's helicopter or plane. You'll need a reason to be there."

"Right," said Dr Kilbride thoughtfully. "Any ideas?"

"You paying for ideas?" asked Gerald Geraint, faintly annoyed with himself for having been so cocksure about the identity of the woman he had found.

"Damn right."

"Tell them you're writing a book about isolated mines, historical and modern, and you've chosen that one to write about if they'll let you come up and do research on the spot for a couple of days."

"You should be writing fiction if you're this inventive."

Gerald Geraint laughed. "Wish I could. I've got plots galore by now, but I can't string two words together on paper. Well, so long, doc, I'll hear from you soon no doubt."

....

Charlie Demchuk was waiting—and waiting and waiting—for his chiropractor. He hadn't realised what a change getting older would make to his back; the days when he could sit comfortably for hours driving his truck were long gone. But he had found a great chiropractor who made all the difference in

The Tosca Taunt

the world to his aching back.

Today, for the first time since Charlie had been coming to him, the chiropractor was making him wait. It had been an hour now. Charlie had read everything in the waiting room, except for a coverless, wrinkled magazine he found behind the lamp. He took it, sat down with resignation, and began to read.

In the centre of the magazine he came across a photo of one Antonio Amato, who was, according to the caption, a tenor taking his kids into some chapel for his wife's funeral. Idly Charlie began to read the article. Poor guy, his wife Jenetta disappearing, burned to death; Charlie could scarcely imagine the feelings he would have if he knew his wife Barb, of whom he was very fond, had died like that. *Geezus. Burned!* The article said the couple had a great marriage, and that the tenor was devastated. He didn't look so hot in the picture, in Charlie's opinion. And he turned the torn page.

"Holy shit!" he said out loud, and the startled receptionist looked up from her computer.

"Scuse me," Charlie said. But he could scarcely believe what he saw, for staring up at him was a picture of the woman he had picked up on the logging road two months ago, Jen she had said her name was. He was sure it was the same woman—the name even fit; Jen—Jenetta. Had to be her, blonde, looked like that Catherine Deneuve woman. *Only—only how could it possibly be?*

He hastily looked at the facing page to read the rest of the article. But the consecutive page was missing. Still, he did get some facts from a scrap of print left under the picture of the woman; this Jenetta Amato had been listed as missing and then declared dead when her effects were found in the ashes of a fire.

The next page would have told him where, among other things.

Geezus.

"Can I have this magazine?" he asked the receptionist. "I'll buy it from you."

"Is it a new one?"

"No, it looks real old."

"Just take it then. You found something interesting in it, Charlie?"

"I sure did," he said.

....

When Charlie arrived home after his chiropractic treatment he consulted his wife. "What do I do now, Barb? I'm sure it's the same woman, but how can it be when the article says they're sure she's dead? But what if it is her? I can't remember the name of the mine she said she was going to. She seemed kinda mixed up, almost like she couldn't remember stuff, ordinary stuff, you know? What if it is her and she has amnesia or something and doesn't know she's this Amato woman?"

"But Charlie, think a minute, your hitcher had a name, she seemed sure of where she was going, I'd think if that Mrs Amato had amnesia she would just be confused, she wouldn't imagine she was someone else, on her way to be a cook in a mine. I mean, a woman like that, a professional artist and married to that rich singer, all that high society living, where would she get the idea she was an assistant cook?"

"I remember she said she liked opera," he argued, beginning to doubt his own reasoning.

"Oh Charlie, come on, people like this kind of music or that kind of music, it doesn't mean they're married to opera singers or rock singers. Old Mrs Nikiforuk likes opera; she was married to a grocer, for heaven's sake. You're just imagining things. It's just because the woman in the picture is so good-looking and you said the woman you picked up was good looking too; honestly Charlie, men!"

"Barb, that's stupid. I seen lots of pictures of good-looking women since I picked up that hitcher; I never thought any of them was her until today. I still don't know what to do."

"I don't see that you can do anything. There's lots of mines in northern Ontario. You can't hardly get a list of all of them so's you can ask them if two months ago they might have hired a new assistant cook who might have had amnesia and who might have been in a fire and who might be this dead artist. And anyway Charlie if it turned out it was her, except I'm sure it isn't, you'd have to admit you were picking up hitch-hikers, and you know how the company is about that. I'd just leave it alone if I was you."

So Charlie left it alone.

Until, that is, his wife came home one day as pale as a lily.

"What's the matter, Barb, you look awful. You not feeling good?"

"I feel terrible. But not how you mean."

"What's the matter?"

"I was really early to pick the kids up at school, I had an hour to wait, so I went into the library and I looked at some magazines. I found an old one, with an article about that Jenetta Amato, you know, the one that was burned. Charlie, did you know where the fire was that she was supposed to be burned in?"

Jean Dell

"Haven't a clue."

"It was—oh, Charlie! It was the hotel at Hadley's Ridge."

Charlie stared at her, realisation seeping in. "Geezus, that's up—way up—the mountain from the road where I picked up my hitcher. What should we do? What if it really—I better get me a list of mines and see if I can remember where she was going. Unless you can think of something better to do."

"I can't. Only—if it is her, maybe—maybe she was running away from something. Maybe she doesn't want to be found. Should we just pretend you never picked up that hitcher?"

"I can't, Barb, I can't. If it's her—I mean, if it was you that was lost, and I thought you were dead and you weren't, you think I wouldn't want to know? The article said these guys had a great marriage. There aren't that many around; us, we've been lucky. We've got to do something about this."

Twenty-Four

Julian LeComte was astounded when his father told him that he had finally decided this was the right time to run for Governor of Louisiana. This notion of Leonard's, of running for Governor, had been discussed for so long, more or less in secret, that Julian had come to believe it was a fantasy. But today Leonard had dropped in at Julian's townhouse, unannounced, to tell his son that he and his crony Victor Macready Kilbride had been quietly assembling a political "machine", and that he would make his official announcement at a press conference the following day.

"But Dad, I never really took it seriously—do you really think—aren't you afraid of the investigative press?"

"Why? What've I ever done that wouldn't wash in this state?"

"You've been a member of the Klan." Julian knew he was unsuccessful at keeping the anger from his voice.

"So what, son? If that gets out, you think it will hurt me—in

Louisiana? Fact is, I *used* to be a member of the Klan; both sides can take that up and see it as positive for me. Those as sympathise will think I still believe in the Klan's ideals but just don't broadcast them so much any more, and they'll vote for me because of it. Those as don't sympathise will believe that because I haven't been to a meeting in years I saw the error of my ways, and they'll vote for me because of that. No, son, I've got it made, as long as I have you on my side."

Julian took a long while answering. Finally he said, "Are you on *my* side?"

Leonard put his hand placatingly on Julian's arm. "I worded that badly. I know you're not on my side in everything. What I need from you is your word that you'll not oppose me. Do nothing, if that's how you have to be, but don't set yourself against me. Can you at least do that?"

Julian thought, *It won't help Val and me if I oppose him. Nothing will help Val and me.* But he found it interesting that his increasing fame as an author gave him this unexpected power over his father.

"I won't oppose you," he replied, "and I won't campaign for you. If questions are asked, you can say I'm much too busy with my writing to involve myself in politics, but that I am with you in spirit. But don't say more than that; I'll deny anything else."

"I expected more from you, Julian."

"And I expected more from you, Pa."

They stared at one another.

"Oh for Chrissake you're not still on about that black dame, are you?" Leonard looked scornful. "Isn't it time you forgot her? Lots of good white women dying to marry you, Julie. Look

The Tosca Taunt

around. Take off the black glasses and ogle the merchandise, boy."

Julian was appalled. "Let's change the subject. This one will go nowhere. Tell me more about your campaign; I never could believe you really wanted to be Governor. Why? You're the man who has everything—money, challenging work, a gorgeous wife, a terrific lifestyle—why do you want to take on anything as difficult and troublesome and even sometimes dangerous as being Governor?"

Leonard laughed. "You don't understand, do you, son. It's the power, Julian. Power and fame. Nobody can ever have enough of either; I know *I* can't. First the governorship, and then, who knows?"

Julian had a sudden disquieting vision. He thought he could see where this campaign was going. Quietly he said, "You want to be President, Pa?"

Leonard looked at his son, his eyes opaque, expressionless. Finally he said, "What do you think? Of course I do eventually. I've got all the qualifications—self-made man, beautiful wife not so bright that she'll turn off the men but bright enough to appeal to the women, attractive intellectual son, already a famous writer, what more could I need to achieve my goal?"

Julian saw his opening. "I'll tell you, Pa. Has it occurred to you how useful it would be in these times if you had a black daughter-in-law and mixed race grandchildren?"

Leonard's response was to grab Julian painfully by the shoulders. "I've heard enough about that goddam woman to last me twenty lifetimes! The answer is no, boy, no, no, no! Don't mention her again to me, never!"

Jean Dell

Leonard released Julian, and the two men stared at one another with concentrated malevolence. Then the father turned and left Julian's townhouse, slamming the door so hard that even the neighbours shut in their houses were startled by the crash.

Twenty-Five

Mia and Tony hurried down Manhattan's wide Park Avenue to Cedric's apartment, from where she would leave immediately for the airport on her way to England.

"Stay with us in England," Mia said. "Cedric and I would love to have you."

"I am not good company these days, Mia."

"Don't be silly, we're not inviting you to be comic relief."

An attractive woman with long straight red hair suddenly appeared in front of Tony. His assistant, walking behind, was abruptly alert, vigilant.

"Mr Amato, I'm so sorry about your wife's death." She held out her hand as though to shake his; he put his hand into hers and found himself unexpectedly pulled forward and kissed fervently on the mouth. He pulled away. She smiled and said, "If I could do anything to help—" Tony's assistant pushed between them and said, "Very kind of you, madam," and effectively blocked her further progress while Tony and Mia escaped.

Tony shook his head. "Jen sometimes laughed at all these women, and sometimes not. You would think they would leave me alone for a little while at least." He wiped his mouth with his hand. "Is a miracle I don't catch rabies or something."

Mia laughed at him. "We're healthy creatures, we singers, or we couldn't do what we do. I'll leave you here then, love. In two hours I'll be on the Concorde again. So, will you stay with us?"

"Yes, *grazie*. I would like that. And it will be convenient to go from Cedric's, as often as I can, to see Thomas Graham Lanville; you remember him, Mia—Jen's and my good friend. He is ninety-eight years old now and very ill. I thought his mind was still okay but now I'm not so sure—he can't seem to understand Jen is dead. In my phone conversations with him he keeps saying no, she is not."

"Is that a good idea, Tony, visiting Lanville? Isn't that where you and Jen—"

"Where we met. Yes. It has to be a good idea; I see Jen everywhere. I have to get used to it."

"Shall I have a car pick you up at London Airport Friday?"

"*Per favore*."

"Tony darling, there's got to be a glimmer of light at the end of this awful tunnel."

They reached the canopied doorway that led into Mia's apartment building. Throwing her arms around Tony, Mia kissed him firmly on both cheeks, and was dismayed by the desire that welled in her.

....

Tony and Eric arrived early at the recording studio for the

The Tosca Taunt

rescheduled CD recording session. The rotund blonde producer "smirking Dirk", as Jen used to call him, was all smiles as he pumped Tony's hand.

"Have a look at the changes we've made, Tony; you'll be pleased. You said the songs we had chosen were too happy for the title. We've remedied that."

"Is late, no? You expect I should rehearse and record them all on this day?"

"Let's go over them; you know them anyway, but you just tell us what you need before we start recording."

Several songs were recorded without incident. The recording engineers had Tony re-record two entire stanzas. By this time the hard-working singer was soaked in perspiration. He picked up one of the towels available, wiped his face and then draped a dry towel around the back of his neck.

He recorded two of the newly chosen songs, *I'll Be Seeing You* and *It Never Was You*. Then he began the third, *The Shadow of Your Smile*. He sang with his usual intensity, "The shadow of your smile when you are gone will colour all my dreams and light the dawn."

Abruptly he stopped singing as he realised he was being naive. Tearing off his earphones, he hurled them against the glass partition. The sound engineers jumped as the unexpected noise hit their eardrums.

Tony threw open the cubicle door and said to Dirk, "You are exploiting me!"

He hurled the sheets of music to the floor. Grabbing his now cringing producer by the upper arms, Tony yanked him out of his chair. "You did not choose this music because I said we had too many cheerful songs. You chose it because Jen is dead. You *liked* Jen—and now you would make a profit from her death? I quit, Dirk. You make never again a record with me. And I will stop you selling this one if I can."

Dirk gulped. "Don't threaten me, Tony, we have a contract, remember? You want the truth? Sure I decided to sadden up the selection of songs because of the publicity about Jen's death. Tell me, Tony, in my shoes who wouldn't do what I did?"

Tony held Dirk's arms tighter. But the producer continued, his voice quavering only slightly, 'Don't get mad at me, for Chrissake. What performer hasn't chosen to perform certain material based on events in his personal life? Why do you think your performances of *Romeo et Juliette* were such crowd-pleasers? I hear tickets were scalping for more than five hundred bucks. You think it's because your vocal technique is so superb? Don't be a fool. They came hoping to see you break down. It's 'throw the Christians to the lions' time, baby. Get smart, Tony. What makes you think you should be excluded from the voyeurs? What makes *your* grief so special?"

"What—makes—my—grief—so—special? I will kill you, Dirk!" Tony stood toe to toe against Dirk; and Dirk felt the back of his neck prickling. Tony was a strong man with a fast temper, usually tightly controlled; he was not known to be violent but who knew with these volatile artists? Now Tony's assistant, who had been momentarily shocked into immobility, rushed across the studio and forcefully inserted himself between the two men. Pulling Tony's arm, he said, "Come on, let's go and have a cup of coffee and then come back and talk about this when everybody has cooled down."

The Tosca Taunt

Tony slowly let go of Dirk and said to Eric, "They can cool down or heat up all they like. *Il diavolo!* What does he mean, what makes my grief so special? The special person I lost, of course. Goodbye, Dirk. I don't come back."

Tony ran out the door and down the stairs. His assistant snatched up the coat Tony had forgotten in his flight, and quickly followed.

He found Tony leaning with his back against the wall outside the building, breathing hard as though he had been running.

"Come on," Eric said placatingly. "We'll go home."

Tony glowered at him.

"I know, I know," Eric continued. "That was pretty unpleasant. But when you think about it you'll realise it will be okay. I think the album will be great. In any case you can't stop it now, you've laid down all the tracks except that last song. They've got enough music without that one. Why don't you dedicate the CD to Jen?"

"Why don't you shut up?" said Tony, turning away and striding down the street so fast his assistant had trouble keeping up with him. But Tony had little time to brood, for early the next morning he was booked on the Concorde to London. Soon he found himself settled in at Cedric's home, and hurrying daily back and forth with Mia to London.

....

Rehearsals at the Royal Opera House in London had finished for the day, and Tony and Mia had returned to Cedric's to sample the cook's special paella. Tony had changed for dinner—"casual, darling," Mia had instructed—and he came downstairs to the open doors of the long dining room. Beautiful in its way, it still seemed cold to Tony, despite the warmth of the wood and the cheeriness of the bright, carefully chosen romantic paintings.

Tony stopped at the door. Mia and Cedric stood, arms around one another, heads bent towards each other, foreheads touching. They were laughing; Mia put up her hand and caressed Cedric's cheek, and he surprised Tony by breaking into a dance with her. Tony stepped back into the shadows. He remembered doing similar dances with Jen, spontaneous jigs of explosive joy. When you loved someone as he had loved her, it welled up inside you until sometimes you thought you would burst if you had no such release.

He found himself hoping again that Mia and Cedric would have a union like his and Jen's. He stepped back into the doorway. Now the lovers were kissing. Tony waited and then cleared his throat noisily. The lovers jumped back from each other like guilty children. Tony knew they would not have displayed their tenderness had they known he was there; he was aware of how careful, how thoughtful they were about him and his lonely pilgrimage.

He realized sadly that he could stay with them no longer. He would only make them unhappy too. Until he could be good company, until he could laugh again and joke again and give again, he could be with people only to work with them.

After dinner, during which he had tried and failed to be lighthearted, he said, "I thank you for the hospitality, I have very much appreciated, but I go now to stay in London."

"But why, Tony darling?" Mia, dismayed, put her hand over

The Tosca Taunt

Tony's. "Surely you have everything you want here; what is it?"

Cedric felt surprisingly out of sorts at the notion of Tony leaving. Remembering how he had despaired when he and Mia had parted for a year, Cedric empathised with Tony's loss, and wanted to be helpful to him. But he also liked to have what he thought of as the competition, under his roof, under his control.

Tony continued, "I am truly sorry. I need now to be alone—except of course for the rehearsing and the work. I am not yet good company."

"Is that all, Tony?" Cedric's voice was soft, coaxing, the voice with which he convinced adversaries that he was a nice guy. "If you need more privacy, we can put you in another part of the house; I can have your things moved into the Siddons Room in the East Wing. You can eat your meals alone if you'd rather; you don't need to see nearly so much of us. I—and I'm sure Mia—would be happier about you if you were here with us, under the circumstances."

"*Grazie,* is very kind, I appreciate. But I must go."

"But where, Tony darling? Not the Dorchester, surely." Mia knew Tony had a special fondness for the Dorchester, which was where he had given Jen the engagement ring later found blackened in the ashes at Hadley's Ridge.

"No. I thought to go there; I cannot for the rest of my life avoid what reminds me of Jen. But it is too soon for the Dorchester. No, I will go to that hotel on Park Street with the funny name, Forty Seven. It is very quiet, and I can have room service from Le Gavroche next door."

"They likely don't do meals any better than my chef, Tony."

"You are right. But I go all the same. *Per favore,* do not let this make a difference in our friendship. I think I am still not quite—" His voice petered out.

Tony settled in to a luxurious suite at Forty Seven Park Street. He was busy; rehearsals for *Tales of Hoffmann* were well under way, and in his free time he had to prepare for other upcoming performances. Determined to take care of his health and the musical instrument that lived in his throat, he worked out often and hard at a gym recommended to him by the hotel concierge. He sat down regularly for meals, but without his usual enthusiasm, and he spent the requisite seven hours a night in bed, often staring at shadows moving across the ceiling.

At rehearsals Mia and his other colleagues were dismayed to find him increasingly moody. A long way from the old Tony with whom it had been such a pleasure to work. But once they were in performance, he sang with his usual skill and received his usual complimentary reviews. He flew to Vienna to give a concert, and again was well received by the critics. Soon he was back in London, in rehearsal for a second opera, *Manon Lescaut* with Valentina Welles. These days Tony was relieved when he had occasion to sing with either Mia or Valentina, the two understanding sopranos who had helped him get through his first operas after Jen's death.

Meanwhile Mia had finished several Paris performances of *Carmen*, an experiment for her since she was not a mezzo-soprano. Her reviews for this attempt had been mixed, ranging from grudging approval to raves. She had just returned to Cedric's home, when she received a phone call from the conductor of Tony's *Manon Lescaut*, Sir Sheldon Wasserman.

"Mia! How is my favourite soprano?"

"You favourite soprano is very well, Sir Sheldon, and is hoping Valentina Welles is out of earshot."

"Of course, of course, I am not that much of a fool. Truth be known, she is my favourite soprano too. I use that line with several of you."

"Shameless of you, Sir Sheldon."

"No doubt, my dear. And how is Cedric? When do I finally come to your wedding? I did think it was good of you both to postpone it to help Amato. We all seem to have done a good job of saving at least his voice."

"Cedric is very well, very busy as always, and I'm not sure when we will be married, but soon, very soon. I hope. What ... what do you mean about Tony, that we have saved his voice *at least?*"

"That is what I am phoning you about. The director of *Manon Lescaut* and I are worried and we wondered who might talk to Tony. We decided you or Cedric would be best; you are his good friends and he will resent it less from you. He certainly would not take it from me."

Mia bit her bottom lip uncertainly. Her relations with Tony at the moment were tenuous. He seemed to be avoiding her except in work situations, but then he seemed to be avoiding everybody. After his long period of needing people around him, now apparently he needed to exorcise his demons alone. And because he was so well liked by friends and colleagues, they were willing to let him recover on his own difficult, prickly terms.

"I don't know if he'd listen to me right now, Sir Sheldon.

There was a time when—but not any more. What is it you want me to say?"

"First let me tell you about the rehearsals. If I did not know I were working with Tony Amato I'd swear I was rehearsing Carlo Paoli—you know Paoli very well of course; well, Amato is being *that* temperamental. Not throwing things and shouting like Paoli, but negative, almost uncooperative. I thought I would never live to see the day."

Mia was not pleased with the reference to how well she knew Carlo Paoli. As it happened, it was very well indeed; but now she would sooner that part of her life be forgotten.

"Go on, Sir Sheldon."

"Amato sounds good; he looks good—at least he looks 'lean and mean.' He has lost weight; it becomes him; but I suspect it is less because of the amount of working out that he's doing, than that he's not eating properly. I had one lunch with him last week when he ate about half of a small salad."

"Tony reacts that way to stress, and you have to admit he's stressed."

"I know. We all liked Jen so much. This is a sad enough business even if you don't consider the hideous way she died. But that's not all. Tony is turning into a recluse outside of work. I was surprised to learn he isn't staying with you and Cedric. I would have thought that would be the best place for him right now."

"It would. We tried. He left. He said he was not good company, but I suspect it hurt him to see Cedric and me being affectionate together. We tried not to when he was around of course, but he often caught us just the same."

The Tosca Taunt

"Well my dear, the bottom line as the Americans say is that I—we—think Tony is in a clinical depression, that he is hiding it perhaps even from himself, and that he needs help. I tried to introduce the subject, but backed off in a hurry when I saw how he reacted. I have to work with him and I need his good will. Can you help?"

Mia's heart began to pound disagreeably fast. Tony in a deep depression. Tony refusing help from everyone. Tony wanting to be alone. A solitary Tony, spiralling down, down—how far, and to where?

"I'll talk to him, Sir Sheldon. And I promise I won't back down if he doesn't like what I say. Tony and I have a long, solid friendship, and this shouldn't damage it—I hope."

From having worked with Mia and Tony over the years, Sir Sheldon thought what Mia described as a long solid friendship could very well be something more serious, more dangerous. And because Sir Sheldon realised she was taking a risk for him, he thanked her with more warmth than was his usual wont.

....

Tony, Valentina Welles, Bruce Grey and bass Hendrick Perkin were required for a special rehearsal over the lunch hour with the stage director of *Manon Lescaut*.

"Hamburgers?" asked the stage assistant who was delegated to fetch lunch.

Valentina grimaced. "We had hamburgers yesterday."

Hendrick Perkin said, "What about that Chinese takeout? It's not bad."

Soon the assistant returned with the white cartons of food, and the four singers gobbled lukewarm chop suey and egg rolls.

They spent the afternoon studying new blocking, and co-ordinating movements. All afternoon Tony was unpleasantly aware of the taste of the egg rolls.

Mia had made an appointment to meet Tony after his rehearsal. She waited impatiently for him in The Ivy Restaurant, watching desultorily for other famous performers, so often to be found here relaxing on the leather benches set against the oak panelled walls. Tony had refused her invitation to have a *tete-a-tete* dinner, repeating once more that he would not be good company.

She had sung with him only a month before, but she was dismayed by his appearance when he strode quickly into the room, all hard nervous energy, stared at with adulation by those other customers who recognized him. It was his face that arrested her. Lean, yes, with lines in the right places to give him that world-weary look so beloved by women, but pale, and darkly smudged around the eyes. She stood to greet him, and he enveloped her in a tight, long hug. She was again miserably aware that she had to fight down a longing for him. Sitting down, they ordered coffees. He enquired about her and she filled him in on her and Cedric's lives.

"But when do you get married? Do you not have a space in your schedule right now?"

"If I cancel my appearance at that concert in Barcelona, yes I do. But I should have thought of it earlier; we need time to get the invitations to the banquet out."

"What do you mean, you should have thought earlier? How come you don't know your own schedule?"

Mia stared down at her cup. "I—I didn't exactly let Cedric

The Tosca Taunt

know I could make this time available."

Tony frowned at her, concerned. He covered her hand with his cold one; she grasped his tightly. "What is wrong, Mia? You have doubts? You don't want to marry Cedric all of a sudden? Is late for such a decision, no?"

"Very late, Tony. Too late." She ran a finger around and around the rim of her cup. "No, it's not that I don't want to marry Cedric, of course I want to, it's—oh, I don't know. I've been so upset about Jen and you, and I can't get back into the spirit of things. I just need a little time." She still held his hand. "I don't know how I dare say that in front of you; that *I* need time to get over what's happened." She watched him, slumped morosely in his chair, his face slack. "Tony, you're not drinking your coffee."

"It tastes terrible."

She picked up his cup and tasted it. "But it's exactly the same as my *cafe latte*, darling, it's delicious. What's wrong?"

He shook his head. "*I* am what is wrong, I think. Don't fuss at me, Mia."

Now for the first time in the years since she had known Tony, conversation with him became hard going. Finally Mia again took his cold hand between hers.

"Tony darling, how long can you go on like this?"

"Like what? What are you talking about?"

"You. You look awful. And you're getting thin. You've lost at least twenty pounds."

"I know." He smiled, looking gratified. "I have been trying for years. Is good, yes? The trainer at the gym is happy with me. Everybody comments how much I lose. Is nothing like exercise for losing weight."

"Tony, I know you. That's only half the story."

"So? So you know me?"

"Nobody loses weight that fast just exercising. You're stressed and you're not eating properly. Be truthful now."

"You sound like my mother when I was a child. I don't have to answer to you, Mia."

More's the pity, she thought. But what she said was, "You're acting like a child these days from what I hear."

He frowned and withdrew his hand from hers. "What do you mean? Who have you been talking to?"

"Darling, what does it matter? What matters is that we all love you—and we are all worried about you. I have to talk to you seriously. We—I—don't think you should be trying to do this all by yourself."

"Do what?"

"Recover. Jen's death was too sudden, darling, too traumatic. I mean, it's terrible to lose someone slowly to a lingering illness, I know that only too well—but at least you get a little warning. You can try to erect some barricades against your grief. But Jen's death was such a shock. Tony, please listen to me, you simply can't go on like this, not eating, probably not sleeping properly, turning yourself into a moody hermit."

"*Cielo*, Mia, what business is it of yours? And who is telling you this?"

"It doesn't matter, darling. What matters is—" How do I say this, she wondered. "What matters is—have you thought about taking something like an anti-depressant?"

"Anti-depressants are not for me, they are for people who

The Tosca Taunt

are depressed."

"You're not depressed?"

"Of course I am depressed. But, I mean, those pills are for people who are depressed and don't know why. I *know* why. In my circumstance is normal to feel like I feel. Why is it everybody's business?"

"Because we care about you, and you're not functioning, Tony."

Now she could see he was angry. "Not functioning? Of course I am functioning. I do my work properly, have you read my reviews? That is what matters, nothing else. I keep fit, I do what everybody counts on me to do, I do it well, why can't people leave me alone?"

Rubbing a hand tiredly over his face he said abruptly, "I have to go, Mia. I will call you."

He rose from the table and strode out, leaving Mia going over in her mind how she could have worded her message better. Tony was angry; had she damaged the friendship she valued more than any other?

....

Tony picked up his assistant, who was tactfully finishing a scotch and soda at a table behind a large potted palm, and they decided to walk back to the hotel. Tony hoped a walk would help lighten his growing nausea. Finally he said to Eric, "I will have supper by myself in my room tonight. I will study for *Manon* and for the concert in Hamburg; I will not need anything; go and enjoy London."

"Thanks, Tony. You're sure you're okay? You look a bit green."

"I feel green. Is nothing. Have a happy evening."

The assistant was uneasy, but these days he disliked confronting his prickly employer. His job was to protect Tony, to smooth the way for him, not to play nursemaid. Still, he had never before been as concerned over his famous employer as he was these latter weeks. Like Tony's manager Gareth, Eric had figured that the one thing that might break Tony would be the loss of Jen. He hoped Tony was out of the woods, and dark dangerous woods they had been, but he was not certain yet. He walked away, glancing back once at Tony.

I don't feel well, Tony thought, entering the foyer and making for the elevator. He rushed into his suite just in time. Still wearing his trench coat he dashed into the bathroom, and with one arm held tightly across the pain in his stomach, he was very sick. After a while he stumbled into the bedroom, shaky and sweating. Slowly he undressed and put on his brown silk pyjamas. He pulled back the covers and piled up the pillows. He remembered that Jen gave the children ginger ale when they became thirsty after they had been sick, so he went to the minibar in the sitting room and bent over to open it. But bending over was not a good idea, and again he had to rush for the bathroom.

Afterwards he crouched down in front of the minibar, took out a bottle of ginger ale and opened it. He went over to the bed, and, putting the bottle on the table beside him, he lay down. He was drenched in perspiration, and even being sick twice had not relieved his sharp pain.

His body felt like it was rejecting everything. He didn't blame it; his mind wanted to reject everything and just be empty and numb, so he was not surprised that his body had finally joined in. He knew if he moved he would be sick again. It all seemed unbearable. If he could now trust neither his mind nor his body to behave, what was left?

....

Mia, driving her own Jaguar, was on the outskirts of London on her way to Cedric. But her uneasiness increased by the mile. She kept thinking of Tony, of how he had looked and how angry he had been.

I can't leave things like this. What if I've done real damage to our friendship? I'm going back to see if I can find him and talk to him.

She took the first available opportunity to make a highly illegal turnaround, and she headed for Tony's hotel. When she was on a long stretch of uncrowded road she pulled over and tried to phone Cedric, using her cellular telephone. But the phone was not working, and she realised belatedly that she had not charged its batteries recently. She made a mental note to phone Cedric as soon as she arrived in Tony's suite.

Mia pulled her car up in front of Tony's hotel and dazzled the doorman with her widest smile. She handed him the keys to her car; he could deal with parking it. She knew Tony's room number from having phoned him several times. The elevator took her up to his floor. Arriving at his door, she put her hand up to knock when she was unnerved to see that the door was ajar. She slowly pushed it further, calling softly, "Tony? Tony, are you there?"

She was answered by "M-m-m-h-m-m-m," which sounded more like a groan than a word. Feeling slightly more confident, she walked through the dark living room, her way lighted only by a faint light from the bedroom.

"Tony?"

"Mia, come. I am in here."

At the door of the bedroom she got her first glimpse of him, lying on the bed, spent and perspiring. She dropped her coat on the floor and flew across the room. Feeling his forehead hot against her cool hand, she said anxiously, "Why didn't you tell me in the restaurant? Do you want me to call a doctor?"

"No. I have only the bad indigestion. Tomorrow I will be okay—"

He clapped a hand to his mouth and lurched up from the bed into the bathroom. Mia went after him, and held his forehead as he retched miserably. When he had finished and had stumbled back to the bed she wiped his face gently with a cloth wrung out of cold water.

And reluctantly, fearfully, acknowledged that her body ached with longing for the suddenly vulnerable Tony.

"I have such a pain."

"Where, darling?"

He rubbed his arm across his stomach and grimaced. She put her hand there and stroked gently. He closed his eyes. Now Mia took her hand away.

"No, *per favore,* that feels good. Don't stop."

"Maybe you have appendicitis." Mia, never one to underestimate the dangers inherent in any situation, was beginning to panic. "Let me call—"

He produced a wan version of the famous little-boy smile. "I have no appendix. It got taken out when I was nine. Now you remind me, this hurts just like that did."

The Tosca Taunt

She continued to massage gently, his vulnerability bringing her almost to the point of losing control. *Oh Cedric my love, my dearest love, are you right about me and Tony? But I love you, Cedric, I do, I do...*

Only ... Jen is dead.

And ... Tony is free.

Oh dear God.

"*Per favore,* don't stop."

"I'm getting a cramp in my hand, love. I'm in an awkward position."

"Lie down beside me. That will make it easier."

She looked into his face to see what he meant. But his eyes were guileless. She could discern only pain, not all of it physical. Jen was a fearsome presence, a formidable competitor, even dead.

Competitor? For what? Mia was about to marry Cedric, as soon as they could set another date. She wanted that so much—didn't she? Didn't she? She loved Cedric. *Loved Cedric.*

She kicked off her shoes and lay beside Tony on the bed. He was right; it was easier from this position. Being exaggeratedly careful not to let any other part of her body touch any of his, she moved her hand softly across his pain, back and forth, back and forth, willing her self-control not to fail her. But she felt as though she was on fire.

On fire. Jen's body had been on fire, and that fire had killed her. *Would this fire do the same to me,* she wondered, ruefully aware she was being operatic. Jen had been Mia's friend. What would Jen want now for Tony?

Finally Tony said, "Why did you come back to see me?"

"I didn't like the way we parted this afternoon. I don't ever want to lose you, Tony. You're my best friend."

"You will not lose me. I have no better friend than you either. And—and Cedric—I have been surprised at his generosity to me."

"He admires you. Cedric isn't given to admiring anyone except great artists, and those he holds in awe." She asked herself why. "Probably because he knows an artist is the only thing he can't become, even with his formidable intelligence and all his money."

"You are sure you will be happy with him, Mia?"

"Of course I will ... I hope ... how can anyone be sure, Tony?"

"Who knows? I wish for you two to be like me and Jen." He was quiet for a long time. She thought he had fallen asleep. She stopped moving her hand, and let her arm lie across him. But she was in great peril. She drew her arm back.

"Leave it, *per favore;* it helps."

"I thought you were asleep."

"No. I was just thinking."

"About?"

"About me and Jen. About how sometimes it is hard to go on." He smiled at her, shaking his head. "Especially hard tonight—my mind wants to reject everything and now tonight my body does the same. What is that word in English? Heart—heartbreak. The heart breaks, and then everything else inside falls apart."

Yes, thought Mia, *yes. The heart breaks ...*

"Tony darling, tell me the truth, are you—you're not

The Tosca Taunt

suicidal, are you? You would tell me, wouldn't you?" Mia feared she could not meet the challenge of losing yet another person about whom she cared deeply. For when one of her young sons had died, a long slow death from cancer, the pain had nearly destroyed her. She believed she had used up her lifetime's ration of courage.

"The truth?" Tony's voice was little more than a whisper. "The truth is, yes, I wanted to kill myself; you remember the premiere night of *Romeo et Juliette*? You all were right when you panicked about me. That was why I got so angry; I wanted that nobody should know. But since then, this sadness becomes like an ache that I have to live with for the rest of my life. No, Mia, I am not happy, but I am not suicidal any more. I have too many duties to do—including bring up my Anton and Nina."

Mia was uncertain, wondering what to do now. Tentatively she sat up and swung her legs off the bed.

"*Per favore*, don't go," he said. "I need you." There was nothing of the suggestive in his invitation. Mia thought he was like one of her children needing her touch to quell the pain of too many sweets. Only with Tony it was not too many sweets; it was, she believed, too much grief.

"Have you something I could put on, Tony love, I'll make such a mess of my clothes if I keep lying on them."

"Of course. What do you want? I have in the drawer more pyjamas, and I have in the closet a dressing gown, put on what you like."

In the bathroom she undressed down to her bra and panties and put his long yellow silk pyjama top. She had intended to put on the pants, but Tony was a tall man, and his top came almost to her knees. When she came out he looked at her and laughed. She lay down once again beside him, being careful not to touch his body with hers. He took Mia's hand and put it once again on his stomach.

"*Dio,* this pain can stop any time now, I have had enough." he said. But presently he slept.

I must leave, she thought. *I'll just lie here a little while longer to be sure he's really going to be all right, and then I'll phone Cedric and go home.* Trying to stay awake, she, tired now, fell asleep. In her sleep she turned towards Tony and tucked her body tightly against his. So that later in the night when he half awoke, he turned and put his arm around her, awakening her with a murmured, "I love you, Jen."

Mia was shocked awake. Had she been Jen for him all through this night of sickness? Of course he knew who she was, but had she been merely a substitute for the tender Jen? It was not to be endured. The press called her "Magnificent Mia," the diva with whom half the musical world was in love, and yet here she could not compete with a woman who was dead.

Having thought that, she was deeply disappointed with herself. She was about to marry a man she loved; she was spending a night with a friend who was ill and who had not invited her but who was glad she was there all the same. What more did she want? What did Tony have, what could he give her other than friendship, that would not imperil her future with Cedric? Unless ... Unless her future were with Tony. But it was late, late to think of that; she was committed to her lengthy relationship with Cedric. She had vowed to Cedric that she was not in love with Tony Amato. And at the time the words were

The Tosca Taunt

uttered she had believed them.

She muffled the cry that came unbidden, for she realised she had loved Tony Amato for years. Indeed, realised she loved two men, but perhaps loved Tony the more.

She was stifling sobs now, wanting not to awaken Tony. He moved his body against hers and tightened his arm around her. He mumbled, "Jen? Why do you cry?"

Mia could stand this no longer. She jumped off the bed and cried, "Tony, wake up! I'm not Jen; Jen is dead. I'm Mia!"

He shook his head and opened his eyes. He looked at her, and said, bewildered, "But of course you are Mia, I know that; why are you shouting at me?"

"Don't you know what you called me?"

"I did not call you anything; I was sleeping."

She sank down on the bed, sobbing, "No, no, you called me Jen! I'm not Jen, oh God Tony, I'm not Jen ..."

Tony was completely at a loss. Of course she was not Jen. Why was she so upset? He sat up slowly, thinking he felt better for his sleep. But what on earth was the matter with Mia? He put one arm around her and pulled her to him in a consoling gesture. Gently he stroked her tousled hair.

"*Per favore,* don't cry, there is nothing wrong, Mia, you see, already I am feeling better, this pain is almost gone, you have been a big help to me. If you cry for me, you must not; I will be okay. Did I really call you Jen?"

But Mia was out of control now. She took Tony's face between her hands and stared at him. "You called me Jen," she sobbed, and kissed him.

He was ill, but not that ill. And Jen was dead. He responded with a passion fuelled by lonely despair. Now Mia moved her hands down from where she had touched him earlier. His body was hard, muscled, altogether desirable.

He kissed her over and over, caressing her, undoing her lacy brassiere, slowly pulling off the lacy panties, until she was naked beside him. He was ready. At last she was to experience what had been so long denied her.

Because Jen was truly dead.

And Tony was truly free.

But suddenly he faltered, and, turning away from her, lay on his back, staring unhappily at the ceiling.

"What, what, Tony darling? Is it just that you are not well?"

"Mia, I am sorry. I should never have started."

"But why, darling? What's wrong?"

He turned and lay on his side facing her, not touching her anywhere.

"Is not you, believe me, you are the most attractive woman I know. And is not that I don't care for you, because I do. But ... oh Mia, you are ... you are not Jen ... "

"But darling, nobody will be Jen, not ever again."

"You think I don't know?"

"What about ... later? Later when you've had time to ..."

"I don't know anything about later. I only know I have to get through today without Jen, and tomorrow, and the day after, one day after another, for all my life—and you are not Jen, and you are going to marry Cedric ... "

Mia hung her head, her tousled, curly brown hair falling about her face so that Tony could not see her expression. "Don't you understand what I'm asking you, Tony?"

The Tosca Taunt

"No. I—I don't think I do. I understand that now you feel sorry for me, Mia, you want to comfort me, ... *grazie,* I am grateful, but maybe is too much ... "

There was a knock on the door. A peremptory knock. Mia jumped from the bed, and, grabbing her brassiere and pants, dashed into the bathroom where she had shed the rest of her clothes, and shut the door. Tony got off the bed and walked—slowly, for he was still shaky—from the bedroom through the sitting room to the door and called out, "Who is it?"

Cedric's voice answered. "It's me, Tony. I can't find Mia anywhere—let me in, will you?"

Tony let the chain off the door and opened it. *"Per favore,* come in. Mia is here. She—"

But Cedric slammed the door hard against the wall and confronted Tony as Mia came out from the bathroom. She had rapidly dressed and fixed her hair which fortunately was worn in a casual tangle. But Cedric knew her too well. Knew her expressions. Knew their hidden meanings.

Cedric was a dirty fighter. The ends justified the means, and Cedric had to win. Always, in whatever context. Before anyone could say anything Cedric hit Tony hard in the stomach, right into his pain. Professional opera singers often have stomach muscles as strong as those of weight lifters, but Tony had not had warning enough to tense himself against the blow. He doubled up, lurching against the wall to keep himself from going down.

Cedric wiped his hands together in a good riddance gesture. "Not much of a man, your Tony," he said acidly to Mia, who had rushed over and put her arm about Tony, still bent over, grimacing and trying to catch his breath.

"My God Cedric what have you done? Tony, are you all right?" She looked helplessly up at Cedric. "Help him!"

"I'm not touching him. Why should I?"

"You don't understand." Mia was barely controlling tears.

"No, I don't. You swore to me that you loved me. And yet at the first opportunity after Jen's death you spend the night with Amato. You're right, I don't understand."

Tony swallowed hard and spoke, needing to rescue Mia. "What is the matter with you, Cedric? I have been sick all night and Mia has looked after me. *Dio*, I am sick again—" He struggled upright with ineffectual help from Mia, and made his way unsteadily to the bathroom. He waved Mia off and closed the bathroom door.

She returned to Cedric and, grabbing him by his sleeves, confronted him. "How *could* you, Cedric? He's been in a lot of pain, God knows what you've done to him, you're so damn strong, you've likely ruptured whatever it is that's hurting him. If you've done him harm ... "

"Go on. If I've done him harm, what? What will you do to me? And what about me? Did you think of the harm you were doing to me when you spent the night with him? Do you ever think of me before him? I don't believe he was sick all night. I made him sick when I hit him." Cedric sneered, "Your hero."

Mia looked at this man, this man she had loved enough to promise to marry, this man she still loved after her fashion. "Cedric, nothing happened between us, I swear it."

She did not feel like a liar as she swore this; in deed if not in desire she had been faithful to Cedric, even though she could scarcely take credit for it. "You either say you believe me or I leave you for good. I know we've parted once before, but this time I promise you I will do my best never to see you again."

This was the one threat Cedric could not bear. Could this be true, could Amato really have been ill and in need of the help of a friend all through the night? But if it were true, why couldn't Mia have phoned him? What had distracted her so much she forgot all about him? Could he believe Mia, since she had that look about her, the I've-been-making-love look he knew so well?

If Mia had made love to Tony Amato, Cedric would kill him. It was as simple as that. Mia belonged to him.

But now Tony stumbled out of the bathroom and fell back on the bed. He held one arm tightly across his middle, and squeezed his eyes shut.

Cedric began to feel uncomfortable. He did not think he had hit Tony hard enough to cause this amount of damage; Tony was a fit, strong man. Cedric's spirits lightened slightly; maybe, just maybe the story they were telling him was true.

The phone on a table near Cedric rang. Automatically he picked it up and said hello.

"Amato?"

"Cedric Tyhurst. Can I give Mr Amato a message?"

"Sheldon Wasserman here. You are well I hope Lord Ridlough. I'm calling to see how Mr Amato is feeling. He and three others in the cast had Chinese take-out food yesterday, and the three others are quite ill with food poisoning; as a matter of fact Valentina Welles is in hospital but should be released later today."

What have I done, wondered Cedric, feeling doubt, an

emotion he rarely felt. Locking his eyes with Mia's, he said into the phone, "Tony has food poisoning too; I don't know whether he's up to talking to you."

Tony nodded that he was, and picked up the phone by his bedside. After a few minutes he said goodbye and hung up.

"At least I know what's wrong with me," Tony said, speaking to Mia. "I was beginning to think something serious was happening." He closed his eyes. Then he continued, talking now to Cedric, "You see? I *told* you I needed help in the night."

But because of what had nearly happened between him and Mia, Tony was uncomfortable with this situation. To be sure, Mia was not yet anybody's wife, but still ... Cedric looked angry, uncertain, unhappy. Cedric was rarely uncertain. Tony knew him to be a man of energy and decision, seldom confounded by any difficulty. But the challenge of wooing Mia Mitsouros had at times undone even Cedric.

Tony could only hope no permanent harm had been done by the unexpected events of this night.

Now Cedric took Mia's arm and began to urge her out the door. "Come, darling. Tony will be fine now. Surely your business here is finished."

"Stop it, Cedric, don't manhandle me. After what you did I won't leave Tony until I'm sure he's all right." Mia pulled herself away from Cedric and looked at him with distaste.

"I will be fine," Tony said. "My assistant is supposed to be here any minute now so I will have company."

As if on cue Eric knocked on the open door and walked in. He was dismayed to hear of the food poisoning.

"I told you you looked green yesterday," he said, faintly

The Tosca Taunt

accusatory.

"That's why I keep you—to let me know about these important things." Tony and Eric grinned at one another. When Tony turned his head to thank Mia, only the open door to the hall met his eyes. Mia and Cedric had gone.

Twenty-Six

The pale cream Rolls Royce belonging to Cedric Tyhurst, Viscount Ridlough, hummed as it idled, complete with impassive chauffeur, waiting for him to emerge from the London hotel so oddly named Forty Seven. The doorman would have preferred to have the Rolls park elsewhere and leave the loading zone clear, but even he, who saw altogether too many people overly imbued with a sense of their own importance, was intimidated by Viscount Ridlough. It was as though the Viscount were surrounded by an invisible armour of spikes that would impale you if you got too close and tried to thwart him.

The elevator doors leading into the hotel lobby glided open and Viscount Ridlough charged out, his female companion tripping and nearly falling as he propelled her along, his hand grasping her upper arm. The doorman, interested but far too worldly to show it, noticed how flushed Viscount Ridlough looked, how pale his companion, the diva Mia Mitsouros. Fascinating. But then the doorman was privy to many intriguing

The Tosca Taunt

scenes.

"But Cedric, my car is here, I can't just leave it," Mia protested.

"Of course you can't leave it. Blackwell will drive it back. You come with me."

She struggled ineffectually in his grasp, not wanting to make a public scene. "I don't want to come with you. Not when you're in this mood. I prefer to drive alone in my own car. Maybe by the time we get home you'll have cooled down."

"I won't let you out of my sight. Let you drive home? I know you—you wouldn't even get the car out of the garage—you'd go running straight back to Amato."

Cedric opened the passenger door of the purring Rolls and shoved Mia into the car. He ordered her to give the claim check of her car to Blackwell, and he instructed the chauffeur to drive Mia's car back to Ridlough Hall. Cedric climbed into the grey leather driver's seat. He put the car in drive gear and it roared forward with a squeal of tires. Mia gasped, but said nothing; if they were to arrive home safely, Cedric scarcely needed to be further upset. She could see his hands grasping the steering wheel so tightly his knuckles were blenched, as beads of perspiration slowly rolled down his face. He had been flushed when he left Tony's apartment; now slowly he became ashen.

As she often said to Cedric, she did love him after her fashion. Indeed one of their shared private jokes consisted of her singing to him from the musical *Kiss Me Kate*, "*I'm Always True to You Darling in my Fashion*". There was so much about Cedric that she cared about, esteemed, wanted. She was privy to his gentle side, a side few people knew he had. Mia, whose love comprised so much of the maternal, wanted—needed—to soothe, to comfort, to protect.

Suddenly Cedric said, "God, Mia, I'm so bloody sorry. You know I don't often lose my temper; I—" He swallowed hard several times, and for a scary moment Mia thought he too was going to be sick. She put her hand on his thigh and caressed it comfortingly; he gripped it hard enough to hurt her, and lifted it to his lips. Turning to stare at her, he pressed his mouth to her palm. She saw through her own welling tears that his eyes were filling too; then they heard the scream, the metallic thud, the screech of powerful brakes, the shriek of tires.

Cedric had been looking at Mia, not at the light which had turned red. The Rolls hurtled forward as Cedric tried to control it, tried to avoid cars and pedestrians who were leaping out of harm's way. Cedric finally brought the car to a halt after it had sped through the intersection. The first parking space on the left was free and Cedric, shaking now, glided the Rolls up against the curb as Mia, looking back to see the damage, cried, "What happened? Oh, Cedric, what have we done?"

Just pulling out of the intersection behind them was a large truck, whose driver, eyes on the road and one hand steering his rig, gave Cedric a sign of disgust with the other hand. But as the rig cleared the intersection, Mia saw a frightening scene. In the pedestrian walkway was an overturned baby carriage, near which a distraught black woman sobbed, holding a baby close against her, while a black man, one arm tightly around the woman's shoulders, caressed the child's head as he peered closely into its face. An angry looking group was gathering around, pointing across the road at the pale Rolls.

The Tosca Taunt

"Cedric, I think you hit a baby carriage," Mia's voice shook.

He stared at her, and she saw her tough Cedric become paralysed with the fear that he might have hurt—or perhaps even killed—a child.

She took his hand. "Come, darling, come, we've got to do something." She climbed out of the car and he quickly joined her. Running across the road as soon as they could, they reached the knot of people surrounding the black man, the woman and the baby. The crowd was restless, staring, muttering. A short ill-dressed man wearing a tweed cap sized up Cedric and Mia, their clothes, their agitated looks.

"You the blighter with the Rolls?"

"I am. Please, let me through. What can I do? Is the baby—"

"You're lucky, you bleedin' sod. Baby's fine, far as we can see, mate. But you could have killed 'im."

The crowd was angry. They surged menacingly around Cedric and Mia. Forcefully breaching the crush of people, Cedric confronted the young mother, still weeping as she clutched her baby who, to Cedric and Mia's vast relief, was now wailing lustily.

Cedric spoke to her. "I am the driver of the car, of course I'll make amends, come with me now and we'll have the baby checked over at the nearest hospital."

The tall black man, undoubtedly the father of the baby, said angrily, "Someone's calling the police, man; we don't need help from you. You one of those that thinks you own everything? You could have killed my son, man, you realise?"

"Of course I realise; you have no idea how sorry I am. It was completely my fault. Please let me make some sort of restitution."

The onlookers muttered ominously. The father said furiously, "Restitution? Restitution? Big words, fancy talk, where it get you if you killed my son, man? You be careful, or I'm going to restitute you."

The seething group surged closer to Cedric. Mia clutched his hand tightly, wondering where this was leading.

"Kill the bastard," someone shouted. "The Frenchies had it right when they guillotined this lot."

"Toffee-nosed gits," said someone else.

Cedric abruptly realised into what danger he had put himself and Mia. What to do? He was a skilled boxer, but this crowd was unlikely to fight by the Marquis of Queensberry rules. Then he thought of a solution; his effective weapon in this situation, he believed, was money. He pulled out his wallet, and, taking out the considerable amount of cash in it, he tried to hand it to the baby's father along with his card.

"Here, please, take this and my card; I will do whatever is necessary to restore your child to health if he is found hurt in any way. Money is no object."

As a ploy this seemed less than successful. Someone said, "He's insulting you, he is. These posh toffs think they can buy their way out of anything." Mia saw a couple of men with clenched fists making menacing gestures at Cedric. One of them grabbed Mia and pulled her away, saying, "Ere, we don't want to 'urt 'is woman, she had nuffink to do wiv' it, it was 'im that was drivin', 'im and 'is bloody Rolls." Mia struggled, desperately trying techniques she had learned in a self-defence course, but she was a slight woman and the man holding her

The Tosca Taunt

was strong. Now two men grabbed and held Cedric's arms, urging the baby's father to "Give it to 'im, dad, 'e bleedin' near killed your kid, give it to 'im good then."

The baby's father was an enraged man but a fair one. "I won't hit while you holding him, man, but you just watch me when you let him go."

Cedric thought, *I've a chance if they let me go, but what are they doing to my Mia?*

Muttering angrily, the two men who held Cedric's arms released him. As soon as he was free Cedric tensed his stomach muscles further and began to move his arms into a defensive position, but the young black father was amazingly quick, and he hit Cedric hard in the solar plexus. Fortunately Cedric had been prepared; unlike Tony Amato this morning, Cedric was scarcely hurt.

The crowd had been so focussed inward on the action at their centre that they had not heard the approach of the two policemen.

"Here now, what's going on? You there—" this addressed at the black man, "—leave off, what do you think you're doing?"

But Cedric, catching his breath, said quickly, "No, officer, this is all my fault, these people have nothing to do with it."

....

Some hours later, Cedric found himself charged with reckless driving endangering life and limb; the baby's parents found themselves vastly relieved that their firstborn son was unhurt, though a little aggrieved at all this sleep-depriving attention; and the young parents found themselves utterly astonished to discover that Cedric would set up a generous trust fund for their son which would ensure his future.

Cedric was sufficiently unnerved by this experience to send for Blackwell, who drove Mia, Cedric and the Rolls carefully to Ridlough Hall. Cedric and Mia entered silently together through its massive oak doors. Mia looked searchingly at Cedric when they reached the top of the stairs, but his look was cold, inscrutable. Each longed to forgive and be forgiven; each was too proud, and too ashamed now, to make the first move. At the doors to their adjoining suites, they silently went separate ways.

Mia shut her door and, leaning against it, burst into tears. Cedric shut his door and, leaning against it, put his head back and grimaced in pain. He had barely made it here without showing Mia that the pain in his chest, that which had so frightened them both earlier this year, was back. But he would not show her tonight, not after this impossible day. If she came to him now it would be because she loved him, wanted him, and not because he was in pain and needed her. Tony Amato had attracted Mia and kept her with him last night with illness and need; Cedric would be loved for himself alone, and not because he fulfilled some sort of maternal requirement for his woman.

Mia trailed from her sitting room into her bedroom and slowly began to shed her clothes. The last time she had shed these particular clothes had been very early this morning, when she had lain beside Tony and had helped him while she herself disintegrated. And then—and then—what exactly? What had happened between them?

Mia, now in a lavender negligee, sat at her antique dressing table and stared at herself in its Venetian mirror. Her turquoise eyes stared back, cold, mysterious even to herself. She picked up her silver-backed brush and began slowly to brush her bright brown hair.

She loved Cedric. She would marry Cedric. Must marry Cedric. Nothing had happened between her and Tony Amato to change that. Nothing had happened between her and Tony Amato. Full stop. Tony had said she felt sorry for him and to help console him she had been willing—willing to—yes, it must be that. She had to be right about her feelings for Cedric after all these years, did she not? She had certainly given Cedric a lot of time, a lot of thought.

So this aching longing when she thought of Tony was only compassion, only a desire to comfort. *It had to be only that. Oh God, it had to.*

She needed to be reassured. She needed Cedric's arms about her. She strode to the adjoining double doors between her suite and Cedric's. But Cedric's door was locked. She tried the doorhandle again, at first disbelieving, then suddenly angry. They had had a terrible, frightening day. Did he not know she would need him, did he not need her?

It did not cross her mind that he might be ill and not want her to know. Angrily she left her apartment and tried the corridor door into his rooms. But it too was locked. She went slowly back into her room. What did he mean to do? He had been hurt, jealous, out of control, and then desperately remorseful about the accident to the baby—but to reject her now? Yet in the car he had apologised, just before they had gone through that red light. Had he since had time to think, had he reconsidered?

She contemplated pounding on the adjoining door and

demanding to see him. But by now there had been time for her pride to overcome her longing and she did not. She could not know that he lay on his bed in a haze of pain, not realizing his doors were locked, wishing she would come to him, needing her, afraid he was dying, afraid she loved him no more. Afraid she loved Tony Amato.

Maybe it would be simpler if I were dying, Cedric thought, and then despite his pain had to laugh at himself for such a melodramatic notion. *But at least dying would put me out of my misery.*

Twenty-Seven

Doctor Victor Macready Kilbride was on the phone, speaking long distance to Mark Reinhard. He had his story well-calculated so he hoped he could not be tripped up.

"Yeah, the weather here in New Orleans is better than up there in Canada this time of year," he said in reply to Mark's comment. Then, "That's right, I'm a dentist, but by avocation I'm a non-fiction writer. You may know my book, *Buried Treasure, Silver and Gold?* It's about silver and gold mining. I self-published it a while back, actually it didn't sell well at all. But I'm fascinated by mines and mining."

"I'm sorry, I don't know the book." Mark tried unsuccessfully to sound regretful. "I don't get much time for reading."

"Anyway," continued Victor, "now I'm writing a book about mining throughout the ages, and I want to finish it with a chapter on the most modern mines operating today. Yours—that is, the Delson Mine—has been pointed out to me as a particularly fine example of the modern mine, and I was hoping I could come up and observe, you know, do research for a couple of days. I would enjoy a guided tour, and after that I would just—with your permission of course—wander around and take notes and photographs."

Mark Reinhard considered this request. Security at a gold mine like theirs dictated that they could not let just anyone wander in and observe, "case the joint" as it were, so he was obligated to ask for references from this Doctor Kilbride. Otherwise Mark saw no reason to deny the request, except that it was generally a nuisance having outsiders wandering loose.

"Oh certainly, no problem there," rejoined Victor, speaking of the references. "Just write or Fax to the American Dental Association and they'll tell you whatever you need to know about me. Now, you say there is no village nearby where I could stay in a hotel overnight; so what would you suggest? Day trips in and out to the nearest town that has a hotel?"

"If your references check out, Doctor Kilbride, and if you plan to come soon, we have a cabin not being used right now and I see no reason why you couldn't use it for a night. You'd have to make up your own bed of course, we don't have maid service here, but I'm sure that wouldn't be a problem."

The conversation ended. Victor hung up the phone, rubbed his hands together in glee at his successful ploy, and went into the library to his liquor cabinet where he poured himself a celebratory bourbon.

....

Dear Charlie;

The Tosca Taunt

I apologise for taking so long to write you. I'm sure I didn't thank you properly for your incredible kindness to a total stranger. I've settled in well here at the mine, and have met many nice people. You said I didn't look like a sous-chef, but I'm managing all the same; never forget, as the mine boss up here says constantly, you can't tell how far a frog can jump from looking at him!

(Do I tell him I've got amnesia, Jen wondered? Could he possibly help me? No, how could he?)

I hope everything is going well with you and your large family. Thank you once again for your help and kindness,

Sincerely,

Jen Noonan

Now I'd better print the address, thought Jen; *I have such small handwriting, so hard to read. Maybe I should have printed the whole note. Do you suppose I'm a doctor? Nobody can read their writing either.* Amused at the thought, she carefully printed Charlie's address on the envelope. Then she remembered the letter she had hand printed—at least she believed it was she who had hand printed it—to the woman she addressed as Mama. Her artist's acute visual memory caused her to sense an anomaly. She rummaged in her desk and found the letter. Just as she thought—the print on the letter and the print on the envelope were completely different from one another, obviously not printed by the same person.

She felt a sudden chill. Whoever had printed that letter to "Mama", it was certainly not she, Bridget Jennifer Noonan. But if she had not written that letter, who had? And why did she have it in her possession? Holding it in her hand, she stared unseeing out the window towards the rugged, treed terrain and the freezing lake, a wilderness as vast and unknowable as her own mind, as her own submerged identity.

....

Victor Macready Kilbride had devised two plans of action, one in hopes that he could surprise Bryony alone, and another contingency plan if he came on her when he was being shown around the mine. He was hoping fervently that it would be plan A, with Bryony alone, that he could make operative.

He had time to savour his delicious ideas on the journey up to the mine. After a surprisingly long and arduous trip to Timmins, and an unnerving helicopter ride in to the landing pad belonging to the mine, he at last found himself being shown around the site itself by the mine boss, this Mark Reinhard fellow to whom he had first spoken. Victor was introduced to engineers, geologists, and some staff. Needing to make a convincing impression, he nodded courteously to everyone he passed on paths, in rooms and corridors and of course in the mine itself.

Although appearing to listen intently to descriptions and explanations, and despite the taking of photographs and of copious notes in a large blue notebook, he was actually searching everywhere for Bryony. His thoughts were in disarray; he was going to take pleasure in thumping her hard so she would understand once and for all that this type of behaviour would not be tolerated, but he kept thinking of her beautiful round breasts, of the soft moisture of her body, of the thrills he used to have, forcing her to make love to him.

Gerald Geraint had said Bryony worked in the kitchens, but

the only woman Victor had seen there, pretty but definitely not Bryony, was dressed in a white coverall, with her hair covered in a chef's cap. The wiry head cook had said cursorily "Hi, I'm Steve, this's Jen," and had gone on with his work. The woman called Jen looked at him with beautiful dark blue eyes, nodded, and continued stirring something. Victor would have liked her for a patient.

As he was escorted upstairs to the staff living quarters, he saw that each bedroom had a number, and under that number, a name. And finally he found number 17, and under the number a card with the name Noonan printed on it. Exulting, he knew he was nearly to his goal.

....

The day Victor Macready Kilbride arrived at the mine, Jen received the oddest letter from Charlie Demchuk.

Dear Jen;

I was real glad to get your note and to know youre okay. Ive wondered about you, and just the other day me and my wife Barb that I told you about, learned something that might be interesting to you. I dont want to say more in a letter, but do you think we could meet somewhere and talk confidential, Im kind of concerned about this. I dont want to scare you or sound mysterious, please dont get worried, but phone me when you can.

Me and my family are fine, the kids are growing up too fast.

All the best,
Charlie Demchuk

Jen read this letter with both excitement and foreboding. Was there a chance she was about to learn from Charlie what she had been doing on that logging road, whether she had been raped, and maybe even who she really was? Likely not who she was; where would Charlie find that out? But he could have learned something about whoever had left her on that back road. Walking quickly down the corridor to her room after work, intending to phone Charlie immediately, she remembered he had said he went to bed very early and got up early. It was already ten o'clock. Charlie had given her both his home phone number and his mobile phone number, but she decided to wait until the next day to call.

....

Jen could not know that Victor Macready Kilbride, lurking out of sight for some time, had glimpsed her back retreating down the hall. His gut quivered with anticipation, for that was Bryony all right, wearing the grey cashmere slacks and sweater she had bought just before he'd hit her a bit too hard because of her extravagance. It was after she got out of the hospital that time, that she left him. But what else could he have done except discipline her? She had forgotten the rules. She had no right to buy anything without him saying she could. She had a whole wardrobe full of designer clothes, beautiful expensive stuff, had he ever said she couldn't buy them? Well, maybe once or even twice. But otherwise he had been generosity itself to her. After all, he needed her to look good when they were hobnobbing with Leonard LeComte's society crowd. But why did she go out and buy those cashmere things without his permission?

As the woman in front of him progressed down the corridor, he noted that she had bleached her hair, kind of a pretty blonde colour. It sure did look natural. Bryony would fuck him tonight, right now. He would see to that. And tomorrow she would come home with him. He would make her an offer she could not refuse—well, a threat, actually. Call a spade a spade.

And if she did refuse? He was turning a possible refusal over in his mind just as his hand was turning over the folding utility knife in his pocket. If she refused this time, that effing disrespectful spendthrift flirtatious Bryony, she would learn once and for all never to refuse him again. He would start on her with his hands. But if they were ineffective, then he would whip out the knife. That would get her receptive. Violence always got Bryony receptive except when he miscalculated and rendered her unconscious. But he would not miscalculate tonight. On the periphery of his thought were the possible consequences of his violence to Bryony. He found it strange to realise how little that mattered to him tonight.

He thought she would turn into her room but she did not; She walked to the end of the corridor and down the stairs. He hoped she was going out to take a walk in the crisp night air. Outside, yes; so much the better. If she cried out, who would hear in this godforsaken place? He followed her down the stairs and out the door, quietly closing it behind him.

The fresh-smelling air was cold and still. Victor could see Bryony's back retreating down a path towards the partly frozen lake. It was late enough that nobody was around out of doors but Bryony and Victor following her, ducking from shadow to shadow. Wasn't she cold in just that sweater and slacks? He guessed the answer had to be no, for she could have picked up a coat as she had passed her room.

The pines whispered their sibilant messages. A wolf howled

and was answered by another. Victor saw Bryony sit down on a large rock at the edge of the lake, and stare out at its surface, roughened now by the ice forming. He crept from shadow to shadow until he was directly behind her. She raised her head at another cry from the wolf. From behind, Victor quickly slipped his big hands around her throat and tightened his grip. She made raucous sounds, gasping, choking, clutching at his hands, struggling ineffectually against her powerful assailant.

Breathing heavily, he growled out, amidst her writhings and his attempts to keep his hands tightly fixed, "Okay, Bryony, you've played this game once too often. I'm going to loosen my grip, and you're going to promise to come home, or I'll kill you right now and weigh you down with rocks and dump you in this lake where nobody'll ever find you."

Victor slowly released his grip. Limp now, the woman fell to the ground, face down. He turned her over roughly. And looked in shock at the unconscious woman he had choked; it was the *sous-chef* he had met briefly in the kitchen. Quickly he felt her pulse, he hadn't killed this woman for Godssake had he? No, thank goodness, he had not. He saw she was coming around, and he lifted her into a sitting position. She was making ugly choking sounds as she fought to regain her breath. Victor decided to pretend he had found her lying there. He would play doctor.

"Are you all right?" He feigned great professional anxiety. "Do you know who you are? What is your name?"

"My name? My name, it's—it's Jenetta Maclean." She stopped, bewildered. "No, that's wrong. It's Bridget Jennifer Noonan. No, I—I don't seem to know. What happened? Who are

The Tosca Taunt

you?" She felt her throat gingerly. "My neck hurts. It's hard to breathe."

"I'm Doctor Kilbride, I'm visiting the mine doing research and I was taking a walk when I came on you lying here, you must have fainted, can you get up? I'll help you inside."

"I didn't faint, my throat was hurting, I choked, isn't that what happened? Could it be my allergies?"

What allergies? Have I just remembered something else? I told this doctor my name is Jenetta Maclean, but that doesn't seem right ... but ... there was a ... a city, they spoke French, it was ... was it Montreal, I seem to remember, I was a child, I'm sure I was called Jenetta Maclean, I ... my parents, why don't I remember my parents? ... I played on a swing, a rope swing tied on a tree with my ... my sister, what was her name, Alice, no, it was ... it was Allison ... and then ... and then, oh there must be more, but I don't remember.

'I'm remembering!" she clutched at Victor's arm.

"You're remembering what happened to you?" Victor was wary, apprehensive.

"No. I'm really remembering. I'm sorry; you won't understand what I'm talking about. It doesn't matter. Will you help me back to my room? I feel a bit sick."

Victor supported her as they returned to the building. She led him up the stairs to the room with Noonan on the door.

"Is that your name, Noonan?" Victor asked, as bewildered as she by the turn of events, but also very angry at Bryony and at that stupid Gerald Geraint.

"No. I mean, yes. I am Bridget Jennifer Noonan."

"You don't seem very sure," Victor said, wondering how badly he had hurt her. Had he cut off the blood supply to her brain for a bit too long? "Will you be okay?"

"Yes, thank you, I feel better now."

But Victor was unable to contain himself. He blurted, "But you have Bryony's clothes on."

"Pardon?" Jen frowned, wondering whether what he had just said fit into the puzzle of who she was.

"I thought you—from the back you looked just like my wife Bryony. You even have exactly the clothes she had."

By this time they had crossed the threshold and were in Jen's room. Not always a tidy woman, she had left the closet door open, and one of her handbags, the Louis Vuitton, was on the desk. The clothes that Victor could see hanging in the closet were similar to Bryony's more recent purchases, and the splendid blue handbag was like the one he had bought for her some months ago. Even the battered luggage looked like Bryony's, except hers had been new last time he saw it. He stared at Jen in anger and puzzlement.

"Who the hell *are* you? Dammit, you must know where Bryony is—you have her things. Where the—where did you steal them from? Where is she?"

Self-control was not his forte. He could not contain his frustration, his fury. He grabbed Jen tightly by the upper arms, and shook her violently as he kicked the door closed behind him. Then, remembering himself, he stopped shaking her but still held her.

Choking still from the injury to her throat, she struggled. She tried unsuccessfully to knee him. She managed, "No! Stop it! You've got it wrong, I got these clothes—" and then realised that she really did not know, and that maybe he had it right after all.

The Tosca Taunt

He released his grip slightly.

"Will you let me go? I don't know how I got these clothes," she rasped. "I only know where. They were in a suitcase, I thought they were mine." She had an inspiration. "Let go of me, I have to show you something, maybe you can help me."

"Help you? Help you do bloody what?" Breathing hard, Victor released her.

For a moment Jen rubbed her arms, grimacing. Then she hit him hard across the face. His arms shot towards her but he mastered his temper and slowly lowered them. She said, "You're a brutal bastard! Don't even think of touching me again—what's the matter with you? But—but I have to tell you, because you might just know something that will help me. You see, I—I don't know who I am. I have amnesia. All I can remember is that I came to, near a logging road with this suitcase beside me. I was badly bruised and scratched up. The purse was there, and there was a letter—I have to show you the letter."

She rummaged in her desk and pulled out the letter. She held it out to Victor, and he discerned a wild hope in her eyes.

Quickly he read its contents. Had it been handwritten instead of printed he would have recognised its author more easily. He was unsure, except that the style and content were so Bryony, and unfortunately so fitted the situation. He sank down into a chair.

Jen backed against her bed. "You?" she asked. "You're the husband?

"Yes, but you don't understand. Bryony is—" *What is Bryony?* What could he say to win this woman's confidence? If he could believe the amnesia story, she might be some sort of link to Bryony even though she did not know it. "—is mentally ill. She imagined I was a sadistic husband, but I wasn't, not really."

Weren't you, thought Jen? *But you have just been vicious to me for no reason.*

"She was always trying to get away from me," Victor continued, "even though I gave her a good life, everything a normal woman could want. She's ill, you understand. Very ill. Maybe you can help me find her. Where was this logging road where you fetched up with the suitcase?"

"Near the sawmill at Meilleurville." She saw the name meant nothing to him. "That's about in the middle of Ontario. It was on October 11. Is that any help?"

"Absolutely none, except that Bryony had left me just before. But our home is in New Orleans, and Bryony's a real city girl. Can't stand country living, can't stand cold weather, what the hell would she be doing way up in Ontario in the wilderness and cold? It doesn't fit. But how can I be sure you're telling me the truth?"

"It's the truth as I know it. I told you, I have amnesia. Although just before we came in here I suddenly remembered what might be my real name and something about being brought up in Montreal." She put her hand to her throat and sat down on the bed. "I don't feel well. Please leave—I can't help you any more than this."

Victor looked at her pallor. He considered his role in this bizarre incident—a much heavier role than apparently she could remember, and decided he had better go. In spite of himself, he believed her story. She didn't look like either a common thief or

The Tosca Taunt

a liar – her eyes were too clear, too honest, her expression too open. But just in case she remembered any more, including more specific details on the whereabouts of Bryony, he gave her his card and asked her to let him know. Meanwhile, he said he would go to the spot she mentioned, and see what he could find. She extracted a reluctant promise from him, that if he learned anything that could help her, he would reciprocate.

At this point these unlikely collaborators parted. And, Victor thought, he'd keep looking for Bryony, but he wasn't going to bother about this stupid but innocent broad any more. His opinion of Jen's idiocy was reinforced when, on his way home to New Orleans, Victor rented a car and drove down the road to the sawmill at Meilleurville. But none of that cold, dripping wilderness could have anything to do with the Bryony he knew. Obviously the woman at the mine was a nut case, even though the puzzle of what appeared to be Bryony's luggage and clothes niggled at him as he sat on the plane that was taking him home to New Orleans. The only solution that made any sense was that Bryony's luggage had been stolen, not by Jen but by someone who, once they opened it and looked in, were disappointed with the contents and dumped it where Jen said she found it. But this mystery would remain unsolved, and would niggle at him for years.

....

The next morning when Jen opened her eyes, she thought for a moment she was replaying the scene when she awoke on the mountain, so battered did she feel. She struggled stiffly from her bed, dressed, wondered how she had managed to bruise her throat, and put on a concealing scarf. She decided before she went in to work to phone Charlie Demchuk. Her voice at first sounded rough and strangled, even to herself. "Charlie, hi, it's me, Jen Noonan, how are you, what's the mystery?"

There was a hesitation. Then Charlie said, "I'm fine, we're all fine, I'm glad to hear from you. Listen, Jen, I feel real funny trying to tell you about this over the phone. Like I said in my note, it would be better if—is there any chance you could come out to Meilleurville and see me? I know you guys have to leave those isolated mines every few weeks; could you come on your way home for your next leave? This is important. Please trust me."

"I do trust you, Charlie, you likely have no idea how much. Yes, we're supposed to leave here every month for two weeks; I didn't leave last time because I don't have any—I mean—Charlie, I just didn't leave here. But my next leave is coming up on Saturday, and I'd love to come out. Is there a hotel near where you live? Could I stay there and meet with you?"

Charlie said, "Actually if you'd like, my wife Barb says she'd be happy to have you come and stay with us. I finished the attic; we have a nice guest room up there with a little bathroom and all, that's where my parents and the in-laws stay when they visit. You know we have a bejillion kids and all their friends, it's not restful but it's fun, and I'd kinda like you to meet Barb. Would you come? I mean, we gotta talk about this thing, it's real important."

Jen calculated quickly. She felt she could trust Charlie; he had been so good to her, so straight and kind and generous. She accepted the offer.

"Charlie, yes, I'd be so pleased. Truth to tell, I don't exactly have a place to go on my time off, so I'd be glad to spend some time with you all." She made a sudden decision about her amnesia. "I have to tell you something too, when we meet."

"Maybe the two somethings have to do with each other," Charlie said. "Well now, how do you want to arrange this?"

....

Jen decided not to tell Mark about Charlie's mystery. All she said was, "Mark, I'm taking my next leave properly—I'm leaving for two weeks, I'm going to stay with friends, you remember, I told you about Charlie, in Meilleurville, for a few days."

It was very late, and they were the last two people in the lounge, enjoying an old film, *A Tale of Two Cities* with the British actor Dirk Bogarde. Now Mark said to her, "Our leaves are the same time; I have to do business and I have to speak at a conference in Toronto during the last ten days of my two weeks out, but the first three days, the long weekend, I'm free. There's an Inn called Langdon Hall, not far from Toronto, it's a *Relais et Chateaux* Inn, Jen, you'd like it. Would you come there with me?" He was sitting beside her on the long chesterfield, his arm around her shoulders.

She rested her head on his shoulder, longing and doubt warring together, dictating her first response. "Oh, Mark, I want to—and I don't want to. It's so hard not knowing whether I'm free!"

He tightened his grip on her shoulders. Reflectively he said, "It seems to me your mind has set you free. If you have no recollection of a man you may or may not be married to, who seems by the evidence of your letter to be a brute, you can hardly be unfaithful to him, not in any emotionally significant way. Please, Jen. You've said 'no' long enough. It's time we explored this—this—" He interrupted himself by kissing her.

She responded with all the warmth he had sensed in her from the beginning. And decided she had to tell him that the "Dear Mama" letter was not written by her. She was not quite ready yet to tell him about that Doctor Kilbride who had rescued her when she apparently fainted out by the lake, nor that this doctor believed the "Dear Mama" letter was printed by his wife. Because the rest of his story seemed to indicate that Jen was a thief. She could not bear to give Mark a reason to think her dishonest, a reason to have her fired from her job because she might be a criminal, unless and until she absolutely had to. She already feared she might be implicated in violent death; now it appeared she might have to add theft to that.

So she merely said, "I've realised I didn't write the letter to Mama, the one I showed you; it's not printed in my printing."

He looked at her, dismayed. He hated to admit it to himself, but it suited his plans for her to have, or to believe she had, a brutal, unsuitable husband, if she had one at all. "But that could mean—"

"It means that 'T', whoever he is, is now a blank slate for me. He could be a marvellous person. And have I any right to betray him, until I learn what kind of man he is?"

"Or you could be a widow, or divorced—"

"I could be a lot of things. The point is, I don't know. And something in me says not to betray what might be beautiful, before I *do* know ... "

Mark removed his arm from around her shoulders. He

The Tosca Taunt

stared at the floor.

"This doesn't say much for your feelings about me, does it. You're automatically assuming that what we have, and what is yet to come, will be less than—"

She stopped him with a long passionate kiss. And said, "I assume nothing, Mark. But if I'm not true to my instincts, how am I ever going to know who I really am? How are *you* going to know? You think you want me, but don't you need to know who that 'me' is?"

"You think I can't tell? Your soul shines through, whatever you know or don't know about yourself. Come with me, Jen. Please. I'll book separate rooms for us. Just to show you that my—" he burst out laughing and had difficulty finishing the phrase, "—my intentions are honourable."

She laughed too. "We sound like a pair of proper Victorian lovers. Just ... bear with me on this, Mark, please; it can't be too much longer. I've remembered things; I'm going to spend some of these two weeks seeing if I can trace more about myself; surely there will be a record somewhere of Jenetta Maclean, artist, who lived in Montreal as a child and who has a sister Allison. I'm feeling quite hopeful; my memory seems to be coming back in great chunks. And, yes, of course I'll come with you on condition of separate rooms ... "

Then they pooled resources, trying to think of ingenious ways Jen might find out who she was, without going first to the police. But even together they were unable to conceive of much more than what Jen had already tried.

So the next day she phoned Charlie to tell him she would be later arriving than she had anticipated, since she now had to add the three days of the weekend with Mark to her allotted days to research her past. She did not tell Charlie why the extra three days had been added to her stay in southern Ontario.

After nightfall on Saturday, Mark and Jen arrived at Langdon Hall, a pillared and porticoed red brick Georgian building in a setting of dark pines, quite suitable, thought Jen, for their Victorian tryst. Her rooms were sumptuously furnished, with an enormous bed in the bedroom and a handsome blend of real and pseudo-antique furniture in the sitting room. On the coffee table was a tall arrangement of flowers. Mark had a small bedroom with double communicating doors, adjoining Jen's apartment.

After a long leisurely supper and a great deal of wine, they climbed the stairs to her apartment. Jen was floating, floating on far too much champagne as Mark kissed her and began, almost imperceptibly to her in her state, to undress her gently. But as he pulled down the strap of her blue lace brassiere and bent to kiss her in places she did not want to be kissed—at least until she knew about "T"—she finally realised through her mist of champagne that Mark hoped she had changed her mind about separate rooms. Laughing, she pushed him away, trying to discourage him, but he, tender though he was with her, was not about to be discouraged so easily. Finally she pushed him hard, still smiling but very dizzy, in an almost altered state from the wine. And then she said the terrible thing. "No, Tony my darling, not tonight, please ..."

Mark stopped abruptly. He withdrew his body so that he touched her nowhere, and said, "You called me Tony-my-darling. Who the—who is darling Tony?"

The Tosca Taunt

She was abruptly sober. She had no idea who Tony was; she knew only that the initial inside her wedding ring was "T". She looked at Mark's face, his expression an impossible mixture of compassion, anger, frustration. "Oh Mark, I don't know. I'm so sorry. But—"

"I know." His voice was sardonic. "Like you said before, you can't make love to me until you find out. Whoever you are, you're obviously a loyal type. Okay, okay, if you'll forgive me for trying my luck when I promised not to, I'll forgive you—for—for what?" He hit his forehead lightly with his fist. "God Mark you ass, now you're going to forgive her for *remembering?*"

"What's to forgive—for either of us?"

"Right, maybe I worded that badly. Do you want to go on with our weekend or should we get out of here tomorrow morning?"

"You mean you'd be willing to stay even if I won't—"

"Sure. We always have fun together. I won't push you, not until you're ready; this time I really mean it. I do understand your problem, even though it would be easier for me if I didn't. But there are plenty of things we can do here. We can ride horseback, we can explore the countryside, we can watch videos, they seem to have a video library here—"

"Oh Mark, you're such a good man; you don't deserve anyone as confused as I am."

"You let me decide what I deserve. You have to know by now that you're no one-weekend stand as far as I'm concerned, Jen. I've tried to keep the lid on it, but I'm getting dangerously serious about you. So the sooner you regain your memory the better—I hope!"

Jean Dell

They adjusted their dishevelled clothes and sat together in the living room. They both hoped fervently that she would be able to trace who she was from what she had remembered so far, if she did not spontaneously remember the rest of her life soon. Because what was between them was becoming unbearable, with all this unknowing.

The following evening after a happy, strenuous day riding, hiking, exploring, they decided to watch a video of the comedy *When Harry Met Sally*. Mark put the video into the machine, and, unfamiliar remote control in hand, pushed the wrong button; for a moment whatever was on television came on the screen.

It was a dark man, with his back to the camera, standing on the roof of a building that, judging by the distant skyline, was in Rome. Music swelled, shots rang out, the dark man fell, covered in blood. Mark pushed another button just as Jen cried, "Get it back, get it back, quickly!"

Seeing the urgency on her face Mark began to push buttons on the control. But he had lost the channel, and by the time he found it again there was nothing left of the broadcast but the technical credits superimposed and crawling down the closed curtains of some theatre.

"Mark, Mark, that was my nightmare! How extraordinary! It was only an opera! Maybe I'm not a murderess, maybe I haven't killed anyone after all! But why would I keep dreaming about an *opera*?"

"What are you talking about? Did you actually believe you were a murderess?"

Stumbling over her words, so relieved was she to learn what her recurring nightmare was about, she explained.

The Tosca Taunt

"Only who was the dark man? I keep seeing that same man—at least I think it's him—in other dreams too, not just the dream where he is killed, the same back, the same shirt, the same curly black hair, but I can never see his face, I always wake up before I can identify him, oh Mark! What opera singer was that?"

"You're asking me? I don't know opera singers. What opera was it? I don't even know that."

"Why, it was *Tosca*, of course. Is there a *TV Guide* around?"

Eagerly she thumbed through the Guide she found with other information on hotel amenities, sure she would learn the names of the singers. But when she found the listing, all it said was "*Tosca*, Puccini opera of political intrigue." Oh, but she had come so close, so close! She was both excited and afraid. She was on the brink, she knew it. If only she knew of what she was on the brink! She took Mark's hand, and they began to watch their video. But she could not have described the plot afterwards; fear and a mysterious longing so filled her imagination.

Twenty-Eight

"But darling, nobody will be Jen, not ever again," Mia had said to Tony just before Cedric knocked so peremptorily on his hotel suite door. And those words and their context had gone around and around in Tony's head ever since, blocking conversation, blocking action, almost blocking coherent thought. He knew that nobody would ever again be Jen, of course; that was not the issue. But did this mean he would never again be able to make love to a woman because she was not Jen?

At the moment he believed that if he absolutely had to, difficult though it would be, he could survive even that; he could survive on just the memory of Jen. He realised he had, perhaps foolishly, put her on a pedestal so high that no woman in his life would ever equal her. He could not imagine falling in love with anyone else. But still, to live a life of celibacy because no woman was Jen? Logic told him this was likely not desirable. But having arrived at this point, he again confronted the phrase that would

The Tosca Taunt

not stop, "But darling, nobody will be Jen, not ever again."

These thoughts filled his time until he arrived at the rehearsal hall two days after having been poisoned by the egg rolls. This would be the first rehearsal for the four principals since their illness. Tony greeted the now fragile looking Valentina Welles with "You don't look so good. Should you be here?"

"No. But I need the rehearsal, Tony. Besides, do you think you look any better than I do? You're such a lovely shade of green. At least I don't *look* green." She grinned. It was hard for a black woman to look green.

"Is an unfair advantage," Tony said, laughing.

After a hard session which left the four still queasy principals even more wan than before, Sir Sheldon and the stage director called it a day. As the singers were getting their possessions together preparatory to leaving, a concerned Tony said to the drawn Valentina, "You look really bad, you know. I will see you to your hotel if you like. I feel worried about you."

"I'd be glad of the company, Tony. I may be just hungry—I confess I feel pretty wobbly; what an awful, sick time I've had!"

"You were alone when you got sick? Not—not that it is my business—" Tony was embarrassed at his tactless question.

"I was until I got sick enough that I phoned the emergency number. Then there were so many people around I could hardly take it in. And the ambulance and so on, I've never had such a frantic experience."

They climbed into the car they had ordered, and Valentina gave the name of her hotel, The Russell, in Russell Square. Once there, she said to Tony, "Come on into the brasserie with me—I think I might just be a bit hungry finally, and they make a great chowder here, almost as good as in San Francisco."

"Why not? I am not hungry either but we have to keep up the strength for the singing."

They emerged from their car, and ambled through the tawny marble foyer of the large Victorian building. Soon they were sitting across from one another in the Virginia Woolf brasserie, eating crusty French rolls and a marvellous fish chowder, much too spicy for their battered digestions but so good they were both willing to gamble. Indeed a willingness to gamble went with their profession; each night they performed, they played the odds that their voices would not betray them.

Valentina looked up from her soup to find Tony staring at her.

"What, Tony?"

"I have not said something."

"I know. What is the something you have not said?"

"Not my business, I was just thinking ... " He stopped and smiled.

There ensued a silence, broken finally by Valentina. "Come on, Tony, we've become such good friends lately. Just say it."

"I am only thinking that you are always alone. Is it that you have someone at home in San Francisco? You are maybe committed? Because I see everywhere men wanting to be with you, and always you are saying no. You have maybe a mysterious secret?"

She smiled her exotic smile, and then was suddenly serious. So serious indeed that she looked as though she were going to cry.

Tony hurriedly backpedalled. "I see I have been not tactful. I apologise. You don't tell me any more, *per favore,* I understand—"

"Yes, you probably do, having lost so much yourself..." She covered her mouth with her long rosy-tipped fingers. Tony could see she was troubled and determined not to show it. It was obvious to him he should not have questioned her, especially when she was still feeling weak and vulnerable. Grinning the famous little-boy grin he said lightly, "We change the subject, okay? I have wanted to talk to you for a long time about our *Fanciulla,* to ask have you been happy with the DVD and video? I think it has been cleverly done."

She did not answer him. Finally she said, "Tony, may I change my mind? I'd like to tell you my little story. I know you'll understand, and you'll see why I want it kept a secret ... Come on up to my room, if you've time ... "

And presently Tony found himself in Valentina's hotel room, lounging beside her on the rich dark blue fabric of an overstuffed couch, the scent from port in his glass wafting up at him, while she told him a tale about herself and the writer Julian LeComte which astonished him. He remembered the quiet, attentive Julian hovering around Valentina, when she and Tony had performed in the filmed *Fanciulla del West* in Canada.

But he had not realised that Julian and Valentina had fallen so deeply in love, nor of course that Julian's bigoted father had used all his wealth and power to separate his only son from the black singer. Valentina said that despite not having seen one another for more than two years, she and Julian still could not forget each other and get on wholeheartedly with their separate lives.

Tony's arm was behind Valentina on the chesterfield when she finished her tale and looked at him, her eyes bright with tears. He drew her to him. She put her head down on his broad, comforting shoulder.

"I'm foolish, I know; there are obviously other attractive men around," Valentina said, but her voice caught in the middle.

"Not foolish, Valentina; just a normal woman caught in a sad love story. I have to agree with you that as things stand there is not much hope for you and Julian."

He reflected on the mystery of love, how fragile and yet how enduring it is. He said slowly, "This is why operas like *Tristan and Isolde* and *Romeo et Juliette* are so popular. One way or another we have all lost someone we cannot forget."

Tony was quiet for a moment, and then blurted, "I can imagine—" His voice cracked. He cleared his throat. "—how *I* would have felt if Jen and I had been stopped from experiencing what we have together—" Tony swallowed hard. "Had, I mean, *had* together—" He stopped.

Valentina was staring at him. She drew away from him, then reached out and drew one finger slowly down his cheek. "This may be 'Send In The Clowns' as far as timing is concerned, but, as I said, there are other attractive men around ... "

He laughed and stared at her, for a millisecond not quite taking her meaning. Then he brought his lips down on hers, at first gently exploring, and then hard, passionate.

She responded with the pent-up passion of her frustrated love for Julian LeComte. She had found Tony Amato attractive from the moment they had met, but had not considered him a

The Tosca Taunt

potential lover because he was happily married and she had scruples about that. Besides, at that point she had just met Julian, and she was decidedly intrigued.

But now, Jen Amato was dead, and a lonely Tony would have to create a different life without her. And since Valentina could never have Julian, she could do a lot worse than to explore what Tony Amato was all about.

A lot worse.

She began to unbutton his shirt. Already he had pulled up her sweater; his hands caressing her small, firm breasts.

Once more Tony thought of Mia's words, that no one would be Jen, not ever again. He knew himself well; he knew he would function better in his busy, stressful life with someone understanding at his side. *If he could not have Jen -- if he could not have Jen — not ever again — O Madre de Dio! — he could do a lot worse than this attractive, sympathetic colleague.*

A lot worse.

Valentina stood, took his hand, and pulled him up. Their kisses became frenzied. They hesitated only long enough to go into the bedroom where they quickly shed clothes and tumbled onto the bed.

Afterwards, they lay there entwined. Abruptly Valentina burst into tears.

"I know, I know," Tony said, remembering his night with Mia. "I'm not Julian."

She said huskily, "You're right, how did you know? But it was still good — I'm so sorry, just for a moment I couldn't seem to — but I hope — was it good for you too?"

"It was good for me too," Tony said, and thought *Jen ... Jen ...*

Jean Dell

Jen ...

He recognised what he had done—he had tried to erect a bulwark against his grief. But without love, this was not the way—this experiment was a failure. He was relieved to surmise that it had failed for Valentina too, however gratifying had been the sheer physical release for both of them.

But, he thought, *no one, no one will be Jen, not ever again.*

Twenty-Nine

Light snow fell from a gloomy grey sky as Jen crossed the street and with a wild hope entered the Metro Toronto Reference Library. She was about to do research on Jenetta Maclean, artist—except that she had no idea of when she was born or even how Jenetta Maclean was spelled, since the sound of the name had come to her but no corresponding visual clue. Ginetta, Jeannetta, Janetta Maclean, McCline, MacLaine, McLean—the task seemed more than a little daunting. Her thoughts were momentarily arrested as Jen, the artist, admired the woolly woven mural hanging above an angular pond.

At the information desk she was directed first to the main floor where she found reference books of all sorts, as well as microfiche. Finding little, she asked again and was redirected to the stairs that led up to the second floor, the arts section. She wondered how well she would get to know all the floors she could see above her, surrounding the open central space, before she had finished her research.

Presently, armed with reference books listing artists, she sat down at a carrel and began her search. She had decided to research back twelve years, because she and Mark figured she was likely between thirty-five and forty years old, and, given her considerable artistic skills, if she were known at all she must have been known at least in a minor way for five years. They had decided to add five more years to that, on general principles, and at the library Jen had put in two more years for good measure. Several hours later, after she had researched both printed lists and lists on databases, she had no choice but to admit defeat, at least temporarily.

She could not know that if she had extended her search back thirteen years instead of the twelve she had arbitrarily chosen, she would have found herself listed under Maclean, Jenetta. Nor could she know that despite all her ingenious ways of spelling the name she remembered, she would not have found herself during the past twelve years under any spelling of Maclean, for she was actually listed in most of the books and databases she had so thoroughly scrutinised, but under the name Amato. She had, unremembered by her amnesiac self, proudly taken the name Amato when she married Tony.

Disappointed but not discouraged, for she had been so hopeful and a lot of hope remained, Jen left the library. She returned to the Westin Harbour Castle Hotel to check out, leaving Mark a message saying she must now go to search in Montreal, and that afterwards she would travel directly to Meilleurville to visit Charlie Demchuk. She would see Mark back at the mine. She knew he would be disappointed that she had not waited to tell him all this in person, but she was far too

The Tosca Taunt

wound up in her search to pause now.

In Montreal, once again using the arbitrary cutoff of twelve years, she sought herself in city directories, street directories, electoral lists. And again she was frustrated. Until, miraculously, after a long day spent wandering the city in hopes of jogging her memory, she came upon a street called Sherbrooke which seemed to attract her. But nothing else came to her, until that night when she had a dream. For once, it was not about the last act of *Tosca*. She dreamed of a townhouse whose address she saw clearly. Awakening with a start, she quickly made a note of the address, thinking that her wanderings had triggered a subconscious memory after all. She would go looking for that townhouse, and since she had felt at home on Sherbrooke Street, she would begin there.

Too excited and hopeful to sleep any longer, she dressed and went down to become the first hotel guest to breakfast that day. Afterwards she started towards the concierge's desk to ask him directions, when she realised she did not need to enquire, because she felt so sure she could find her destination on her own. She left the hotel and ran for a bus.

The townhouses on Sherbrooke Street, in a comfortable middle class neighbourhood, were just as she remembered from her dream. She walked slowly up the street. She was overjoyed to realise she could recollect details about these surroundings that she would scarcely have noticed had she driven casually along this street in her past life—her real life?—rather than perhaps having lived here. It felt natural for her to be in this place.

Now she found herself facing the townhouse whose address

had presented itself to her in her dream. How was she going to go about her quest? For a moment she wanted to run away from what her next queries might reveal. But she must not run, partly for Mark's sake, because if she were about to hurt him with revelations about her past, she would prefer to do it now, quickly, before he—no, not only he, they—were too deeply involved with one another. *I am kidding myself,* she thought. *We are already deeply involved.*

She noticed that one of the lace curtains, in the window to her right, moved as she climbed the front stairs to the door. She lifted the bright brass horse's head knocker—which she did not remember—and soon heard two bolts being drawn back. The door opened slightly, fastened still by a heavy brass chain. An elderly face, lighted by an aureole of heavy white hair and incongruous multi-coloured dangling earrings, appeared in the aperture. "Yes? Can I help you?"

"I hope so. Do you—do you know me?"

The faded green eyes peered closely at her. "No, I don't think so. Should I?"

"No, maybe not." How should I approach this, Jen wondered, suddenly filled with misgivings. She struggled onwards. "I'm looking—that is, I believe a woman named Jenetta Maclean either lives here now or used to; I'm trying to get in touch with her."

The elderly face assumed an expression of puzzlement. "There's nobody by that name here. Are you sure you have the right address?"

Doubtful now, Jen said yes, she was. Then, knowing she was being awkward, she added, "Maybe it's just that she used to live here; I'm sorry, I'm not being too clear."

"I don't think so, we bought the house three years ago from people named Harriman, and they bought it from the Freebody family. It may have been rented out at one time, I don't know. What do you want to see this Maclean woman about?"

"About—actually it's about a person who is missing."

The elderly lady, an avid reader of the more classical mysteries, looked apprehensive. The phrase "missing person" conjured up for her the police, suspense, foul play. She wanted none of this conversation. "Why don't you try the houses on each side of mine? They might know something." And the door was abruptly shut in Jen's face. She immediately became aware of being watched again from behind the curtain to her right.

Not yet disheartened, she tried the house next door. There the door was opened wide to her by a red-haired man with a long tawny beard and strange oddly focussed brown eyes, who said cordially, "Hello, how are you, we haven't seen you in a while."

Her stomach contracted painfully. She blurted, "You know me?"

He grinned hugely. "Of course I—" Then he hesitated. "Shouldn't I? Aren't you—no, perhaps not. What did you say your name was?"

"I didn't. It's Jenetta Maclean. Please, oh please, you do recognise me, don't you?"

He lost his smile. "No, I can't say I do. I thought I did for a moment—"

"But when you opened the door you said you hadn't seen me for a long time—"

"A manner of speaking. I thought from your perfume you were my cousin Marilyn."

"But couldn't you see I wasn't your—" and Jen stopped, realising that the man had not looked directly at her throughout this entire encounter. His eyes were fixed on a point slightly to the right of her head. "Oh, I'm so sorry, you're, you're—"

"Blind, my dear. Don't be embarrassed. I've been blind all my life; it's not such a tragedy for me. Now, is there any way I can help you?"

But he could not; he remembered no Jenetta Maclean, no Macleans of any kind, although he had lived here for six years. He suggested she try the townhouse on the other side of the address she remembered. He did not know those neighbours, who kept very much to themselves, but he understood they had been there for a long while.

So Jen knocked on the third door, which was opened by a middle-aged woman in a black shirt and slacks, with a frilled white apron tied about her waist. Jen said, "I'm looking for information about a Jenetta Maclean who may have lived in the townhouse next door, I'm not sure how long ago. Can you help me?"

"Not really, I'm the housekeeper, and I've only been here two years. But maybe the man I work for can help you out. Would you like to come in? He's always glad of company. He's confused and forgetful sometimes but he's lived here forever so he might know something. Who shall I say is here?"

"Actually my name is the same as the person I'm enquiring about, I realise that seems very peculiar ... "

"Mr Runciman, Mr Runciman!" the housekeeper shouted as

The Tosca Taunt

Jen followed her into a dark green, book-strewn library. There, seated in a wheelchair with a blanket across his knees and two books astride one another on top of the blanket, was an elderly, wizened, totally bald man.

The housekeeper shouted, "Here's someone to see you, Mr Runciman, a Miss Jenetta Maclean."

He examined her closely from her hair to her shoes before he spoke. "You related to the rest of those damned Macleans?"

Jen's hopes rose. "What Macleans, Mr Runciman? The ones next door?"

"Of course they're not next door, you fool!" He grabbed his cane and slashed with it; she stepped back hastily to avoid being hit. "Would I live here if those damned Macleans were next door? Wouldn't live in the same damned city with people like that. You related to those Macleans?" He raised the cane again.

Jen, standing well clear, said, "I don't think so, I—"

"What do you mean, you don't think so? Girl's a half-wit, Mrs Calvet, why'd you bring her in here? I don't want to talk to half-wits. Get her out of here."

But Jen had to try one more time. Risking the ever ready cane, she moved closer to him, and bent down, her hands on the arms of the wheelchair. "Please, Mr Runciman, please, can you tell me anything about the Macleans? Did they ever live next door? Where are they? I understand you don't care for them but—"

"Don't care for them? Good God, girl, I can't tell you anything about any Macleans, fool girl's dull-witted, doesn't catch on, give her a glass of water, give her an aspirin, Mrs Calvet, get her out of here for God's sake."

Mrs Calvet said, softly enough that her employer couldn't hear, "We'd better leave him. He gets excited and then he hits out with his cane as you saw, he doesn't much care what or who is on the receiving end."

She and Jen left the room. The housekeeper said, "I don't think he even knew anyone named Maclean, he was just acting up. He does that sometimes to keep from being bored; he's such an intelligent man, and trapped in that helpless body. I'm sorry we can't help you more. Would you like a cup of tea?"

"No, thank you, but can you tell me what schools people would go to who lived here? It seems to me the girls wore a uniform at the school I'm looking for, and there were no boys around ... "

Mrs Calvet told her she was likely thinking of Trafalgar School, a private school for girls, and Jen left, determined to try what seemed to her that last avenue.

As Jen was hurrying down the street and around the corner, Mrs Calvet immediately went in to her employer to see whether he needed anything. He said to her, "Damned Macleans. Lived next door for years, you know. We had an argument over the property line and the apple trees. The Macleans were completely wrong, damn fools. They're dead now, frightful sudden illnesses they had, serves them right. That half-wit you brought in here, she's their daughter, you know. Serves them right to have had a half-witted daughter. Funny though, I didn't remember her being retarded. Twins, they were. Looked different from each other, good-looking girls. This dullard you just brought in, she's still a looker. Wait! Where are you going? It's time for my tea. Where's my tea?"

The Tosca Taunt

For Mrs Calvet had rushed out of the library to the front door and down the steps in an attempt to catch her caller. But Jen had disappeared from sight.

Soon she arrived at the Trafalgar School. But when she enquired as to whether the school kept records of people who would have attended when she herself judged she might have been there—a rather dodgy question given that Jen did not know her age—the secretary said they only kept records for ten years. Then the records went into archives and it was a whole production to get at them. Was Jen in a hurry?

It was Jen's last day of leave, in Montreal. So she told the secretary she would come back in a month or two and try to instigate a search then. She asked if there were public schools in the area near her townhouse, and was given the names of two, a primary school and a secondary school. At the primary school she met a blank wall.

Her quest in the high school had similar results, except for one event. After Jen had determined that she would come back and instigate a search there as well, the secretary to whom she spoke said, "Would you like to look at an old school annual? One of our ex-students brought it in last week. It's missing some pages and a cover so we can't tell what year it is, except by the clothes it looks like about twenty years ago. Here, sit down and have a giggle."

So Jen sat where she was instructed, feeling far from giggling. Eagerly she scanned the faces of the groups of students in grades nine to twelve; but she found nobody remotely resembling herself. Then, as she cursorily glanced at names under the pictures, she came across the tantalising list of students missing from one photograph on that day; Missing; Q. Vervent, G. Malesherbes, J. Maclean, R. Smythe.

Was that how her name was spelled. Could it be she? So close, maybe so close, and yet...

Jen thanked the secretary and, both frustrated and hopeful, went back to the Queen Elizabeth hotel, from where she phoned Mark in Toronto. She intended to leave a message saying she was on her way, and would have breakfast with him tomorrow morning before she went up to stay with the Charlie Demchuks. She was surprised that Mark himself answered the phone; he told her he was dressing for the final banquet of his conference, at which he was to deliver an address.

"I was hoping you'd call," he said. "I called the mine today and they said did I know where you were because there was an urgent message. I said I'd try to find you—did you know you left without telling me where you'd be in Montreal?" He sounded reproachful. "The message is that Charlie Demchuk and his wife can't see you right now; her mother died and the whole family has gone to Saskatchewan for the funeral. Charlie says he'll phone you as soon as he gets back."

Jen was only partly disappointed. "Then I guess I'll spend the next three days with you if you want me; it being the weekend I can't get any further with my research here. No, Mark, no, I've found out nothing."

"Don't lose heart, love. I've got to run. Speech time. See you later."

"*In bocca al lupo,* Mark."

"What?"

Jen could not quite believe what she had just said. She knew

The Tosca Taunt

what it was—it was what one said to opera singers to bring them good luck. But why was she using it, and to Mark? What *was* this operatic connection? She explained to him what she meant.

"Phew, you must be a real opera buff in your other incarnation. Just my luck to marry two women in succession who are nuts about opera."

Jen was momentarily stunned. "Who—who said anything about marriage?"

"I did. Jen, I'm late, I've got to go."

And before Jen could say anything more she was greeted by the dial tone.

Thirty

Warm winds gave the inhabitants of New Orleans illusions of summer, and all who could were enjoying being out of doors, but Julian LeComte was in writing mode. He had closed the windows of his home office to keep out extraneous traffic noise, and he had turned off not only the bell on his telephone but also his answering machine. He was working on the beginning of the third novel of his Louisiana trilogy and the prose was flowing from his fingers. After several days, he came slowly out of his creative spell, turned on his phone and his answering machine, and looked at the calendar. He wondered whether his nerves, always edgy when he was writing, could stand going to a meeting to hear his father give an important political speech.

Julian decided he was too emotionally fraught from his days and nights of writing. But since his father's meeting was to be televised on a local cable channel, Julian did not need to miss it altogether. He would watch it so that he could if necessary

The Tosca Taunt

discuss the speech later with his father.

Julian switched on his television set and surfed until he found the channel he wanted. Leonard's address was being given in the largest meeting room of a local hotel, and the public had been expensively exhorted to come by Leonard's public relations people. On the screen, Leonard's friend and financial supporter Victor Macready Kilbride was just beginning a fulsome introduction for Leonard, who sat behind the podium with a small group of dignitaries. Included among them was Leonard's resplendent second wife Delphine, dressed for the occasion in a fashionable navy Chanel suit sporting a multitude of gold buttons and chains. She sat with her knees together and her superb legs a little to one side, finishing school style, although she was anything but the product of a finishing school. Victor, his introduction finally over, turned and sat down on one of the armchairs behind the podium. Leonard rose and walked with dignity to the microphone.

How dearly I once loved my Dad, thought Julian wistfully. *I almost revered him. I could have been so proud of him if it hadn't been for ...* Julian's reverie was interrupted by the action on his television screen.

The camera had pulled back to show the large crowd; the room was overflowing. As Leonard began his speech the camera stayed on the crowd, so Julian saw the back of a tall dark haired woman as she walked purposefully up the aisle, doubtless looking for a seat at the front. From Julian's vantage point he could see that her quest was fruitless. Then he thought how much the woman looked like Valentina from the back. She had Valentina's sinuous walk. But it couldn't be. Although Valentina had sent him a photo of herself wearing a pantsuit just like that one; he recognised the pattern on the blouse. Odd. He felt vaguely uneasy.

The woman arrived at the front of the room. Looking neither right nor left, she stepped in front of the stage, and took her hand out of her pocket. It clutched a revolver. Now she steadied it with both hands, and pointed it straight at Leonard. As some people in the front rows rose fearfully and Leonard's handlers rushed to get to her, she said calmly to Leonard, "Make them stop."

Leonard put his hands up and shouted, "Nobody move—"

Movement stopped; there was an uneasy murmuring. He said, his voice firm, "Miss Welles. What on earth do you think you're doing?"

Julian's heart skipped painfully. He would die, he was already dying. *Was it really Valentina? Had she actually snapped?* Only her back was visible on the screen. The woman laughed. "Mr LeComte, isn't that nice, you know who I am." She heard a movement behind her, for she glanced back and called out, "No, stop moving or I'll kill him."

Julian let out a breath. He would have sworn that was not Valentina's voice, but then his fear began again, for microphones can deform voices and hers was recording at a fair distance.

The woman kept the revolver trained on Leonard. "Did you know you'd be this easy to kill? You're never safe, nobody's ever safe. So you should live right. Make life better for my valley, you understand? I'll do this for my valley."

"Are you really going to kill me? Get on with it then," said Leonard, facing her down. Julian was amazed that there was no

The Tosca Taunt

tremor in the voice, no hint of fear in Leonard's demeanour. Still, he had to admit that cowardice had never been among Leonard's faults.

"You have to promise," the woman said. "You have to promise you won't hurt my valley any more—"

Three policemen had silently crept up behind her, revolvers drawn. There was a sudden scuffle as they grabbed the woman, and a shot rang out. Leonard clapped one hand to his chest, but it was Victor Macready Kilbride who uttered a high-pitched scream and clutched his crotch. Blood stained his trouser legs. The tall black woman was hurled to the ground, as pandemonium broke loose. Julian tried to see the woman's face and could not.

For a moment the television images swayed precariously, then settled again on the policemen struggling with the black woman. One held the gun aloft; he shouted, "It's not real, it's just a toy ..."

Now the camera turned to a reporter who breathlessly tried to describe what had just happened. " One person has been wounded in what appears to be an assassination attempt on the life of the candidate for Governor of Louisiana, Leonard LeComte. Doctor Victor Macready Kilbride, a prominent New Orleans dentist, appears to have been shot in the lower abdomen or upper legs..." The reporter was handed a piece of paper. He glanced at it, and continued; "The gun used in the assassination threat is a toy. This brings into question the identity of the person who shot Dr Kilbride. We will report on his injuries when more is known." Yet another paper was handed to him. He continued, "The identity of the woman who threatened Mr

LeComte may be known. Mr and Mrs LeComte and two other people on the platform say she closely resembles the American operatic soprano Valentina Welles."

Julian could not bear it. He muted the sound and dropped the control as he sickened. The control hit the floor and the sound came back on. The reporter was still shouting into the microphone as people milled around on the stage behind him. Like an automaton Julian shut off the television. He was in shock. But why would his sweet Val commit an act of such obvious madness? Surely she was nothing if not overwhelmingly sane.

He got up from his chair, trying to convince himself this was not happening; it had to be a bad dream. Finally after what seemed to him an aeon he decided to turn on the radio, to listen to the news. The television images were too disturbing to go back to, that replay of Val going up the middle aisle, of her words, of his father facing her down, of the cruel way she was brought down by the police, of Victor shrieking and clutching his crotch.

A newscast was in progress. Julian heard, " ... and during the melee prominent local dentist Dr Victor Kilbride was accidentally shot; his injuries are not considered life-threatening. Mr LeComte suggests that the woman who threatened him may be the American opera singer Valentina Welles. According to police the assailant has not spoken since the attack. Included in her verbal threats to Mr LeComte were several references to a valley, so it is speculated her motives may be ecological. It is known that a large part of Mr LeComte's fortune was made in oil ventures. But up to now Valentina Welles has not been

The Tosca Taunt

known to actively support ecological concerns. In other news ..."

In a few minutes the radio began to play an Elton John song, but soon broke in with another news bulletin. "Further to the breaking story of the assassination attempt on Leonard LeComte, police have asked us to broadcast the contents of a note, signed Tina Welles, and found in the assailant's pocket. The police are now asking anyone who has any knowledge that might be useful to please come forward. Here is the text of the note.

To Whom it May Concern;
Dont think anybody told me to do this, its all my idea. I am going to do it for my Valley, so my beautiful wonderful Valley will be happy again. My Valley is worth dying for. Remember me.

Julian had to know. He grabbed his phone and dialled "0". When the operator came on he asked her to dial Valentina Welles' number in San Francisco; he was confused to the point where he could not remember it. But Valentina's phone rang its requisite four times and then the answering machine came on.

"There's no answer, sir. Sir, do you mind me asking, is it the singer you're calling?"

"It is."

"Well, if you'll pardon me for interfering, I was just talking to my sister in San Francisco, and she said she was going to the opera tonight to hear Valentina Welles sing. So Miss Welles is likely at the Opera House."

"Oh Jesus, let her be there," Julian whispered.

"Pardon?"

"Could you try that number for me?"

"Of course, one moment please."

Presently he heard a woman's voice saying, "San Francisco Opera House."

"This—" Julian's voice broke. He tried again. "This is Julian LeComte; I'm calling from New Orleans. I would like to speak to Valentina Welles please."

"I can take a message for you and get Miss Welles or her assistant to call you back."

"You mean—you mean she's not there?"

"Of course she's here. What *are* all these calls from New Orleans asking me whether she's here? At the moment she's on stage singing the first act of *Madama Butterfly*."

"You know for sure she's there?" Julian's voice broke once more on the last word.

"Sir, I can take a message for her if you would like."

"Is she there or are you just assuming she's there because she's scheduled to sing?"

"Sir, there's no need to shout at me. Miss Welles is here—I have seen her with my own eyes—she came in two hours ago for makeup and she certainly has not left, so where would she be but on the stage? What's the matter with you people? First some New Orleans police detective snarls at me on the phone not ten minutes ago, and now you, whoever you are. Look, I have other things to do besides get yelled at by you; would you like Miss Welles to call you or not?"

"Yes, please, get her to call Julian LeComte. As soon as possible."

Valentina was surprised to receive a message to call Julian, delivered to her during her first intermission. She was having unnerving vocal problems again tonight, so she believed it was necessary not to use her voice at all during intermissions. Therefore she would not call Julian until she had finished singing the arduous finale of this opera. No news, no radio disturbed her silence, as her assistant ensured that she would be protected while she waited for her call to go back on stage. Valentina had no idea what a sensation her very name was causing in New Orleans.

Oh God, thought Julian, *it was not Valentina who had threatened his father, it was not her, oh God thank you God ...*

He sat immobile in the chair, holding the receiver in his hand, paralysed, and preventing anyone from dialling him, including the frantic Leonard. Julian was completely unable to deal with his thoughts. Who was this woman, this Tina Welles, who had so much of his sweet Val about her? The radio announcer was now saying there had been an error, that in the confusion after the assassination attempt it had been mistakenly believed that the assailant was Valentina Welles, but Welles had been located in San Francisco where she was performing etc. etc. Meanwhile it was being reported that the bullet that had wounded Dr Kilbride came from a police revolver that accidentally discharged.

Julian came out of his trance and hung up the phone. Immediately it rang. It was Delphine, his stepmother.

"Julian, we've been trying to reach you, the police are sending a car around to bring you here, of course you'll want to be with Leonard, he's badly shaken up."

"I'll be right there, Del, I saw it on TV, I was horrified, poor Dad, I'll come as soon as I can."

Julian slowly hung up the phone. And again it rang

immediately.

"Val?" Julian said.

"Yes, yes Julian, it's me, I just heard, darling are you all right, what a ghastly business, and how appalling that they could think it was me! But Julian my love I think I know who it is, I think it's my cousin Evangelina."

Julian was too stunned to take this in. "What?"

"My cousin, she's been mentally ill for years, she looks a lot like me, she showed up one night recently when I had drunk too much and was feeling sad about you, and I couldn't seem to stop myself from blurting it all out to her, but she must have, oh Julian, she must have—" Valentina stopped, swallowed, started again. "—she always loved me. When we were kids, before she got sick, we were such good pals, she always said she'd do anything for me. I've just heard the contents of the note; Julian, if it's Lina, she's not talking about a valley; she's talking about me. Valley was always her name for me. What should I do?"

"The only thing you can do is call the police, Val, you'll—we'll have to tell them."

"But—but they'll find out about us—"

"Yes, I guess they will. So what? We can't be any worse off than we already are. I have to go, the police are at the door to take me to my father's place; do you want me to tell them to contact you or will you talk to them in San Francisco?"

"I'll do it, Julian, she's *my* cousin, in a way she's my responsibility. I mean, if I hadn't cried all over her —"

"I'll call you tomorrow, my love. Once you've spoken to the police, try to get some sleep. Goodnight, darling."

The Tosca Taunt

First thing the next morning, Valentina called the police to add to what she had already told them, the fact that a letter from her cousin Evangelina Welles had just arrived, and she would like to open and read it in their presence. Two detectives were dispatched to her apartment, where in front of them she opened and read the letter.

Valley;
Dont be mad at me Valley. You would say no if I told you what Im going to do, so I wont tell you. But youl know after. Im going to scare him so much he will leave you alone to love your man. Call one of your babies Evangelina for your Lina that loves you. Thank you, Valley, your the kindest of all the Welles. And thats saying a lot, theyv all tried to be kind to Lina.

I love you. Dont be mad for what Im doing, and dont forget your loving Lina.

Valentina read this aloud with the detectives peering over her shoulder. And by the end, she wept for all the different and moving manifestations of love.

"Now what's this about, Miss?"

She had to tell them something. So she said that, although she and Julian had not met for years, they had once been infatuated with one another. She did not say why they had separated. She explained that Evangelina had only vague notions of time, and must have thought the affair was still on and that in some way Leonard LeComte was impeding it. Valentina, wording her phrase with great care, said she was not completely sure why Evangelina would think that. But the detectives, scarcely naive in the ways of the world, were in the next day or two able to ascertain that neither Valentina nor

Julian was seeing anyone else, and they correctly deduced that these two believed they were living out a *Romeo and Juliet* tragedy. With a little digging about, they uncovered some possibilities as to why.

It also did not take the investigators long to figure out that an impressionable, childlike, sick woman like Evangelina Welles could be moved to pity on her beloved cousin's behalf, and could take matters into her own hands in a mistaken belief that she could help out.

Badly shaken now, Julian and Valentina retreated into shells of silence. Since the detectives had filled in many of the gaps in their story, the couple decided that it would be better for a time to cut off all communication between them.

Thirty-One

The unseasonable fog spread out from London until it touched as far out as Cedric Tyhurst's grounds. In the chateau itself, the morning after Tony's food poisoning and the mishap with the Rolls and the baby, Mia ran down the long staircase after taking breakfast in her rooms. She heard the heavy front door shut with a clang. Thomson came from the entryway into the great hall as Mia reached it.

"What was that, Thomson? Who was leaving?"

"Viscount Ridlough, Miss Mitsouros. He said he wanted to get up to town early."

Mia's face felt icy. "Did he leave any message for me?"

"No. He said he expected to spend the night in town, but he did not say that was a message specifically for you."

"Do you—did he happen to say where—will he be at his office?"

"He did say he is expecting a call from Saudi Arabia which should go to his office but due to its nature may come here. He left me a number where he will be this morning."

The ice had descended into Mia's chest, into her stomach. What was happening? Yesterday had been such a terrible day—last night Cedric locked her out of his room—this morning he went off without a word to her. She wanted to ask Thomson for the number where Cedric was to be this morning, and knew the loyal butler would not give it to her.

The phone rang; Thomson answered it. From what Mia could hear of Thomson's side of the conversation, it was the call from Saudi Arabia he had just mentioned, and she heard Thomson say Cedric could be reached in a few minutes at—and here Thomson gave out the number. No, said the butler, Viscount Ridlough did not wish to be reached on his cellular phone, as he was not certain of its privacy.

Mia ran upstairs and hastily wrote down the number as she remembered it. She waited impatiently in her rooms until she was certain Cedric would have reached London. She dialled, and was answered by a crisp female voice repeating the phone number. Mia asked for Cedric.

"I'm sorry, Madame, he is with the doctor now. May I have him call you when he is finished?"

"The doctor?"

"Doctor Morgan, yes. Is your call urgent?"

Mia said no, hung up the phone, and frantically searched in her London telephone directory. Yes, there he was, on Harley Street, a cardiologist with the telephone number she had just called. But Cedric had not spoken to her about conferring with a cardiologist. And he had had no further trouble since that frightening time in the potting shed. He had consulted nobody

The Tosca Taunt

over that episode, and together he and Mia had concluded that it must have been an attack of severe heartburn or a muscle spasm. He had seemed so well since. So what was going on today?

....

"Certainly angina; I'll need to do a work up on you to find how compromised your heart and arteries are." Dr Morgan told Cedric. "How soon can you—"

"Straight away," said Cedric, ever decisive. "Can you start today?"

"Of course. You can go into the clinic this afternoon, stay overnight and we can finish the tests tomorrow."

"Let's proceed then."

....

Mia drove herself into London. She had her hair trimmed slightly and her nails painted deep red at her beauty salon, and at Harrod's chose a black lace negligee and nightgown as well as an elegant pale green silk suit to dine out with tonight. Then she went to Cedric's London townhouse, put on her handsome new suit, and waited for him to come after his workday was over.

But he had not appeared by eleven o'clock. So she changed into her new negligee and waited, first in the sitting room where she had spent the evening, and then in the big bed, its width a painful reminder of how alone she was. Finally she fell asleep, only to waken at intervals throughout the night, unhappily aware that Cedric had not returned. Yet he had told Thomson he was spending the night in town. So where could he be? What was happening to her—to them?

Next morning at eight-thirty she called his London office. His private secretary said to her, "No, Miss Mitsouros, he didn't come in at all yesterday. But I have a number where he said he can be reached in an emergency." The private secretary laughed in vague embarrassment at her, saying, "Are you an emergency?"

"Yes, Samuel, I am. Please?" Mia said, aware that the brilliant young secretary found her extremely tempting. He rose to the bait. "I hope I don't get fired for this, but here's the number."

"Thank you, Samuel. Of course you won't get fired ... " *I hope—unless by any unlikely but dreadful chance this is the number of another woman ...*

Cedric had ordered a telephone installed in his room at the clinic, which would be answered at the nursing station if he were out of his private room. When Mia dialled the number, it was answered by a woman with a high lilting voice. A recently graduated young nurse just hired at the clinic, she forgot for a moment she was supposed to say, "Viscount Ridlough's room," and she merely said softly, "Hello, may I help you?"

Mia's throat tightened painfully. What was going on? Who was this woman? "I am Mia Mitsouros, and I wish to speak to my fiance, Viscount Ridlough," she said in her coldest voice.

The nurse suddenly remembered how she had been told to answer the phone. "Oh, yes, this is Viscount Ridlough's room, but he's not here right now, can he call you back?"

Mia could not stop herself. She said, "What are *you* doing in my fiance's room?"

"Pardon?" The young voice sounded unsure now. "I—I'm not actually in his room, I just answer the phone if he can't."

"I don't understand."

The Tosca Taunt

"If he's doing his tests I answer his phone."

"Tests?" Mia was now completely bewildered. "But—but are you a college of some kind?"

"Oh no, this is not a teaching hospital, it's a diagnostic and treatment clinic."

A clinic? What was Cedric doing in a clinic? Was he ill? Why had nobody informed her? Surely she was the first person who should know when he was ill. She steeled herself to ask a question which likely would not be answered, given the rules of patient confidentiality.

"Can you tell me when Viscount Ridlough was admitted, and how he is, please?"

"But—but I thought you said you were his fiance; how do you know he's here if you don't know any of those things—just a minute, I'm sure my supervisor will want to speak to you—"

The supervisor was preoccupied, and when the phone was handed to her without explanation, she barked into it, "Traynor Clinic, Mrs Rowbotham here," and found she was listening to a dial tone. For Mia had learned what she wanted to know.

But when she arrived at the clinic, Cedric had finished his tests and had gone. She rushed back to his townhouse, but he was not there. She called Thomson, who said yes, Viscount Ridlough was expected at home tonight. Only then did Mia become angry. What did Cedric imagine he was doing? Mia deliberately did not tell Thomson that she would be spending another night in town, at the townhouse.

Miserably she decided to treat herself to the theatre. But she walked out in the middle of the play, unable to concentrate on the travails of a group of men with AIDS. She took herself to the townhouse where she spent a miserable, wakeful night. In the morning she decided to go to Bournemouth for a few days, but when she had driven herself halfway there she turned her car around and headed back to Ridlough Hall and to Cedric.

....

Mia arrived at Ridlough Hall by nightfall. Thomson was at the door to let her in.

"Yes, he is here, he is at supper in the dining hall, Miss Mitsouros. He will be glad to see you, I'm sure. I think he was a little worried about you."

"*He* was worried! Really, Thomson!"

But she dashed towards the dining room nevertheless, not even taking off her coat, and stopped on the threshold, like an abashed child. Cedric looked up from the newspaper he had been reading to keep him company as he ate. The light played tricks on his face; just for a moment she saw his skull, his bone structure, the skin stretched tightly across it. No, no, she would not allow herself to succumb once more to pity, to her maternal instincts; she would not let sympathy for his haggard look blind her to the dreadful misunderstanding they were having. Except—except–

"Mia, my dear, where have you been? I've been concerned."

"*You've* been concerned? What is this, are you trying to put me on the defensive so I won't accuse *you*?"

"Accuse me of what?" Cedric's voice was as weary as his face.

"Cedric, stop it. I know you've been in a clinic, I don't know what's going on, I know you rejected me rather cruelly the night of the accident—"

The Tosca Taunt

"Rejected you? On the contrary. I needed you, I wanted you to come to me of your own accord, and you didn't come, Mia. You went to Tony Amato when he needed you, but you did not come to me."

"Of course I didn't come to you, how could I, both your bedroom doors were locked when I tried them."

"They were?" Cedric was incredulous. "I had no idea. Damn the maid, damn the pushbutton locks—but I thought you—I thought—" He rose from his place at the long table. But Mia took no step towards him.

"I don't believe you." Her voice had a bitter edge. "It all sounds convincing now, but how is it you didn't respond when I tried the doors and you realised they were locked? You can't have missed hearing me."

"But I did."

"You're lying."

"I'm not, Mia. I missed hearing you because I was—" he cleared his throat. Why was it so hard to tell her, to admit that he was human after all? "—I was—ill, I had that pain in my chest again, it lasted almost all night."

She stared at him. He was pale, his eyes ringed in shadow. Even someone who did not know him would say he looked unwell. She could see he was likely telling her the truth. But why had he not trusted her enough to call out, to tell her? Had she so irrevocably damaged their relationship with her complicated feelings for Tony Amato? She took a step towards Cedric; he rose and took one towards her, and then they clung tightly to one another.

"Let's marry next week, next week Mia my darling, before

Jean Dell

I—" Cedric realised he was about to say, before he died. He did not know why he had this sudden premonition of death. Yes, he had some coronary artery blockage, yes, he needed surgery, but people lived normally for many years after such surgery. So why this dark forewarning?

She was weeping now, but whether they were tears of fear or relief even she did not know.

"Cedric my love we can't, not next week, but we can in three weeks, I have a huge window in my schedule, yes, yes, let's do it then, oh please yes."

They kissed one another with a passion sufficient to give Cedric a disagreeable twinge in his chest. But at the moment he did not really care. Three weeks. He would certainly live for three weeks. And then Mia would be his.

Thirty-Two

From his hotel in London Tony called Ridlough hall, two days before he was due to leave for New York. Speaking to Mia, he said, "I need to talk with Cedric. Things are bad between us, I will apologise."

"*You* apologise? Are you insane? He hit you so hard I thought he—"

"With good reason, Mia. How do you think the situation looked to Cedric? In his shoes, well, I have to tell you if it had been my Jen with some sick man all night, if she had been with Cedric, for instance—"

"Men! You all think we're your possessions! Anyway, Jen is—was—your *wife*, Tony; I am not Cedric's, not yet, but that's what I'm calling about; we have finally set the date." She gave him the details. "Does that work for you?"

"Does Cedric still want me to be best man?"

"I think so—maybe you'd better talk to him. Would you be free at that time if he does?"

"I have that weekend free—I sing in New York Thursday night and in Boston Monday; you marry Saturday. I will come on the Concorde Friday, it should be fine, I will leave Sunday or Monday morning, the Concorde should get me to New York in time to get to Boston."

"Phew, Tony."

"Phew is right. But you know me," Tony said, his voice filled with pride for his well-known stamina. "I can do that, is not really too hard. I will come to see Cedric tonight?"

"Of course. Come to dinner, the usual time. I also wanted to tell you, Tony darling, that I am quite worried; Cedric is ill, something to do with his heart, he's scaring me. He won't want to talk about it of course. But you'll see it on his face."

"I will be tactful. I see you at dinner time."

Later, when Thomson the butler ushered the slightly late Tony into the small sitting room where Cedric and Mia were having cocktails, Tony was dismayed to see the change in Cedric. His usually rosy British complexion was grey-tinged and dark smudges underlined his eyes. He stood up to give Tony a welcoming handshake, as the butler served Tony a very dry gin martini, straight up with olives just as he had learned to like them.

Conversation was strained, like trying to run through waist high mud, thought Tony. He was amused by the ever direct Mia who finally said, "You two have something to say to one another. I'll leave you to say it." She swirled from the room in a flutter of peach chiffon.

Cedric stared into his glass; Tony stared at him. Finally, without raising his eyes, Cedric said, "I believe I may owe you

The Tosca Taunt

an apology. If what I did was unwarranted, I am heartily sorry."

Tony thought, *my English is not perfect but that is the most qualified apology I have ever heard. It seems to me Cedric would be better not to apologise at all. On the other hand, given what almost happened, maybe Cedric has a right to be doubtful.*

"Cedric, maybe I owe you too an apology. If the tables were turned, as you say, if it had been my Jen all night with you, I might have been ... I am sorry, Cedric."

"Shall we try to—"

"Yes." Cedric stood up, then Tony rose from his chair, embarrassed, awkward. He would have known what to do next if Cedric had been an Italian. Cedric reached out first; Tony responded and they shook each other's hands. Then they sat, not meeting one another's eyes. Finally Tony spoke again. "Cedric, I will understand if you want one of your brothers to stand up with you at the wedding, and not me, under the circumstances."

"Don't be ridiculous, of course I—we still want you. Please. Unless it would be too difficult for you, because Jen was to be Mia's attendant and Jen is—"

"And Jen is not." Tony finished for him, his voice tight. "It is *all* too hard, I was addicted to her you know, and the withdrawal is so—I had no idea how it could be—but I just have to go on."

"Putting one foot ahead of the other and soldiering on until it gets easier?"

"Something like that."

Mia came back into the room and examined their faces. Each smiled at her. She knew dinner would be a more relaxed meal now, and taking their arms she ushered them into the dining room.

Jean Dell

Fourteen years before, Jen and Tony had met at a banquet given by philanthropist Thomas Graham Lanville in his English chateau. Elderly even then, he at a fragile ninety-eight still remained their close, good friend. Since Jen's death Lanville and Tony had been in contact by phone and with occasional visits. Each contact with Lanville was painful now to Tony, because Lanville steadfastly refused to believe in Jen's death. He simply repeated, over and over, that she was not dead.

Before Tony left London for New York, he phoned to see how his old friend was feeling. And the conversation ended with Mr Lanville saying softly into the phone, "Jen's coming soon, Tony."

"No, no, Mr Lanville, I have bad news for you. Jen is dead; she died in a fire. Remember, we've talked about this?"

"*You've* talked about it. I tell you it's nonsense. She's no more dead than I am. Do I sound dead to you?"

Tony found these conversations difficult. But it was not in his credo to abandon a friend because that friend had perhaps become senile. So he persevered. "You sound quite well, Mr Lanville. But, *per favore,* you must try to believe about Jen. She really is—she's dead—I know it seems impossible, even to me, sometimes I feel her thoughts still, just like I did the night we met and I knew she was in your maze and lost. I don't know how I can feel her thoughts when she is dead, but—"

"But that's the whole point, Tony my lad. She's not dead. It's just some misunderstanding. You'll see, she's coming soon; you mustn't ever give up hope. My Francesca, now, she comes to me, almost every night..."

The Tosca Taunt

Dio, thought Tony, *Francesca Lanville has been dead for years, and my Jen, she is dead too but she does not come to me every night, these conversations with Lanville are impossible. Hope? How can I hope? For what? I could hope to dream of Jen every night, that would be wonderful, but I don't even have that. How fortunate for Mr Lanville that he dreams...*

"One night soon, Tony my boy, Francesca will take me with her when she goes. And then I'll have her always with me, not just at night. You will see. Don't lose hope."

He is so confused, thought Tony sadly as he ended the conversation.

Thirty-Three

The latest news on the LeComte-Kilbride shooting saga was greeted with laughter in the office of the New York based tabloid for which journalist Keith Craig worked. The story was that Kilbride was suing the New Orleans police force for some millions, because his ability to have children was compromised by his wounds.

Keith Craig's editor put him, the paper's star investigative journalist, on the first plane to New Orleans, where Craig was to begin his interviews with the press conference given that afternoon by Leonard LeComte. Craig listened carefully, sensing a good story behind LeComte's constipated performance. When asked why he would assume the diva Valentina Welles could possibly be threatening him with a revolver, LeComte had no explanation.

Did he know Miss Welles?

Well, actually, yes he did, she had replaced Mia Mitsouros at the New Orleans Opera a few years ago, and of course it was

The Tosca Taunt

well known that he was a great benefactor of the opera.

Was that the extent of his acquaintance?

Yes, unless you counted listening to her CDs and watching her on television.

Chewing hard on his gum as he watched this interview, Keith Craig thought it was incongruous that on the strength of so slight an acquaintanceship Leonard LeComte could imagine that his menacer was Valentina Welles.

No. It didn't wash. But wait, wait just a minute here.

Very beautiful, Valentina Welles, if you liked the type. Very beautiful, very unmarried, with a reputation for brushing off would-be suitors with chill efficiency.

Why? Craig was pretty sure she was not gay, so why the standoffish attitude? Unless--unless she loved the married Leonard, and he had "done her wrong." Done her so wrong that he could believe she might hate him enough to want to kill him.

Keith Craig chewed that over for a while. Then he made a phone call to an acquaintance who worked for the LeComte corporation. The response was not encouraging. His acquaintance merely said, "Boy, would I be surprised if old Len LeComte had an affair or anything else with a black woman. Nobody says much about it, but African Americans aren't exactly Len's favourite people. I've even heard he's been a member of the Klan, but of course he wouldn't want that rumour spread around too much now he's running for Governor. So I doubt you'll find any evidence to show he ever got near that Welles woman, but never say never, eh, Keith?"

Then as an afterthought, Keith's pal said, "Now there's Julian, you know, Len's kid, well he's not a kid any more of course, what about him? If there is any romantic connection between this Welles woman and the LeComtes, I'd think it's more likely to be to the kid. Nice guy, one hell of a lot more liberal than Len. Anyway, it's a thought. Hey Keith, good to hear from you. Let's have a drink sometime."

The son. The writer, whose books Keith Craig enjoyed enormously. These days he waited for another Julian LeComte novel as eagerly as he waited for those of John Grisham.

The first two LeComte novels had been excellent, the writing crisp and detached, the observation clinical. Then something changed. The next two books each contained a minor subplot of *Romeo and Juliet* type love—obsessive, hopeless love, so beautifully written that even Keith Craig was faintly moved.

Obsessive love.

What if? And if so, what would keep the two apart? There seemed no obvious impediment.

Keith Craig now made a lengthy phone call to an insider on LeComte's campaign team, a woman who loved gossip and who owed Craig more than a few favours. After that, he called Julian LeComte, and asked for an interview.

Julian's first instinct was to slam down the receiver, but having taken a degree in journalism at university, he decided to be at least polite. After all, what harm could one interview do? Julian was certain he could out-manoeuver any practising journalist. So later that day Julian found himself serving coffee in his living room to the sturdy, grey-haired Keith Craig.

Whose first question, after a small speech of commiseration for the fear Julian must have experienced over the bogus assassination attempt, was, "I'm trying to figure out why your

The Tosca Taunt

father would assume Valentina Welles, of all people, might want to kill him. That's a strong assumption; I mean, if some husky stranger with a beard waved a gun around and threatened me, I wouldn't automatically assume it was Luciano Pavarotti. There has to be some connection here. Can you help me out on this?"

Julian did a quick mental calculation. He hoped Evangelina would not elaborate too much on her reasons for threatening Leonard, but he had doubts. If she were tried in court instead of committed for care, Evangelina might have to divulge details. In order to protect herself; she would have to establish her motives and indicate what she was trying to get Leonard to do. Julian was on an uncomfortable knife edge. *What to do?*

He did not want to harm his father, but he was weary of his own pain. *Would it be better for some of the truth to be generally known?*

He chose his words with care.

"I can help you out a bit, although what I'll tell you doesn't explain why my father assumed that woman was Valentina Welles. The cousins are very like, of course, and the truest explanation may be the simple one—that in a life-threatening situation the protagonists are not necessarily thinking logically. I mean, if it looks like Luciano Pavarotti trying to kill me, it must *be* Luciano Pavarotti—I don't have a lot of time to reason it out."

Julian stopped, pleased with this line of reasoning. But Keith Craig continued to fix him in a searching stare, and finally said, "Fine, that's as interesting a theory as I've heard so far; is that what you meant when you said you'd help me out a bit? Because I still believe there has to be a connection between your family and the Welles woman, and if I get no help from you on this I'll certainly broaden my base of interviews. Wouldn't you rather tell me yourself than have me interviewing your father's staff and his enemies and yours if you have any?"

I sure as hell would, thought Julian miserably. Suddenly doubtful of his ability to control this interview, he took a deep breath and said, "Of course you're right. There is a connection between Valentina Welles and the LeComtes, namely me. We had a short love affair about three years ago now. It ended, but we're still friends."

Keith Craig let the silence prolong into discomfort. Then he said, "I'm a fan of your novels. The books you write have changed in those three years. You're doing *Romeo and Juliet* type subplots. Why?"

Julian was becoming increasingly unhappy. He said as lightly as he could manage, "Writers like to try new themes; I decided to—to get in touch with–uh-- the sensitive side of myself in my writing."

Silence.

Julian would not let himself be drawn into babbling by this man's manipulative stillness.

Keith Craig and Julian LeComte stared lengthily at one another. Craig spoke first. "Thank you for your time, Mr LeComte. If you have nothing more to offer me, I'll leave you to get on with expressing the sensitive side of yourself in your writing. Oh, before I go, do you by any chance know where Valentina Welles is performing at the moment? Naturally she will be my next interview, and she's findable, of course, but maybe you can save me some trouble."

Julian's heart gave a painful thump. "Sorry."

"No problem. Goodbye then."

....

Although warned by Julian, Valentina was not nearly as skilful at fending off journalistic questions as he was. So when Keith Craig arranged with her for lunch and a chat, she was, at least in his view, surprisingly forthcoming. Because from her he heard the phrase that put all the puzzle pieces into place.

In response to questions about her relationship with Julian, she had described their romance in exactly the succinct way he had.

So Keith Craig asked, " Was there a precipitating factor in your breakup, I mean was it just a natural drift apart or—?"

"N-not really. I mean, it was impossibly awkward in light of my busy schedule—"

"Opera singers don't have relationships?"

"Of course we do, but ... "

"But what? Your family didn't approve? His family didn't approve? What?"

She smiled. "My family thinks Julian is great."

Keith Craig pounced. "His family then. You say his family didn't approve?"

"No, no of course I'm not saying ... "

"Because you're black and they don't approve of mixed marriages? Is that what tore it for you?"

"No, I, you're twisting my ... "

"Dammit Miss Welles I'm twisting nothing." (*Time to put in the knife and turn it,* thought the skilled muckraker.) "I put it to you that your love affair broke up because Leonard LeComte is a bigot who hates blacks and who acted to keep his son from marrying one."

"You're putting words in my mouth, I never said that ... "

"What will your sick cousin say when the authorities ask her these same questions, or worse? And after, when the press gets hold of her, then what? This is your chance to have a balanced article written, before the vultures get to you all. Your breakup was Leonard LeComte's fault, true or false?"

Confused now, Valentina did not know what would do the least harm to her and Julian. She realised she had not yet thought through all the consequences of having told her story to Evangelina. She had hoped Evangelina would understand that she should keep some of Valentina's confidences to herself, but that was doubtful; Evangelina's sanity was so fragile.

Never a shrinking violet, she decided a little truth had to be the best defence.

"If you promise not to make a major scandal out of it, I'll answer your question."

Keith Craig scarcely knew what the word "promise" meant any more. What he did know was the importance of getting a saleable story, by whatever means. So he promised.

"It's true that Julian and I ended our relationship because his family did not approve."

"His father, you mean? I don't see it mattering a damn to whatsername, Delphine, the young trophy wife."

"His father, yes."

"You and Julian are not minors; how could Leonard LeComte stop you from being together?"

Valentina stared at her hands, clutched together in her lap.

"He had his methods."

The Tosca Taunt

Craig laughed; he thought he saw his headline. "Bought you off, did he?"

But that infuriated Valentina. "That is extremely offensive, I wish I hadn't told you *anything*. This interview is terminated."

"Ah. Not bribery of you then. Bribery of his son? Threatened to cut him off without a penny, is that it, and your charms were unequal to the charms of poppa's money?"

Valentina knew she was attractive to men; she did not in any sense underestimate herself, and she resented anyone who did. "That's insulting. In the first place Julian has independent means, and in the second place he's the kind of man who would never give up someone he loved just for financial gain. Julian's not for sale."

"Oh? So for what would this paragon of virtue give up a woman like you, if, say, he really loved her?" Craig was homing in now.

Valentina was confused. Could she obfuscate? She could certainly try. "Well—this is just a for instance, it didn't happen, but say if someone Julian loved was in danger because of the relationship, that kind of thing would prompt a man like him to—"

"Of course! The old man threatened to hurt you! Now that one didn't occur to me—thanks, Miss Welles, this is great stuff."

Valentina felt the blood drain from her face. "No, that's not what I said, it was just hypothetical—"

Keith knew when to end a good interview. "Right, then! Well, goodbye Miss Welles, and thanks. You're a great interview."

"Candidate for Governor Against Interracial Marriage", one tabloid headline screamed.

"Gubernatorial Candidate Uses Threats Against Interracial Romance", a second tabloid blared.

"Writer's Affair Ended by Prejudiced Father", shouted yet another.

And Leonard Lecomte, besieged by the press, saw his lifelong ambitions for political power slowly being thwarted. His political enemies would make the most of this spectacular opportunity to derail his campaign before it got seriously under way.

A desperate Leonard, now a wounded animal at bay, sought a way to save his campaign. And like that wounded animal, Leonard was prepared to do almost anything.

....

As soon as Julian realized the extent of the damage being done to his father he was upset; he was not by nature a vengeful man. Swallowing his pride, he hurried to the LeComte mansion where he found Leonard locked in his study. He banged on the door with his closed fist.

"Open the door, Dad, we have to talk."

"Judas," Leonard shouted. "What about? You and that goddam woman have just ruined what I've worked for all my life."

"Not necessarily. Let me in, Dad. I'm not your enemy; I wish I could say you weren't mine. You have to believe me, I did my best to control those interviews."

Leonard, flushed, dishevelled and with a half empty glass of Bourbon in his hand, unlocked the door and confronted Julian.

The Tosca Taunt

"Oh for godssake come in, Julie, I guess what's done is done. The question is, can we salvage anything from this godawful mess? If we can't turn this around I'm done for."

"Nonsense, Pa, you're hardly finished, even if you don't succeed in politics. You're still head of the LeComte Corp—that'll keep you busy enough for the rest of your days."

"I know, Julie, but I've been there, done that, they were all stepping stones on the path to the Governor's Mansion and the White House, haven't you realised that yet?"

"But that's just dreams, Pa. The LeComte Corp is reality."

Leonard exploded. "Reality? What the hell do you know about reality? You think LeComte Corp didn't start out as a dream too? I came from nothing, son, nothing! I never want you to know what I had to do to even get myself out of the boonies, let alone to where I am now, and to where you and Del and all of you that live off me could have this great life. And now you have the colossal gall to tell me I don't have a right to dream higher? I can dream as goddam high as I want."

Julian said quietly, "I don't live off you, Pa."

"Who cares? What I'm talking about, is that it was way further from the beginning up to LeComte Corp, than it is from here to the White House. And I want it, son, I want it whatever I have to do, do you understand?" Leonard was breathing hard.

"Calm down, Pa, you'll have apoplexy."

Leonard sat down heavily in his big leather chair. Father and son looked balefully at each other.

"Look, Pa, I want to help. Which is a bloody lot more than you've done for me in the past few years. So, what can we do? How can we get around this?"

"Christ, son, I don't know. Any ideas?"

"Maybe."

"Shoot."

"The one thing that would prove all these rumours to be a lie."

"And what's that, son? I mean, we can be honest in here; the rumours are *not* a lie."

"But what if you had a black daughter-in-law and mixed race grandchildren that you looked like you approved of?"

"You think I haven't thought of that since the shit hit the fan this morning?"

"Okay, so you've thought of it too. Well?"

"Julie for godssake you know how I feel."

"Yes, I do, Pa. Only you say there's nothing you want more than to succeed in your political dream. I can maybe give you a shot at that, and the way may not be as bad as it seems. I mean, I know I'm your only son, but has it occurred to you that Delphine could give you a second family? I know neither of you has wanted that, but maybe other sons would be more satisfactory than I've been. Meanwhile the son you've got can take away these terrible rumours about you."

"Jesus, Julie."

But Leonard saw the chasm yawning before him. Denials of the headlines would not be believed now; they might even tarnish him further if he were proved a liar; and certainly such proof existed if a clever investigator looked far enough.

No, the solution was simple and painful. He could remove his objections to the romance between his son and Valentina Welles, and, quickly imagining how future publicity might be handled, he could be photographed beaming enthusiastically, first at the diva, next at her wedding, then at her pregnant, and later at his mixed-race grandchildren.

Furthermore Julian had a good point. There was no reason why Leonard and Delphine couldn't have a family. *Photogenic children in the Governor's mansion and in the White House, like Caroline and John-John Kennedy. Why ever not? And surely they would not all grow up to marry black spouses.*

Julian was unsuccessful in hiding his burgeoning hope. "It's your only chance, Pa," he said, his voice shaking.

"I know. I know." Leonard put his head in his hands and sighed an operatic sized sigh. Slowly, slowly, he looked up at his son. "Okay, Julian, go for it."

Julian's heart was pounding so hard it actually hurt. He said, "You won't oppose it, not now, not ever? You'll stand with us for good? You swear it?"

"I'll not oppose it. And I'll stand with you for good. I swear it. But never ask, Julian, never ask what I really feel. Now go, find that woman, propose to her, phone the bloody journalists with your announcement, tell them they've got the wrong end of the stick. Tell them it was her profession I objected to, that'll wash, not the fact that she has a career of course—I'd lose most of the women's votes if I objected to that—just that she spends her life singing all over the world. Tell them I figured that was no way to run a successful marriage."

"You won't be popular for it."

"I'll be a hell of a lot more popular than I am with *these* goddam headlines. Go, Julie, go and do it before I—"

Julian felt the blood drain from his face. "Before you change your mind? Pa, you promised; are you—"

"Yes. I promised. Get going, son."

....

Julian got a ticket for speeding his Porsche on the way home. And cared not a bit. He was shaking so badly he could scarcely get his key into the lock. Once into his townhouse, he grabbed the library telephone and dialled Valentina in San Francisco.

"Val! You singing tonight?"

"Julian, hello! What a stranger you've been! Of course, why?"

But he realised there was a better way than on the phone. So he extemporised with, "No reason, I just wanted to say *In Bocca al Lupo.*"

"Julian, you *are* foolish, but thanks. I'm sorry, I can't talk, I have to run. Bye, love."

Julian savoured his words. "Au revoir, love."

He hung up, and phoned the florist.

....

When Valentina entered her dressing room that evening, she was amazed to find it so filled with roses of every colour and kind that she could find no surface on which to put her purse. Nor on perusal could she find a card from the sender. She thought ruefully that she had a new admirer, obviously rich and intemperate, and that she would have to use her increasingly skilled methods to discourage him. She was both flattered and exasperated. She loved being adulated for her singing—that was one reason why she sang—but not courted to this exaggerated extent. There were more sensible ways to spend money—like sending a dozen roses and donating the rest of the money to

The Tosca Taunt

charity, for instance.

Still, as she put on her costume and makeup, she could scarcely ignore the lavish display of floral beauty she saw behind her in the mirror.

She noticed nobody special in the front rows, no man whose loud *bravas* stood out as had often happened in previous situations like this. She assumed as she took her last curtain call, at the end of a fairly successful evening, that the identity of her latest pursuer would be made known to her soon enough.

But those who waited at the dressing room door were regulars, a few old friends and acquaintances who had been in the audience.

Odd, she thought. *Imagine sending a fortune's worth of flowers and not even showing up after the performance to be, at the very least, thanked for them. Ah well, it takes all kinds.* She determined to have the bouquets delivered to two nearby nursing homes in the morning.

She had ordered her usual taxi with her usual driver, and when she was sure he had arrived at the stage door, she threw her coat over her shoulders and left the increasingly deserted opera house.

There was her cab, and there was someone in it. Exasperated that her very own cabbie would allow himself to be bribed by the donor of the flowers, Valentina threw open the back door of the cab and began to say, "What do you—" when the man turned around and she saw his face.

"Julian? Julian!"

He climbed out of the cab, holding one perfect red rose. Wordlessly he handed it to her. Then he took her by the shoulders.

"Will you marry me?"

"What? What are you talking about?"

"What kind of a response is that?" He touched her lips softly with his. "I said, will you marry me?"

"But Julian, what about—"

"It's over." He smiled at her. "The way is clear. Our problems will be our own, not his. I promise, Val."

The cabbie glanced in his side mirror, and saw his diva slowly put her arms around the man's shoulders. The lovers drew together. The cabbie slumped down in his seat and turned up his radio. He guessed he was going to be here for a while yet.

Thirty-Four

"Geez, Barb, I don't know," Charlie Demchuk said to his wife as they flew home to Ontario from the Saskatchewan funeral of his mother-in-law. "I can't leave it until Jen gets her next leave, they only come out once a month, if it was you alive and I thought you were dead, that poor guy Amato, you saw his face in the picture, no, I've got to find some way to tell her before the month is up."

"But Charlie you can't just tell her on the phone, how could you? It would be so hard for her—I'm sure she needs to see the pictures to help her remember, if that really is her I mean. So what can you do?"

"What if I say I need to see her and can I come up to the mine for a day? I s'pose they have some kind of accommodation for visitors; if I can't go for a weekend I could always take a couple days off my holiday time, I've still got two weeks left. I better do it that way."

So when Charlie, Barb and their children finally arrived

home, glad to be there but sad to be forever without their dear Grammie, Charlie dialled the phone number Jen had sent him, and left a message asking her to call him back when it was convenient.

Charlie's phone rang two hours later.

"What trouble we're having getting together, Charlie. I was so sorry to hear about your wife's mother."

"Yeah, it's been kinda tough, but listen, Jen, that thing I've got to talk to you about—"

"I don't have leave for a month now, Charlie. Can I come to see you then?"

"That's too long to wait."

"Couldn't you tell me over the phone?"

There was a pause. Then, "No, it wouldn't be right."

Jen was dismayed. What could he have to tell her that was so upsetting he didn't dare do it over the phone? "Good heavens, Charlie, what on earth is it? You've got me so curious!"

"Yeah. Uh, I was wondering, since this is important and I can't do it on the phone because I have to show you something along with telling you, I'd like to come up to the mine if that can be arranged."

"I don't see why not. There's one helicopter in and out each day, you'd have to stay overnight, but I'm sure Mark—he's the mine boss—he'd let you sleep in the empty cabin if I asked him."

So it was arranged that Charlie would come up the following Monday and leave Tuesday. Monday evening the weather was unsettled and the helicopter from Timmins was late arriving. After supper Jen and Mark waited for Charlie in the television room, idly channel surfing, when suddenly Mark said,

The Tosca Taunt

"I completely forgot, when I was in Toronto I went to a video store and bought out all the versions of *Tosca* they had, they're a present for you; I thought one of them might be the one we saw. I'll get them."

He hurriedly fetched the videos and handed them to her. "Here, a surfeit of tenors, maybe one of these will be your nightmare man, here's Luciano Pavarotti, Placido Domingo, Antonio Amato. And the sopranos are Hildegarde Behrens, Maria Ewing and Mia Mitsouros. Do you suppose opera singers are ever named Smith?" He handed her the three cassettes. "We'll look at them while we wait for Charlie, if you like."

"I know there's a soprano named Jones—Gwyneth Jones; how do you imagine I can remember that and not more important things?"

He put his arm briefly around her shoulders. "It's probably important to her."

They put in the first cassette, which featured Luciano Pavarotti singing *Cavaradossi*. Jen was quite sure he was not the tenor of her dreaming, but she still wanted to fast forward to the shooting at the end to be absolutely certain. When Pavarotti entered and began to sing *Recondite Armonia,* she was mesmerised by the beauty of his voice, and she listened, absorbed.

"Turn up the volume, Jen—I think opera should be loud or not at all," said Mark.

"And mostly not at all, right, Mark?" Jen smiled fondly at him.

There was a sudden commotion outside. Because of the music, Jen and Mark, sitting on the sofa holding hands, had not heard the helicopter arriving, so they did not make up a proper welcoming committee for Charlie, who had been directed down the hall. He came hesitantly into the room; Jen sprang out of her chair and impulsively hugged him.

"Charlie! I'm so glad to see you! Please, come and join us, I'd like you to meet Mark Reinhard. Would you like something to drink, are you hungry, I could—"

"Whoa, Jen, whoa! I've ate, I'm not thirsty, I'd just like to talk with you."

"Well then, sit down, tell us how your trip went."

Charlie sank gratefully into a big comfortable chair. He had been enthusiastic about his trip, believing he was about to make a miracle for Jen, but now, having seen Jen holding Mark's hand, and observing the way the couple looked at each other, he was uneasy. He felt out of his depth, uncomfortable about his mission, assailed by sudden doubts as though what he were about to do were wrong. He wondered if there was a way to put off his session with her until later. He glanced at the television, still bellowing opera, and thought of a clever way to postpone his disclosures.

"Hey, there's that big guy, Pavrot, you and I talked about him, Jen. You said you liked the other guy better, the guy that acts, Domingo. You got Domingo on a video, maybe I could see him too, before we get down to serious talk? It's classical music study time." Charlie grinned at Jen.

Jen felt slightly let down. She was eager to learn what Charlie had come to tell her. But she supposed she had to let him do it in his own time. "Actually, yes, I do. Are you sure, Charlie? I mean, you've just arrived, don't you want to just relax and chat

The Tosca Taunt

for a while?"

"Nope, I'm sure. Show me."

"All right. I'll show you him singing the same bit Pavarotti just sang, you'll see what I mean about their different styles."

"Sure, why not? I'll get an education, take my mind off that damn helicopter, pardon my French."

Mark laughed. "Rough ride tonight, Charlie?"

"I'll say. Do you ever get used to them things? I'll take my rig any day, weird brakes and all. Oh, there he is, that Domingo guy, yeah, I recognize him. I see what you mean, they both sound good but they sure have different styles."

After the aria Jen said, "We've got a third tenor here, let's give you an in depth course; do you want to see someone different do the same aria?"

Charlie was not sure all this would turn him into an opera enthusiast. But what the hell, it postponed his announcement about which, as he surreptitiously continued watching Mark and Jen, he felt increasingly perturbed. Jen put in the third operatic cassette and pressed play and the fast forward button. She was listening to Charlie, who had just told her a long joke, and she was laughing so hard she forgot to tell him the name of this third tenor. She released the fast forward button and looked back at the television screen just as the tenor came on and began his version of *Recondite Armonia*.

Jen gave a little cry. Startled, Mark and Charlie swung their heads to look at her. With her hand over her mouth, she gave another cry, then stood up. She put her hands out in front of her, palms up in a gesture of total submission. The tenor's voice soared, honeyed gold, beautiful. Jen's knees began to buckle, she put one hand to her head, and Mark grabbed her as she crumpled. He gently helped her down onto the couch.

"For God's sake turn off that racket," he said to Charlie, gesturing with his head at the television set.

Charlie shook his head. "No. You don't understand."

"What the hell are you talking about?" Mark grabbed the remote control and pushed the mute button.

And Jen cried, "No! Let him sing!"

Bewildered now, Mark stared at her. "Here, take the remote, do whatever makes you feel better, what on earth is wrong?"

Jen released the mute button so the music soared again, and gazed at the television with fierce concentration. Mark glanced at Charlie, who unaccountably chose this moment to take an envelope out of his pocket and pull from it some crumpled printed pages.

Jen got up and stumbled towards the television set in front of which her legs gave way and she fell to her knees. Mark started towards her to help her, but Charlie grabbed his arms from behind and stopped him.

"What the hell?" said Mark, struggling. But Charlie was a strong man, stronger even than the fit Mark.

"Leave her alone," Charlie said.

"You don't know her from Eve, let go of me you idiot, she needs help—"

Jen stared at the screen from about two feet away. Charlie held Mark in a firm grip, and for a moment they watched Jen, mesmerised.

Mark tried again to wrestle free. "Let me go, what the hell do you think you're—"

The Tosca Taunt

"Mark, no, I know what's happening to her. She has amnesia, doesn't she."

"Yeah, how do you know? And what's that got to do with her and this video, for God's sake?"

"I'm going to let you go; don't move until I can show you something."

Charlie loosed Mark and handed him the magazine clippings, first the picture of Jen, with under it the caption, "The Late Jenetta Maclean Amato", then the previous page, the one with the picture of a grim Tony Amato and his children going to their mother's memorial service.

"Oh God," said Mark. "You—she's—oh God."

Charlie took his eyes off Jen long enough to look at Mark. And saw for certain that Mark was in love with Jen, and that Charlie and the video had just delivered a vicious blow.

"She's—do you think she's remembering?" Mark whispered.

"Damned if I know, but something's happening, and we've got to leave her be. Maybe she'll have to see the opera right through. We've just got to stay with her and make sure nothing bad happens to her—"

Jen, still on her knees in front of the television set, clutched her hands together so tightly the fingers were blenched. Amato-*Cavaradossi* had come on the scene after having been tortured; he was a superb actor, and his stage pain was convincing even to Charlie and Mark.

But the effect on Jen was curious. As the soprano tried to comfort the tenor, Jen whispered, "No, no, Mia, nobody can help Tony but me, ohgod ohgod ohgod Tony, oh Tony!"

The two men stood together, mesmerised by Jen's ecstatic

agony. She stayed on her knees, her hands now held as though in prayer. But for Charlie there was a third drama besides Jen's and the one on the video. There was the drama of Mark, visibly pale even in the dimly lit room, trying to deal with this discovery. What dreams had he entertained about Jen? Had he dreamed of a life with her? Charlie figured this was one hell of a way to get dumped.

On the television the firing squad was about to shoot the tenor, and Mark now recognised this as the video they had glimpsed in Langdon Hall. The soprano realised the tenor was truly dead, and, unwilling to face the rest of her life without him, committed suicide by jumping from the parapet. Jen let the video run all through the credits until it faded to snowy black. Slowly she stood up. She put one hand on her forehead, grimacing as though in pain, and turned to Mark and Charlie, her face glistening with tears.

Mark put his arms around her, and she clung to him.

"Mark, oh my dearest Mark, I—that tenor—I remember—I know who I am."

"I know. That's why Charlie came. Don't say anything more, just sit down here and see what he's brought. I've already seen them."

"You look ill, Mark." Confused, she gently touched his face. "Is it bad news?"

"Not for everybody. Only for me."

"Oh Mark. I'm so sorry."

She sat down between him and Charlie, and stared at the picture of herself. Then she saw the other one, the one of Tony and her children on their way to say a final "goodbye" to her.

The Tosca Taunt

She whispered, "All this pain, all this pain! How can I have forgotten for—how long?—that I have these beautiful children, this husband—whatever happened to make me forget?"

"I know that too, Jen," Charlie said, and from his other pocket he pulled a clipping about the fire, and about Jen being one of the four people missing and almost certainly dead.

"This hotel at Hadley's Ridge, it's miles away, up above the road where I found you, it's—that is, it was—on a cliff with what they advertised as the world's most beautiful view."

Jen sat with her head on Mark's shoulder, his arm around her. "I don't remember anything about the fire, or why I would be there in the first place. But Mark, I'll have to go now ... I'll have to go home. I need ... " her voice diminished until it was a barely audible whisper. "I need ... Tony."

"And me, Jen?" Mark said, the hopelessness already in his voice.

"Oh Mark I'm so sorry." She rubbed her hand across her forehead. "I think ... I think now I understand why I couldn't make love to you even when I couldn't remember. It's because ... oh, it's because Tony is ... he's the other half of me. It's like the song; *Someone to Watch Over Me*. We watch over each other, Tony and I. Oh Mark, I'm so tired. "

....

Tony Amato had an early plane to catch, so he had gone to bed in the hope of getting a few hours sleep. But he was disturbed by dreams; he was performing in *Tosca,* with Mia Mitsouros as his *Floria Tosca*. In the dream he performed badly, partly because Jen was on stage with him, only she was almost transparent and nobody could see her except him. She kept throwing her arms around him and putting her face against his, so that all his stage movements were hampered. He should have minded, but somehow he was so glad to see Jen, nuisance though she was being, that he did not care. He finished the dream opera singing *Someone to Watch Over Me* to the phantomlike Jen. He awoke in a state of confused misery.

This makes no sense, he thought. *After Mia and Cedric's wedding, I will go to see Thomas Graham Lanville again, and I will tell him I think I understand what he is trying to tell me. It's that Jen—and Francesca—are dead as the world understands death, but for we who loved them so much, they can never really die as long as they are in our memory.*

....

Charlie and Mark helped Jen to her room. She seemed almost catatonic in her exhaustion, so Mark put her on the bed, undid the buttons and zipper of her blue jeans, and covered her with a blanket. She fell immediately into a deep sleep.

Mark took Charlie out to the unoccupied cabin he was to sleep in, where they sat together and had a talk about Jen's future. Mark told a worried Charlie that he would go with Jen to her reunion with Tony Amato if she needed him to, and saying that, he realised the emotional cost to himself, and that unfortunately he loved Jen enough to pay it.

Before he went to bed, Mark alerted the mine nurse, told her Jen had had an emotional shock and seemed unwell, and asked her to look in during the night.

Once in bed himself, Mark stared at the darkness, knowing he had not found the cure for his loneliness, and wondering now, given the depth of his love for Jen, whether he ever would.

And then, abruptly, came an oddly welcome thought; yes, she was Mrs Antonio Amato, but she had not yet met Mark when she married Amato; what if her affection for him were now stronger than her feelings for Amato? Was there still a chance for him? He knew it was a faint hope, but it gave colour to his dark thoughts of the future.

By morning Jen had a fever. Influenza, said the nurse; she pointed out to Mark that they seemed to be having a mini-epidemic at the mine. The victims felt ill for a week, tired for another, and then were fine. Mark was almost glad to see Jen flushed, feverish, and sleeping constantly. It put off the inevitable day when she would decide how to tell her husband and children that she was not dead. But he strongly suspected that her illness was not only due to the 'flu epidemic that was spreading virulently through the mine buildings. For he had seen her ordeal.

Thirty-Five

There were many secrets Cedric kept from Mia. One of them was that he needed a coronary bypass operation. But he would say nothing of that to her until after the wedding. He had waited too long, suffered too much, given up too much, not to get his prize. Mia would be his wife. And if he died immediately afterwards, he wasn't certain he cared. To die on a high, that was all he asked of death; he would not ask when, or by what means, even if he could have had answers. It was not that Cedric was suicidal; he loved life, and had only begun all that he hoped to achieve. It was simply that he was a realist; life is a terminal illness, and there are never any guarantees, not even for men like him.

He wanted to believe Mia saw little or nothing of his illness, wanted to believe she was at last rushing headlong into nuptials like a happy girl. But still, unreasonably he knew, he hoped that she was aware he was ill, and that his illness pulled her ever closer to him in love and compassion. *How perverse the human*

The Tosca Taunt

heart, he thought.

And how perverse mine. Just let me live until my wedding day. That sounds so emotional. This making an opera out of the big events of one's life—I thought only Tony and Mia and their delightfully dramatic ilk did that, and here I am, making an opera out of my illness and my marriage. I begin to see why they self-dramatize like this; it gives an unexpected excitement to life, a heightening of the already theatrical.

The notion that Mia did not see what was going on was nonsense, she thought, covertly watching him going about business as usual. Because of course it was in truth anything but business as usual. He was grey-faced now, with a darkness around his eyes and a weary slump to his shoulders that she had never seen there before. Sometimes he would perspire though the room was cold; sometimes he would shiver though the room was hot; altogether there was no way she could have missed seeing that he was not well.

But, since he confided in her no further, she did what he wanted her to do. She went ahead with plans for the small wedding, to be held in the private chapel at Ridlough Hall, and for the large lavish reception to be held in the great hall. There would be the most sumptuous food Cedric's chef could devise, there would be an orchestra, there would be dancing, and Antonio Amato singing love songs for the bride and groom; there would be toasts and replies, there would be splendour, there would even be, for as short a while as possible, the media.

Above all Cedric wanted splendour; he wanted all the world to know that Mia was at last his. His. Not the musical world's; not the widower Tony Amato's—despite the years of rumours—

no, his, Cedric's wife. He had extracted from Mia the promise that she would wear a white gown, because somehow, incongruous though he knew it to be, he felt that her marriage to him wiped from her his own stain and the stain of other men. For him, on their wedding night, she would be a virgin.

So Mia, feeling more than a little foolish, had asked one of the fashion designers renowned for dressing certain of the more fashionable royal British women, to create a gown suitable for a sophisticated career woman in her mid-thirties, twice divorced, three times a mother, who had had a well publicized love affair with tenor Carlo Paoli as well as other love affairs about which the prying media had never learned. She did not of course express all this to her designer; she simply let it be known that she expected a gown suiting all aspects of her.

Great was her astonishment when she went to see his first drawings and realised that he had conceived a gown so simple it could have been worn by a virginal seventeen year old bride. She demurred.

He said, "Trust me. Have you ever seen a gown of mine that was a failure, or that did not suit the wearer?"

At her first fitting the designer said, "May I take down your hair, and show you how I want it worn on your wedding day?" He pulled the pins from her bright hair, and it cascaded around her shoulders in an unruly mass. He pinned up the front in an Alice-in-Wonderland sweep, a style she had not worn for ten years other than on stage, believing herself to be too mature and far too worldly. But now she looked young, sweet, bridal. The designer had her slip on the dress, her back to the mirror. He adjusted various zippers and hooks, and turned her around. She was amazed.

The mirror reflected a slender dark woman in a deceptively simple full-skirted floor length silk dress, with a sweetheart neckline and short puffy sleeves. The top was completely beaded with pure white pearls and sequins. She was wearing, as the designer had requested, the pearl necklace given her by Cedric, a necklace that had once belonged to the Empress Josephine. Mia was astonished at the look the designer had given her. Not too young, not mutton dressed as lamb as she might have thought had she only looked at the gown on its hanger, but sophisticated simplicity, a look of worldly maidenliness if such a thing could be. Impulsively she threw her arms about the designer and kissed him.

"Am I to take it that you like the dress, Madame Mitsouros?"

"Like it? You're a wizard, a magician!"

"May I say that a lot of the dress's success is you. I have simply enhanced your beauty, Madame. That gown, seen only on the hanger, is nothing."

After telling Mia that most of the brides who wore his gowns had happy marriages, a tale about which she was sceptical, he instructed her to have the finished dress picked up the day before the wedding. And she, enchanted and quite bemused, left his studio.

....

Mark Reinhard was having an evening conference with Sue, the mine nurse, in her office. "I don't know what to think, Mark," the nurse said to him. "This is the oddest case of flu I've seen. If we weren't having this 'flu epidemic, I'd say her illness had a psychological component."

"It does," said Mark morosely. "But she doesn't want me to talk about it yet. Everybody will know soon, but I won't break the faith with her on that account."

"Should we fly her out?"

"She'll go of her own accord soon enough, Sue. More's the pity."

Sue searched her boss' face. A middle-aged widow who had done a lot of living, she had no problem seeing that Mark had fallen 'head-over-apple-cart,' as they used to say in her Nova Scotia home, for Jen Noonan. Now she wondered whether what had looked so promising on both sides, had just been terminated by Jen. She ill, he white-faced, sombre—it fit the nurse's scenario. But it was not in her mandate to seek confidences; if they came unsolicited, that was something else again.

"I'll just go along and see how she's doing," Mark said. "Maybe if this fever doesn't go down soon we *should* get her out of here. But there are some peculiar problems that I'm damned if I know what to do with. If she can't make a decision soon I'm going to have to do it for her, and it's a bugger, Sue, it's a real bugger." He shook his head, rose, and walked slowly to Jen's room.

"Come," she said, when he knocked and called out.

She sat on the edge of her bed, her hair uncombed, her face scrubbed clean of makeup. She was flushed, her eyes glittering, but when he touched her hands they were icy and she was trembling.

"How goes it, my dear?" He longed to put his arms around her, to kiss-her-and-make-it-well, to tell her to come away with him to the ends of the earth and be his love forever. And he

The Tosca Taunt

could not.

"It doesn't go very well, Mark, every time I sit up I'm dizzy—but I've been thinking, and—" Her dark blue eyes were huge in her pinched face. "—I think I've subconsciously made myself ill because I don't know how to go back, oh Mark, I want my children, I want Tony, but I'm so afraid."

"I'm not sure I understand what you're afraid of; you say you love this man, you see from his pictures how shattered he is thinking he has lost you, why can't you just phone him and tell him? Why give him more days of agony?"

"I don't know, oh ... what if by now it's not agony, what if he has adjusted finally to life without me?"

"How could he stop wanting you so soon if you had the wonderful marriage you say you had? If you were *my* wife, do you think I would forget you so quickly? God, Jen, you're not my wife, you're not even my mistress, and how fast do you think I'll forget you when you've gone where you—where you *say* you—belong? Unless—" Mark allowed himself a glimpse of hope. "—unless you're not sure; unless I count for something in this equation—"

He saw from her expression that he was close to the truth. He knew at the very least that she cared for him, in a confused way, and that she trusted him utterly.

"You mean you agree that maybe I'm making myself sick because I don't know which way to go? Oh Mark, help me; surely I *have* to go back—"

"You have to go back, of course, but do you have to stay?"

He took her cold hands and warmed them between his. They sat together in silent misery for a long while. Then Mark, seeing how utterly forlorn she looked, needed to distract her. He suggested they watch a bit of television on the small set he had brought into her room. What turned up was one of those gossip shows that purport to be news.

The visuals were of Mia Mitsouros getting out of a Rolls Royce in London with Cedric, Viscount Ridlough, behind her. The voice-over announcer was saying, "The American diva Mia Mitsouros and her British tycoon Lord Ridlough are finally putting to rest the rumours that the widower Tony Amato had come between them. Mia and her Lord will tie the knot at his ancestral home this Saturday in a private ceremony, followed by one of the most lavish receptions of the decade. And just to show there are no hard feelings, the apparently still grieving Tony Amato will dance the night away with his old friends, and will, we are told, sing love songs for the newly-weds at the big ball."

The visuals cut to Tony Amato, smiling at photographers as he too emerged from a limousine. The unctuous voice-over continued. "All this should put paid to the rumours that have circulated about Amato and Mitsouros for years; if there had been anything to the stories, surely Amato would have taken advantage of his recent tragically won freedom to stop Saturday's nuptials and to grab the lovely Mia for himself."

Now the visuals showed a desolate looking Tony and his children leaving their apartment for The Cloisters the day of the memorial service for Jen. The announcer continued, "—which goes to show you that what we said all along is true; Tony Amato continues to carry a big torch for his beloved late wife Jen, the woman he can never have again."

When Jen saw Tony's set, white face, she squeezed her eyes

shut and covered her face with her hands as though she could not bear to look. She opened her eyes only when she heard the item end and a commercial blaring.

"That was a message," she said to Mark.

"What are you talking about?"

"That was a message telling me to go home now."

Good grief, thought Mark, *she's worse off than even Sue and I imagined.*

Jen looked at him. "Will you really take the time and come with me? I'm so mixed up, Mark." She faltered, then continued. "That program said Tony would be in England next weekend for the wedding. Come with me and be my strength, this is so hard, you can't imagine. "

"But what on earth do you plan to do? You can't just show up at the wedding like a revenant, you'll give everybody heart attacks, Jen, dear Jen, be logical. At least phone your hus—" Mark cleared his throat. "—husband, let the poor guy know you're alive."

"But don't you see, that's just what I'm not able to do!"

"You surely you don't expect me to—do you want me to tell him for you?" Mark tried to steel himself against her answer. "Is that what you're trying to say?"

"Oh no, I must be the one to tell him, but I don't know how."

He cast about for a way to help her. "What about consulting a psychiatrist on the best way to do this? I happen to know a good doctor; one of my sisters had a severe post-partum depression, she was treated by a Tom Grayme in Toronto. Would you—"

"Thomas Graham Lanville!"

"What?"

"Thomas Graham Lanville, you know, the—"

"Of course I know of him. The old man, the great benefactor to the arts and various charities, the one who's dying? What's he got to do with anything?"

"He's not dying."

"But Jen, he must be almost a hundred years old, he's got to be dying."

Frowning, she reflected for a long moment. "No. He won't die until I get there. He has something to do yet for me."

This is bloody voodoo stuff, Mark thought helplessly.

"He's been my last resort before—he once helped Tony and me out of a terrible situation," she continued. "He'll help me. Come with me, we'll go to Mr Lanville, he lives in England not far from Cedric, the man who is marrying Mia Mitsouros..."

"Of course I'll come. Let's phone your friend Lanville right now."

"No. I'll just go to him. He'll know what I should do."

"You'll give him a heart attack, Jen! Everybody thinks you're dead, you could do harm to an ailing old man if you just appear out of the blue, it's irresponsible."

"No it's not. I won't hurt him, of course I would never hurt him, don't be ridiculous, Mark! You see, he knows. He knows I'm alive."

"What are you talking about?"

"How can I explain to you? I just know he knows. Francesca told him."

"Who the hell is Francesca?"

"His wife. She's been dead for years."

Mark stared at her, afraid for her sanity, wondering whether he should call psychiatrist Tom Grayme on his own. But he knew if he did so without Jen's assent, he would lose the chance he hoped he still had, of winning her.

He picked up the telephone in Jen's room and dialled his travel agent's number in Toronto.

....

In the end, since Mia could never again be attended at her wedding ceremony by Jen Amato, she chose as her attendant her own daughter Gilda, aged seven and reasonably well-behaved. Mia could not bring herself to ask another adult woman; it hurt her too much that her dear friend Jen was dead. Besides, she could not imagine what it would do to Tony to see another woman attending Mia. So pretty, wilful Gilda, in a long yellow dress of her own choosing, walked into the chapel ahead of her mother, as the trio culled from the orchestra for tonight's reception played a cheerful *partita* by Bach, and Mia's serious son Simon watched nervously from a front pew. Simon had many reasons to know that Gilda did not always behave as she should. But today his apprehensions were baseless; Gilda's poise was unshakeable for the entire evening.

Nobody gave Mia away this time. Her widowed father had done so for her two previous weddings, but he, retired in Greece, said he was now too crippled with arthritis to come to this wedding. Mia suspected that this lameness was partly diplomatic; her father detested Cedric. In any case, the superstitious Mia wanted nothing similar to either of her previous weddings, which had preceded marriages ending in bitterness and grief.

Mia had not worn a white wedding dress before. For her first wedding she had considered herself too sophisticated for such nonsense; she had worn a turquoise dress that matched her unusual eyes. For her second she had worn a pale grey lace suit. And traditional wedding music had accompanied each of those ceremonies.

But not this time.

Cedric, and Tony who was his best man, waited in the chapel dressed in their white ties and tails. The ceremony was, at six-thirty in the evening, a little early for such attire, but since they would be going immediately in to the banquet and dance after the small wedding ceremony, they had elected to dress only once rather than change for dinner after the service.

Cedric knew his Mia was beautiful, but even he was unprepared for what he saw when the music began and he and Tony turned to face the entrance through which Mia came. She was so exquisite that looking at her hurt him, quite literally gave him a painful twinge in his chest. As she came slowly up the short aisle, he smiled at her, but she did not respond to him. Yet she was smiling, with a fixed smile, almost trance-like. *She is transported with happiness,* Cedric thought, as she came up beside him. Gilda stepped to Mia's left, her gaze never leaving her mother.

Finally Mia turned to Cedric as he took her hand, and smiled her best stage smile at him, fully aware that he never knew when she was sincere and when she was acting.

For as she walked into the church, it was Tony Amato she had seen first, Tony towards whom she walked, Tony, the

The Tosca Taunt

inadvertent spoiler...

Now the Anglican minister began the service. Mia felt Cedric's eyes on her, knew they did not leave her throughout the entire ceremony. The wedding ring he put on her finger was a total surprise for her, a wide band of pave diamonds and emeralds set in platinum.

He kissed her as gently as though he were kissing a young virgin bride. *How men do deceive themselves,* she thought as she kissed him back. Cedric had closed his eyes as he kissed, but Mia stared over his shoulder at the sombre face of Tony Amato. Tony was staring back, seeing, and yet it seemed to Mia, not seeing. As Cedric kissed her once more, obviously entranced, she continued to look at Tony, appalled at the Rogers and Hammerstein song which had just hurled itself into her consciousness, "*This Nearly Was Mine.*"

Tony. Tony. Tony.

Now the wedding was over; the wedding party left the chapel to the strains of a melody by Handel. They hurried across to the great hall where the assembled guests cheered as the wedding party walked in, this time to the triumphal wedding march played by an orchestra on a raised platform. The large group would eat seated at tables placed at one end of the great hall, but the dancing and general festivities would undoubtedly fill the large space.

The guests were dressed as though they were at a Coronation. Royalty was present. Ball gowns had been brought out, family jewels had been taken from vaults and encircled smooth necks and crepey ones alike; tiaras sparkled in white, black, brown, blonde, red hair; diamond studs embellished evening shirts. Cedric had wanted splendour; pomp was what he got.

Just before dessert the master of ceremonies, a noted English television interviewer, announced that the tenor Antonio Amato had been asked by the bride and groom to sing two songs, one for each of them. Apparently the bride had been too excited to choose her song, so the groom had chosen for both of them; his choices were *All the Things You Are,* by Kern and Hammerstein, and *Be My Love,* by Cahn and Brodszky.

Tony was determined to give Mia and Cedric their heart's worth, and he put everything he had into his singing, to the point that when he had finished, the wedding guests, disconcerted by the emotions he aroused, had to collect themselves for a moment before they erupted into wild applause.

Tony acknowledged their applause with his usual grace, but declined to sing any more. He had spent his emotional currency. He would have to be alone for a few minutes now, alone with his memories, before he could join once more in the festivities. He unobtrusively left the room, and walked from the chateau out to the front drive, where he stood looking at the full moon that seemed to sit in the branches of an ancient oak.

"Oh my Jen," he whispered. "Did you hear my songs? Mia and Cedric think they were for them but—" He stopped. He needed to believe Jen could hear him when he talked to her, hear him when he sang to her. Why not? Who could ever know these things?

He had not heard Mia come up behind him. She slipped her arm into his.

The Tosca Taunt

"Cedric sent me to fetch you, Tony darling. He says to thank you for the songs; he says he knows what singing like that must still cost you. Funny, I hadn't thought of Cedric as that sensitive; I guess I don't know him, even yet."

He smiled at her. "You know what I keep wishing for you both, Mia. I wish for you to be like Jen and me."

"I know. I know. Only I have a problem that I think Jen never had."

"What is that?"

"Oh Tony. It would be better if I didn't say it, not to you, not on my wedding night to—" She had been about to say "to someone else," but stopped herself. Leaning forward, she stretched up on tiptoe and kissed him on the cheek.

"Part of my soul will always belong to you, Tony darling." She bent her head so he would not see her tear-filled eyes. Then, not a little afraid, she knew she must lighten the mood. "Forever friends, promise? Now come back in, Tony; you owe me the next dance. You promised me the Viennese waltzes, remember?"

Soon they were swirling gracefully about the floor, two people who had obviously learned a lot from their training for dancing on stage. Half way through the second waltz, Cedric cut in.

"My turn, Tony. I'm claiming my bride. All the rest of her dances are mine."

Thirty-Six

Not far from Cedric's home but much closer to Glyndebourne, Mark Reinhard emerged from a rented car, and rang the bell on the stone pillar beside the wrought iron gates of Thomas Graham Lanville's country estate. A disembodied, plummy male voice said through a loudspeaker, "Who is it? Speak slowly please, we are having some difficulty with the intercommunications systems."

Mark now followed Jen's instructions. They had decided, in deference to Mr Lanville's age and state of health, to begin their interviews with the long time butler. Mark spoke into a small metal grille in the pillar with the sign underneath saying, "Speak Here".

"My name is Mark Reinhard, I'm a mining engineer from Canada, and I'd like to speak to your butler, please, I believe his name is Bradford."

"I am Bradford; can you state your business; I have not the pleasure of your acquaintance."

The Tosca Taunt

"It has to do with the Amatos."

"I'm sorry, I can't hear you very well, but we don't need tomatoes, we grow our own here in the greenhouse."

"Not tomatoes, Amatos, the Amatos, he's a singer."

There was a silence. Then Bradford said doubtfully, "I don't know what you are talking about, I can hardly hear you, something about tomatoes and a singer, I'll send the chauffeur down to the gate."

There was a click. Mark went back to the car. He said, "Jen, won't you let me tell them you're here? We're going to have trouble getting in."

But Jen, shaking with fear, could not speak. She was virtually paralysed.

Presently a large, heavy-set man appeared and stared at the car through the bars.

"What do you want?" he called.

Mark came back to the tall gates and again said who he was and that he had business with the butler.

"We can't let every Tom Dick and Harry in that says he has business with the butler, we have to think of security."

Mark was unsure of how to proceed, but obviously Jen's idea would not work.

"Just a minute," he said to the chauffeur. He walked back to the car and opened the door, revealing Jen sitting staring straight ahead of her, only her profile visible to the man inside the gates.

"This is about her," Mark said.

"Good heavens, I'd swear that was Mr Amato's wife if I didn't know for a fact she was killed. Dead ringer for Mrs Amato your friend is."

"Jen, please," Mark pleaded.

Jen turned her head towards the chauffeur. "Hello Hadlam," she whispered.

"Good God," Hadlam exclaimed, grabbing one of the wrought iron bars of the gate as though to steady himself. "Mrs—Mrs Amato? Is that really you? But you're dead! Mr Amato has come several times, he's that upset about you—"

"She's had amnesia," Mark said to the bewildered chauffeur. "She's been out of sight since a hotel fire in which she supposedly died; she hasn't known who she was. Her memory didn't return until just a few days ago. She hasn't yet told anyone from her 'real' life that she's alive; she wants first to talk to her friend Mr Lanville. She hopes he can advise her. Please, you can see she's not at all well. Won't you let us in? She needs help."

The chauffeur was convinced. He said, "I can hardly wait until Bradford sees her; he prides himself on not showing his emotions. I'll drive up with you."

Hadlam briefly communicated with Bradford on a cellular phone, telling him that he and the Canadian engineer and his party were on their way up to the house.

The ponderous gates slowly swung open; Hadlam slipped into the back seat of the car as Mark drove up the long oak framed drive to the classical Georgian mansion.

"How are you going to do this?" Hadlam asked as they got out of the car. Bradford, curious, opened the door before there was a chance to ring.

Mark started to say, "I'm Mark Reinhard, I have someone with me who wants to see Mr Lanville—" but Jen had stepped

The Tosca Taunt

from the car behind him. Bradford's eyes opened in such classic astonishment that Hadlam laughed out loud.

"But—but that woman—I would swear she was—but she cannot be—I—I think I must sit down." Bradford abruptly sat on the stone bench beside the door as Jen said quietly, "Hello, Bradford. I know, this is a confusing way to do it, but I don't know what else I can do."

"She's had amnesia," Mark explained, as Bradford finally collected himself enough to ask them in. "I'll order tea," he said in a strangled voice.

"We must talk about how best to approach your employer," Mark said worriedly over tea. "At his age a shock like this could do him real harm."

"I think you will be surprised at his reaction, Mr Reinhard, Mrs Amato. You see, he has said all along that Mrs Amato was not dead, that it was simply some sort of misunderstanding. He insists on this, each time Mr Amato telephones or comes to visit, and poor Mr Amato leaves him and goes and sits in the maze for a long while, trying to pull himself together before he has to leave. Mrs Amato, you cannot imagine how terrible losing you ... er ... has been for your husband."

Jen bowed her head. Then she looked up at Mark. "I told you Mr Lanville would know I wasn't dead."

Mark and the butler exchanged puzzled glances. Bradford realised that Mrs Amato must not be entirely recovered from her head injury, because of course there was no way she could have known that Mr Lanville thought she was alive. *No way. Was there?*

"So, Bradford, should I just go up to Mr Lanville? If you

really believe he will not be too surprised to see me, then perhaps you can just announce me without a lot of explanations, and let me do the rest."

"I feel confident that will be the best, Mrs Amato. Please understand you will find him sadly changed from when you saw him last; he is now completely bedridden. But his mind, of course, his formidable mind has diminished very little."

They climbed the staircase together, that staircase which had seen many of Jen and Tony's pivotal moments; their first meeting, their successful reunion once when they had believed their marriage was over, and now—and now?

They arrived at the door of Mr Lanville's bedroom. Bradford knocked, and Mr Lanville's nurse called, "Come."

Bradford opened the door. Jen, sure she could not be seen in the shadows of the hall, peeked in at the spacious bright room, at the huge four poster bed piled with colourful bedding, and at the thin, frail man who lay there unmoving, eyes closed.

Bradford went in and began to say, "Mr Lanville, I have a thrilling surprise for you. You have a visitor—"

Without opening his eyes Thomas Graham Lanville said, "Of course I have a visitor. What took her so long? Tell Mrs Amato to stop hiding and come in." Only then did he open his eyes.

Jen moved into the doorway as Bradford turned to her, and she shrugged in a gesture which said, "I told you he would not be shocked." Smiling, Bradford left her and Mark with Mr Lanville.

"Jen, my dear, it's about time you came back to us. Where have you been? Your Tony has been well nigh annihilated by your disappearance. And who are you, young man?"

Jen introduced them. Mr Lanville appraised Mark, and said, "And you love Jen too, do you not."

Mark, discomfited, said, "I'm her friend, Mr Lanville. She has only just recovered from a head injury and complete amnesia. I've come with her ... she ... she needs support as she tries to return to her new ... her old ... life..."

"Don't be ridiculous, young man. A friend, nonsense. You love her and you want her. She is like my Francesca. I believe almost every man who knows Jen falls in love with her. Why should you be any different?" Mr Lanville reached out and touched Mark's hand. "But I think tonight you will weep, because Jen belongs with Tony. You will stay with me tonight, young man, and we will weep together and rejoice together as well."

Mark was momentarily speechless. Mr Lanville said, "Well, are you going to tell me, Jen, how this happened to you? I have been waiting for months for you to come and tell me why you left us. I knew there had to be a good reason."

So Jen, aided by Mark, told her adventure to her cherished old friend.

"—and I'm frightened, Mr Lanville, I'm frightened of Tony and yet I want him so. I don't know if he still wants me— how do I see him again for the first time since my—and where do I see him?" Jen's voice was rising hysterically. "Please, please help me, you have helped so much before—"

Mr Lanville looked at his grandfather's clock, ticking hollowly in its alcove. For he knew something Jen did not. He said gently, "I am tiring, my dear. Please, stay nearby until I can decide what should be done; give me an hour. There is something I want you to do while I think about all this. I want you to go into my maze, and wait there until I send for you."

"But you know I have no sense of direction," Jen said, her voice shaking. "I'll be lost in the maze and I'm so claustrophobic and there's no Tony to find me like he did the first night we met here—"

"But, child, there are maps of the maze; ask Bradford, he will give one to you; you will have no trouble getting both in and out." But he had not reckoned on Jen's claustrophobia; he could see now that in her present state she could not cope with being in the maze alone. So he said, "Mr Reinhard will look after you; go right to the centre, there is a bench there, you will see my lovely rose bush, it is a rare Talisman rose, did you know that? There are only a few of them left. Bring me one of those roses when you come out. Please. Indulge me. I promise I will have found a solution for you when you return to me. But hurry, hurry into the maze now."

Jen and Mark looked at one another, puzzled at this injunction. They left Mr Lanville's room intending to comply with his odd wishes. Bradford encouraged them in this; he even ordered a thermos of tea and some cake in a picnic basket for two, for them to take into the maze; he thrust it into their hands and practically pushed them out the door. For Bradford too knew something they did not.

Silently Jen and Mark walked into the maze, that maze where Tony had first kissed Jen. Mark wanted to touch her and did not know whether he should; finally he reached out and she let him hold her small, cold hand.

The Tosca Taunt

The maze was framed in hedges of yew, with here and there a flowering bush to relieve the dense green. They explored slowly, following the map to the centre where, as Mr Lanville had said, they found a flowering Talisman rosebush and, surprisingly, a black wrought iron Parisian park bench on which to sit and admire the coral and gold blooms. Still silent, they poured cups of tea. Mark, though not hungry, forced himself to eat the piece of fruitcake. Jen tried, almost gagged, gave up. They sat quietly, in an outward cocoon of beauty, in an inward torture chamber. They heard, distantly, the rumble of a car motor, the slow squeal of brakes.

....

Today was the Sunday after the wedding, and Tony Amato had promised himself he would visit Thomas Graham Lanville once more before he went back to sing in Boston. Feeling stressed after the party and knowing how badly he drove when he was tense, he hired a car and a driver.

Once he had arrived at Lanville's home he bounded up the broad inside staircase two steps at once, knowing he had little time to spend here and wanting to make the most of his visit. He was ushered into Mr Lanville's room by the nurse, and he took Lanville's cold hand into his as Lanville slowly opened his eyes. Tony wondered how many more visits he would have with his valued friend; it seemed to him that Mr Lanville looked more transparent every time Tony saw him. Today, the elderly man was particularly fragile, yet there was an excitement about him, a glitter to his eyes.

"Tony, Tony lad, she has come back at last! I told you she would!"

Tony was never sure whether Mr Lanville was referring to Francesca or Jen when he started in this vein.

"Who has come, Mr Lanville?"

"Why, Jen, of course. I told you she would come. I've sent her into the maze with her friend. It seemed to me that would be the best place for you two to meet again after Jen's resurrection. The resurrection of your life too, Tony my lad, I told you it would happen. Don't worry about that man. He loves Jen too, but it doesn't matter."

Worried by this, Tony glanced around to catch the eye of the nurse, but she had unobtrusively left the room.

"Now, go, go, Tony my boy, go into the maze," Lanville continued. "Go right to the centre. There is a Talisman rose bush there, you will see, bring me a rose. There are thorns there too, but the thorns are not for you. The thorns are for him, he will feel the stab of them. But bring me the rose, for I want to go to Francesca with her rose in my hand. She planted the bush, you see."

The old eyes closed. Tony felt close to panic. Was his friend about to die? Lanville opened his eyes and stared at Tony. The nurse was now back in the room. The old man said almost angrily, "Yes, yes, Jen is alive, go, go, get me the rose, promise, bring it back as soon as you dare, please—"

Deeply concerned, Tony looked up at the nurse, but she only smiled and nodded, mouthing the words, "Go, please do what he asks."

"I will go now into the maze, I will come back as soon as I find the rose," Tony said to the now closed old face. "Wait for me—" And wondered why he had said that.

The Tosca Taunt

He loped back down the stairs where at the bottom he met Bradford. Tony said, "I'm going into the maze to get a rose," and Bradford replied, puzzlingly, "Of course, Mr Amato. I'm so happy for you both. Good luck, or should I say *In Bocca al Lupo?*"

Tony looked at him in astonishment. What was the matter with everybody here? He needed good luck now to go and pick a rose? How feeble did everyone think he had become? *Cielo!*

Turning right as he left the chateau Tony entered the maze. At first his steps were quick, but always memories assailed him here, memories of rescuing his hysterical, claustrophobic Jen, lost in the maze on the night they had met. He had kissed her, telling himself it was to comfort her; yes, he had found her and kissed her and lost himself.

He walked on. He admonished himself that it was time now, time to get control over this anguish, time to put it behind him and try to find some joy in life, if only because it was not good for his children to feel his sadness even though he did his best to conceal it. He told himself he was being weak and cowardly to still allow these moments of desolation, these moments when he could feel Jen still so close to him, these moments alone when he did not have to hide his grief.

He let his tears flow unchecked as he continued ever more slowly towards the centre of the maze. He would sit for a moment on the Parisian bench, collect himself, pick a rose for Mr Lanville and take it to him. What an unsettling day. He would be glad to get back to America and to his busy singing schedule. It gave him less time to think like this.

In the heart of the maze Jen and Mark had drunk their tea and had put the cups away in the basket. They sat hand in hand on the surprisingly comfortable bench. Jen spoke softly, for the maze, like a church, induced whispering.

"Is someone coming? Do you hear those sounds? That must be Mr Lanville sending for us. I hope he's had time to consider my troubles. Do you find this maze scary?"

Mark grinned. "Hardly. I've been caught in a mine collapse. It gives you a point of view about what's scary."

He looked at her. But she was no longer attending. Slowly she stood, staring at the opening which led out of the centre of this maze. Mark's head swivelled. There was nothing there.

Jen took a step. Mark stood up now, holding firmly to her hand.

"Tony," Jen said. But there was nobody there, just the sound of trees in the wind. She pulled her hand from Mark's though he held on as long as he could.

"Tony," she said, and started to run from the clearing. As she reached the opening which led back out of the maze, Mark saw a man come around the corner, and stop stark still, an expression of horror on his face as he stared at Jen.

Mark recognised Jen's husband Antonio Amato.

With a panicky movement Tony covered his face with his hands and rubbed his eyes hard. He lowered his hands and whispered, "*Dio, I've gone mad, Madre de Dio!*"

He closed his eyes tightly and opened them again, but Jen was still there—still there, standing before him, holding her hands out in a gesture of supplication.

"*Madre de Dio,*" Tony breathed, and lurched against the trunk of a tree. Bending his head, he once again covered his face and began to sob, great heaving agonized sobs. Mark could see

The Tosca Taunt

that Tony believed he had lost his mind.

Suddenly Jen knew what to do. For this was her Tony in trouble, and he needed her as he had always needed her, would always need her. She put her arms around him and said quietly, "Tony, Tony, I'm real, you haven't gone mad."

"I don't believe it—you are only a wonderful hallucination. You are saying what a mirage would say—"

"She's real, Mr Amato. Believe," Mark interposed, feeling his own hopes die. But he could not stand to see Tony Amato's pain.

Tony had not until that moment noticed Mark. "Who are you?"

"My name is Mark Reinhard, I'm a Canadian mining engineer. I brought Jen here. By way of convincing you this is real, why would you hallucinate *me?*"

Tony looked at Jen, still doubting all his senses but needing desperately to believe.

"*Cara mia*, is it really you—are you—I—I have felt you in my mind, I could not believe you were dead until I had to, when they found your rings in the fire and even then—oh, *cara mia*, where have you been?"

But Jen put her lips on Tony's and kissed him with all the passion that was for him, only for him. And he knew at last that she was real.

"She had amnesia, Mr Amato," interrupted Mark. "Jen, remember the rose—" he said, but neither Tony nor Jen heard him speak or leave.

Presently Tony and Jen sat down together on the bench, holding each other as though if they let go all this might disappear.

"Anton, Janina, oh Tony, tell me, are they well? Did they—however did they—"

"They are well, but they have forgotten how to play, my Jen. Like me. But now, we will all learn again together, oh my Jen ..." He touched her face as though he was still convinced that she might vanish.

She began to tell him, caressing and kissing him all the while, what she knew of her story. Tony listened intently, and only after she had finished did he remember why he had come into the maze in the first place.

"Jen, I promised Mr Lanville a rose from his bush, we should go back now, how strange, I always say you are my talisman and Mr Lanville wants a Talisman rose..."

"I too promised him a rose."

Holding their two roses, they made their way hand clasping hand back through the maze and soon entered the chateau. Bradford came to greet them, pale, grim faced.

"What is it, Bradford?" asked Tony, suddenly afraid.

"Mr Lanville has taken a very bad turn; the doctor is on his way."

"I did wonder," said Tony. "He was—Bradford, he wanted these roses, for Francesca, he said. Do you suppose we could—"

"Of course. I think he is beyond helping or hurting now. By all means take him the roses."

So hand in hand Jen and Tony went one more time up the great staircase and into the room of the dying Thomas Graham Lanville. Already his breathing echoed with the death rattle. But when they put their roses beside him, he opened his dimming eyes and whispered, "Ah, my children, my happy children, you

The Tosca Taunt

have brought the roses for my Francesca. Thank you, thank you. Do you see, here she comes for me, oh my dear, and in your bridal gown, oh, Francesca! How beautiful!"

They thought he was gone. But he opened his eyes one last time and whispered, "Goodbye, my happy children. I leave you to your bliss."

The End

Jean Dell is a first generation Canadian of English and French descent. A sometime free-lance journalist, she now writes suspense novels set in the theatrical and musical worlds. She also writes and illustrates children's books.

Attending university in mid-life when her two daughters were growing up, she obtained degrees in English and French literature, and journalism.

She has played the violin and viola in several Western Canadian symphony orchestras. One of her musical passions is opera, to which she was introduced in France by her Parisian mother.

Jean Dell has travelled, mostly in North America and Europe, and has lived (too briefly) in France. She now lives in Vancouver, Canada.

ISBN 141206793-6